ZETTA'S DREAM

ZETTA'S DREAM

An Appalachian
Coal Camp Novel

SANDRA PICKLESIMER ALDRICH

• BOLD WORDS •
COLORADO SPRINGS

Published by Bold Words, Inc.
P.O. Box 51351
Colorado Springs, CO 80949-1351

Library of Congress Cataloging-in-Publications Data has been requested.

Scripture is from the *King James Version*.

Printed in the United States of America
ISBN: 0692357505
ISBN-13: 978-0692357507

DEDICATION

With gratitude for the encouragement from my Birthday Friends,
who insisted I read the latest chapter at our dinners:

Libby Paddle
Mim Pain
Elizabeth Robinove
Mary Wells

Chapter 1

Zetta stopped the clock above the fireplace. With her fingers still grasping the cold metal pendulum, she whispered, "No need to waste your pretty chimes in an empty house."

She ran her hands over her protruding abdomen and turned away from the cold fireplace. She smiled at Rachel, who sat on the travel satchel near the door. The three-year-old clutched her rag doll, her eyes wide with unspoken questions.

"We'll be back, honey," was all Zetta managed before her father strode in, carrying two-year-old Micah.

Paw Davis scowled and didn't look at his daughter.

"I got the crates in the wagon," he said. "I don't know why you think you've got to traipse off to that place. It was bad enough Asa got your brothers to go with him. He shouldn't be wanting you to travel now."

Zetta ignored his comment, refusing to argue. Instead, she pulled her black bonnet over her hair, re-tied the wool scarf around Rachel's head, then stooped awkwardly to pick up the small hickory basket holding her coin purse and hoe cakes and fried chicken from last night's supper.

"You and me have talked about this 'til we're both tired, Paw. Asa misses us—and we miss him. He's been down at that coal camp since he got the crops laid by. The youngins are gonna forget what he looks like. Besides, it isn't forever. We'll be back before planting time."

Paw touched his rough cheek to Micah's pink face.

1

"Well, I still wish you was waiting a week or two—at least 'til after Christmas."

Zetta shook her head. "Now that would put the travel all the closer to my time. I'll write you and Mama Becky as soon as we get there."

Paw made a sound that was close to a growl as he scowled again, but allowed his expression to soften as he gestured for Rachel to go onto the porch.

He picked up the satchel with Micah still clinging to his neck. Zetta took one last look around the room, straightened the picture of Jesus near the window and pulled the door shut behind her.

Outside, she stood for several moments on the porch, breathing deeply of the cold mountain air. The hills of Eastern Kentucky hovered over her little home like comforting sentinels. Asa had planted the pear trees on either side of the porch steps a few weeks before Rachel's birth saying there was no better place for either trees or children to grow than in these hills. The next fall when she told him about Micah's expected arrival, he planted two apple trees at the gate. Next spring, he planned to put out peach trees by the smokehouse in honor of the new baby. He had teased her, saying at this rate they would have the finest orchards in all of Magoffin County.

Paw settled Rachel and Micah in the middle of the wagon seat before holding out his hand to help Zetta climb next to them. As he pulled himself into his own place and gently slapped the reins across the mules' backs, Zetta could tell by his set jaw he was through talking. The ride to the Salyersville train station would be without comment, but that would give her time to think about seeing Asa again—and enjoying his welcoming kiss.

Zetta studied the mules' breath hanging in the crisp air as she folded the wagon quilt over the children's legs. The chestnut trees stood by the lane, their bare branches framing the gray sky. Zetta tipped her head upward, remembering when Asa left the leaves had been thick, forming a canopy above his head.

Lord, you know all of us need to be together. Keep us safe as we travel, please—and keep Asa safe in the mines. And help the time pass quickly 'til we can come home, she inwardly prayed.

Before Zetta could add *amen*, the baby inside her kicked hard. Zetta leaned back and rubbed her side. I know, honey. I don't want to leave, either, she thought.

* * * * *

At the station, Paw wordlessly helped Zetta down from the wagon, then motioned for the baggage handlers to collect the satchel and crates of household goods, salted hog meat, canned vegetables and potatoes while Zetta bought one-way tickets.

The agent quickly averted his eyes as he noticed Zetta's expanding belly beneath her gaping coat.

"Hazard, huh? Your man working coal down there?" he said.

Zetta nodded. "Near there. Just 'til spring though."

The agent smiled. "Five years ago, during the Great War, I was in France," he said. "All I could think about was getting back to these hills. I hope y'all make it back safe, too."

Zetta started to reply, then merely nodded her thanks as he pushed the tickets and change of silver dimes toward her.

As she turned, Paw had both Rachel and Micah in his arms as they watched the steam hiss around the wheels of the train.

At Zetta's approach, he jerked his head toward the third car.

"I'll carry the youngins on," he said.

He turned, leaving Zetta to take a deep breath and follow. Inside, Paw eased the children into the closest seat, patted his daughter on the shoulder and strode off the train without looking back.

Zetta didn't dwell on her father's abrupt departure but unbuttoned the children's coats as the train began its laborious chuffing away from the station. Within minutes, Rachel leaned against her mother and soon was lulled to sleep by the rocking motion of the wheels. Zetta reached for Micah, but he preferred to stand by the dirty window, fascinated by the barren trees and brown hillsides sliding by.

For a while, Zetta watched with him as the familiar hills slipped away, but a knot began to form around her heart. Finally, she took a handkerchief from her sleeve and pulled Micah to her.

"You're getting your face all dirty against that glass," she said. "Let Mommy wash it."

Reluctantly, the toddler stood at her knees as Zetta spat into a corner of the cloth and ran it over his face.

"There! That'll do for now," she said. "Sit up here, and we'll read Poppy's letters."

As Micah dutifully clambered onto the seat, Zetta pulled several folded papers from her coat pocket and, mindful of nearby passengers, softly read aloud:

" 'Dear Zetta Berghoffer, my dear wife. I write you again. I wrote last week and haven't heard from you yet. Please write me often since I worry when I don't hear from you. This letter leaves me okay. Hope all is well with you and the children. What have you been doing? I think about you all the time. I recollect how you'd smile at me when we was in school together. I like remembering the time you kissed me on the cheek after I kept the Allen boy from killing the baby bird that fell out of the pear tree. I decided right then someday I'd kiss your pretty lips. And sure enough I did. To this day I can't pass a pear tree in bloom without thinking about that time. Sometimes I still can't believe that pretty little girl grew up to be my beautiful wife. When the driver of the mantrip takes us into the dark of the mine each morning, I close my eyes and think it's a summer evening. And after Brother and Sister are in bed, you and me sit on the porch and listen to the whippoorwills calling back and forth across the creek. It kills me being away from you, but you know I'm looking for that four hundred dollars to pay off the farm. I don't like being beholden to anybody, especially somebody holding title to the land I'm plowing. I want our children to have a life better than I did. I want you and them here with me. Then we can go back home together come spring.

" 'Well, I got $76.50 in my pocket now that I've been paid again. I have not spent much since I been here other than what the company makes me buy and my board and all. Did the Reed boys get the last of the corn in? I miss your cornbread. I miss your fried sweet potatoes. I miss Brother and Sister. I miss everything. Most of all, I miss you. Love your husband, Asa.' "

Micah blinked solemnly at his mother, then rubbed his nose as Zetta smiled at him and unfolded another letter.

" 'Mrs. Zetta Berghoffer, my dear wife. Was glad to get your letter, so I take the pleasure to write you back. Hope all is well at home. As for me, I'm okay, just working like a mule. I will be glad when this comes to the end and I can be home with you and the children. If I was back at our place, right about now I'd be finished with our butchering and would have all the meat hanging in the smokehouse. And come evening, you and me would sit by the fire and talk while you worked one of your quilts and I fixed the harness. Then I'd yawn and stretch and you'd smile that sweet smile and say it was bedtime. As I'd bank the fire, you would turn the lamp down. In the glow from the fireplace, I would watch you step out of your dress and pull your gown on before you take down your hair to brush it. And I'd put my arms around you and feel you all warm against me. Well, I reckon I better think about something else right about now.

" 'A man quit his job down here, and I got it. Right now I make $4.80 on a full shift instead of the $3.50 I started with. The boys and me each pay the boarding lady $1.25 a day. She's got five of us staying here. If you and the children was here, I could rent us a company house, and your brothers could pay us board. That sure would help us get the farm paid off. Think about what I said about coming down here. There's a good granny woman here to help when the baby comes. Being with you and the children is the only thing that will suit me. I'm not satisfied now and won't be as long as we are apart. Love your husband, Asa.' "

Zetta leaned against the seat, picturing Asa bending over the paper as he wrote, his hair the color of creek sand and flopping across his left eye. She smiled, thinking about seeing him in just a little while. As she unfolded another page, she watched Micah rub his nose again.

She put the letters away. "Your daddy sure is a good hand to write. And you sure do have his blue eyes. But I reckon you want your nap. First, let me get you some chicken. That cold breakfast wore off fast."

After a bite of fried chicken and half of a hoe cake, Micah fell asleep. Within a few minutes, Zetta tried to doze as well but couldn't get comfortable in the upright seat. As she listened to the harsh grinding of the train wheels against the metal tracks, she pictured Asa, tall and blond and still fresh from his Saturday night bath, waiting at the Hazard station. She imagined him, one foot up on a wooden trunk, watching the tracks curving out of the mountains. She was glad they'd be arriving before it was fully dark.

At last, the conductor walked through the train, calling, "Hazard next stop. Next stop Hazard."

Zetta eased Micah off the seat and stood the sleepy child before her, then gently shook Rachel.

"Come on, Babies," she said. "We're about there. Poppy's probably pacing the boards off the platform. Stand up now."

5

Micah blinked and yawned. As the train announced its slow approach with a series of short whistles, Rachel rubbed her eyes. Zetta could see the roof of the station ahead. Quickly she thrust the handle of the hickory basket over her arm and clutched a hand of each child, ready to stand as soon as the train stopped.

As the engine settled into the station with one final hiss of steam, Zetta could see Asa through the window as he rushed forward, almost knocking the conductor down as the man set a wooden step onto the platform. Zetta steered the children along the narrow aisle, her heart beating faster.

At the top of the steps, Rachel squealed, "Poppy! Poppy!"

Micah stared for a moment, then smiled in recognition and put his arms out. Asa swooped both children into his arms as Zetta carefully descended the two steps. Finally she stood before him, and he kissed her soundly in front of the other passengers. Then he nodded toward her bonnet.

"Take that thing off for a minute," he said. "I've missed seeing your Indian gal hair shining in the sun."

And he kissed her again before she could protest.

Her tall, dark-haired brothers, Loren and Luttrell, stood grinning by the mule-drawn wagon at the side of the platform, ready to collect the luggage and crates Zetta had brought from the farm. Both of them gave their sister a quick hug, patted both children on their heads and began to unload the crates from the baggage car. By Loren's third trip with an overloaded crate, he paused to rub the jagged scar on his chin.

"You musta brung every bit of food in the county with you, Sis," he said. "I reckon you forget we can buy whatever we need at the company store."

"Yes, and pay a war price for it," Zetta said. "Besides, this is better than any store-bought. And I wanted Asa to eat what he planted before he came off down here. Now you hush. I know you like my beans and cornbread. You can't get *that* at your store."

At the mention of her cornbread, the brothers moved a little faster. As they stacked the crates, Zetta turned to look at the buildings near the train platform. Asa, with a child in each arm, watched her study the outlines of the nearby two-story warehouses. The muddy road that ran from the station into town was filled with mule-drawn wagons and an occasional motorcar.

"It's just 'til spring, Zetta," Asa said. "Before you know it, we'll be back on our own place. And this time it will be ours. Working another man's ground darkens even the brightest day."

Zetta nodded. It was not the first time she'd heard this speech. "Is the camp near here?"

"Well, not exactly," Asa said. "We have a little ways to go. The train goes on to it, but you would have had a layover here. This way, I could see you sooner, and we'll still get there about the same time the train arrives at Golden Gate."

Loren handed the last crate to Luttrell, who stood in the wagon to secure each one against the side.

"Golden Gate! Now ain't that some name?" Loren said. "It's called for the owner, Harold Golden. But *Rusty Hinge* would be more fitting."

Asa frowned at him. "I swear you'd complain if you was being hung with a *new* rope!" he said. "Come spring, you'll have enough jingle to buy that piece of bottom land at Foraker and marry Sarah—if you quit throwing your money around. And she'll have to put up with you claiming you mined more coal than all the rest of us put together."

At the mention of his sweetheart, Loren grinned as he reached for Rachel and Micah to hand them up to Luttrell. "I reckon you got that right."

Zetta watched as her brothers settled into the wagon bed, each with a child held tightly on his lap. Only then did she accept Asa's outstretched hand to help her into the wagon seat. As she watched him cross in front of the mules, she took a deep, ragged breath.

CHAPTER 2

With everyone settled, Asa climbed onto the wagon seat, released the pole brake and guided the mules onto the southwest road. He held the reins tighter as a motorcar chugged past, throwing mud and slush, then allowed the animals to set their own gait before he spoke.

"Our section boss let me borrow the wagon," he said. "So I thought maybe you could bake him a sweet later on to say, 'much obliged.' I hear tell his woman ain't much of a cook."

Zetta nodded. "It'll probably take me a day or two to get used to the other kitchen, though," she said.

Asa watched the twitching of the mules' ears then said, "The house is costing $15 a week, but each of us was paying almost $9 staying at the boarding house, so this is better."

Loren snorted from the wagon bed. "Wait 'til you see what the Rusty Hinge Camp is charging $15 a week for," he said. "I'm surprised those old green lumber houses are still standing. And the stove ain't nearly as big as yours back home."

For the first time since greeting his sister, Luttrell spoke. From his tone, Zetta knew his brown eyes held warning.

"Loren, nobody put a gun to your head and made you come here," he said quietly. "Now let Zetta be. She could conjure up a fine meal over a pit fire if she had to."

Asa ignored the interruption. "This camp pays more than some of the others around here and don't run Sunday shifts," he said. "So as long as we load our quotas each day, we can do pretty good.

On a full week, I work ten hours a day for six days and make $4.80 a day times six days, which is $28.80 a week, minus the cost of the supplies and the house—and that still leaves me with any place from $55 to $78 a month, plus what the boys will pay you for boarding."

The numbers swirled through Zetta's head, and she had difficulty keeping them straight.

But as she waded through the arithmetic, she smelled smoke. Just then Asa pointed toward a hollow between two sandstone ledges. Dirty snow hung over the top of the rocks.

"That's our turn-off," he said. "Pretty soon we'll be at the camp."

Zetta coughed from the dirty air and turned to check on Rachel and Micah. Both of her brothers had opened their coats and pulled their shirttails over the children's mouths. As Zetta pulled the handkerchief from her sleeve to hold across her nose, Loren spoke.

"Oh, yeah, we're getting close all right," he said. "You can smell the coal dust from Rusty Hinge even before you see it."

Everyone was quiet as the mules pulled the wagon across a narrow wooden bridge deeper into the hollow. A dirty white building stood to the left. A sign with "Golden Gate Store" was nailed above the porch, but its yellow letters were faded and cracked. Straight ahead was a wide building that seemed attached to the mountain towering above its left side. The right side tapered into a narrow horizontal V over a shed, under which an open train car waited.

Asa gestured toward the structure. "That's the tipple," he said. "That's where the coal is sorted and washed and dumped into the cars for transport. It's pretty noisy around there during the week. But you get used to it."

Zetta's breath was coming in short little jabs despite the handkerchief at her mouth. She had never seen a building that large or that dirty.

Lord, this is worse than I imagined, she thought.

Asa turned the mules onto a narrow lane between several unpainted houses stacked so closely together their thin porches almost touched. He gestured to the far left.

"Over there is Shucky Bean holler," he said. "You probably can't see it real good right now in the twilight, but the colored miners and their families live there. And up on top of the ridge ahead is Silk Stocking Row for the boss and owner. I hear tell they've even got water pumps right in their kitchens. The biggest house belongs to the owner, but he's not been here since we arrived. The other house belongs to the supervisor, Edwin Gray."

Zetta barely heard him as she wondered how she was going to keep everyone clean.

Asa's command of "Whoa!" interrupted her thoughts. "Well, here we are," he said. "Here's our home for the next three months."

As Asa jumped down to tie the mules' reins to the banister, Zetta fought a panicking wave of homesickness.

Asa came around to help her from the wagon, then reached up as Luttrell handed first Rachel, then Micah, down to him. He led them onto the porch and had just started to open the front door when a shrill whistle blasted the air.

Rachel and Micah burst into tears, but Asa bent down and pulled their heads to his chest. "It's okay, Babies," he said. "Poppy's here."

As the whistle faded away, Asa turned to Zetta. "That's the call for the afternoon shift."

Zetta's hand was over her heart. "You mean to tell me that noise starts up at every shift?"

Asa nodded. "Afraid so. But you'll get used to it."

"I don't know about that."

"Remember, we'll leave as soon as I get paid the last day of March," he said. "Keep thinking of that four hundred dollars."

Zetta looked around at the rows of unpainted houses covered with coal dust. March thirty-first suddenly seemed an eternity away.

* * * * *

The winter sun was beginning to disappear behind the mountain, so Asa stepped into the house and lit the kerosene lamp on a small table near the door. Then he held it high and gestured for the others to enter. Inside, it didn't take Zetta long to inspect the house. From the front porch, they stepped into a small curtainless room holding a few straight-back chairs. The two walls facing the outside were covered with overlapping newspaper and magazine pages that formed crude wallpaper.

Loren pointed to the pages on the walls. "See what I mean

about green lumber?" he said. "Houses need more than paper to keep the wind out."

Zetta ignored him as she glanced at the unpainted, warped floor boards and thought of her own front room with the braided rugs against the smooth dark green painted floor.

Asa's forced cheerfulness interrupted Zetta's thoughts as he gestured toward two small bedrooms on the right.

"The boys will sleep in the second one," he said. "Ours is closer to the kitchen."

Still holding the lamp, he pulled Zetta to the first doorway.

"See? This is our bed," he said. "Sister and Brother's bed is right next to ours. As soon as we unpack your quilts, it'll be just like home."

Then Asa motioned toward the lidded graniteware behind the door.

"I bought a new chamber pot for you and the children," he said. "Since you're in the family way, I'll empty it each evening."

He pointed beyond the back door. "The boys and I will meander up the lane to the outhouse."

Zetta nodded, then turned toward the kitchen, which was beyond the front room archway. The worn cook stove, accompanied by a full coal bucket and kindling box, leaned toward the corner. A small galvanized bathing tub hung on the wall nearby. A square table and more straight-back chairs were positioned near the dingy window. Beside the table was a narrow bench holding two large gray enamel dishpans and a filled water bucket. That's where she would wash the dishes, which would be stacked on open shelves nearby. To the right of the bench was the door leading to a tiny porch. Even in the dimming light, she could see a grassless yard. Crushed shale kept the winter mud at bay.

Asa gestured toward three large cloth sacks in the far corner.

"See? I already got flour, sugar and cornmeal for you," he said.

As Zetta studied the kitchen, Loren spread his arms. "Well, here you have it, Sis," he said. "What more can any coal miner and his family want?"

Asa scowled. "Why don't you and Luttrell start unloading the wagon instead of working your jaws," he said. "I'll be along directly."

* * * * *

11

Even as tired as she was from the trip, Zetta straightened her shoulders and took charge of the unpacking.

"Luttrell, whilst I get the fire going, bring in the can goods first—the crate with the sack of dried apples on top," she said. "Loren, bring in the dish barrel so I can get us fed. Then stack the vegetable crates over here next to the wash bench."

Asa started toward the door, but Zetta gestured toward a chair at the kitchen table. "No, Poppy. You light another lamp and sit right here and keep the youngins from under foot," she said. "Besides, I've missed your sweet face."

Loren shook his head. "How can you call that ugly face sweet? You can't even see it, what with those big ears."

Zetta kissed Asa's cheek before answering. "Loren, you sure are mouthy for somebody who's hoping for more than one piece of cornbread."

"Can't argue there," Loren said. "You're the cook."

He reached for the first lamp as Asa lit the one on the kitchen table.

"Let me have some light for the porch," Loren said. "I don't need to be banging my legs dragging heavy crates up the steps."

Asa handed him the lamp then sat down at the table and pulled both children onto his lap.

He crossed one leg over the other and slid Micah to sit on the upraised boot. "Here, Brother. Ride the horsey."

As the toddler giggled with each bounce, Rachel leaned against her daddy's chest, reaching up to pat his clean-shaven face every few moments.

"How'd the butchering go?" Asa asked. "I sure hated leaving that up to you."

Zetta shrugged. "It was fine," she said. "Jim Reed brung his boys early and stayed all day. I offered him the usual fourth of the good meats, but all he would take was a ham for Christmas. I reckon he's never gonna forget you standing up for him that time."

Asa pulled his eyes away from the bouncing toddler.

"He don't owe me a thing," he said. "That was the decent thing to do. Well, next butchering, I'll make sure he accepts more."

As Luttrell carried in the crate of canned goods, Zetta gestured toward the kitchen corner, then pulled out a quart jar of green beans.

"These beans will have to do," she said. "Tomorrow I'll make a proper supper."

Asa smiled as he bounced Micah higher on his boot.

"Having you and the youngins here makes any meal a feast," he said.

Loren came through the front door and grunted as he set the dish barrel down near the bare shelves. After she opened the top, Zetta pulled yellow flowered plates from within the folded towels and sheets and set them on the table.

"Next year, Jim will take his rightful share of the meat with you there," Zetta said. "Seems like overnight that girl of theirs turned into a real beauty. They're gonna be giving a wedding supper before long."

Loren went back to the wagon as Luttrell stacked the meat crate near the stove. Zetta pulled her favorite skillet from on top and greased it with a piece of fatback, which she tossed into the simmering beans.

After several more trips to the wagon, Luttrell carried quilts and pillows into the bedroom while Loren pushed the final vegetable crate into the corner.

"Well, that's the last of it," he said. "Me and Luttrell's taking the wagon to the stable—and hoping to eat when we get back."

His sister gestured toward the table as she cracked an egg from a straw-filled crate into the bowl of cornmeal.

"Everything will be sitting right there in just a few more minutes, so you better hurry," Zetta said.

Loren was out the door before she finished the sentence.

Zetta slid the skillet into the oven, then retrieved the hickory basket from the dish shelf.

"Here, Asa. Feed the youngins the rest of last night's chicken whilst the cornbread's baking," she said. "I've got to get them to bed. Poor babies are dead on their feet."

Asa tore chunks of meat from the bone and handed them to each child. As they chewed thoughtfully, he gnawed the remaining scrapes from each joint.

"I swear, you fry the best chicken around," he said. "If you get a hankering for a frying hen or fresh eggs, the granny woman I told you about has chickens up her way—and a good cow. I paid her already to bring milk for the youngins several times a week."

Zetta unwrapped newspaper from around a large red tomato that had been plucked green and stored since the September harvest.

"I'm glad to hear that," she said. "I gathered the last of the eggs before Jim Reed's boys came over to get Brownie and the chickens. The oldest boy put a piece of wire around the legs of ours so they'll know which ones to fetch back to us. I hope they lay good and that Brownie gives plenty of milk for their family."

Both children had finished eating and leaned drowsily against Asa as he rubbed their backs.

"This is all I want," he said. "You and me and our youngins. You know I'm working here so they can have a better life than I did."

Zetta nodded as she set the sliced tomatoes on the table.

"Here, let me have Micah," she said. "He's asleep already. You bring Rachel in. Don't forget her rag baby."

* * * * *

As Asa eased Rachel out of her dress and onto the bed, the little girl snuggled next to her sleeping brother and put her arm around him. Within seconds, she fell asleep, too. Just as Zetta pulled the blue and white quilt over the children's shoulders, Loren jerked open the front door.

"I beat Luttrell here," he said. "Let's eat."

Zetta hurried out of the bedroom to hush him.

"The youngins are asleep," she said. "You can't be calling out like that."

Loren opened his mouth, but immediately closed it. Wordlessly, he sauntered to the table and sat down.

Just as Zetta moved toward the stove, Luttrell opened the door. He glanced at his silent brother and sat down without comment. As Zetta set the steaming cornbread and bowl of beans into the middle of the table, Asa sat down and leaned forward, breathing in the hot aroma. Only then did Loren venture to whisper.

"Pray," he said. "My stomach's starting to think my throat's been cut."

Asa smiled at Zetta, then bowed his head. "Lord, thank you for bringing Zetta and the youngins safely here," he said. "Thank you for being with them and with me and the boys whilst we was all apart. Thank you now for this good food. Bless it to our bodies and bless the hands that prepared it. Help us serve you better. In Jesus' name. Amen."

Loren was reaching for the cornbread before Luttrell had raised his head.

For the next few minutes, no one talked as the three men hunched over their plates, pushing beans and fatback onto the forks with fist-sized chunks of cornbread glistening with fresh butter. Zetta smiled as she pulled the white cloth from yesterday's gingerbread cake and set the dessert on the table. It was good to see Asa enjoying her cooking again, but she knew she would count the days until they could be back home.

CHAPTER 3

Zetta watched Asa swing the ax against the tender bark of the saplings near the creek. His back muscles rippled beneath his torn shirt as he struck each thin trunk. Then in one swift motion, he swooped up the timber and tossed the entire stack onto the mound of fresh dirt beside him. A cold wind rustled the leaves, causing the saplings to moan, *Too soon. Too soon.* The fresh sap on the blade glistened and then turned red as drops of blood fell onto the soil. Asa lifted his face and looked longingly at her.

Zetta awoke with a start, her heart pounding.

For a moment, she gulped air, disoriented and frightened as she tried to shake off the mountain belief about dreams of new timber and fresh soil being signs of coming death. She looked toward the window but the light from the waning moon offered no comfort. Then Asa's gentle snore pulled her to full consciousness, and she moved closer to the warmth of his back as she whispered, "Lord, thank you that Asa is right here. Protect him—and us—please. Help me know I dreamed about the trees and dirt because I'm homesick, and nothing more."

Asa turned in his sleep then, rolling onto his back. Zetta eased away to give him more room, then bent to kiss his cheek before pulling the quilt over his bare chest. Even though she wanted to snuggle against him, she could tell from her longtime practice of early rising that it was close to five o'clock—getting up time for the miners. She looked toward the little bed just an arm's reach away where Rachel and Micah slept, their breath coming in unified puffs. Rachel's arms were folded around the rag baby doll.

Well, I'd better get a jump on fixing breakfast and packing the dinner buckets before the whistle blows, she thought as she changed from her nightgown into a shapeless dress.

At the kitchen window, Zetta rubbed her arms for warmth as she looked toward the outhouse standing in the eerie shadows up the lane and was thankful Asa had thought to buy the chamber pot. Then she lit the lantern on the table and pulled kindling from the wood box, which she poked into last night's embers in the cook stove. As those caught fire, she added small chunks of coal.

Trying to stay ahead of the whistle, Zetta filled the gray enamel coffee pot from the water bucket near the door and set it on the back of the stove. As she mixed biscuit dough, the mine whistle blew. At its shrill cry, Zetta shook her head, knowing she was going to hate hearing that sound every morning.

She looked in on Rachel and Micah, concerned the whistle had awakened them. But Asa was leaning over their bed rubbing their backs and whispering, "It's all right, Babies. Go back to sleep."

As Zetta turned back toward the stove, she heard the corn shuck pallets on which her brothers slept rustle as the men stretched and yawned. She sliced fatback into a hot skillet, then cracked six eggs directly into the hot grease. One egg had a double yolk. She would put that on Asa's plate.

The three men made quick trips up the lane, then splashed cold water on their faces at the wash bench. By the time they sat down at the table, the biscuits were ready.

With his elbows on the rough table, Asa leaned his head against his folded hands. "Lord, thank you for the good night's sleep," he began. Zetta, standing at his shoulder, clinched her hands together, remembering her disturbing dream.

At Asa's *Amen*, Zetta set their plates before them heaped with fried apples, fatback and eggs. She turned the biscuits onto another plate and set a jar of her blackberry jam next to them.

The men ate in silence for several minutes but occasionally made smacking sounds to let her know her cooking was appreciated. When they were finished, each man wiped his plate with a final bite of biscuit.

"What did y'all eat before I showed up?" she asked.

Asa smiled. "Nothing nearly as good as this."

Loren stood up and stretched until his fingertips touched the uneven ceiling.

"I'll fill the lamps and see if I've got clean shirts for work this week."

The hint was not lost on Zetta. "Haven't y'all done any washing?" she asked.

Loren smiled. "You know I'm not about to do women's work," he said. "Perton's wife used to take in washing, but now that she's in the family way I reckon she won't be doing that. It's a good thing Asa had you come here."

Zetta turned toward Asa, but he shook his head.

"You know better than that," he said. "But if you reckon you feel up to washing the shirts today, Luttrell and I will get the wash kettles out from under the back porch and fill 'em for you."

As Asa and Luttrell went out the back door, Zetta watched Loren pull a box from the back of the top shelf and line up three brown canvas caps on the table. On the front of each cap was a rectangular metal compartment into which he carefully poured tiny black granules.

"What's that?" Zetta asked.

Loren never looked up. "Carbide," he said. "We'll add the water at the mine to get light."

"That's about as clear as mud to me," Zetta said as she put fatback meat between biscuit halves. "But I'm glad you know what you're doing."

After she cut three large chunks of gingerbread cake for each man, Zetta sliced raw sweet potatoes and folded them into a small piece of wax paper. Those would go into Asa's bucket. She turned to Loren.

"There are only two buckets here," she said.

Loren nodded, "Since we work the same section, Asa always packs his dinner in our buckets."

"He does? Why?"

"Oh, you know Old Gotta-Save-Every-Penny Asa," Loren answered. "He said he's not paying for something just to haul his food. I swear he's been saving every extra cent—except for what he bought for this house and that Christmas surprise for you."

At Zetta's startled look, Loren tried to cover his telling of Asa's secret.

"A while back, that man of yours wouldn't go to the new Tom Mix flicker show over in Hazard," he said. "And that was even after I offered to pay his way. He said he'd druther not waste any money. Not even mine."

Zetta reached for the little basket that had held the chicken and hoe cakes for yesterday's trip to the camp.

"Well, I'll just put his dinner in this basket," she said.

Loren stood up to put the carbide back on the top shelf.

"Nope, can't do that," he said. "The rats will get into it. That's why our dinner buckets are metal—and covered."

Zetta stopped, stunned, "Rats? In the mine?"

Loren nodded. "Oh, yeah," he said. "And it's bad luck to kill one. In a cave-in they'll run for the opening. If a man's trapped, he can follow the rats out by listening to their scurrying even in the dark. Yeah, I won't kill a rat, but I ain't about to share my dinner with him, either."

Zetta paused, the biscuits and fatback in her hands.

Loren shrugged. "Go ahead and put Asa's dinner in my bucket," he said. "But put it all on the top tray. Drinkin' water goes in the bottom. I'll see about getting him his own bucket since you're liable to be packing more than what the boarding lady did."

Luttrell stepped into the kitchen just as Zetta closed the dinner bucket lids.

"We got both wash kettles filled," he said. "Asa's lighting the fire under the one now."

Loren picked up his bucket. "I saw a jar of blackberries in one of the crates," he said. "If you took a notion to make cobbler for supper, I reckon I could choke down a bite or two."

Zetta smiled and patted him on the shoulder. "You stay out of trouble today," she said.

Loren winked at her and went out the front door just as Asa walked in the back. Zetta watched him position his cap.

"I put sweet potato slices in the bucket for you. The boys don't like them raw," she said.

Asa nodded. "Yeah, buddy. Sweet potatoes from our ground beats any store candy."

"I appreciate you filling the kettles for me," Zetta said. "I just hope the weather stays clear enough so I can hang everything on the line."

"Well, you'll find the work duds piled on the back porch, under the wash bench," Asa said. "Don't try to get all the coal dust out of 'em, they're pretty bad."

He leaned over, kissed her and then hurried to catch up with her brothers. As Zetta stood at the open door, she could hear the conveyor belts starting their loud rumbles at the tipple. She watched the three men trudge toward the mine and disappear into the predawn darkness.

Thinking of her bad dream, she whispered, "Oh, Lord, please keep them all safe."

* * * * *

After feeding Rachel and Micah, Zetta pushed the disturbing dream aside as she poured boiling water over the dishes in the pan until later. Then she put the children's coats on them and handed Rachel her doll.

"Now, Mommy's gonna wash the shirts, so I need you to stand right here in the doorway and watch," she said. "If you mind, I'll give you a sweet later."

Zetta pulled her work apron over her dress and stooped to pull the men's shirts from under the bench. As she straightened, she saw a woman with braided silver hair coming down the lane. A bright blue apron showed below her open brown coat. Even though Zetta didn't know who she was, there was something strong about the older woman that made her watch as she descended the steps toward the kettles. The woman carried a canning jar of milk in the crook of her arm and poked a twisted walking stick in front of her with each step—more like it was a snake-killing club instead of a cane. Her bonnet hung down her back, and she looked up at the sky, ignoring the noise from the coal cars at the tipple.

She smiled when she saw Zetta. Still on the path, she raised her stick to point at the largest wash kettle over the wood fire.

"I'm glad you know to fill the kettle before you light the fire," she said. "We had a woman here last year who thought she'd get the fire going whilst she toted water from the pump. By the time she poured the water into the hot kettle, that metal popped open like a hog's bladder on butchering day."

Zetta just stood there, not knowing if she should say *Thank you* for the compliment or cluck her tongue over the ruining of that other kettle. Then whilst she was deciding if she should confess Asa and Luttrell had toted the water up from the camp pump, the woman leaned forward.

"I'm Clarissa Farley," she said. "But folks call me *Clarie*. Asa told me you'll be needing me come next month. I catch babies around here. Been doing that even before my man was killed by slate. I own my place up the holler, so the boss lets me hang around as long as I'm some use. If I lived in the camp, I woulda been turned out. A man getting hurt or killed means his family leaves, too."

Suddenly her smile widened, and the lines at her mouth and eyes seemed to run together into a pattern.

"Lands, I haven't let you get a word in edgewise," she said.

Her gray eyes reminded Zetta of the morning mist rising out of the hills around the farm at home, and she smiled back.

"I'm Zetta Berghoffer," she said, shyly.

Clarie handed Zetta the jar of milk.

"Why, honey, I know," she said. "Asa asked me to bring milk around whenever I've got extra. He's already paid me, so's you don't have to worry."

As Zetta stammered her thanks, Clarie nodded toward Rachel and Micah peeking around the door frame.

"And that's the youngins," Clarie said. "Asa thinks right smart of them."

While Zetta was trying to think of something to say that wouldn't make her sound addled, Clarie stepped forward and took the shirts Zetta was clutching in one arm. Seeing the older woman's wide hands wrapped around the material comforted Zetta as though she was seeing them helping her new baby into the world. Clarie poked the shirts into the kettle of boiling water with the wash paddle then turned back to Zetta.

"This your first time in a coal camp?"

Zetta nodded as she shifted the jar of milk to her other hand. "Yes, but we don't aim to stay long," she said."

Clarie looked down the hill toward the tipple.

"Well, it's a hard life no matter how long you're here," she said. "We always say the man works the mine, but the woman carries it inside. I worried about my man being under that mountain every day. I prayed to the good Lord, of course, but it helped me do things just so for him. I'd fold his clothes across the back of the bedroom chair—pants always on the bottom—and I'd always try to have a little twig of spearmint to add to his dinner bucket, since he liked it. Doing all that made me feel better—like I was helping him be safe."

Zetta smiled, remembering the sweet potatoes in Asa's dinner bucket.

Suddenly Clarie frowned as she looked down the lane. Zetta turned, but saw only a little blonde girl, about eight years old.

Clarie lowered her voice.

"That's Julia, the supervisor's girl," she said. "Don't tell that child anything you don't want the whole camp to know in sight of ten minutes," she warned.

"I'll go check on one of my other girls," Clarie decided. "Polly lives just below. She's not bound to have her youngin 'til long after you but this is her first one, so she worries a right smart. I boil her up some red chestnut tea now and then and just talk to her. A good birthing needs a calm mother, so I try to encourage the first-time ones. Seeing how this ain't your first one, I reckon you'll do just fine."

She pulled her dangling bonnet onto her head.

"I'll bring Polly to meet you directly," she said. "Mind what I said about this child coming up the path."

Then with a nod, she thrust her walking stick in front of her.

Suddenly the little girl was right in her way.

"Well, Miz Julia. How are you this pretty morning?" Clarie said.

The child stopped and thrust both hands onto her own scrawny hips. "You delivering a baby today?"

Clarie laughed. "No, child. Not today," she said.

Zetta watched the tall form meander down the path, then turned to face the little girl's muddy green eyes glaring at her.

CHAPTER 4

Zetta squared her shoulders and bit the inside of her cheek as Julia scowled at her for several moments.

"You're new here!" the little girl said. "And you're going to have a baby!"

Zetta's cheeks flushed at the child's words that seemed like accusations.

"Yes."

As Julia turned to stare at the toddlers watching her from the doorway, Zetta saw Rachel clutch her doll to her face.

"You've already got two children," Julia said. "Mama says you hillbillies don't know how to do anything more than work coal and have babies."

Zetta stiffened. "Well, now," she said. "I don't know what you mean by hillbillies, but the way you say it, it don't sound like a nice word."

"Mama says if Daddy had any ambition, he'd take us away from here and back to civilization," Julia said.

Zetta set the milk jar on the bottom step, then pushed the shirts under the boiling water with a wooden paddle. As she pondered how to answer the young visitor, she pulled lye soap chunks from her apron pocket and added them to the wash water.

"And where might civilization be?" she said finally.

"In Lexington," Julia answered. "That's where Mama and Daddy met. Mama says this is a godforsaken place."

Zetta gave the shirts another push with the wooden paddle.

"No. God's here, too."

Julia turned toward the children in the doorway. "What are their names?"

Zetta wished she'd left them inside. "Rachel and Micah."

Julia frowned. "What's *your* name?"

"Mrs. Berghoffer."

Julia frowned again. "That's a strange name," she said. "You look Indian. Mama says all you hillbillies are half-breeds."

Zetta pushed her lips together before responding.

"I'll have to remember that when I meet your mother," she said. "Perhaps at church?"

"When she goes," Julia said. "She says this sooty air gives her a headache."

At least we have that in common, Zetta thought as she punched the shirts under the water again.

"I'm surprised you're not in school today."

Julia shook her head. "Mama teaches me. She said I'll learn more in two hours with her than I would all day in a hillbilly classroom."

"Well, I can tell you've learned at least one favorite word from her," Zetta said.

Zetta gave the shirts another poke under the boiling water, marveling at the black scum that rose to the top, then glanced toward the doorway where Rachel and Micah stood.

"Well, the shirts need to boil a while, and I need to do some work inside," she said. "Perhaps you can visit another time."

Julia frowned but finally said, "Okay. See you soon."

Zetta sighed. Already she dreaded that visit.

* * * * *

As Zetta picked up the jar of milk and climbed the steps to the children, she heard someone calling a breathless "Good morning!" She turned to see a plump young woman with bright red hair rushing down the path and barely nodding at Julia as the child stood watching, hands on hips again.

The young woman stopped at the bottom step and looked up at Zetta. Her left hand fluttered to her throat as she leaned forward.

"I'm Dosha Conley," she said. "Jack—my husband—saw Asa and Luttrell filling the wash kettles and said y'all musta moved in last night. I was aiming to bring a buttermilk pie down to you later, but seeing how I was about to get company, I had to come empty handed."

She jerked her head in the direction of the child still standing on the path behind her.

Zetta nodded. "You come right on in. You don't need to be bringing anything anyway."

She steered Rachel and Micah inside the kitchen where Dosha swooped to smile at them.

"What sweet babies," she said. "Me and Jack ain't been married long enough to have youngins yet, but one of these days we want a house full. I'd like to have a passel of boys for Jack. But if we was to have girls, I'd name them all after flowers—Rose and Iris and Pansy and Violet and Blossom."

During Dosha's prattle, Zetta seated the children at the table, then handed each a small slice of the leftover gingerbread.

"That's for being good whilst I was starting the wash," she said.

Then she placed a piece on a saucer and set it in front of Dosha.

"After I get fully settled, I'll try to have more sweets on hand," Zetta said. "I baked this day before yesterday—back in my own kitchen. Lands, that seems like a month ago now."

Dosha plopped a hunk of the cake into her mouth then worked it around, savoring the spice.

"Oh, this is so good it about makes me swallow my tongue," she said. "Mine never raises like this, though. What do you do?"

Zetta pulled the coffee pot to the hottest part of the stove. "I just beat the daylights out of the eggs," she said.

Dosha licked a crumb from her finger. "I'll have to remember that," she said. "Do you care which one you get this time?"

At Zetta's confused look, Dosha giggled, her left hand fluttering at her throat again. "Oh, listen to me," she said. "I mean do you care whether you get a boy or a girl this time around?"

Zetta smiled. "Oh. Well, no," she said. "Long as it's healthy, we don't care what the Lord gives us."

As Dosha nodded, the call of "Hello in the cabin" came from the front. Zetta glanced at the remaining supply of gingerbread, then hurried to open the door. Clarie stood at the bottom of the steps, thumping her walking stick against her shoe. Behind her stood a young woman with downcast eyes.

Clarie pulled the woman forward. "This here is Polly Muncy," she said. "Her man, Perton, works the same shift as Asa and the boys."

Polly barely glanced at Zetta as she nodded a timid greeting. It struck Zetta that Polly's hair was the color of stale mop water—and a stark contrast to the brightness of Dosha's hair. Immediately, she scolded herself for the thought and gestured toward the open door.

"I'm proud to meet you, Polly," she said. "You and Clarie come right in. Dosha's here, too. We was just fixing to have coffee with some dried out cake."

Clarie took Polly's hand and pulled her up the steps. "You don't have to twist my arm when it comes to anything sweet," she said.

She stomped coal dust from her feet before stepping into the front room.

"Now, look at those pretty babies sitting there," she said. "You, too, Dosha, honey. You doing all right?"

Zetta shut the door, marveling how Clarie's presence filled the room.

* * * * *

As Clarie sat down at the table, she waved her arms toward Polly and Dosha. "You two know each other, I reckon."

Dosha laughed. "Of course, we do." But Polly merely nodded, her eyes still downcast. Clarie turned toward Rachel.

"This old lap needs a pretty little girl and her dolly to sit in it," she said.

The child turned questioningly to Zetta.

"It's all right, honey. That's Miz Clarie," her mother said.

With the needed approval, Rachel scooted down from her chair and stood in front of Clarie, who promptly pulled the little girl onto her ample lap. Then Clarie held out her hands to Micah, but the toddler leaned back in his chair and rubbed his nose.

Zetta stooped to pick him up. "Oh, somebody's ready for his morning nap. I'll be right back," she said.

As his mother carried him, Micah whispered, "Snug bug, Mama?"

She lowered him onto the bed and tucked the quilt under his hips.

"Yes, Baby. Now you're snug as a bug in a rug," she said. "Snug as a little bug in a great big rug."

* * * * *

Zetta sighed as she entered the kitchen, "I swear Micah is still worn out from yesterday," she said.

Clarie nodded. "Traveling wears a body out, all right."

Then she took Rachel's hands into her own. "Show your mama what we've been doing," she said. "Here, lace your little fingers together this way again."

She intertwined the child's fingers so they were pointing to the inside of her hands.

"Here's the church." Then she gently pulled the child's index fingers upward.

"Here's the steeple." Then she turned the little hands palm upward and wiggled the still intertwined fingers.

"Open the doors and see all the people."

Rachel pulled her hands together in an attempt to repeat the action.

Clarie laughed. "You about got it."

As Zetta moved to the dish shelf, Dosha jumped up from her chair.

"Here I am letting you wait on me when I ought to be doing for you," she said.

Dosha pulled four cups off the shelf. "Oh, these are right pretty," she said. "I like all the flowers."

She turned to show Clarie and Polly the pattern.

Zetta picked up the coffee pot. "They belonged to Asa's mother," she said. "We cared for her when we was first married since she was so poorly. When she died, her girls said I should take them. I don't reckon she ever had the full set."

Dosha giggled. "Do you ever wonder what it would be like to have all the dishes you want?" she said. "One of these days, I'd like to have blue willow dishes—with pretty cups to drink out of. When I was about ten or eleven, Mama boarded me out with a rich lady to work for a couple of years. I'd never seen so many pretty dishes. When I'd wash them, I'd play like they was mine and I was the fine lady of the house. I'd have stayed on for longer than I did, but she up and died with her last baby."

As soon as the words were out of Dosha's mouth, she gasped.

"Oh, I shoulda not said that in front of you two," she said. "That was a long time ago. And she didn't have nobody like Clarie around to help. Oh, sometimes I could just bite my tongue off for saying unthoughted things."

Clarie shook her head. "Now, Dosha, don't go on like that. And you don't need to worry. I've never lost any of my girls, and I don't aim to start now."

Polly stared at her knuckles, then whispered, "You ever had a baby die?"

Clarie took a deep breath. "Well, a few times, yes," she said. "Mostly little bitty ones that had too much wrong with them to survive in this old world."

She glanced down at Rachel who was still concentrating on getting her fingers intertwined.

"I reckon we can come up with something else to talk about."

But Polly leaned closer, her voice still in a whisper.

"When was the first time you had that happen?"

"Now we're getting off this subject real soon," Clarie said. "But it was my own twin girls. Pretty little things. They just came too soon. They'd be y'alls age right about now."

"How did you bear losing them?" Polly asked.

Clarie gave another long sigh. "Honey, there are some things in life that all you can do with 'em is *bear* 'em. But I've learned we can bear 'em a sight better if we're hanging onto the Lord."

For several moments, no one spoke. As the young women stared at Clarie, and Zetta tried to imagine her years younger, Clarie shook herself loose from the long-ago event.

"Now, I reckon that's enough of that," she said. "Dwelling on the past don't do any of us any good. All the bad just has to be given to Jesus for him to carry. We have to be thankful for the good around us right now. In fact, one good thing is the school program this Sunday afternoon. Mr. Golden might even show up since it's Christmas Eve."

She looked at Dosha, who was still holding the flowered cups.

"Dosha, get rid of that hang-dog look and help Zetta with the coffee," she said. "Polly, you was here last year for the party. Tell the girls what it was like."

Polly was still staring at her knuckles. "Oh, it was nice," she said.

Clarie took over. "Oh, it was that all right—and more. The school children sang songs, and the teacher quoted from the Bible," she said. "I never get tired of hearing about little Jesus being born amongst barn animals—and Mary with nobody to tend her. I think about that a lot. Seems to me it wouldn't be fitting for her husband to help, especially back then. I like to think angels tended her before they went to tell the shepherds. Anyway, after the program was over, Mr. Gray said a few words and everybody got an orange."

Dosha's eyes brightened. "Everybody got an orange?" she asked. "Not just the children? I got an orange once. I ate it real slow and made it last a couple of days. Then I kept the peelings under my pillow 'til they dried up to nothing. Oh, I hope they give out oranges this year, too."

Zetta set the last of the cake on the table then studied Rachel, wondering if she remembered the orange in her stocking last Christmas.

"But my children ain't in school," Zetta said.

Clarie shrugged. "Don't matter. Everybody is invited. The women take the babies. The men even go so's they can shake the boss's hand."

Zetta glanced down at her middle.

"Well, now. I don't know if I need to go," she said. "Me this big and all."

Clarie laughed. "Honey, you're in a coal camp now," she said. "If it don't come out of the ground, nobody pays any attention. Besides, if all my girls stayed out of sight as their time got close, nothing would get done around here. You plan on going and just wear Asa's coat if that'll make you feel better."

Zetta smiled. "Well, it would tickle me to hear the little children sing," she said. "And maybe y'all can come back here for sweets afterward? That'll give me a good excuse to catch up on my baking. Besides, Asa wants me to make something for his shift boss since he let out the wagon yesterday to pick us up at the train station. Do you know who that is?"

"Reckon I do," Clarie said. "Fact is, right here is his wife."

She gestured toward Polly.

Bright spots of embarrassment popped onto Polly's cheeks as Zetta managed a startled, "Oh. Well, now. That makes it easy, don't it?"

29

Dosha clapped her hands. "That will be fun. I'll bring a buttermilk pie."

Clarie leaned over to pick up Rachel's doll that had slipped to the floor. "I'll bring my potato candy," she said. "It's about time I stirred up a batch."

Polly, her shoulders still hunched, glanced at Zetta. "I wouldn't know what to bring," she said. "We don't get asked around much. Besides, Perton says I'm not much of a cook."

Zetta and Dosha glanced at each other, stunned a husband would say something so unkind about his wife, but Clarie waved the comment aside.

"Honey, I'll help you mix up a pan of brown sugar sweets," she said. "I've even got a good supply of this fall's walnut meats to throw in. Ain't a man alive that can resist Kentucky black walnuts."

As Polly managed a smile, Clarie put the last bite of cake into her mouth. Then she kissed Rachel on the cheek and eased her off her lap.

"Dosha, let's you and me get Zetta's shirts into the rinse kettle before the buttons boil off," she said. "Then we'll wring them out and show her how to hang a clothes line behind the stove."

Zetta started to protest, gesturing toward the clothes line just beyond the wash kettles, but Clarie shook her head.

"Honey, if you hang your clothes outside, you're liable to wind up with nothing to show for your work but soot," she said. "It's best if you dry them behind the stove. It's a bother, but at least they stay clean 'til the men put them back on."

As Clarie and Dosha went out the back door, Polly began to stack the plates from the table. When she spoke, her voice was barely audible.

"Whilst they're doing that, I'll help you with the dishes, if you'll let me," she said.

"I appreciate your help," Zetta said.

As she smiled at Polly, Zetta breathed a silent prayer: Lord, give this sad woman your hope.

Chapter 5

After the women left, Zetta stood on the narrow front porch and looked toward the mine tipple, wondering how deep inside the mountain Asa and her brothers were. The buildings below looked even worse in the daylight than they had when their wagon passed them in yesterday's waning sunlight. She tried not to think about the nightmare she'd had about Asa cutting timber, but the image of his pleading face stayed with her. Finally, she sighed and stepped back into the house.

Inside, she ran her hands along the blue shirts hanging on the makeshift line behind the stove then turned to Rachel who sat at the table, rocking her rag doll.

"These won't take any time at all to dry. And since I built up the fire, how about we make that cobbler whilst Micah is napping? I might as well soak the beans and put the meat on, too."

Rachel nodded. "Can I make little biscuits?"

"Sure enough," Zetta said. "Wasn't that something about Miz Clarie saying to have a kettle of hot water ready for the men? She said I've never seen anybody as dirty as your daddy is gonna be when he gets home. She said it's worse than tobacca harvest."

As Zetta talked, she opened a quart jar of blackberries and poured them into a gray cobbler pan. Then she stirred flour and sugar together and added a splash of buttermilk from home.

"Do you remember helping me get these berries back in

August? You picked a right smart amount. Micah's sure lucky to have you as a big sister. And it won't be long before you'll be big sister to another little baby."

Zetta placed the biscuit topping over the berries, then scraped the last of the dough from the bowl and sprinkled flour on it before handing it to Rachel.

"Here, now. Pat this out flat."

When the child had pressed the dough into an awkward circle, Zetta handed her a thimble with which to press out tiny circles. Rachel lined them up in front of her dolly, then squeezed them back into a dough ball to begin the procedure again. She would be busy long enough for Zetta to write her father and stepmother the promised letter.

Zetta eased herself into the chair across from Rachel and tapped the pencil against the same pad of paper Asa had used to write her. Finally, she began her letter.

Dear Paw and Mama Becky. I hope this letter finds you both well. We arrived safe and are happy to be together. Asa and the boys are fine and glad to be eating my cooking again.

Zetta looked around her, then decided against describing the house. Instead she wrote, *Right now, Micah is taking his morning nap and Rachel is making thimble biscuits for her doll here at the kitchen table. They sure was glad to see their Poppy at the station last night. And I wish you could have seen them on his lap whilst I fixed supper. I met the granny woman this morning already and two of our neighbor women. They told me about some of the goings-on here and made me feel right at home with helping finish the wash and hang the shirts. We are all going to the camp Christmas party this Saturday and then coming back here for sweets.*

Zetta fidgeted with the pencil for a moment. There was no way she was going to confess how homesick she was and how she longed for her own kitchen with its view of the mountains. She turned back to the paper:

Well, I know this is a short letter, but I want to bake ribs for supper, so I better cut the onions while Micah is still asleep. You probably won't get this before Christmas, but I hope you haven't been worried about us. We are all fine and are happy to be together. Tell Hobie and Frankie hello. Love, Zetta.

She folded the lined paper. She'd leave it out of the envelope in case one of the boys wanted to add a line or two at the bottom.

* * * * *

By the time Zetta had placed the sweet potatoes and onions next to the ribs in the covered skillet, Micah was awake and ready for noon dinner. The shirts were dry by mid-afternoon, so Zetta hung them on the nails behind the bedroom doors. Clarie already had said she needn't bother to iron them. As she lit the lanterns and set the coffee to boil, the shrill whistle announced the end of one shift and the start of another. Just as she looked out the back window to watch for the men, Asa and Luttrell stepped onto the porch.

She jumped, startled at the sight of them so covered in coal dust that only the whites of their eyes appeared untouched.

Rachel and Micah starred at them, wide-eyed and frightened, as Zetta opened the door to hand out a basin of hot water and a chunk of lye soap.

"Mercy! Do you look like this everyday?"

Asa nodded just as Loren ran onto the porch and handed Zetta a new dinner bucket along with his own.

"I told you I'd get another one," Loren said.

Then he turned to his brother-in-law. "Why don't you give her a big kiss now?"

Asa rinsed the black lather from his hands. "Aw, I'll wait 'til she can taste something besides the soot."

Within a few minutes, the men had changed into clean shirts and were presentable enough to sit at the table. Asa kissed Zetta's mouth and Rachel's face, then rubbed Micah's head.

As the men sat down, Zetta placed the pot of ribs, sweet potatoes and onions before them and spooned out a small portion for each child.

"Now let that cool whilst Poppy asks the blessing. Close your eyes, Micah."

The child did as he was told, but immediately held a finger over one eye and stared at his daddy with the other. Zetta bit her tongue to keep from laughing as she lowered her head.

At Asa's *Amen*, Loren was the first to pick up the serving spoon. "Well, Sis, you got the washing done and supper on. You're about as handy as a pocket on a shirt."

Zetta placed the plate of hot cornbread in front of him then sat in her own chair.

"And I met the granny woman when she brung down milk,"

Zetta said. "I swear she never meets a stranger, does she? I had a little visit from the supervisor's girl, too, and heard all about her mama not liking it here."

Asa didn't look up. "Try to put up with her," he said. "I hear tell she got a family run out a while back."

Zetta nodded. "I believe it. Oh, and I met Dosha Conley and Polly Muncy. We talked about the Christmas party up at the schoolhouse this Sunday. Clarie talked me into going, so I invited them all back here for sweets after the program."

All three men, their food at their mouths, stopped and turned to Zetta. Loren tossed his cornbread onto his plate, and Luttrell cleared his throat. Asa lowered the bite of sweet potato.

"Now, Zetta, I wish you'd asked me before you went off and asked Perton and his woman back here."

Zetta looked bewildered. "Why, back home you was pleased to have folks in for sweets," she said. "And I didn't ask Perton and his woman in, I asked Polly and her man. Why is that so wrong?"

Asa looked pained. "This ain't back home. Perton's decent enough in the mine—otherwise he wouldn't be shift boss—but outside he likes his moonshine too much."

Loren rubbed the scar on his chin. "And he likes the fights that come with it."

Zetta frowned as she pulled meat off the cooled ribs for the children. "Well, I can't uninvite them," she said. "I'll just remember that the next time."

For several moments, no one said anything as the men continued to stare at their plates. Finally, Asa picked up his discarded fork.

"I swear, nothing beats sweet potatoes from our own ground," he said.

Loren reached for another helping of ribs. "After Grandpaw Davis got home from the war, he wouldn't eat 'em. Said there was weeks when that and hardtack was all they had. And some nights they could smell the *meat* the Yankees was cooking across the river."

Zetta sighed, knowing the coming argument.

Asa scowled at his brother-in-law. "They were *Union*. It wasn't just Yankees in the ranks. Plenty folks from our part of the country joined up."

Loren shook his head. "That's always puzzled me—how your family could let a bunch of *Yankees* come in and tell us how to run our business."

"Slavery's not right," Asa answered. "One man never should own another man."

"None of your kin ever owned slaves," Loren said. "Ours neither. We picked up rifles at Ivy Point in October of '63 because nobody in Washington needs to be telling us how to run things. And we held our ground."

"Yes, and lost it two years later when the Union came back through," Asa said. "Look, I know all about Ivy Point. Sometimes when I'm plowing, I find buttons or a piece of bone. And I think about those boys who should have growed old to sit on the porch and watch their grandbabies play."

"They was fighting so their grandbabies could play," Loren said. "I just wish I'd been around at Perrysville in '62. I'd made sure we won so Kentucky could go Confederate."

"What ails you? That was the bloodiest battle Kentucky had," Asa said. "And what the bullets didn't take, the drought and dysentery did. I swear, sometimes I wonder about you—and about your granddad for fighting on the wrong side."

Loren glared at Asa. "A man's gotta fight for what he knows is right."

"Well, I can't argue that—wrong side or not," Asa replied. "But it's too bad he put all his money in Confederate bills instead of keeping it in Union gold. I hear tell a trunk full of worthless paper is all he left your daddy. All it's good for is to fill that old dried up well."

Loren's voice took on a sudden harshness. "You think you're pretty smart, don't you?"

Luttrell had not spoken during the argument but suddenly reached in front of his brother for the cornbread.

"It was bad enough the War Between Brothers split the country and families back then," he said. "Let's not let it split us now. Loren, hand me some butter."

For several minutes, no one spoke. Zetta felt the baby move as though reacting to the tension within the room and her body.

Lord, you're gonna have to help me know how to act here, she inwardly prayed. *I got us off on the wrong foot with that whole mess about the sweets.*

Asa interrupted Zetta's thoughts. "Hey, Rachel. Where was Moses when the lantern went out?"

The little girl—and everyone else—merely looked at him.

"In the dark!" He slapped his thigh as he answered his own joke.

"Oh, Asa!" was Zetta's only comment, but at least the tension was broken.

For several moments, the men ate somberly, savoring the peppered meat. But when Zetta held out the blackberry cobbler, Loren grinned as he scooped out a double portion.

"Your cobbler can't be beat. But don't tell Sarah I said that."

"Oh, I won't," Zetta said. "Especially since your every letter is probably bragging to her how hard you work and how hard it is to save money here."

Asa wiped his plate with the last of the cornbread before reaching for the cobbler pan Loren held.

"You'd get your money saved a lot quicker if you tried to hang onto it a little more," Asa said.

Zetta didn't want another argument to start so she quickly said, "Speaking of letters, I left room on mine to Paw and Becky for anybody to add a hello."

Luttrell lifted his cobbler-laden fork. "Not me. Loren's a better hand at writing."

Loren chuckled. "I am at that—even if I do say so myself. Folks know when they hear from Luttrell something bad wrong has happened."

* * * * *

As the men stretched and stood up from the table, Loren gestured toward the remaining cobbler. "Put some of that in my bucket tomorrow. But make sure to put it on top of everything else. That way if the mine caves in before I'm finished eating, at least I woulda had dessert."

Zetta gasped, remembering her dream. "Don't be kidding like that," she said. "Clarie said her man was killed by slate."

Loren shrugged. "Aw, come on, now. That was just a joke. Here, I'll get your water for tomorrow."

36

He grabbed the nearly empty water bucket and strode out the door.

Zetta stood to pour warm water from the kettle onto a kitchen towel, then turned to wash the children's faces. But her hands trembled.

Asa took the cloth from her. "That was a fine meal," he said. "Here, I'll put Sister and Brother to bed whilst you wash the dishes. Then I want to show you what I've been working on."

As he ran the cloth over Micah's face, he turned back to Zetta.

"I saw Clarie on the way home," he said. "Tomorrow morning, she's planning to show you around the camp a little. I thought you'd like that."

Zetta merely nodded as she placed the dishes in the pan of sudsy water. What is there to see around here? she thought.

Asa picked up the children and held them toward Zetta for a good night kiss. As he left the room, Luttrell pulled a cigar box from the top shelf, then sat in his customary spot at the table. He opened his pocket knife before reaching into the box and bringing out several large, dry peach pits.

"What you got there?" Zetta asked.

"I thought I'd whittle out some little baskets for Rachel's Christmas play pretties," Luttrell answered. "And some squirrels for Micah."

Zetta smiled. "They'll like that. You're a good hand to whittle."

"I like whittling because it's like fishing," Luttrell said. "A man can't think of anything else whilst doing it."

With her hands still in the hot, soapy water, Zetta watched her brother deftly turn the pit beneath his knife. Soon a basket with a raised handle began to appear.

"Rachel will take a shine to that, Luttrell. Next year I'm thinking to get her one of those fancy store-bought dolls. But for now, I just made a little quilt to go with the cradle Asa told me he's making for her rag baby."

As Luttrell set the tiny basket on the table to check its levelness, Asa came back into the kitchen and held a wooden figure toward Zetta.

"Look at what I'm making for Micah. I been studying the dancing men the company store has. I reckon I can do just as good a job. See how I put the wire through the arms and legs so they swing? I finished Rachel's cradle. Clarie's keeping it 'til Christmas."

37

"Asa, honey, that little man is right clever," Zetta said.

Asa nodded as he sat at the table. "And when we get home I'm going to make marbles for Micah. I'll set the marble stone under that waterfall behind the smokehouse. It'll take a while for the water to bounce the rough edges off the stones, but he'll have a bagful of marbles by the time he goes to school."

Loren came through the door at Asa's last sentence. "Yeah, and lose them just like you always lost yours to the Allen boys."

Asa shook his head. "Nah. I'll teach Micah how to win. Problem was, I didn't have a daddy to show me things like that."

Zetta bit her lip, remembering the stories Asa's mother had told of the awful Christmas Eve when Asa was twelve.

Loren set the filled water bucket on the work bench. "I hear tell your daddy tried to be a peacemaker. A lot of good it did him."

"I know," Asa said. "But the Patrick boys had gotten into the Christmas moonshine a little early and chased my brother home on horseback. Paw stepped off the porch just as the ringleader fired his rifle. He wasn't aiming at anything, but he hit Paw square in the chest. He made it back into the house but bled to death on the hearth, right in front of Maw. Every time it rained for years after, the blood stains reappeared in the stone."

Asa's voice trailed off. Even though Zetta had heard the story numerous times, it always filled her with fresh sorrow as she imagined Asa's father staggering back into the house and dying as his wife pushed her apron against the pulsating wound and screamed. Young Asa had run from his bedroom and dumped the candy from his shoes, filled German-style by old Santa Claus, before running to the neighbors for help.

As the long silence filled the kitchen, Loren picked up the unfinished letter to his paw and stepmother. Asa and Luttrell bent over the toys in their hands, and Zetta scrubbed the dishes a little harder.

CHAPTER 6

The next morning, Zetta was surprised at how well she had slept despite the evening's reminder of that long-ago Christmas Eve tragedy and her previous bad dream. She had the eggs, biscuits, gravy and hot coffee waiting as the men sat down. After Asa asked the blessing, Zetta poured drinking water into the bottom of the gray graniteware dinner buckets, then folded leftover ribs and cobbler into squares of wax paper and placed them in each bucket's tray.

She held the paper roll toward Asa. "At this rate, I'm gonna run out of food paper," she said. "When Clarie takes me to the store, I reckon I better get some more—if that's all right."

Asa never looked up from spooning jelly onto his biscuit.

"Get whatever you figure we need," he said. "Roscoe, the feller running the company store, will put the charge on the books, and it'll come out of my pay at the end of the month. That adds up pretty fast, though, so don't go hog wild."

Loren pointed the last of his biscuit at Zetta before plopping it into his mouth. "Make sure you pack a spoon with that cobber."

Zetta nodded. "I already did. And I put damp wash rags in the buckets, too, since I packed those old messy ribs."

Loren hooted. "Now that's gonna be a sight. Us sitting in the bottom of a coal mine, wiping our hands after each bite like city folk. Our britches will do just fine."

Luttrell saw Zetta's stricken look. "It's okay, Sis. You saw us

39

yesterday before we cleaned up. Wash rags will just tote more of the mine back up here to the house."

Asa studied the row of dinner buckets on the bench. "Where'd that third bucket come from?"

"Loren brung it in whilst you was washing up last night. He said you ought to have your own," Zetta said.

Asa nodded. "Well, I hate to admit it, but I reckon he's right." He turned to his brother-in-law. "I'm much obliged. I'll pay you back come payday."

Loren shook his head. "Nah, I'll just find a way to take it out of your hide."

"You know I don't like being beholding," Asa said.

Loren drained the last of his coffee. "And you know I don't like hearing about you being beholding," he said. "Just take the bucket and hush."

* * * * *

While Micah and Rachel ate their biscuits and gravy, Zetta washed the morning dishes then rinsed the pinto beans that had soaked all night in the largest kettle. After pouring fresh water over them and adding a ham hock for flavor, she pulled the kettle to the warmest part of the stove where the beans would simmer all day. She stared at the kettle for a moment, then added another ham hock.

As she pulled off her apron, she looked out the back window to see Clarie coming down the hill. As always, the woman's faded brown coat hung open, revealing the bright blue apron with its several pockets.

Zetta bent over Micah, a wash cloth in her hand. "Here, let me help you finish up, honey," she said. "I declare, you've got more gravy on your face than you do in your little belly. Now, Miz Clarie's going to show us around. You and Sister mind your manners at the store. Hear?"

Both children solemnly nodded. Zetta opened the back door as Clarie came up the steps. A wooden basket dangled from her arm, its contents covered with a white cloth.

"You ready to see the sights?" Clarie said as she pointed her walking stick in the direction of the mine.

"Ready as I'll ever be, I reckon," Zetta answered as she handed Rachel her coat, then tugged Micah's on him.

Then she picked up Asa's coat. "Asa said for me to wear his so's I can button it up."

Clarie nodded. "My man had to shovel coal on his side at times, so a bundlesome coat just got in the way. Not that he needed one down there. He liked working underground. Said it was always cool in the summer and warm in the winter."

Zetta put the letter she had written yesterday into her coat, then took Micah's hand.

She nodded to Rachel as they turned toward the front door. "Take Brother's other hand."

Clarie called her back. "I'd druther go out the same door I come in," she said. "Otherwise, the Devil follows me out."

Zetta smiled as she turned the children around. "I haven't heard that since I was a girl," she said. "My mother always used to say that."

Clarie held the back door open. "Used to?"

"Yes," Zetta said quietly. "She died when I was 12."

"I'm right sorry," Clarie said. "What of?"

Zetta frowned. "Purple fever. Two weeks after my baby brother, Hobie, was born."

Clarie nodded. "Now that's a shame. But I don't want you worrying about that in your case. I always make sure every bit of the afterbirth is out. I don't leave anything in there that's liable to poison my girls."

Clarie stepped down the two narrow steps to the hard packed dirt below. There, she pulled two white cloths from her apron pocket and handed them to Zetta.

"If the wind shifts once we get down the hill you might want to tie these over the children's mouths. Right now they'll be okay, though."

Zetta tucked the cloths into her pocket. "Do you ever get used to the soot?" she asked.

"Nah. You just learn to tolerate it," Clarie said. "In fact, my chickens have got so they won't eat a bug unless it's covered in coal dust."

Clarie chuckled at her own joke, then lifted the cloth on her basket for Zetta to see.

"Even though I'm not an official part of the camp, Roscoe— the head clerk—let's me buy at the store," Clarie said. "He always needs fresh eggs, so occasionally I take a few down in exchange for what little I need. The price the store charges the miners for my eggs aggravates me, though, so most of the time I just sell them outright to my girls for the same penny apiece the company pays me."

As they started down the lane toward the mine, Clarie waved her walking stick.

"When I was a girl, this holler was the prettiest around," she said. "My daddy used to let me dig ginseng in the fall with him. And in the spring, this whole hillside was white with the dogwood trees in bloom. My mother and I would come up here to gather sallet greens. To this day, nothing beats fresh greens and wild onions wilted down with a little hot bacon grease."

Zetta looked at the buildings in the distance. They looked even more tired than when she first had seen them. Was it really just two nights ago when we arrived? she thought Clarie waved her walking stick again. "And up yonder was a stand of hickory trees always filled with fat squirrels that made mighty tasty eating," she said. "You could stand right still and hear them hollering back and forth or arguing with the blue jays. And if they was off someplace, the woods was so still you could hear your own heart beat. Now this place is all coal dust and mud and noise."

Clarie jabbed her walking stick toward the building with the faded yellow letters *Golden Gate Store* over the door.

"I reckon you know that's the store," she said. "They built it along with a bunch of buildings just about overnight after they got the tipple put in. Right past the store is the rail station."

Then Clarie gestured to her right. "That little side track goes to the mine."

Zetta stared for several moments at the rail track going into the folds of the mountains. Oh, Lord, please keep Asa safe. Keep them all safe.

Clarie continued waving her stick. "And that little squat building in front of the tipple is the machine shop. Next to it is the lamp house where the men get their lanterns repaired."

She gestured toward a brick building sitting just beyond them. "And that's the school Mr. Golden built last year. He aims to have this camp be as good as the ones over at Benham and Lynch, I reckon, so when they put in school buildings, he had to do the same.

"Over yonder is the ball field," she continued. "Come summer, we have some good games. Those boys from Hazard can get a little rough, though. Does Asa like ball? I reckon Loren does."

"Yes, they all played when we was in school," Zetta answered. "But we won't be here come summer."

"That's right; you told me," Clarie said. "I forgot since I've known so many miners say that but then wind up staying since they're in such bad debt to the company. They bring their families here for the good paying jobs, thinking they're in paradise. They find out soon enough this ain't heaven."

Her voice trailed off as she pointed her stick again. "Well, now, over yonder is the hospital," she said. "I hear tell the doctor was running from some trouble up north, so he's more interested in looking over his shoulder than tending patients. He's happy to have me and Ruthie catch the babies, though, so we just stay out of his way."

"Ruthie? But I thought you was the only granny woman," Zetta said.

Clarie pointed her stick toward the leaning shacks behind the tipple. "Oh, Ruthie catches the colored babies over in Shucky Bean Holler," she said. "We help each other if one of our girls is having a rough go of it, but most of the time we just go about our own business."

She stepped forward to where the path dipped, then held her hand out to the children, then Zetta. "Now be real careful here. You need much at the store today?"

"I want to mail a letter home," Zetta said as she leaned against Clarie's arm for a moment. "And get food paper and a cake of yeast. Maybe cloves for the Christmas ham—if they're not too expensive."

"Think what you'd pay at home and then more than double that," Clarie said.

Zetta gasped. "More than double? For cloves? When Asa was first here he wrote me the company prices were high, but I didn't think they'd be that bad."

Clarie shrugged. "Mine owners like reminding us they ain't in business for their *health*. Ain't this something? The men pull the coal out of the ground to make the iron that makes the railroad ties that haul the coal out of these hills. Reminds me of my man telling about the mules plowing all spring to plant the corn to feed them all winter so they could be strong enough to plant the corn the next spring."

Zetta turned to Clarie, anticipating the customary chuckle. But this time Clarie's face was solemn.

"Funny thing. I dreamed about him last night," Clarie said. "There he was, just standing in my kitchen, grinning at me and asking if I had anything for him to eat. I woke up trying to remember if he'd had his noon dinner before the slate fell on him."

Clarie sighed then raised her stick toward the hill above the store.

"The mine graveyard is up there," she said. "Most folks take their men home to bury them, but my man is up there. Seems only fitting since we grew up around here."

She took a deep breath. "He's buried next to our baby girls. I used to go up there just to be near him. And I'd ask him about heaven and if our girls were still babies or if they was growed up— it being heaven and all. After a while, though, I got tired of talking to the ground and not getting an answer. So I'd just sit and look off across the mountains, remembering how pretty this valley used to be. And I'd talk about whatever was worrying me. Pretty soon, I realized I was talking to God and not to my man...."

Clarie's voice trailed off, and she gave herself a gentle shake. "Well, I declare," she said. "I sure am going on this morning. I reckon I always feel like this when it gets close to the time he died."

Zetta gripped the children's hands, unsure how to respond and wondering how to tell about her own dream. Then before she could form a question, their little group reached the street near the store and met more basket-toting women exiting the various lanes throughout the camp. Clarie looked toward Shucky Bean Holler then raised her hand in greeting.

Zetta turned to see an older woman approaching, her dark skin a stark contrast to the crisp white kerchief covering her hair.

Clarie held out her hand. "Morning, Ruthie. I reckon your ears was burning a little bit ago," she said. "I was telling Zetta here about you and me catching all the babies."

Ruthie gripped Clarie's fingers. "Yessirree," she chuckled. "We get the job done, don't we?"

She gave Zetta's figure a quick assessment. "Well, Miz Zetta, even with that heavy coat, it looks like you've got just a little over a month before you get yourself another pretty baby."

Zetta blushed and nodded as she took the woman's offered hand, marveling at the beige palm that contrasted with the blackness of the rest of Ruthie's skin. As they released fingers, Ruthie leaned forward to smile at the children. Micah quickly hid behind his mother's legs, but Rachel stared gap-mouthed.

Clarie fumbled in her apron pocket, then withdrew a small packet. "I was hoping to see you today," she said. "Since a couple of your girls are gonna be delivering about the same time, I figured you might could use these morning glory seeds."

Ruthie smiled. "Oh, bless your sweet heart," she said. "You know I'm partial to morning glory tea when I've been run ragged."

She turned toward the store. "Well, that line is getting pretty long around back so I better get the bag of flour I've come after."

She turned to smile at Zetta.

"It was nice meeting you, Miz Zetta."

"Uh, nice meeting you, too."

As Ruthie left, Zetta turned to Clarie.

"What did she mean about the line around in back?"

Clarie sighed. "Oh, honey, that's one thing I hate. The colored people can't go inside the store. When one of the clerks has a minute, he goes to the back door, collects the baskets with the lists in them and then fills the orders. Sometimes, though, he gets the orders and the baskets mixed up, so the girls have to swap goods before they go home. And all they can do is hope Roscoe got the charges entered in the books right."

Clarie took Rachel's hand. "When you see Mr. Roscoe, say hello real nice. But don't touch a thing. He can be grouchy about that."

Zetta glanced at the group of women waiting at the back of the store, clutched Micah's hand all the tighter, then followed Clarie up the four steps into the front of the store.

CHAPTER 7

Zetta gasped as she stepped inside the brightly lit company store. Tulip-shaped glass shades covered the light bulbs hanging from the ceiling in three long rows. The heavy air stung her nose with its combined smells of salty cured meat and burning coal. An over-heated pot-bellied stove stood in the middle of the store surrounded by rocking chairs with prominent price tags on the backs. All around the walls were shelves reaching high above her head. Open sacks of coffee beans stood in front of the long counters. Nearby, potatoes, onions and pinto beans filled wooden barrels. The shelves held canned goods, their labels bright with images of red tomatoes, yellow corn, green beans. Toys lined the shelves behind the cash register—mechanical banks in animal shapes, dancing men on sticks, painted wooden horses, little cast iron stoves and dolls with long lacy dresses and golden curls.

Rachel, her eyes on the dolls, tugged at her mother's coat. "Mama, look. They're pretty."

"Yes, they sure enough are," her mother said as she noticed Rachel's rag doll hanging limply from the child's hand.

Zetta sighed as she turned to study the hams and pork shoulders hanging above the cash register. She leaned toward Clarie.

"Our little store back home would fit in this one six times or more," Zetta whispered. She gestured toward the large glass cases holding row after row of candy.

"Chocolate drops, peppermint sticks, lemon drops and more,"

Zetta said. "I've never seen so much all at once."

Clarie nodded. "This is quite a place all right," she whispered back. "Gets folks to hanker after what they didn't know they couldn't live without it 'til they saw it here."

Zetta turned her attention to the several clerks waiting on miners' wives. As each woman told a clerk what she needed, he would move a ladder to the appropriate shelf and get the item. Zetta was trying to take it all in without gawking. But Rachel and Micah stared openmouthed at the wonders packed from floor to ceiling. Clarie gently elbowed Zetta and nodded toward a bald clerk talking to the little girl Zetta had met the morning before.

"That's Roscoe," she said. "We'll wait 'til he's finished with Miz Julia."

The man looked as though he would rather be waiting on anyone but Julia as she stood before him, arms folded defiantly across her beige coat.

"I told you to give me a sack of chocolate drops," she said. "I'm going to tell my daddy if you don't."

Sweat was beginning to form on Roscoe's forehead.

"Now Miz Julia, your daddy was the one who told me not to let you have any more candy unless he's with you," he said.

Julia pursed her lips, pondering that. "What if I told you my mother said I could have it?"

Roscoe nervously ran his tongue over his teeth. "If your mother comes with you, you can have whatever she says."

The child shrugged. "She's got a headache today, so she sent me down here. Said for me to get anything I want."

Roscoe gestured toward the closed door to his left.

"I've got some oranges in the back just waiting for the Christmas party," he said. "How about I get you a big one of those?"

"My mother is going to be mad at you when I tell her."

"Now, Miz Julia, you know I can't go against your daddy," Roscoe said. "How about this? You go home and get your mother to write that it's okay to give you the candy."

The child gave a disgruntled huff, but turned to go. Suddenly, she faced him again. "I'm going to tell her you made me wake her up," she said.

Then Julia noticed Rachel watching her. Julia stuck out her tongue at the startled toddler and stomped out the front door.

Rachel turned to her mother. "She's mean."

"Shush, honey," Zetta said. "You're fine."

"But that's not nice," Rachel said.

"I know. But don't you fret about her. Just make sure you don't act that way." Clarie nudged Zetta forward.

"Well, Roscoe," Clarie said. "You sure had your hands full there for a minute."

Roscoe pulled his handkerchief from his back pocket and mopped his brow.

"I've never seen a child so determined to have things her own way," he said. "What can I get for you, Clarie?"

"I've got eggs to trade, but first I want you to meet Asa Berghoffer's woman and youngins. This here is Zetta and little Rachel and Micah. Zetta needs a few things, too."

Roscoe put both hands on the counter and leaned forward in greeting.

"Welcome to Golden Gate," he said. "What can I get for you?"

Zetta pulled the letter from her coat pocket.

"I'd like to mail this home," she said. "And I need a pack of yeast and a roll of food paper, please." The cloves can wait for another day, she thought.

"All righty," Roscoe said. "First, let me check which mailbox is yours."

He turned to a stack of tall black ledgers on the shelf behind him and selected the one with A-B-C on the spine. He opened it on the counter before Zetta.

"Let's see; Avery, Bailey. Ah, here we go. Berghoff. Asa. Box seventeen."

"Excuse me, Sir," Zetta said. "It's Berghoff*er*. Our name has an *E-R* on the end. Berg-hoff-*er*."

Roscoe shrugged. "I reckon I didn't have room for all that. But what does it matter as long as he gets paid?"

He gestured across the aisle toward the postal cage positioned between rows of tiny boxes, then came around the counter to lead the way. Above the cage hung several graniteware buckets and canvas caps.

"That'll be two cents for the stamp, but we'll add it to rest of your charges," Roscoe said. "Your mail box is number seventeen— right up here. Turn the knob on the glass window and get your mail. But nothing's in there today."

Clarie bent over to check box number fifty-one. When she

straightened, she held up a letter.

"Well, I declare," she said. "It's from my cousin over at Hindman Settlement School."

She smiled as she put the envelope into her apron pocket.

After dropping Zetta's letter into a canvas pouch, Roscoe waved the little group back to the grocery counter. Just then, Zetta saw another clerk come through the back door, holding several baskets, which he lined up on the counter. He put the lists in front of the baskets and started pulling items off the shelves.

Roscoe moved to his usual spot near the register. "What else you need today?"

"Yeast and food paper, please," Zetta said.

Roscoe walked to the end of the counter, pulled a roll of wax paper down from the shelf then called to the young clerk filling the baskets.

"Bring this lady a pack of yeast."

Roscoe leaned over the black book again and read aloud as he entered the charges. "Asa Berghoff—December 19—postal and grocery charge—fifty-two cents."

"Fifty-two cents for the little I got?" Zetta said.

"Yep. Be glad you didn't need meat," Roscoe answered.

Then he turned to Clarie. "How many eggs you got for me today?"

As Zetta shoved her purchases into her coat pocket, Clarie set the egg basket on the counter and withdrew the cloth.

"Eleven eggs today," Clarie said. "In trade for a small box of salt."

Roscoe handed the basket to the young clerk still trying to fill orders. As the young man carefully placed the eggs in a straw-lined crate, Roscoe took a round box of salt from the shelf and handed it to Clarie.

"That's fifteen cents minus eleven cents. You owe me four cents," he said.

Clarie fumbled in her apron pocket. "Well, I see the prices went up again," she said. "I was thinking we'd break even today," she said. "But I shouldn't be surprised since I dreamed about birds last night. Feathers are always a sign of disappointment."

At the mention of dreams, Zetta quickly looked at Clarie, but Roscoe merely shrugged.

"It costs to tote all these goods back in these hills," he said.

"Why don't you just let me put the difference in the book for you? You can settle up later."

Clarie shook her head as she withdrew a worn leather coin purse from her pocket. "Now Roscoe, you know being in debt is one way to have less than nothing," she said.

She handed him a nickel—the lone coin in the snap purse. As he handed her the empty egg basket and a penny in change, she smiled.

"I always like having a little something in here as seed," she said. Then she patted the purse and tucked it back into her pocket.

* * * * *

As Clarie, Zetta and the children left the store, Julia came down the hill.

"Hey, wait for me," she called.

Rachel immediately moved closer to her mother. Clarie glanced at Zetta and shook her head. "That child…" was all she managed before Julia joined them.

Julia flipped her hair out of her coat collar. "What did you buy?"

Clarie quickened her pace. "Oh, cooking things. Did your mother write Mr. Roscoe?"

"Not yet. But she will."

"How's her headache? Still bad?"

"I guess," Julia said.

"Would you like to take a lavender pack to her?" Clarie asked. "She can put it across her eyes whilst she's resting."

Julia sniffed. "She doesn't like hillbilly medicine."

Clarie and Zetta looked at each over the child's head.

"Well, how about you take her a few sprigs from the holly bush I found up in the woods," Clarie offered. "Maybe the sight of the pretty berries will make her feel better."

Julia shrugged. "I guess. Daddy offered to rub her neck this morning, but she told him the first neck rub in Lexington is what started her headaches."

Zetta stifled a chuckle as she stooped to pick up Micah, who was having trouble keeping up with the increased pace. But Clarie laughed aloud. Julia stopped in the middle of the path and put her hands on her hips.

"What's so funny?" the child asked.

"Oh, Miz Julia, I reckon you just have a clever way with words," Clarie said. "Come on, now. We'll get those holly berries."

Clarie gave a half-hearted wave and turned up the lane with Julia at her heels. Zetta was relieved not to put up with the wearying child, but was disappointed she hadn't been able to ask Clarie about dreams.

By the time Zetta and the children had arrived at the house, Micah was yawning. As soon as Zetta put him down for his nap, she came back into the kitchen and put on her apron.

She was pleased to see Rachel clutching her doll again.

"You and me are gonna surprise Poppy with a big supper tonight," Zetta said. "And I'm gonna bake meat and cabbage in bread so's it'll be easier for the men to eat in the mine."

For the rest of the day, Zetta cooked, stopping only to feed the three of them when Micah awakened. By midafternoon, the meat from the second ham hock had been mixed with cooked cabbage and onions and packed inside folded over yeast rolls.

While the meat rolls baked, Zetta ignored the tightness in her abdomen as she measured out half of the contents of a Mason jar of peaches for a small pie. Then she positioned the reminder of the fruit on top of small rounds of dough, which she folded over and sealed. As she fried each hand pie to a golden brown in hot lard, she repeatedly wiped the sweat from her face with her apron.

* * * * *

By the time the mine shift was over, Zetta had the kettle of hot water and soap waiting on the wash bench. When the three men were clean enough to enter the kitchen, Asa kissed Zetta and then stared at the steaming dishes on the table.

"We having company tonight?" he asked.

Zetta shook her head. "No. I'm just planning ahead to pack y'all's buckets."

Asa settled into his place at the table. "Well, you've had a right busy day. What did you think of the store?"

"It's something, especially those fancy electric lights," Zetta said. "But the prices are even worse than I expected."

Luttrell sat down as Loren leaned forward to savor the stream rising from the bowls of fried corn, cooked cabbage and pinto beans.

Asa nodded. "Mr. Gray—the supervisor—is right proud of the Corliss steam engine that keeps the lights on in the central buildings and keeps water out of the mine. Says it took 20 teams of mules to get it off the railcar and into place."

Loren looked at his brother-in-law. "Could this little discussion wait 'til you ask the blessing?" he said. "You two can talk whilst I work on this food."

Zetta put her hands on the children's shoulders. "Fold your hands," she said. "Poppy's gonna pray."

At the *Amen*, Zetta spooned beans onto the children's plates, then handed the bowl to Asa.

"Did you know Roscoe doesn't have our full name in the books?" she asked. "And he didn't seem to care one way or another when I pointed it out to him."

Asa took a large helping of beans, then accepted the bowl of fried corn from Luttrell.

"I know. Mr. Gray calls me Berghoff, too," Asa said. "I tried correcting them a time or two, but finally got tired. I just keep telling myself I can tolerate anything 'til March thirty-first."

Zetta set the plate of rolls on the table.

Loren's face brightened. "Well, looky here! Sunday rolls in the middle of the week. What got into you, Sis?"

Zetta sat in her own chair. "I've come up with a way to bake meat and cabbage inside the rolls for your noon dinner. That way it won't be messy to eat."

Loren reached for another roll before swallowing what already was in his mouth.

Zetta turned back to Asa. "Clarie told me the colored women ain't allowed in the store. I saw them line up around back and wait for their goods. That don't seem right."

Asa nodded. "I know. The men get paid less, too."

Loren spooned a ham hock from the bean bowl. "They've got their own church, and their children go to their own school," he said. "And their families can stay with them. They ought to be happy. Some of the camps don't allow that."

Asa frowned. "We're all the same color under the ground. And under the skin, too."

Loren put his fork down. "Now you're sounding like Jim Reed back home."

Zetta interrupted her brother. "And I've fried hand pies for your dessert, too. The ones for tomorrow are peach. I'm sending six of the best ones to your shift boss, like you said, to thank him for letting out the wagon last Sunday."

Asa merely nodded.

Luttrell looked up. "One of the single fellers saw my cobbler and offered me a nickel if I'd give him half. He looked so pitiful, I let him have it for free."

Loren reached for more bread.

"Wait 'til the boarders see the meat and cabbage all baked pretty in Sunday rolls," he said. "And ain't none of them getting mine."

Zetta stared at him, wrestling with a new thought. Then she turned to Asa.

"The youngins played so quiet whilst I cooked that I got carried away with making the meat rolls," she said. "I've got extra. What would you think about taking them to sell to the boarders?"

Asa looked up in surprise, but Zetta babbled on. "Would fifteen cents each be too much?" she asked. "And I've got a few extra fried fruit pies, too. What if I offered them for five cents?"

"Now, Zetta."

She rushed on, determined. "Those two little items I bought this morning cost an awful lot," she said. "Then all the money I'd make I'd put toward our groceries. Roscoe said I should be glad I wasn't buying meat today. Even with all I brung from home, it's not going to last us 'til the end of March."

"I reckon you've got enough to do with two youngins already and another one on the way," Asa said.

"Well, what if I made them just when I had a little extra time?" Zetta asked. "I wouldn't have to make them every day."

Asa shrugged. "Suit yourself."

But as her husband bent over his plate, Zetta saw the slightest smile.

CHAPTER 8

By the time the dreaded whistle blew the next morning, Zetta had the yeast bread rising in her largest ironstone bowl, the breakfast biscuits in the oven and the dough mixed for gingerbread cookies. After serving the men a hearty breakfast, Zetta breathed her customary prayer as she watched the three trudge down the path toward the mine.

Oh, Lord, please keep them all safe.

She watched as they were swallowed by the damp morning darkness, then smiled as she thought of the three dinner buckets crowded with extra meat pies, and the little package of six peach fried pies Asa carried to give to his shift boss.

While she waited for Rachel and Micah to awaken, she rolled out the cookie dough and positioned the oblong shapes on a flat skillet. As the cookies baked, she washed the morning dishes, humming to herself.

Just as she pulled the cookies from the oven and placed them on a towel to cool, she heard the familiar and cheerful "Hello in the cabin" at the front door.

She hurried to open it. There stood Clarie at the bottom of the steps with Polly at her side. The young woman shyly smiled at Zetta, then lowered her eyes.

Clarie held out a jar of milk to Zetta then waved her walking stick toward the mine. "Me and Polly is on our way to the store for sugar," she said. "I aim to teach her how to make brown sugar sweets today. You need anything whilst we're out and about?"

Zetta smiled as she accepted the milk. "No, but I appreciate you asking," she said. "I'm glad you stopped by. I forgot to give back your handkerchiefs from yesterday. Since the air wasn't bad enough for me to put them over the youngins mouths, I plumb forgot them."

Clarie shook her head. "Hang on to 'em. You'll need 'em sooner or later around here."

Zetta noticed Clarie's basket was empty. A blue cloth was folded in the bottom.

"Didn't your hens give eggs this morning?" Zetta asked.

Clarie pointed to the cloth that was the same bright blue as her ever-present apron.

"Oh, they laid a right smart amount, but I sold them already," she said. "On the mornings I need to trade eggs at the store, I cover them with a white cloth. But when the women see the blue cloth, they know the eggs are available to buy. I sold them all before I got down here to your place. Polly got the last two."

Zetta nodded. "That's a good system. I'm already about out of the ones I brung from home, so I'll take any you can spare for my baking. In fact, I just took cookies out of the oven if y'all want coffee before you set off."

Clarie grabbed Polly's hand and started up the steps. "I was hoping you'd ask. And from that good smell, I'm guessing you made gingerbread."

Once inside and seated at the table, Clarie shrugged off her coat and pulled a letter from her apron pocket.

"I have to read you what my cousin at the Hindman Settlement School sent me yesterday," she said. "She's all the time writing pretty letters about what's going on over there. A couple of level land women started the school a while back, but to hear my cousin tell it, you'd think the good Lord himself came up with the idea. She teaches reading and writing classes and helps out in the sore eyes clinic in between times."

As she unfolded the letter, Clarie said, "Listen to what my cousin says this time: 'Yesterday I asked my students to describe what these mountains mean to them. Here's what Drucilla wrote: I love these mountains that protect me and threaten me all at the same time. I love to see the morning mist rise out of the leafy places and then roll on the brown water of the river toward unknown parts. If I could, I'd ride a ways with the mist just to see where it was going. But I know I can never stay away from these mountains that rise to the sky like purple ridges on a green dragon's back.'"

Clarie waved the letter toward Polly. "Now that's plumb good writing for a youngin who will wind up marrying far too young and getting old before her time."

Zetta set a plate of cookies on the table.

"But that wasn't the news I wanted to tell," Clarie said. "My cousin says they got a whole family to come to their sore eyes clinic. Listen. 'The little boy had the worse infection, and it spread through the family. The mother refused our offer to help, saying God's will had to be done. Well, I snatched up that sweet child and ran out the door with him before the mother could holler for her husband to shoot me!'"

Zetta handed cups of coffee to both women. "Shoot her?"

Clarie nodded. "Yeah, but it turns out all right. Listen. 'Of course, the father came to the school—mad as a hornet—but our director met him at the gate with her Bible in hand. She talked to him about how God wants us to be part of his miracles. She even made him listen to the story of Jesus raising Lazarus in John 11 and remarked that just like Jesus told the bystanders to roll away the stone from the grave and then take the grave clothes off Lazarus, we are to do the things we can do and leave the miracles to God. While he was pondering that, she said helping people with sore eyes was something she could do, but the healing was God's. Well, about then he saw me watching from the clinic window and he waved his rifle and shouted I'd better never carry off one of his children again. But he went home to get the rest of the family for treatment. These are the times I feel as though I'm finally doing some good with my life.'"

Clarie folded the letter then leaned forward to take the largest cookie from the plate.

"Yessir! She's the type I wish all my kin was like," she said. "Not like poor old Granddad selling coal rights to this whole valley."

Zetta slid another skilletful of dough into the oven then turned to Clarie.

"Your people used to own all this?" she asked.

Clarie nodded as she bit into the warm cookie.

"Uh-huh. Owned as far as you could see," she said. "All I

got now is the homeplace."

She swallowed, then spoke. "About the time Granddad's old mule died, and he didn't know how he was going to get the money together to buy another one, a city feller showed up with a man from the courthouse. Real polite he was. Said his company thought there might be coal here in his hills and they was willing to take a risk and buy the mineral rights to it. Said they'd pay twenty-five cents an acre and he'd still own the land."

Clarie took a sip of coffee. "Well, Granddad owned 1,088 acres, and the city feller said yes, he'd already heard that down at the courthouse. Then he opened the little satchel he carried and counted out 271 silver dollars into Granddad's lap."

Polly looked up. "All that cash money right on the spot?"

Clarie nodded. "Yep. Counted it out real slow like, too. Well, Granddad had never seen such a sight. He asked again to make sure he still owned the land, but before you knowed it, he had made his mark on the paper the man had and the feller from the courthouse signed his name next to it, certifying Granddad was who he said he was. Granddad got his new mule, bought shoes for my mama and his other children and stuck the rest back to use a dollar now and again when he needed something. Everybody kind of forgot about the deal 'til I was a big o' girl. Then one morning, men showed up with that paper he'd signed years ago and started digging."

Clarie's voice was tight as she continued. "When Granddad saw how they was cutting up the land, he tried to stop them, but they brung the law out. Said he'd signed a broadland deed that gave the coal company rights to anything they wanted to take from under the ground. It didn't matter they destroyed the hills to get to what was underneath. Granddad didn't live long after that. It was like they tore up his heart when they tore up the land."

Clarie reached for another cookie. "Well, there I go again— rattling on so."

Zetta refilled both coffee cups. "I'm trying to get my mind around them cutting up the land like that," she said. "I sure would hate to think of my pretty little farm being turned into something ugly and dirty like this place."

Clarie shrugged. "Honey, it's happening more than we like to think," she said. "And the broadland deeds stay with the land. A feller can buy a farm with good money and good intentions and then have the coal owners show up years later. Well, the damage is done now. Polly, try one of these cookies. They sure are good."

* * * * *

After Clarie and Polly left, Zetta pushed Clarie's story of the broadland deeds aside as she fed Micah and Rachel.

Then, when the children were finished eating, she gave Micah a spoon to bang against an empty pan and handed Rachel a few scraps of gingerbread dough and the thimble to cut out tiny cookies. As she checked the yeast dough, rain hit the back door. She turned toward the sound, pleased. Surely the rain would keep Julia from making her customary rounds. But as she gazed at the black ribbons of coal dust snaking their way down the window, the ever-present homesickness burrowed deeper into her being. Beyond the window, sooty puddles began to form on the back porch, and tiny rivers of coal dust filled the path. Zetta gave a weary sigh, glad she had settled on cooking and baking for the day.

* * * * *

By the time the men arrived home for supper, the rain had stopped, and Zetta had the wash tin of hot water waiting on the back porch bench.

Asa scrubbed his face, then stepped inside. Even before he kissed his wife, he pulled a handful of coins from his grimy pants pocket.

"Looky here, Zetta. You made $1.85 from the pies you sent," he said. "I ran out of pies before I ran out of takers. The boarders want more. And Perton sure liked the peach pies. He ate two of them right off. Said to tell you much obliged. So I reckon if you feel up to making more, I'll tote them to the mine tomorrow."

Zetta gestured toward the pies under a cloth on the kitchen bench.

"I'm way ahead of you, Asa," she said.

Loren was the next one through the door.

"Boy, Zetta, you should've seen those boarders eating your fancy pies," he said. "You even got a marriage proposal out of the deal if you decide to ever leave old Big Ears."

Luttrell ducked his head under the door frame and took his seat at the table. "I don't know when I've had miners so interested in what I'm carrying in my dinner bucket, Sis."

Zetta smiled as she set the platter of fried sweet potatoes on the table.

"Well, I'm just glad I've hit on something to help out," she said. "Asa, pray, so's I can dish up the rest of the supper."

* * * * *

As the men wiped their plates with the last of the bread, Zetta set the platter of gingerbread cookies before them. As she reached for the coffee pot to refill their cups, she saw the light from a lantern bobbing in the darkness behind the house. Soon she could see a slender young man walking beside Dosha as they picked their way across the muddy path leading to the back step. Dosha carried a cloth-covered basket while the young man held the lantern in one hand and clutched Dosha's waist with the other.

Zetta barely had the door open before the young woman greeted her.

"I made buttermilk pies tonight," Dosha said. "Then I happened to think you hadn't met Jack, so I thought I'd bring him along whilst you taste the pie to see if it's fit for your party on Sunday. Oh, look at those sweet babies."

As Dosha swooped toward the startled children, Zetta put out her hand to the dark haired young man who was a good two inches shorter than Dosha. He smiled as he took her hand.

"Mi-miz Zetta. Wel-welcome to co-coal mining."

"I'm proud to meet you, Jack," she said. She hoped her surprise at his stuttering didn't show.

Dosha straightened from cooing at the children. "We didn't mean to interrupt your supper. I was so anxious to have you try the pie that I stacked our dishes and come on down. We'll just leave this and go on."

Asa stood to pull two more straight-back chairs from the front room to the kitchen table.

"Now, you set right here," he said. "We was just finishing. But I've got room for a piece of that good looking pie."

Zetta poured two more cups of coffee and handed Dosha a knife to cut the pie.

"Jack, Dosha says y'all is newly married," she said.

Jack smiled and turned to his wife, waiting for her to answer.

"Oh, yes," Dosha said. "We got married right after Jack helped my cousin get the tobacca in and then we come off up here. That's where we met—on my cousin's farm. I was visiting one day and noticed how hard Jack was working. Then when I got to know him, I knew if I had to live more than a hand span away from him, I wouldn't be able to breathe."

Loren interrupted her. "Dosha, I'm waiting for a piece of that pie. I reckon we can do without the lovey-dovey tale."

Dosha laughed as she cut into the sugary custard.

"Well, I do get carried away, I reckon," she said. "But I'm just so tickled to have somebody like him."

Jack put his hand on her arm. "I...I ne...never figured some...somebody so pr-pretty wo-would li...like me. An...and can sh...she cook!"

As Loren held his plate toward Dosha, Asa asked, "What'd your family think about you marrying a carrot top gal, Jack?"

Dosha positioned the pie on Loren's plate as she answered for her husband.

"Oh, Jack's mother and little sister—the only family he can remember—both died in the big influenza a few years back," she said. "Jack's area was so hard hit, they had whole families wiped out. Jack was just a youngin but since he didn't get sick he helped the preacher bury folks. Between buryings, the preacher taught him to play the dulcimer."

Loren took a big bite of pie and grunted appreciatively.

"Well, that beats all, Jack. I didn't know you could play the hog fiddle," he said. "I wish I'd brung my guitar from home. We could have a good show—you playing and me singing."

Dosha handed pie to Luttrell.

"Oh, Jack sings, too," she said. "And he don't stutter then. My favorite is "Sweet William." I always wind up crying over those old songs. But he's learning brand new ones for the Fourth of July party. You could sing with him then."

Loren shook his head. "Nah, we'll be long gone by then. But how come he can sing words but can't say them?"

Zetta looked pained. "Loren!"

Loren shrugged. "I'm just wondering," he said. "There Jack is driving us into the mine every morning for less money than the rest of us make. But if he was a regular miner, he'd get us all blowed to

Kingdom Come before he could holler, 'Fire in the hole!' Good thing Asa's the powder monkey."

Zetta looked up from giving the children slivers of pie. "Powder monkey?"

Loren wiped his mouth with the back of his hand. "Yep. He's in charge of the dynamite for the entire section," he said.

She thought of her nightmare. "Asa, you didn't tell me that," she said. "Your letter said you was making more money than you used to, but I just figured it was because you weren't new anymore. Now that worries me."

Asa shot a disgusted look toward his brother-in-law.

"Now, Zetta. You know I'm careful," he said. "Don't be fretting. I'm not about to blow myself up. I've got to get home for the spring plowing."

Then he winked at her as he leaned back in his chair.

"And I've got to start training me a new coon dog," he said. "Of course, I'll never be able to replace that fine old dog I used to own."

Zetta turned back to Micah. She knew the coming joke well.

Asa looked pensive, as though remembering some long ago scene.

"In fact, that dog was so fine I couldn't come up with a name good enough for him," he said. "So I just settled on calling him 'Dawg.' It fit him okay."

Asa paused for a moment, as though savoring the memory.

Dosha leaned forward. "What made him so special?"

Asa had been waiting for that question. "Oh, he was the best coon dog around," he said. "I collected a right smart batch of hides to sell because of Dawg. In fact, he loved hunting so much that if I didn't feel like going out, all I had to do was show Dawg a skinning board the size of the coon I wanted. If I needed a medium-sized skin, I'd show him a medium board. If I needed a large skin, I'd show him my large board. He'd study the board, then take off and bring that exact size coon back a few hours later."

Dosha's jaw dropped. "Why, I've never heard of such a thing."

Asa nodded. "He was something all right. I sure do miss him."

"Why? What happened to him?" Dosha asked.

"Well, Zetta left her *ironing board* on the porch one summer night, and I haven't seen that ambiguous dog since!"

As the others laughed and Jack leaned forward to slap Asa's

back, Dosha looked bewildered. Jack took her hand.

"Da-dawg is lo-looking for a-a coon big as the ir-ironing bo-board."

With the explanation, Dosha broke into good-natured laughter.

"You got me good with that one, Asa," she said.

Zetta laughed along with the others, but she knew there would be no further discussion about the dynamite.

CHAPTER 9

Even after they were alone in their bed that night, Asa dismissed Zetta's concerns about the dynamite—just as she had known he would do.

"Now, Zetta, this isn't like the old days when being a powder monkey meant having to sleep with the stuff to keep it warm," he said.

"*Sleep* with dynamite!"

"Yep. But these are modern times," he said. "Nowadays, all I have to do is drill a hole in the coal vein, put the dynamite stick in, pack clay around it to keep it in place, light the fuse, yell 'Fire in the hole' to warn the other miners to take cover and then run for my own cover."

"But, what if something goes wrong?" Zetta asked. "What if you can't run fast enough?"

Asa laughed quietly in the darkness.

"Those Allen boys trained me pretty good," he said. "I learned early that some days I had to be a good fighter and on other days a good runner."

"But, Asa, dy—"

"Shush now," he said. "We've both got work to do—you here, me at the mine. Scoot closer. Let me warm your cold back."

For the next three mornings, Zetta's prayers centered around that new danger as she watched the men disappear into the predawn darkness with their dinner buckets packed with extra hand pies.

Now it was Saturday morning and even though the rain had stopped days earlier, black puddles of soot still filled the path. Yesterday the air had held the threat of snow, so Zetta had been content to stay inside her warm kitchen.

The air was even heavier now, and Zetta pulled her shawl tighter around her shoulders as she stood on the porch long after the men were gone from sight.

"Lord, please keep `em safe," she whispered. "And please help me quit worrying about that awful dream. Just help me tolerate being here."

She listened to the darkness, straining to hear some encouragement. But she heard only the deep grumblings of the mine. She sighed and stepped back into the house.

The dimes and nickels Asa collected from the boarding house miners were beginning to fill the Mason jar on the top shelf, but having to pull out a few coins even for Clarie's eggs worried Zetta. Before they could leave for home, she would have to buy meat at the company store. She dreaded the price Roscoe would quote for even ham hocks.

She turned toward the sweets she had prepared for tomorrow's company. The dried-apple cake was on the dish shelf, covered with a clean towel. Cooked dried apples, sweetened with molasses, were between five rounds of gingerbread and soaking into the layers. A peach cobbler sat nearby. A few gingerbread cookies remained in her largest ironstone bowl. Zetta made a mental note: With Clarie's potato candy, Polly's brown sugar sweets and Dosha's buttermilk pies, they would have a wonderful party. The mine would be closed tomorrow, Sunday, and again on Monday for Christmas Day, but she already had Tuesday's meat pies wrapped in a vinegar-soaked cloth to keep them fresh.

She lifted the pot of pinto beans from the work bench where they had soaked overnight, rinsed them, added salt pork for flavor and put them on the back of the stove to simmer. She stared at the kettle for several minutes before speaking.

"How many pots of beans have I cooked over the years, Lord? Your Word says you've counted the number of hairs on my head. Do you bother counting pots of beans, too? I miss my own kitchen, Lord. I miss the chimes of our sweet little clock. But we've got more than three months before we can go home."

Zetta rubbed her tightening abdomen for several moments,

then began to count aloud on her fingers. "Let's see. Today is the twenty-third, tomorrow's the twenty-fourth, twenty-fifth, twenty-sixth, twenty-seventh, twenty-eighth, twenty-ninth, thirtieth, thirty-first. Nine more days left in December. Then January has thirty-one days, so that makes forty days. Add February's twenty-eight days and that takes us to sixty-eight days. Then add March's thirty-one days and that's, um, ninety-nine days."

"Ninety-nine days, Lord. Ninety-nine long days."

She put her hand into the small of her back, then reached for the jar of dried pinto beans in one of the wooden crates. She was still counting out ninety-nine dried beans and dropping them into a clean pint jar when Rachel and Micah awakened.

* * * * *

After spooning gravy over the children's breakfast biscuits, Zetta stooped awkwardly to pull a crate from under the kitchen work bench. From the back of it, she selected a jar of corn kernels and held it toward the children.

"Mama's got a treat for you today," she said. "Poppy shelled these out just about this time last winter. He's gonna be pleased to see we've still got a jar left."

Zetta shook kernels into the sizzling lard in the skillet and covered it with a gray lid. As Micah and Rachel watched, she pushed the skillet back and forth across the hot stove top to keep the corn from burning. She listened to the kernels bouncing against the lid. When she thought the last kernel had popped, she took the lid off. Just then another kernel popped and shot through the air, causing both children to giggle. Zetta smiled as she poured white, fluffy corn into the clean dishpan. Two more skilletfuls and the pan was filled—as well as a small gray granite bowl.

"There! This little bowl will be for the tree if Poppy can get us one," she said. "But all this will make our corn balls. Now you watch."

After she had washed the children's hands, Zetta poured molasses into the skillet, added sugar, a dash of salt and a teaspoon of vinegar.

"As soon as that boils, I'll pour it over the corn," she said. "Then we'll shape the balls."

The words were barely out of Zetta's mouth when she saw

through the back window that Julia was coming up the steps.

"Hey, I'm here!" the girl called out.

The greeting startled Rachel. "Momma, it's that mean girl."

Zetta put her hand on Rachel's head. "It's okay, honey. I won't let her bother you."

Then she took a deep breath and opened the door. "Why, good morning, Miz Julia," she said. "You're out early."

Julia ignored the greeting and stepped into the warm kitchen.

Zetta was tempted to remark, "I don't believe you were invited inside, young lady," but Asa's earlier warning about tolerating the child caused her to bite back the words.

Julia gestured toward the filled dishpan. "What's that?"

"Popcorn," Zetta said. "I was about to show the children how to make popcorn balls."

Zetta paused, then added, "Maybe you'd like to help?"

Julia shrugged. "I guess." But she stepped quickly to the table.

Zetta guided her to the chair farthest away from Rachel.

"Now, first you need to take off that pretty coat," she said. "We don't want it getting all sticky. Next, you need to wash your hands real good."

Zetta was surprised at how quickly Julia held out her hands for scrubbing and drying.

As Julia squirmed in her chair, Zetta poured the boiled molasses over a small portion of the white kernels.

"Let it cool for a minute," Zetta said. "Here, I'll get it out for you. Now push it all together into a ball."

Julia quickly shoved the kernels into a ball about the size of an apple. Rachel daintily pushed kernels together with the heel of her hands while warily watching their guest and scowling at her little brother for licking his sticky fingers.

Julia put her ball on the buttered plate Zetta placed before her then reached into the dishpan.

"You hillbillies do funny things for Christmas," Julia said.

Can't that child say two sentences without using that word? Zetta thought. Instead she said, "I'd druther think we do *fun* things."

Then to change the subject, she asked, "What do you hope to get for Christmas?"

Julia shrugged. "I'm getting another doll. I saw Daddy putting it behind his desk."

"Are you looking forward to tomorrow's party at the school?"

Julia shook her head. "No. But Daddy says I have to be there to help him pass out the oranges. He wanted Mama to be there, but she said crowds make her nervous."

Zetta handed Rachel more kernels. "What did your daddy say then?" She hoped she didn't sound eager.

Julia shoveled the kernels together. "He told Mama, '*Breathing* makes you nervous.' That made Mama mad and she said if he was a real man, he'd get a real job."

Zetta waited for the phrase "away from these hillbillies," but the words didn't come. She pointed to the large popcorn ball the child had just placed on the plate.

"When your visit is over, Miz Julia, you can take that one with you for helping."

To Zetta's irritation, Julia merely shrugged again.

* * * * *

Shortly after Julia left, clutching her popcorn ball in waxed paper, Zetta tucked Micah into bed. While he napped, Zetta tore several pages from the writing tablet and cut them into narrow strips. Then she mixed a paste from flour and water and set the bowl in front of Rachel.

"Now we're gonna make a paper chain for the tree," Zetta said. "Watch. You put a little dab of paste on one end of the paper and fold the other end over to it, like this."

Rachel smiled as Zetta continued. "Then you hold the ends together for a minute. Now we put another strip of paper through that one and do the same thing over. See? And like magic, we've got a pretty chain. You ready to try?"

Rachel nodded eagerly and reached for the paper. By the time the end-of-shift whistle blew, the chain was finished. The evening shadows choked the lane as Zetta poured hot water into the wash pan and set it on the back porch bench. Little wisps of steam were still rising as Asa arrived. He scrubbed his face and hands with lye soap, rinsed and toweled off quickly and stepped inside.

He hugged the children, heard about their popcorn balls, pulled coins from his pocket and kissed Zetta all in the same moment.

"The boys are toting water up for our baths, so they'll be a while. But looky here. Your paw sent you a letter."

Zetta steered the children toward their chairs. "You read it to me, whilst I finish stirring up the cornbread," she said. "We're just having soup beans tonight."

Asa sat at his customary place and tore open the envelope.

" 'Dear Zetta and family,' " he began. " 'I hope this letter finds you and yours well. We are fine here. Was glad to get your letter. We got a new preacher. He's all right, but his wife is a big woman who has an opinion on everything. Somebody set Jim Reed's barn on fire, but he got the animals out in time—including your Brownie. His brothers and him just about got a new one up. Your mama and little brothers got the turnips all in. We've been shelling out nuts every evening for Becky's Christmas cake. Wish y'all could be here to eat it with us. Tell everybody hello. Your paw, John D.' "

Zetta poured the cornbread batter into the hot skillet. "It's about time they got a new preacher," she said. "But that's too bad about Jim's barn. If we was home, you'd be helping him rebuild. Wonder who'd do a thing like that."

Asa folded the paper. "Just about anybody who's still holding a grudge," he said.

Zetta put her arm under her heavy abdomen as she slid the cornbread skillet into the oven.

"I wish Paw wouldn't call Becky my mama," she said. "I still miss my own mama and she's been gone 10 years now. Becky's a good enough woman, I guess, but I could never understand her giving her own three little boys to her brother so's she could marry Paw."

Asa nodded as he turned to caress Rachel's and Micah's cheeks.

"I reckon a woman alone has to make tough choices sometimes," he said. "If anything was to happen to me, I'd want you to marry again. But I know you'd never let anybody make you give up our babies to start having his."

Zetta watched Asa lean toward the children, feeling dread creep across her heart.

* * * * *

The cornbread was golden brown as Loren and Luttrell came through the door, the carbide light from their caps reflected in the two buckets of water in each of their hands.

Asa looked up. "Eight buckets? Y'all are carrying a lazy man's load," he said. "Where'd you get the extras? All I had under the back porch was the two gray ones."

Loren set his buckets on the stove, then snuffed the light from his cap with his hand.

"From Clarie. That woman's got anything anybody needs," he said. "We'll take them back later. I was getting tired of toting water with just two buckets. Let me wash up."

Loren stepped onto the back porch as Luttrell set his buckets down. Zetta smiled and added more coal to the stove. They would have fine baths tonight.

The family ate quickly. After his final bite of cornbread and jelly, Loren pulled a nickel from his pocket and gestured toward the galvanized tub hanging on the wall.

"Zetta and the youngins will get their baths first," Loren said. "But I'm not getting in the water after either one of you fellers have been in there with all your coal dust. Call it, forever and always, Luttrell."

He flipped the coin into the air, caught it and slapped it onto the back of his hand.

Luttrell drank the last of his coffee before speaking. "I'll go last," he said. "I'll stand and you can pour water over me after I lather up."

Loren shook his head. "Naw. Call it."

"Heads then."

Loren lifted his hand and grinned. "Tails. You're the last man in the tub."

Then he turned to Asa. "It's you and me now. Call it."

"I'll stick with tails," Asa said.

Loren flipped the coin again. When he lifted his hand, he frowned.

"Well, shoot. It's tails," he said. "You're first man in. I'll go after you, but I'm not sitting in your water. I'll stand up like Luttrell."

His brother reached for his jacket. "Asa *should* go after Zetta," he said. "You could have saved yourself the trouble."

Loren reached for his own jacket. "Naw. That'd take all the fun out of it."

He turned back to Asa. "Whilst y'all are getting slicked up, we'll get that little tree up the mountain Clarie mentioned. Keep some water hot."

Asa nodded. "She's got a shovel for you. Dig the tree up. I want to plant it back home as a reminder of our time here."

Loren shook his head. "Beats me why you'd want to remember this place," he said. Then he lit the carbide on his cap and followed Luttrell into the darkness.

* * * * *

As Zetta turned down the glow from the lantern, Asa poured half a pail of cold water into the tub and added hot water.

Zetta tugged the clothes off Rachel and Micah, then leaned to test the temperature of the water. After helping the children into the tub, she started to get on her knees. Asa stopped her.

"No, you don't need to be bending down like that," he said. "I'll wash the babies whilst you do the dishes."

Zetta moved to the work bench, poured hot water into the dishpan and lathered the cloth with lye soap. "This time last week, I had finished packing and then the babies and me had our baths," she said. "I was anxious to get to bed that night, knowing I'd see you the next day. We sure did miss you."

Asa swished the washcloth over both children as they sat in the few inches of water.

"This old camp is a tougher place than I figured," he said. "It helps having you and the babies here."

Zetta scrubbed the bean kettle, not daring to look at her husband.

"Asa, let's go back home tomorrow," she said. "With four of us packing, we could be out of here right quick. And I'll just tote all the sweets up to Clarie."

Asa's words came slowly, patiently. "Zetta, we don't get paid 'til the thirty-first. If I leave quick like that, I lose all I've worked for this whole month. I've already told Perton we're heading out the last day of March. Worrying me over this isn't gonna help any."

Zetta bit her lower lip and scrubbed the kettle all the harder.

* * * * *

After putting the children to bed, Asa came back into the dark kitchen just as Zetta stepped out of her dress.

"You shut off the lantern," he said.

"Well, yes. With no curtains, everybody would see in," she said.

70

Asa caught the terseness in her tone. He poured more hot water into the tub then held Zetta's elbow as she stepped in.

"Now, we can't be talking about leaving 'til it's time to leave," he said. "In three months time, we'll be glad we stuck it out. Here, let me wash your back."

Zetta gave a sigh of defeat then awkwardly leaned forward. She enjoyed the motion of the rough cloth on her back for a moment, then said, "Asa, are you sure you want me going to the school program tomorrow? I swear I'm getting bigger by the minute."

He squeezed water from the cloth over her shoulders. "Sure, I do," he said. "Besides, the boarders will want to see who's been feeding them so good."

Asa helped Zetta to her feet, then put both hands on her extended belly and leaned down to kiss her abdomen.

"Hello in there, Baby," he said. "This is your Poppy who can't wait to hold you."

He wrapped a coarse towel around Zetta's trembling shoulders.

"When Rachel was born, I couldn't imagine ever loving another baby that much," he said. "Then when Micah come along, I found out a body's heart just grows bigger to hold more love. Pretty soon, there won't be room in my chest for a liver and lungs."

Zetta was glad the room was dark since sudden tears sprang to her eyes.

* * * * *

Asa finished his bath and had the kitchen bright with the glow of lantern light by the time his brothers-in-law arrived with the tree.

Loren thrust the three feet of timber into an empty water bucket and held it out to Asa.

"Well, here's the start of your future forest," he said. "Now I'm ready for that bath."

Luttrell gestured toward the burlap sticking over the top of the bucket. "Clarie put that around the roots," he said. "And she said to keep it damp 'til spring."

As Asa held the tree at arm's length to examine its features, Zetta picked up the lantern from the kitchen table.

"Since you boys know where everything is on your bodies, I'll take the light," she said. "Try not to slop water on the floor."

Loren's laugh followed her into the front room.

"Yes, ma'am," he said. "Still the big sister, huh?"

Earlier, Zetta had placed the small bowl of popcorn, a threaded needle, Rachel's paper chain and short white candles from home onto the straight-back chair nearest the kitchen. As she set the lantern on the floor and leaned over to pick up the needle to begin stringing the popcorn, she could hear her brothers emptying their pockets. Their folding knives and loose change hit the kitchen table. Then she heard Luttrell's low voice.

"Cover that tin. What if Zetta sees it?"

Immediately Asa was by Zetta's side.

"Reckon you could spare a quilt to wrap around the tree bucket and pretty it up?" he said.

As Zetta nodded and turned toward their bedroom, Asa rushed into the kitchen. When Zetta appeared with their oldest quilt in her arms, she could hear Asa whispering to her brothers. But he quickly stepped back into the front room, carrying a bucket of cold water.

He gestured toward the far corner.

"We'll keep water near the tree—just in case the candles catch anything on fire," he said. "I still remember those folks that had a fire on Christmas Day."

Asa picked up the paper chain and began to drape it over the branches. "Sister and Brother are going to be tickled to see the tree," he said. "We never had such a thing when I was growing up. My daddy said it were a waste of a fine tree to chop it down just to look at it. Said it was prettiest outside with the sunlight bouncing off the snow on the branches."

Zetta watched him fuss over the chain. Something wasn't right.

"Asa. . ." she began. But he ignored her.

"That's why we always put our shoes on the hearth for old Santy Claus to fill with candy," he said. "The Christmas my daddy was shot was the last time I put 'em out. I guess I knew my days of being a little boy were over."

Zetta had heard one version or another of that awful event every Christmas. But somehow this year it seemed even sadder.

Chapter 10

When the mine whistle blew Sunday morning, Asa murmured, "We don't work today, honey," put his arms around Zetta and fell back asleep. But she remained awake, staring into the darkness as she quietly prayed.

"Lord, I wish we was up and packing for home right now. But Asa made it plain I'm not to worry him about leaving. So help me bear being here."

Asa stirred and turned to his other side. Carefully, Zetta slipped from their bed and pulled her shawl around her shoulders. Might as well get breakfast started, she thought.

In the kitchen, she lit the lantern then pulled the pint jar of dried pinto beans from the top shelf. As she transferred one bean back into the original gallon jar, she whispered, "Ninety-eight more days. One more day closer to home."

She heard her brothers stirring, then hastily set the pint jar behind the dishes and reached for the coffee pot.

* * * * *

While Zetta fried eggs in the sausage grease, Asa dressed both children. She smiled as she heard the excitement in his voice.

"Now you sit right here," he said. "I've got a surprise. Don't peek."

From the kitchen, Zetta watched as Asa hurried into the front room and lit the candles perched on the branches. He stepped back

73

to admire the glow, then led Rachel and Micah to the tree.

Rachel clapped her hands, and Micah opened his mouth in wonder.

Asa smiled at their response.

"In the morning, old Santy Claus will have toys under the tree for you," he said.

"Toys for me?" Rachel asked.

"Yes. For you, and Brother, too."

Asa stepped behind the children and put his hands on their heads as they marveled at the tiny flames.

"Well, time to blow out the candles," he finally said. "Careful now."

Zetta chuckled as Micah's efforts produced more spitting than blowing.

As Asa turned the children toward their chairs, Zetta spooned gravy onto plates.

"Wait 'til Poppy asks the blessing," she said.

She nodded at Asa, listened for his *Amen* then poured coffee for the men.

Loren spread a thick layer of butter over a hot biscuit. "Since it's the day before Christmas, we don't have to worry about sitting through another servant-listen-to-your-master sermon," he said. "I swear the camp sure is getting their money's worth out of this preacher. He's right comfortable in their back pocket."

Asa reached for the fried apples. "Preacher Howard's a good man."

Loren swallowed the bite of biscuit. "Yeah, but he'd be a lot better if he didn't have to worry about his year almost being up," he said. "Old Man Golden always chooses his preachers based on who offers to work the cheapest."

Zetta halved a fried egg and placed a portion before each child.

"Makes me wonder what our new preacher is like," she said. "I hope he don't shout."

Asa shook his head. "No, Preacher Howard is quiet like."

"I meant our preacher back home," Zetta said.

"Oh," Asa said. "Well, I reckon we'll find out come spring."

Zetta nodded. But spring won't be soon enough, she thought.

* * * * *

While Zetta washed the breakfast dishes, Loren, on his hands and knees, chased squealing Rachel and Micah back and forth between the front room and bedroom.

As Zetta opened a jar of home-canned chicken and dumped it into a pot of water to simmer, Asa held his coat toward her. "I reckon we better get a move on for church," he said. "Here. Put this on. I don't want you catching a cold."

Zetta smiled her acceptance and thrust her arms into the long sleeves. She double knotted Rachel's scarf as Luttrell picked up the child and her doll. Loren set Micah's cap at a rakish angle, swooped him up and charged out the front door. With their arms linked, Asa and Zetta walked slowly on the path rimmed with sooty frost.

Rachel watched her parents from the high perch in Luttrell's arms. Micah giggled as Loren skipped and bounced him against his shoulder.

"Loren, be careful now," Zetta said. "Don't drop my boy."

"I got a good grip, Sis. I'm just trying to shake the vinegar out of him before church. I don't believe Jesus himself talked as long as preachers do."

The path opened onto the main street. When Clarie had taken Zetta to the camp store earlier in the week, they had walked across the road and up the steps. Now the little group turned right, past the hospital.

Loren tipped a giggling Micah upside down and pointed to a flat-roofed room at the back of the hospital.

"That's the death house," he said. "That's where they hold the bodies 'til they're shipped home."

Asa's voice was sharp. "You don't need to say that," he said. "It ain't been used since we've been here."

Loren shrugged. "I'm just saying Rusty Hinge Coal Camp thinks ahead," he said. "They've even got the stones already cut. All they have to do is add the feller's name."

Asa took a quick step toward Loren and took Micah from his arms.

"One of these days that mouth of yours is gonna get you in bad trouble," Asa said.

Zetta held her hand out. "Please, you two. Don't argue on the Lord's day."

They walked the rest of the way in silence.

* * * * *

Beyond the hospital was a grove of hickory trees surrounding a small church. Zetta was pleased to see the building was made of sandstone rather than warped lumber like the camp houses.

As the little group approached, several people standing on the crushed shale in front of the church turned to greet them. They called out the men's names and raised their hands in greeting toward Zetta.

Luttrell gently set Rachel down by her mother and then joined Loren as he meandered toward the men on the right. The women, many holding babies, clumped together on the left. Dosha and Jack stood near the church door, talking softly as their shoulders touched. Jack held something wrapped in a faded quilt.

Clarie stepped forward to take Micah from Asa, who then joined the other men. Before Zetta could feel abandoned, Clarie said, "Wait 'til you hear about Polly's brown sugar sweets. She outdid herself."

Clarie's long brown coat hung open to reveal a green cotton dress. But even as Zetta realized she missed the usual bright blue apron, Clarie kissed a startled Micah on the cheek and pulled a tired looking Polly forward.

"Polly, honey, tell Zetta how good you did with the sweets."

The young woman blushed and ducked her head.

Murmured greetings came from the men's side. Clarie nudged Zetta.

"There's Preacher Howard."

Zetta turned to see a short, round man wearing thick wire-rimmed glasses. He shook hands with several of the miners as he walked toward the church door. Inside, he unwound a rope from a peg by the front window. He gave it several long tugs, and the little bell in the steeple sent its mournful invitation across the camp. As the miners and their families started to file into the sanctuary, a black motorcar pulled up, then turned to back in at the right of the church.

Mothers grabbed their children's hands as the car rolled over the crushed rock.

Clarie watched the car for a moment then turned to Zetta.

"That there is the Grays," she said. "And if Mr. Gray is backing in, it means his wife is with him today. Wonder what he had to buy her to get her to come."

Immediately the miners pulled off their caps and stepped back. Mr. Gray, a tall, dark-haired man, emerged from the vehicle and walked around to the passenger side. He nodded to the waiting group as he reached for the car door.

"Good morning," he said. "See you at the school program this afternoon."

The men murmured low greetings in return.

As Mr. Gray opened the door and held out his hand, a tall, thin woman emerged who ignored his gesture and turned to watch their daughter scramble from the backseat. Even from several feet away, Zetta could see the deep frown lines in Mrs. Gray's forehead. Her coat was the same beige color as Julia's but was trimmed with a wide fur collar the exact shade of her brown hair. Pulling one hand from the matching fur muff, she quickly guided Julia through the church doors before the child had a chance to react to those watching.

Clarie nudged Zetta. "Well, I'll be," she said. "Here it is Christmas and she's still got that sour face on. Maybe she's afraid her skin will crack if she smiles."

The group watched as the Grays disappeared into the building before they followed. Zetta clutched Rachel's hand while Asa took Micah from Clarie. Together they filed into the church behind the older woman and Polly, and headed for the back pew. Even as she helped the children settle between her and Asa, Zetta looked around. Twelve rows of homemade pews lined each side of the narrow aisle. A leaning wooden pulpit stood at the front of the room with two straight-back chairs on each side. A coal burning stove filled the right front corner, but there was no fire in it despite the damp morning. Loren and Luttrell crowded next to single men across the aisle. Dosha and Jack hurried toward the front pew.

As the folks shuffled into their seats, Preacher Howard stood in front of the pulpit, squinting through his thick glasses. His hands were folded across his stomach as he swayed slightly. When everyone was settled, he cleared his throat and stepped forward.

"Well, I'm glad y'all could be here," he said. "And I'm especially glad Mrs. Gray could be with us today."

The supervisor's wife barely nodded as she pulled a white linen handkerchief from her muff and audibly sniffed.

Clarie nudged Zetta. "Reckon we should tell her we all took our baths last night?"

Zetta offered a half smile to acknowledge the comment, but she was struck not only by the unhappy woman's rudeness but by a sudden kinship. *I don't want to be here anymore than she does, Lord. But help me not to be ugly about it,* she thought.

Preacher Howard seemed momentarily flustered by Mrs. Gray's response, but quickly said, "Well, now, let's get started by singing unto the Lord."

Then without announcing the song's title, he launched into the first words of "Blessed Assurance."

"Blessed assurance, Jesus is mine! Oh, what a foretaste of glory divine!"

Zetta recognized the familiar words and, turning her attention away from the silent Mrs. Gray, immediately added her voice to the others.

"Heir of salvation, purchase of God. Born of His Spirit, washed in His blood. This is my story, this is my song. Praising my Savior all the day long."

As the voices faded with the final notes, Preacher Howard nodded.

"That's good singing," he said. "Now, does anybody have a word of testimony?"

Immediately Asa stood up. "I'm thankful my family arrived safely last Sunday evening," he said as he gestured toward them. "This here is my wife, Zetta, and our youngins, Rachel and Micah."

Low welcomes filled the little room: "Welcome, Miz Zetta. Glad you's here."

Preacher Howard smiled. "Yessir. It makes a big difference to have our loved ones with us," he said. "You want to say anything, Miz Zetta?"

Zetta didn't stand but pulled Asa's coat tighter across her abdomen. "Uh, well. I'm grateful to see Asa again—and my brothers," she said.

The preacher nodded. "We're glad you're here. We've got time for one more."

Clarie pushed herself up. "I always feel homesick and lonesome this time of year," she said. "But I thank the good Lord he has given me work to do in my old age."

Encouragement floated toward the woman: "We love you, Clarie." "God bless you." "We depend on your prayers, Goodheart." "Yes, praise Jesus."

The preacher waited for the last comment, then said, "Now before I hold out God's Word, I've asked Jack Conley to sing a song I heard at a revival over in Hazard," he said. "It's called 'A Beautiful Life.' And isn't that what we're all looking for?"

He nodded at the Gray family. "And when y'all hear the first few words, you'll know why I think we ought to name this our Golden Gate song. Jack, you come right on up here."

As Jack stood, he pulled a long wooden instrument shaped like a figure eight from the quilt. Dosha smiled at those behind her as though to say, "Wait 'til y'all hear this."

Zetta smiled back but she remembered how painful it had been to hear Jack speak the night they brought the buttermilk pies. She hoped he wouldn't embarrass himself in front of all these people—especially Mrs. Gray.

Jack pulled one of the straight-back chairs away from the side of the pulpit, seated himself and positioned the dulcimer across his lap.

Rachel, along with several other children, stood up to see him.

The preacher nodded. "Go ahead, Jack. We're ready when you are."

Zetta held her breath as Jack pulled a turkey feather from his shirt pocket and brushed the quill end across the strings. After several strokes, he began:

"Each day I'll do a golden deed by helping those who are in need."

Even though Dosha had previously told them Jack could sing without stuttering, Zetta was astonished at the beauty and clarity of his words.

"My life on earth is but a span, and so I'll do the best I can."

He brushed the feather across lower notes to signal the chorus, then sang, "Life's evening sun is sinking low. A few more days and I must go. To meet the deeds that I have done. Where there will be no setting sun."

Jack paused and looked at the preacher.

"Now let's all sing," Preacher Howard said. "I'll line the words. Ready, Jack? Each day I'll do a golden deed."

Golden! That's why he suggested this as the camp song, Zetta thought. But she, along with the others, sang the words as the preacher said them.

As the last note faded, Preacher Howard put his hand on Jack's shoulder.

"That was mighty fine."

Jack nodded his thanks and returned to the front pew. Dosha scooted closer to him and appreciatively patted his arm.

As Jack rewrapped the dulcimer in the old quilt, Preacher Howard opened a large, worn Bible before squinting toward the group.

"Since we're celebrating our Savior's birth tomorrow, I'm gonna read from the Book of Luke," he said. "Listen now to God's Word."

He pulled the Bible close to his face.

"'And it came to pass in those days that there went out a decree from Caesar Augustus that all the world should be taxed. And this taxing was first made when Cyrenius was governor of Syria. And all went to be taxed, every one into his own city. And Joseph also went up from Galilee, out of the city of Nazareth, into Judea, unto the city of David, which is called Bethlehem, because he was of the house and lineage of David, to be taxed with Mary his espoused wife, being great with child. And so it was that while they were there, the days were accomplished that she should be delivered. And she brought forth her firstborn son, and wrapped him in swaddling clothes and laid him in a manager, because there was no room for them in the inn.'"

Clarie pulled a handkerchief from her sleeve and wiped her eyes. As the preacher finished reading, he put his finger in the text and held it close to his chest.

"Luke tells a good story," he said. "And he puts this report in its right place in history. If he was writing about our time, he'd likely say, 'Now this happened when Warren G. Harding was President of the United States and Ed Morrow was governor of Kentucky.' And he lets us know this was a pretty big event. Just think if we all had to go back to our birthplace right now. Why, I'd have to walk deep into the hills of Harlan County."

Zetta sighed. Oh, Lord, I wish you would send us back to our birthplaces right now.

Pastor Howard continued. "Since Joseph's people started out in Bethlehem, he had to go back there to register. And since Mary was his promised wife, she had to go with him even though she was— like it says here, 'Great with child.' Miz Clarie knows about a woman being great with child. And that's not a time when she wants to be traveling—especially on the back of some bony old donkey."

Clarie smiled at the preacher's recognition as he continued.

"Now I reckon Bethlehem was a back-water place," he said. "Kindly like the holler where I come from. But that was the place God decided his Son was to be born, so it was the right place.

"But one thing has always puzzled me," he said. "If this was Joseph's homeplace, how come they couldn't stay with his people? Why, there's not a one of us here that wouldn't make up a pallet in front of the fireplace for kin. Maybe Joseph's people around there was dead, and the ones coming back was in the same shape he was—with nobody to welcome them. So he had to find shelter amongst the animals. But we know from other places in Scripture that Joseph was a good man. And a good man is gonna take care of his family even if they wind up where they don't want to be."

Zetta turned to Asa, wondering if he had talked to the preacher about her unhappiness at being there. But he was busy pulling a sleepy Micah onto his lap.

She turned back toward the preacher.

"Over in Matthew, we're told Joseph was thinking about sending Mary away privately when he found out she was to have a baby," the preacher said. "He knew it wasn't his. But then the angel of the Lord appeared to him in a dream and told him the baby was God's."

A dream? Preacher Howard had Zetta's full attention now.

"I reckon Joseph was plenty relieved at that news," he said then paused and glanced at the Gray family.

It struck Zetta he was pondering how much he could say about having a baby before marriage in front of the children—especially Miss Julia.

During the pause, Clarie couldn't resist elbowing Zetta. "I always say the first baby can come any time," she said. "The second one usually takes nine months."

Clarie shook with silent laughter at her own whispered joke.

Zetta's attention still was on Joseph's dream. Lord, do you still speak to us like that? Should I tell Asa my awful dream?

The preacher's words pulled her back. "So Joseph trusts God to show him how to take care of Mary and this little baby," he said. "And when we listen to our heavenly Father, we're always provided for—even if it's in a stable. Let's pray."

Zetta barely heard the pastor's comforting voice thanking God for the gift of his son. She was too busy pondering the right time to tell Asa about her dream.

At the preacher's *Amen*, the Grays left immediately while the miners and their families stood respectively until the three had passed. Only when they heard the sound of the motorcar starting did they shake the preacher's hand and thump Jack's back to thank him for the song.

Clarie turned to Zetta. "I'll see y'all at the school after a while."

Next she turned to Asa. "Don't forget to bring a chair for little mama here. Those school benches are hard on a good woman's back."

Then with a wave of her hand, she hurried after Polly.

Zetta watched her go, determined to find a time to ask her about dreams.

CHAPTER 11

After a hurried meal of chicken and dumplings, Zetta and her family left for the school. Luttrell carried Rachel again, but this time Asa carried Micah. The school, a large sandstone building, stood on a slight knoll beside the company store. Just as they reached the stone steps, Loren caught up to them. He was carrying a straight-back chair.

"Hey, Sis, I'll leave this with Clarie for you," he said. "Better hustle, Luttrell, if you want to say hello to that pretty teacher."

Luttrell merely grunted, "Mm-hmm." But Zetta noticed his face reddening.

She couldn't resist teasing him. "Maybe we should invite her back for sweets."

Luttrell gently set Rachel on the bottom step. "I'd druther you didn't," he said.

Asa shifted Micah higher on his shoulder, then took Zetta's arm.

"Luttrell's right," he said. "We're gonna have trouble enough with Perton there."

Zetta sighed. *What have I've gotten myself into?*

She thought about the table now in the front room and the sweets waiting under clean towels as she followed families through the open school doors. As they entered, she saw frayed basketball nets at each end of the large room that served as both gymnasium and program hall. Under one hoop was a platform with burlap-covered crates stacked beside it. Backless benches were lined haphazardly toward the front. The room was lit with four rows of un-shaded bulbs hanging from long ceiling cords.

As Zetta and her family paused to look for Clarie, fathers stepped around them to join the other miners along the walls. Mothers seated in chairs or on the benches, held babies and waved back at the children sitting cross-legged in front of the platform.

Clarie, wearing her usual bright blue apron, stepped out of the sweet chaos.

"I was watching for y'all," she said. "Loren's put your chair next to where I'm sitting."

She glanced toward the door as more families arrived, then reached into her pocket.

"There's Mildred. She's been having trouble sleeping so I brung her some lavender. I'll be right back."

As Clarie hurried away, Luttrell tucked Rachel's hand into Zetta's, then joined Loren leaning against the side wall. Zetta eased herself into the chair and gestured for Rachel and Micah to sit on the bench next to her. As she did so, she noticed Jack and Dosha talking quietly on the front bench. Jack's dulcimer was across his lap.

Zetta turned to Asa. "Looks like Jack's gonna be playing here, too."

Asa nodded as Clarie reappeared.

"Looky over yonder. Perton showed up with Polly, after all," Clarie said. "Probably wants to make sure Mr. Gray sees him."

Zetta turned to see Polly standing awkwardly by a tall, broad-shouldered man. His dark eyebrows were pulled together in a scowl as he quickly surveyed the room. Then he abruptly joined miners at the back wall, leaving Polly standing alone.

Clarie hurried to the abandoned woman and led her toward Zetta.

Asa acknowledged Polly with a nod, then patted Zetta on the shoulder.

"Program's about ready to start," he said. "I'll be over there."

As he joined the other men, a small, pretty woman in a white outdated dress approached Jack and gestured toward the chair by the crates. Her tiny waist was bound with a wide unwrinkled blue ribbon.

As Zetta wondered if she'd ever regain her own waist, Clarie nudged her.

"See that little bitty thing talking to Jack?" she said. "That's the teacher. Came here from Knott County. The young ones don't last long since they always wind up marrying a miner."

Zetta turned toward her brothers just as Loren nudged Luttrell and nodded in the teacher's direction. Both men were smiling.

The young woman stepped forward and daintily cleared her throat to ask for silence.

"Welcome," she said. "For those of you who don't know me, I'm Miz Pryor."

One of the miners gave a catcall. Zetta knew it was Loren.

Miss Pryor waited for the accompanying chuckles to die down, then said, "The children have worked hard to bring you this special program. We hope you enjoy our version of the Christmas Story. Children, take your places."

As the youngsters scrambled to position themselves on the left of the platform, the teacher held a finger to her lips. When all was quiet, she nodded to a young miner near the door. He pushed three wall buttons to turn off all lights except for the bulbs over the platform.

As Miss Pryor said, "Now Jesus was born in Bethlehem," a little boy and girl, about eight years old, stepped onto the platform, wearing their parents' clothing as ancient robes. The child portraying Mary held a doll wrapped tightly in a much-used baby blanket. As she eased onto the floor, the pretend Joseph spotted his mother sitting on the front bench, grinned broadly and waved. The teacher cleared her throat, and Joseph became solemn again and stood behind Mary and the doll baby. He protectively gripped the sawed-off broom handle, which served as his staff.

Once the substitute Holy Family was in place, the teacher nodded to Jack, who brushed the turkey quill across the dulcimer strings. Rachel stood on tiptoe next to her mother and watched the children fidget as they bobbed their heads to the music and shifted from foot to foot. But at the teacher's one-two-three count of her raised hand, their sweet voices begin to sing:

Oh, little town of Bethlehem!
How still we see thee lie;
Above thy deep and dreamless sleep,

The silent stars go by.
Yet in thy dark street shineth,
The everlasting light;
The hopes and fears of all the years,
Are met in thee tonight.

At the end of the song, the audience applauded joyously. Micah, standing on the bench next to Zetta's chair, watched his sister applaud with the others. Then he clapped as hard as his little hands would allow. Zetta shushed him as the teacher spoke.

"After the birth of Jesus, the angel of the Lord announced the news to the shepherds abiding in the nearby fields."

She again raised her hand, and the children's voices sang:

Hark! the herald angels sing
Glory to the newborn King;
Peace on earth, and mercy mild,
God and sinners reconciled;
Joyful all, ye nations rise,
Join the triumph of the skies,
With angelic hosts proclaim,
Christ is born in Bethlehem.

As Zetta smiled at Micah's renewed applause, she noticed Mr. Gray, Julia and Roscoe enter the room and stand by the door. The miners quickly moved aside to make room for the trio.

Miss Pryor turned toward the audience and said, "Now when Jesus was born, there came Wise Men from the East."

At her announcement, three young boys appeared, their dads' long jackets serving as robes and their mothers' kitchen towels wrapped around their heads for turbans. Each carried a festive small box.

As the self-conscious lads stepped onto the platform, Clarie whispered, "Those boys will be working coal come summer."

"Working coal?" Zetta asked. "But they're just youngins."

"I know, honey."

Zetta turned from them to look at Rachel and Micah who were watching the program with shining eyes.

Oh, Lord, let us get home soon.

As the teacher said, "And they brung him gifts of gold,

frankincense and myrrh," the young Wise Men awkwardly knelt before Mary and the baby. At another one-two-three hand signal, the children waiting on the platform sang:

O come, all ye faithful,
Joyful and triumphant,
O come ye, O come ye to Bethlehem.
Come and behold him, born the King of angels
O come, let us adore him,
O come, let us adore him,
O come, let us adore him, Christ the Lord.

As Micah and Rachel clapped this time, Zetta wanted to hold them tightly and keep the hard future away from them.

Miss Pryor waited until the applause faded.

"Thank you," she said. "We're glad you liked our program."

She turned to her young charges fidgeting on the platform and said, "Y'all may go sit with your folks now."

Like puppies let out of a box, the children jumped off the stage and ran to their mothers, their thin shoes sounding against the wooden floor.

The teacher held up her hand. "Quietly, children. Quietly. Remember what we practiced."

It still was several moments before the scene was calm enough for her to be heard over the excited inquiries of "Did you see me, Mama?" "Did you hear me singing loud?"

Finally, after the maternal hushes, the room was quiet again. The teacher smiled.

"Now, we're privileged to have Mr. Edwin Gray say a few words."

Mr. Gray came forward to polite applause.

"Thank you, Miz Pryor," he said. "Well, here we are celebrating another Christmas even though it seems we did this just a few weeks ago. Time seems to pass quicker the older I get."

He paused, as though waiting for appreciative chuckles. When they didn't come, he continued.

"Well, men, even though Mr. Golden couldn't be with us today, he asked me to express his appreciation for your work. So, Merry Christmas."

While the audience again applauded politely, Mr. Gray gestured to his daughter and Roscoe. Julia stepped forward to stand arrogantly by her father while Roscoe lifted the burlap from the crates.

A quiet *ahhh* fluttered around the room as the oranges were uncovered. Each crate displayed a colorful label showing a green valley stretching toward faraway snow-capped mountains. A small white house stood in the foreground near rows of trees heavy with ripe fruit.

Mr. Gray gestured toward Julia. "My daughter, Miz Gray, will hand out the treats today," he said. "I think you all know her."

Clarie and Zetta glanced at each other. No one applauded.

Mr. Gray paused for an awkward moment, then spoke again: "Well, like I said—Merry Christmas. Come on up and let me shake your hands."

Zetta remained seated, waiting for Asa to make his way back to her.

Clarie gave a mighty heave and stood up from the bench.

"Next year, I'm gonna have to bring me a chair," she said.

She put her hand on her lower back. "I'd offer to fetch your orange so you didn't have to stand in line," she said. "But we're not allowed to do that. Here's Asa. I'll meet y'all back at your house directly."

She took Polly's arm, and then they were gone.

As Asa picked up Micah, Loren appeared, tossing an orange into the air.

"Luttrell got his orange and hightailed it home without saying a word to the teacher," Loren said. "That boy better start taking lessons from me!"

He picked up Zetta's chair. "I'll take this back to the house," he said. "I'm ready to dig into that cobbler."

As parents thanked the teacher for the program and shook the supervisor's hand, Roscoe moved full boxes of oranges next to Julia and carried away empty ones. Children breathed deeply as they held the oranges to their noses.

As she moved forward with those waiting in line, Zetta could see the disgusted look on Julia's face as she handed out the fruit. The child never looked at the recipients even as each one murmured appreciation.

When it was Rachel's and Micah's turns for the treat, Zetta said, "Say thank you to Miz Julia."

As the two little voices piped their thanks, Julia merely huffed.

Zetta and Asa acknowledged the gift of their own oranges then moved toward Mr. Gray. Zetta pulled her coat tighter as the supervisor nodded when Asa stepped forward.

"Good to see your family in church with you this morning, Berghoff," he said. "Nice to meet you, Mrs. Berghoff."

"Please, Mr. Gray" was as far as Zetta got in an attempt to remind him of the missing *er* on their name.

Asa quickly thrust his hand forward and said, "Mr. Gray, pass along our appreciation to Mr. Golden. We're much obliged."

As they walked away, Asa said, "Don't worry about our name, Zetta."

In reply, she offered a huff similar to the one Julia had produced minutes before.

* * * * *

Once they were back at their house, Zetta busied herself with stacking the oranges in a large bowl, which she set on the dish shelf. As she pulled the coffee pot to the warmest part of the stove, Clarie, Dosha and Jack arrived.

Holding a buttermilk pie, Dosha cooed as she looked at the cheerful scene.

"Oh, look at your pretty little tree," she said. "And those pretty babies standing right next to it just like little angels."

As Zetta made room on the table for Dosha's pie and Clarie's potato candy, Perton and Polly arrived. He opened the door without knocking, then swayed slightly as he stepped inside.

"We would have come right on," he said. "But old scaredy pants here wanted to stop by the house and get a lantern for when we leave. I told her even if something got her, it would let her go come daylight when it got a good look at her."

As Zetta reached to take the plate of brown sugar sweets from Polly, Asa's look plainly told her what he had meant about Perton being trouble.

Perton turned to Zetta. "So this is the pretty little lady who keeps my men supplied with decent vittles," he said.

Zetta caught the stench of moonshine, then stammered for something to say.

"Thank you for letting Asa use the wagon and team last week," she managed. "I've enjoyed getting to know Polly these past few days."

Perton shrugged. "Yeah, she'd be plumb pretty if she put a bag over her head," he said. "Nobody will ever love her except her mother—and then only on payday."

He again chuckled as Polly hung her head. Before a stunned Zetta—or anyone else—could react, Loren strode to the table.

"My stomach growled all through that school thing just thinking about what was waiting up here," he said.

He plopped a piece of Clarie's potato candy into his mouth then scooped a large portion of the cobbler onto a plate.

Clarie took Polly's hand and led her to the table. "All this looks so good, I don't know which one to try first."

Perton swayed as he laughed. "Don't look like you had trouble making such decisions in the past."

Clarie ignored the comment as she put a brown sugar sweet onto her plate.

"Missed you in church this morning, Perton," she said.

He snorted. "I had enough of that get right with God stuff when I was a youngin."

Clarie handed a plate to Polly. "Too bad it didn't take," she said. "You missed a good service. Jack sang a new song, and Preacher Howard did a good job of holding out the Word of God for us."

She cut into Dosha's pie.

"The Christmas Story always touches my heart," Clarie said. "And to think of little baby Jesus growing up to have his sweet skin beaten and tore by the Roman soldiers."

Perton snapped his fingers at Polly and pointed toward the cobbler.

"Save your testifying for next week's church, Clarie," he said.

But even as he spoke, he stumbled into the nearby wall.

Clarie shook her head. "You'd think you could leave off the moonshine on the Lord's day."

His dark eyebrows came together in a deep scowl.

"Don't you be scolding me," he said. "You've been known to buy some, too."

"You know I keep that around in case it's needed," she said.

"Oh, I know you say you keep it to keep dead babies' skin from turning dark," he said. "I bet that's just your excuse."

As Clarie shook her head in disgust, Zetta noticed Rachel staring at Perton.

She quickly offered the child a sliver of pie.

Polly hadn't spoken since they arrived, but now she whispered, "Perton, honey, let it be."

He glared at her. "Are you telling me what to do, woman?"

"No, Perton." Her voice was barely audible.

He took an awkward step toward her. "I ought to slap you."

As she cowered, the other men put down their plates, and Zetta stepped closer to both children. But while the men paused, waiting for Perton's next move, Clarie strode forward and thrust a finger at his face.

"Don't be threatening one of my girls, Perton Muncy," she said. "Even if she is your woman, I won't have it."

Perton forced his eyes to focus. "Now, Miz Clarie, you don't scare me," he said. "You're a God-fearing woman."

She took a step closer. "I'll slap you silly if you hit Polly and then I'll ponder if I should ask God's forgiveness," she said. "Don't test me on this."

Perton stared at the old woman, then shrugged. "Ah, can't you take a joke?"

No one moved for several moments. Dosha glanced around, her little hands fluttering at her throat.

"Did y'all like Jack's singing this morning?" she asked. "I'd travel all day to hear him and not even notice if I was standing with my feet in the fire."

Dosha looked to Zetta then Asa, wordlessly asking for support.

Asa took a deep breath. "He's good, sure enough, Dosha," he said. "But you mentioning travel reminds me of the feller who was taking his first train trip a while back. After he bought the ticket, the agent asked, 'You got any luggage?' The old boy thought a minute, then asked, 'What's luggage?'

" 'Oh, kindly like a box with a handle,' the agent answered. 'You put your clothes in it.'

"The country feller looked right shocked, 'What? And travel naked!?' "

As the others chuckled, Zetta turned to Asa, horrified.

"Asa! Don't say that word in front of the children."

He looked bewildered. "What word? Naked?"

"Asa!"

Perton punched Asa's shoulder. "That one's worth remembering."

Even though the tension was broken, Zetta knew she wouldn't plan another sweets party. And she couldn't wait for this one to end.

CHAPTER 12

That night, Zetta lay awake long after Asa had fallen asleep. She tried snuggling against his warm back and settling a pillow under her expanding abdomen, but her misery remained.

Lord, I thought a sweets party like we used to have at home would be fun, but I couldn't have come up with a worse idea.

She punched the second feather pillow beneath her head, remembering how relieved everyone had been when Perton gulped down another helping of cobbler and abruptly left. Polly had hurried after him, the lantern swinging at her side.

Trembling, Zetta had watched the bobbing light through the window, then turned to wipe Rachel's and Micah's faces and steer them toward bed.

After an awkward silence, the others left. Asa walked Clarie home to collect the doll cradle she had been keeping for Rachel. As Zetta returned to the kitchen, Loren had gestured toward the table holding the empty plates.

"Well, I don't reckon you'll be inviting Perton back anytime soon."

Luttrell's voice had been low as he turned toward their bedroom, but Zetta still heard him murmur, "No need to say that. Let's set out the toys for the youngins."

Zetta punched the pillow again, remembering how when Asa returned, he strode past her to put the little cradle in front of the Christmas tree. Zetta had tried to ignore his grim face.

"That's right pretty, Asa," she had said. "Rachel's gonna love that for her rag baby."

93

Asa had merely grunted, so Zetta spoke again as she draped the little quilt she had made back home over one end of the cradle.

"I see what you mean about Perton," she said. "I never dreamed anybody would be like that. I won't invite them again. I was just trying to—"

Asa interrupted her. "It's all right, Zetta."

Then he stood to admire the cradle in front of the tree as Luttrell and Loren came back into the room. Luttrell handed Asa the wooden dancing man Asa had finished for Micah. When Asa set the toy man in front of the tree, Luttrell placed five carved peach seed squirrels nearby. Then he pulled five little peach seed baskets from his shirt pocket and arranged them beside the cradle. Behind the cradle, Loren had set a doll-sized cast iron stove and a mechanical bank in the shape of a man holding a pig. Zetta remembered seeing both items on the company store shelf.

She punched the pillow again, remembering the appreciative whistle Asa had given as her brothers positioned the toys they had for the children.

"These youngins are sure enough spoiled," he had said. "All we got when I was growing up was candy in our shoes. . . ."

Zetta drowsily turned to her other side, remembering how his voice had trailed off then.

Lord, the pain of loss never quits, does it?

* * * * *

The crow was on the dish shelf. Its black feathers shimmered in the moonlight as he strutted across the clean dishes to where the bean jar was hidden behind the stack of plates. The bird's eyes glowed with orange fire as he pushed the jar from the shelf. Zetta lunged forward, hands outstretched, but the container shattered, mixing glass shards with the beans rolling across the wooden floor. The evil bird gave a hoarse victory cry and swooped to gobble the beans even as Zetta waved her arms, her cries stuck in her throat.

With a start, Zetta awakened. Confused, she looked around the room and listened for the crow's tormenting calls. But she heard only Asa's gentle breathing as he lay beside her. She pulled the quilt over his chest, then leaned toward Rachel and Micah as they lay with their arms entwined. Through the window, she could see quarter-sized snowflakes lazily falling on the black ground. She groped for her shawl, then hurried into the kitchen. A shaft of moonlight spilled through the dirty window and fell across the table. Zetta stopped, her hand on the back of a chair, and studied the shelf holding the pint jar with the beans representing the number of days until March thirty-first. Heart pounding and remembering the orange eyes of the bird, she took a deep breath before reaching behind the stack of plates. When her hands encountered the pint jar in the far corner, she pulled it forward and set it on the table.

She glanced toward the bedroom, then eased herself into the chair. She held the jar up to the moonlight, looking at the mound of beans. Carefully, afraid the lid would squeak, she opened the jar and tipped it toward her hand. A speckled bean rolled onto her palm. One more day closer to home, Lord. One more day closer to home.

She pushed herself up from the table to drop the lone bean into the gallon jar holding beans to be cooked. As she did, she saw a dark figure leaning heavily on a walking stick. The snow falling around her was quickly swallowed by the sooty lane.

Zetta opened the door and whispered, "Clarie? That you?"

The woman stopped. "Lands, honey, you like to have scared the living daylights out of me!" Clarie said. "What you doing up this time of night?"

"I had a bad dream," Zetta answered.

Clarie moved toward the steps and whispered. "Well, there's been a lot of that lately."

Zetta's voice was just as soft. "What you doing out?"

Clarie's shoulders sagged, startling Zetta at how the woman had aged in just a few hours.

"Mildred, the one I gave the lavender to yesterday at the program, miscarried again tonight. She's had nothing but bad dreams these whole two months."

Zetta sucked in her breath. "How'd you know to go to her?"

"Her man came just after I went to bed," Clarie said. "When he told how bad she was bleeding, I knew all's I'd be able to do would be wash her and hug her whilst she cried."

Clarie waved her hand in front of her face. "I'm sorry," she said. "I shouldn't have said anything. It's just that she's wanted a baby from the minute they got married."

Zetta took a step forward. "Come in. I'll stir up the stove fire."

Clarie shook her head. "No, honey."

She held up the black sachet Zetta hadn't noticed until then.

"I promised Mildred I'd take the little clump of remains to my spot up the mountain come morning—where her other babies are," Clarie said. "Some granny women burn the bloody rags when this happens, but I bury them up near that big dogwood tree. You go on back to bed now."

Clarie turned away as Zetta quietly shut the door. Then stifling a sob for a grieving woman she didn't know, Zetta crossed her arms across her abdomen.

* * * * *

After a restless and dreamless two hours of sleep, Zetta eased out of bed, dressed quietly and slipped into the kitchen. The snow was still falling. She watched the soot absorb the flakes, then turned toward the stove. There, she stirred the ashes within the fire compartment and added several small chunks of coal, all the while glancing up the lane toward Clarie's house.

How awful to lose a baby on Christmas morning, she thought. Lord, please be with Mildred and with Clarie. And please protect my little one as well as the rest of my family.

After placing the filled coffee pot on the hottest part of the stove, she stooped to lift the ham from the meat crate. She stared at the empty space where the ham had been. The crate was only half full now.

I'm gonna have to start buying meat from Roscoe sooner than I wanted, she thought.

She sighed as she held the ham over a dishpan and poured a dipperful of water over the skin to rinse away the salt. She rubbed dried mustard into the meat and positioned it in her largest skillet, which she pushed to the back of the oven. Then she pulled an orange from the bowl on the dish shelf, held it to her nose and breathed deeply. Smiling, she cut it into twelve slices. Three slices went on each man's plate and one each on hers and the children's. She would divide the remaining oranges like that until the fruit was gone.

After mixing the biscuit dough, Zetta reached for her favorite skillet as Asa came into the kitchen and kissed the back of her neck.

"Christmas Gift, Mrs. Berg*hoff*."

Zetta turned and put her hands on each side of his face, relieved to hear the teasing forgiveness in his voice.

"And Christmas Gift to you, Mr. Berghoff*er*," she said. "The coffee's about ready. Wipe that silly grin off your face, and I'll get you a cup."

Asa shook his head. "Let that wait. I'm gonna light the tree candles and get Sister and Brother up."

"Asa, I swear, you're a bigger kid than anybody I know. I want the youngins to eat a good breakfast before they start playing."

"They will."

Before Asa had finished lighting the candles, Rachel emerged from the bedroom, clutching her rag doll.

"Sister, looky here," Asa said. "Come see what Santy Claus brung."

Zetta smiled as Rachel's eyes widened at the sight of the toys.

Asa took the child by the hand. "The cradle is for your doll baby, and the dancing man is for Micah," he said. "And looky at the play stove and the little baskets for play pretties."

Rachel smiled and stooped to place her rag baby in the cradle, then reached for the peach seed baskets. Zetta heard the corn shuck mattresses rustle as her brothers awakened. Luttrell stepped into the room first, smiling as he watched the child. Loren followed, buckling his belt.

"You'd think you'd let a feller sleep in on Christmas," Loren said. "But instead you're out here yammering enough to wake the dead. That dang whistle hasn't even sounded yet and here y'all are acting like it's the middle of the day."

Zetta smiled. "I swear you spent too much on these youngins."

Loren held up his hands in feigned surprise. "I didn't buy a thing," he said. "Those gifts are from Santy Claus. Hey, since it's Christmas, how about making chocolate gravy?"

"Chocolate gravy? I swear I've got a houseful of youngins today," Zetta said. "But all right. I've got some cocoa powder to stir in. Oh, here's sweet Micah."

Asa swooped up the child and held him close. Then with his son in one arm, he picked up the stick attached to the back of the dancing man and bounced the toy against the bare floor.

As Micah watched the swirling legs of the toy, Loren danced several shuffling steps in rhythm then pointed toward the mechanical bank.

"Hey, come over here," he said. "See how you balance a penny on the pig's snout? Then you push this level behind the man, and the pig kicks the penny into the man's mouth. Watch now."

As Loren pushed the lever, the penny sailed into the mechanical man's mouth, who promptly stuck out his tongue. Rachel frowned at the sight of the metal tongue, but Micah giggled. Loren slapped his thigh and laughed.

"That look on your face beats all," he said. "Let me see if I've got another penny."

Asa shook his head. "That bank's gonna have more money than you do at this rate. Why'd you have to go and spend your wages on fool stuff?"

Loren balanced another penny on the pig's snout. "Maybe I got tired of hearing you yammering all the time about those pitiful Christmases when you was growing up."

He turned to Micah. "Watch now."

Asa shook his head. "Whoever said a fool and his money are soon parted sure knew you."

Loren shrugged. Then as he dug in his pocket for another penny, the mine whistle blew.

* * * * *

Rachel and Micah fidgeted throughout breakfast, often turning to look at the treasures under the tree. Even the shiny orange slices didn't hold their interest. Finally, Zetta released the children to return to their toys and then refilled the men's coffee cups.

Asa watched her for a moment then said, "You're awful quiet. You still upset about the sweets party? I said it's all right."

Zetta eased into her own chair. "No, it's just that I got up in the middle of the night and saw Clarie coming back from helping a woman who miscarried."

Loren reached for another biscuit. "Miscarried? Well, that's not so bad," he said. "It ain't like she lost a real baby."

Zetta tried to keep her voice level. "From the minute that baby is started, it's *real* to the mother."

Loren shrugged as he reached for the jam.

Zetta started to comment again but saw Clarie coming up the back steps. She hurried to open the door.

"Christmas Gift, Clarie! Come on in."

Clarie stomped sooty snow from her shoes. "Christmas Gift to y'all, too," she said. "Here's your jar of milk for the youngins—and some snow cream. I know it's better suited for noon dinner, but it was starting to melt and I was afraid the soot would seep in. I know we breathe the soot, but I didn't want us *eating* it."

"Snow cream! Why I haven't had that in ages," Zetta said as she reached for saucers from the shelf. "Here, let me dish it up before it melts. Where'd you find snow this clean?"

Clarie glanced at the men before answering. "Oh, I went way up the mountain early. I knew the snow would be pretty up there."

Asa stood up and gestured toward his chair.

"Here, I'm finished eating—all except for the snow cream," he said. "You sit right down."

Zetta spooned snow cream into the dishes and handed them to the men, then called Rachel and Micah away from their toys.

"Miz Clarie made this special treat just for us," she said. "It's real cold, so don't swallow it too fast. Brother, turn loose the toy squirrels. You can play with them in a little while."

Reluctantly, both children came to the table but smiled as they touched their lips to the coldness. Zetta held a portion toward Clarie. "I know you've got room for sweets."

The woman nodded and accepted the dish. "When I was a youngin, we had snow cream every time it snowed as long as the cow was giving good milk and we had a dab of sugar," Clarie said. "But once the camp opened and soot covered everything, I give up on that. Christmas is the only time I make it anymore—if it snows. Last couple of years, we got rain instead."

Zetta watched as the woman savored a cold, sweet bite, as though remembering those long ago years.

"Will you have dinner with us?" Zetta asked. "I meant to ask you earlier, but with the sweets party and all, I plumb forgot."

Clarie shook her head. "I appreciate that. But I always have Christmas dinner with Ruthie. It being Christmas, nobody notices."

Loren frowned. "Ruthie? The colored granny woman? What's this world coming to?"

Clarie shook her empty spoon at Loren. "Now, don't you start. A long while back, one of my girls was taking too long birthing. Ruthie showed up with bitter mugwort and got the baby here. We've been good friends ever since."

She leaned forward, ready for an argument. "It don't matter what color Ruthie is."

Loren shrugged as he took the last bite of his snow cream.

* * * * *

Clarie didn't stay long, and the children quickly returned to their new toys. But as Zetta began to clear the breakfast table, Asa pulled her to the living room.

"Let the dishes be," he said. "The boys and me have gifts for you."

As Asa steered Zetta toward a chair near the tree, she stammered, "Now, I wish y'all hadn't gone and done that."

Loren grinned and pulled a tortoise shell hand mirror from behind the bucket holding the tree. "Asa's all the time bragging on your hair," he said. "So I wanted you to have this."

Zetta motioned for him to bend down and then kissed him soundly on the cheek. "And did you buy another one to give to your sweet Sarah?" she asked.

Loren's grin widened as he turned toward his bedroom. "Already sent it to her, Sis."

Then Luttrell held out a smooth board marked with black lines. A small bright blue cloth bag lay on top.

"I thought maybe you'd like to teach Rachel the Fox and Geese game," he said. "I recollect you teaching me when we was little. Clarie made the pouch for the stones."

Just as Zetta motioned for Luttrell to bend down for a kiss on the cheek, Loren came back into the room with his hands behind his back.

Zetta looked at the three men. "This summer I knitted y'all mittens, but if I'd had half a brain, I would have realized digging coal would chew up your hands. I should have made you tallow salve instead."

Asa smiled. "No. The mittens will be fine."

Then he looked at Loren and Luttrell. "Are all the presents give out?" he asked. "Good then. Zetta, I got you something special."

He nodded at Loren, who still kept his hands behind his back.

"Sis, here's old Asa's surprise I slipped and told you about," Loren said. "It's the only thing he's spent money on—other than things for the house and what the company forced him to buy—the whole time we've been here."

With his back to Loren, Asa accepted what his brother-in-law had been holding. Then with the item still hidden, he said, "When Perton sent me into Hazard a while back to pick up some tools, I saw a woman outside the Beaumont Hotel wearing one like this. I thought of you right away and thought how it would look so much prettier on you than it did on her."

He pulled his hands from behind his back and held up a red sweater.

Zetta was startled by the color but managed to stammer, "Why, that's right pretty, Asa."

When she didn't take it from her husband's outstretched hands, Loren laughed.

"What'd I tell you, Asa? I told you the woman you saw was a street walker," he said. "Nobody but women like that wear red."

Asa looked bewildered, looking first at Zetta then at the grinning Loren.

"But with Zetta's dark hair, I just figured...."

Zetta stood up and took the garment from his hands.

"Asa, I'm right pleased you thought of me," she said. "I can't wear it just yet, what with the baby and all. But I will soon. Real soon."

Then as Zetta hugged her husband, she looked beyond his shoulder to the dish shelf where the crow of her nightmare had stood.

CHAPTER 13

The next morning, Zetta was in the kitchen before the dreaded whistle sounded. She ran her hands lovingly over her abdomen, lit the kerosene lamp on the table and reached behind the stack of plates for the jar holding the dried beans. As a lone bean rolled from the tipped jar, Zetta tightened her fist around it, then tossed it into the kettle of beans that had been soaking all night. As she reached for her apron, she whispered, "One more day closer to home, Lord. Thank you."

Tying the material around her middle, Zetta studied the little Christmas tree in the moonlit front room—the toys still under its branches. Through the window behind the tree, she could see the black slush left from yesterday's snow. She shook her head and turned toward the bag of flour. As she mixed the biscuit dough, she pondered the previous afternoon. After the ham dinner, Asa sat on the floor with the children, feeding them orange slices and talking about Christmas on the farm next year. Then as he reached for a popcorn ball, he turned toward Loren.

"Hey, can your Sarah cook as good as Zetta?" he asked.

Loren grinned. "I don't plan on finding out for a while," he said. "I'm more interested in what all else she can do."

Then he turned to wink at Luttrell.

"You better get a move on with that school teacher," Loren said. "Sarah and I will have a houseful of youngins before you even introduce yourself."

Luttrell had merely shrugged, but Zetta noticed his face reddening.

Now as she kneaded the biscuits, Zetta whispered a prayer. "Luttrell is my tender brother, Lord, always watching out for others. But, he's bashful and not forward like Loren. So would you help him speak to the teacher? Maybe if Rachel was in school, I could arrange a meeting."

In the midst of Zetta's plotting, the shrill mine whistle sounded, making her jump. She quickly fried eggs as the men made their trips up the lane to the outhouse, then plunged their hands into the pan of warm water set out on the back porch for them.

As the men ate breakfast, Zetta filled their dinner buckets with the meat and cabbage rolls she had baked two days earlier. The rest of the rolls she wrapped tightly in a cloth for sale to the boarding miners. Then as she sliced raw sweet potatoes for Asa's bucket, she breathed a prayer for safely for all three men.

* * * * *

When Rachel and Micah awakened, they ate their breakfasts quickly, anxious to play with their new toys. As Zetta kneaded the bread dough for the next day's meat pies, she smiled as she watched the children. Micah tried to hold all his peach seed squirrels in one little fist so he could thump the dancing man against the floor, but he kept dropping them. He'd frown, put down the dancing man, pick up another tiny squirrel, drop two more and pick up the dancing man. Occasionally, he'd push the lever on the metal bank and giggle as the man stuck out his tongue. Rachel was content to line her peach seed baskets across the toy stove top, kiss her rag doll, lay her in the cradle, cover her with the tiny quilt, then realign the little baskets.

Zetta smiled as she placed the bread dough into the ironstone bowl to rise. "You youngins are being so good, I believe I'll write Paw and Becky," she said.

But as she wiped her hands and reached for the writing paper, an unwelcome voice called from the back porch.

"Hey, open the door!"

Julia. Zetta sighed as she turned the knob. The child stepped immediately into the kitchen.

Before she could stop herself, Zetta said, "Miz Julia, the polite thing to do is wait 'til you are invited in."

Julia shrugged. "You opened the door. Besides, I've come to see what you hillbillies did for Christmas. We had important company yesterday, so Daddy wouldn't let me leave."

Thank you, Lord, for that blessing, Zetta thought.

At the sight of the other girl, Rachel pulled her rag doll from the cradle and clutched it to her face. As Julia stepped toward the children, Zetta was right beside her.

"Your tree is little," Julia said. "Ours reaches the ceiling. Two men had to carry it. And it took our colored maids all afternoon to decorate it."

Zetta took a deep breath to hide her disdain. "Well, now," she said. "That sounds impressive, all right."

Then wanting to draw Julia away from the children, Zetta gestured toward the table. "Would you like a cookie?"

Julia shrugged again. "I guess."

But before Zetta could reach for the cookies left from Sunday night's party, Julia spied the Fox and Geese game under the tree.

"What's that?"

Zetta tried to keep her voice level. "Oh, just a game."

"How do you play?"

Everything within Zetta's being wanted to send the child out the door. But she remembered Asa's earlier warning about Julia's power to get families turned out of the camp. Suddenly, a new thought entered her mind: If I get us kicked out of here, we can go home. But she sighed at the next thought: Asa would have a fit if I did that.

As Zetta wrestled with the delicious thought of being forced to leave, Julia spoke again.

"Hey, I said how do you play the game?"

Zetta sighed as she pulled the board and blue bag from under the tree, but she smiled at Rachel and Micah.

"It's okay, Babies," she said. "You just stay with your play pretties."

Julia sneered.

As Zetta placed the board on the kitchen table and poured the pebbles from the blue bag onto the board, Julia sneered again.

"Those are just rocks!"

"No, they're smooth pebbles," Zetta said. "The brown one stands for the fox. The 15 white ones are the geese."

She put the brown stone in the center of the board.

"The fox starts here in the middle and then move by move chases the geese," she said. "If he jumps over eight geese, he wins. And if the geese can pen him into one spot and keep him from moving, they win."

Zetta took a deep breath, wishing Julia would leave. Instead she said, "It's a game that makes you think. Would you like to play one time so you can see how it works?"

The child gave her a disdainful look.

"Nobody but hillbillies plays with rocks," she said. "Where's that cookie?"

Zetta quickly put her hands behind her back. If that girl was mine, I'd paddle her good, she thought. But she turned toward the cloth-covered dish holding the leftover cookies.

"Here you go," Zetta said as she handed the child a cookie and then opened the door.

"It's a good thing you hadn't taken off your coat yet," she said. "This way, you don't have to bother to put it back on, do you?"

Julia shrugged and bit into the cookie as she went out the door.

* * * * *

Throughout the gray afternoon, Zetta often glanced out the window toward the dampness as she shaped hand pies around the slivered ham, chopped cabbage, potatoes and onions.

"I wish Clarie would stop by," she said to Rachel, who ignored her. "I'm about out of eggs."

And I want to ask her about these dreams I've been having, Zetta thought. Funny she's not out and about this morning.

Zetta glanced out the window again. Come to think of it, she hadn't seen anybody but Julia on the lane all morning. Well, I guess nobody needs anything from the store the day after Christmas, she thought.

She pinched together the edges of the hand pies and thrust them into the waiting oven. Then after glancing again toward the empty path leading from Clarie's house, she awkwardly bent to help Micah gather the peach seed squirrels.

The day seemed even longer without the men there, but finally the shift-ending whistle sounded. Zetta poured cornbread batter into the hot skillet as Rachel and her rag doll watched.

"Your daddy will be tickled to hear how much you played with that cradle today," Zetta said. "He sure worked hard on it. Well, him and old Santy Claus."

She thrust the skillet into the oven. "I'm glad he never complains about whatever I fix for supper. Tonight we're having leftovers from yesterday. I've got to slow down on the meat if I don't want to have to start buying it from Roscoe pretty soon. Oh, here's your daddy now."

After the men had washed, Asa stepped into the kitchen and smiled as he dropped two dollar's worth of nickels and silver dimes into Zetta's hand before kissing her and greeting the children.

"The boarders said to tell you they sure missed your meat pies the last two days," he said. "I've got orders for 15 more if you feel up to sending some tomorrow."

Zetta smiled and gestured toward the platter on the stove's warming shelf. "Even after I pack y'all's buckets tomorrow, I'll have twenty to send with you," she said.

* * * * *

As soon as Asa said *Amen* after the blessing, Loren broke off a chunk of cornbread.

"Did you notice how Mr. Gray was snooping around today?" Loren said. "He normally spends all day in his office, but he was breathing coal dust with the rest of us all morning."

Asa nodded his thanks as Zetta filled his coffee cup. "Yep. I heard Perton telling a couple of the men Mr. Golden and the missus was in town yesterday," he said. "Even had Christmas dinner with the Grays yesterday."

Loren reached for the beans. "Maybe they got wind of the union meeting tonight."

Zetta poured coffee for her brothers. "Was Perton still drunk?" she asked.

Loren didn't look up. "Nah. He's always sober in the mine. He'd get himself killed if he wasn't."

She turned to Asa. "Did Perton say anything about the sweets party? I hope he's ashamed of the way he acted the other night."

Asa shook his head. "He probably doesn't even remember his shenanigans," he said. "He was all business today. And he was watching Mr. Gray's every move."

Zetta handed Asa the bowl of sweet potatoes. "At the school program Clarie told me those little boys playing the Wise Men will be working coal come next summer."

Asa nodded. "Yep, they'll be under the mountain before long. But they'll start out oiling the big engine or picking rocks out of the coal. Some mines have boys as little as four years old picking rocks, but here Mr. Golden won't let them go in before they're eight."

Zetta gasped. "Four! Why that's just a little older than Rachel!"

"I know," Asa said. "But within three, four years after they start here they're all working right alongside their daddies. Some of the clever ones will handle the mules."

"Mules?" Zetta asked.

"Yep. Got a whole stable under the ground."

As Asa reached for his coffee, Loren spoke. "The only difference between the men and the mules is that the mules are treated better than the men. Everybody knows they can *hire* a man, but they have to *buy* a mule."

* * * * *

Asa had just drained his cup when heavy footsteps sounded on the front porch. He sat straighter, his eyes on the door. Zetta saw Loren and Luttrell glance at each other as a gruff call of "Hello in the cabin" rang out.

Loren snorted. "That's Perton. What's he doing here? Didn't he cause enough trouble the other night?"

Zetta poured warm water over a clean cloth and nervously ran it over Rachel's and Micah's mouths and hands and quickly steered them toward their new toys.

Asa opened the door. "Well, Perton," he said. "Something the matter?"

Perton looked beyond Asa's shoulder.

"Good," he said. "Loren and Luttrell are here, too. I need to talk to all three of you boys."

Asa stepped back and gestured toward the kitchen. Perton entered, then took off his cap as he saw Zetta standing with the children near the tree.

"Good evening, Miz Zetta," he said. "You doing all right?"

Zetta barely nodded, remembering how he had acted at the sweets party. She glanced at Asa, who pulled a chair out from the table and gestured for Perton to sit. His shift boss waved Asa aside and remained standing.

"I want you boys to attend the union meeting up in the woods tonight," he said. "Old man Golden had Christmas dinner yesterday with Ed Gray and his family. Something's up, and we'd better be ready for it."

Asa slowly poured himself more coffee and gestured to ask if Perton wanted a cup.

Perton shook his head. "Well?"

Asa took a slow sip. "That meeting has nothing to do with me," he said. "I'm leaving the last day of March and don't want trouble. And I sure don't want a strike between now and then."

Perton leaned forward and put his hands on the table.

"This meeting has everything to do with you—and everybody in this camp," he said. "Old Man Golden never bothers with any of his coal companies unless something is going on. The last time he was down here was last year just after Sid Hatfield and his deputy were shot in cold blood right in front of their wives on the Matewan courthouse steps. And Golden didn't come alone then. He had enough hired guns by his side to kill every one of us. And those thugs would just as soon shoot a miner as say howdy."

Asa glanced at Zetta, who stared at him. "That whole Matewan thing happened over in West Virginia," he said. "Like I said, it has nothing to do with me."

"It has everything to do with you," Perton said again. "A sheriff and his deputy are gunned down by hired guns just because the mine owner didn't like the jury's verdict declaring them innocent. Sid Hatfield didn't start that fight with the Felts-Baldwin detectives but he didn't back down either. He was protecting the miners and their families who got pitched outta their homes just because the miners wanted to join a union."

Asa shook his head. "Look," he said. "I might not agree with what the mine owners do, but that's just it: They're the mine *owners.*"

Perton's jaw tightened. "That don't give them the right to cheat workers. A union would make sure the weight scales are honest. A union would make sure we got a decent wage for our long hours under the mountain. A union would make sure we worked in safer conditions."

As Perton leaned toward Asa, Zetta held her breath.

"You say last year's murders had nothing to do with you," he said. "Well, plenty of other miners thought it did. We marched together, proud to wear the red bandanas to show whose side we was on."

Perton began to pace. "That big-time New York reporter called us a bunch of Rednecks because of the bandanas," he said. "Didn't have the decency to call us soldiers or even miners! But we sure fought hard enough at Blair Mountain even though the mine thugs had the higher ground and was using submachine guns!"

Asa glanced at Zetta, who still stared at him with wide eyes, then said softly. "Look, Perton, I read all about Blair Mountain in the paper last year. Yes, that was the worse battle fought here since the War Between Brothers, but it's over now."

Perton's right hand hit the table. "It's not over. It'll never be over 'til decent workers are treated like men! They brung the U.S. Army in to drop bombs on us. Dropping bombs on the miners fighting and on the houses where their families were. The U.S. Army dropped bombs on its own citizens! I want you at that meeting tonight."

Asa leaned back in his chair and hooked his thumb over his belt. "How's a meeting going to help?" he asked. "Working under a mountain is still working under a mountain."

Perton frowned. "We're being cheated at the weigh station. And right now our pay don't start 'til we hit that first lick against the coal. Our pay ought to start the minute we step into the mantrip instead of after it delivers us to the coal face. That's an hour or more of lost pay for us every day."

At the mention of the money, Loren's eyes brightened.

"That makes sense to me," he said. "Riding in the dark is still part of our job."

Perton moved closer to Loren.

"And too many of our machines are outdated," he said. "The air donkey that pulls the mantrip is dangerous. Who in the world ever heard of having to stop an engine by throwing it in reverse? I'm telling you, the union will make a big difference."

Asa shook his head. "And I'm telling you, I'm not getting involved. Besides, if Mr. Golden is in town, what if his thugs are with him? What you gonna do then?"

Perton gestured toward the lane.

"We're meeting at seven o'clock in the woods up above Clarie's house," he said. "She'll be on the lookout. Outsiders won't know the back way. They'll come straight up the path toward her house. If they show up, she'll light her lantern and pretend she's checking on a woman about to deliver. But just to be on the safe side, she and some of the other women have been watching that back way to make sure no outsiders have discovered it."

Zetta gasped. So that's why I didn't see anybody out and about today, she thought.

Perton turned at Zetta's ragged breath then faced Asa again, his face dark.

"You're acting like working the mine is some Sunday school picnic," he said. "That tin in your pocket should remind you otherwise."

Asa glanced at Zetta. "No need to mention that."

Perton leaned forward. "Empty your pockets."

Asa's voice was low. "Come on. Not in front of Zetta."

"I told you to empty your pockets," Perton said. "I decide who goes into that mine, so if you want to work tomorrow—empty your pockets. All of you."

Slowly the three men pulled out the contents of their pockets and placed them on the table. Zetta stepped closer as Perton picked up a small tin next to the pocket knife and a few pennies in front of Asa, who hung his head. Then she looked at the items in front of her brothers. Before each man was a small identical metal tin.

Zetta leaned over the table. "Asa, what's that?"

Asa's head remained down as Perton tapped the table with the tin.

"This here is morphine, Miz Zetta," Perton said. "I wouldn't be making my men carry it if the mine was a safe place. When my brother and three of the men on his shift died over at Jenkins five years ago, they was found with their hands all bloody from trying to dig through the slate blocking the tunnel and with their mouths hanging open trying to draw one more breath."

Perton clinched his fist. "If any of my men get trapped like that, they can swallow the morphine and die in sweet sleep."

Zetta's hand flew to her throat. Heart pounding, she remembered last Saturday night when Loren and Luttrell were in the kitchen taking their baths. So the tins were what they hadn't wanted her to see. Zetta put her hand on the wall to steady herself.

SANDRA P. ALDRICH

"Asa, you didn't tell me about—"

Perton interrupted. "Now Miz Zetta, this is *men's* business."

Asa quickly stood up. "You don't speak to her that way."

Zetta stepped away from the wall. "I'm all right, Asa," she said. Then she turned toward Perton, her voice low. "Anything that involves Asa or any of my family is my business," she said. "I'll thank you to remember that."

Loren's words quickly rolled over Zetta's, pulling Perton's attention back to him. "Well, if the union's trying to get us more money, I'll be at that meeting."

Luttrell spoke for the first time since Perton had arrived.

"I reckon I better go along to keep an eye on Loren."

Perton turned toward Asa. "I'll expect to see you there, too."

Asa merely jerked his thumb toward the door, motioning for his boss to leave. And this time he didn't tell a joke.

CHAPTER 14

Zetta watched Perton slam the door behind him, then turned to Asa as he stood up and shoved the little tin of morphine back into his pocket.

"Asa, you never told me about that," she said.

Asa turned away from her to stare at his reflection in the back window.

"No need," he said. "Perton makes us carry it, that's all. We ain't gonna talk about it."

Zetta griped the back of her chair.

"Asa Berghoffer, I want us out of this place!" she said. "And don't give me that March thirty-first malarkey."

Asa turned, his face red. "Malarkey? So that's what you call trying to make a better life for my family?"

Luttrell touched her hand. "Sis. It's okay."

Zetta whirled toward her brother. "And you! The one I could always count on to tell me the truth even when you was little!"

Luttrell shook his head. "Sis, Asa's right. We carry the tins because Perton makes us."

He turned to Asa, looking for support. But his brother-in-law already had opened the back door and pulled the two gray buckets from under the wash bench. As he came back into the kitchen, his voice had a hard edge.

"Zetta, whilst you put the youngins to bed, I'll tote the water so you can do the wash tomorrow. I don't reckon Mr. Golden brung his thugs along this time, but just in case, they'll see me doing something besides hiding up in the woods."

Loren stood so quickly, he knocked his chair over. "Hiding?"

Luttrell put his hand on Loren's shoulder, then gestured toward their jackets. "We might as well head for the meeting."

As Asa left through the front door, Zetta watched her brothers leave through the back and disappear into the darkness. She turned toward Rachel, who was hugging her rag doll.

"I swear all this makes me plumb tired," Zetta said. "In all my twenty-two years, I don't reckon I've ever felt this old."

Rachel looked up. "Micah's rubbing his nose, Mama."

"You're a good big sister to see how tired he is," Zetta said. "And I reckon you're tired, too, honey. Come on. It's bedtime."

* * * * *

As Zetta put the children to bed, she could hear Asa slosh bucket after bucket of water into both kettles—one for washing, the other for rinsing. When he had finished, Asa put the buckets back under the wash bench and stepped into the kitchen just as Zetta came from putting the children to bed. He stood awkwardly for a minute. Finally he spoke.

"Both kettles are filled, and I got the kindling laid under the one. I'll light the fire for you before I go to work in the morning."

Zetta merely nodded.

Asa puffed out his cheeks, before drawing in a long breath. "Look, I don't want us fussing," he said.

Zetta sighed and rubbed her abdomen. "I don't want it either, Asa," she said. "I swear the baby jumped with every contrary word."

He wrapped her in a hug. "Just three more months and all this will just be a bad dream."

Dreams. With her head still against his chest, Zetta set her jaw. "Asa, speaking of that, I've had bad dreams since I've been here," she said. "Let's go home. You can use what you've earned so far to pay on the land. And next year's tobacca crop surely will pay the rest."

He pulled back, his hands gripping her shoulders.

"This argument is like beating a dead horse," he said. "It won't get us nowhere."

"But you carry that tin," Zetta said. "And what if there's trouble tonight at the meeting?"

Asa released her shoulders and ran his hand through his hair.

"There won't be any trouble unless Loren shoots off his mouth," he said. "Where's that tablet of paper? I want to figure how much I'm liable to get paid come Saturday."

His release of her and abrupt change of subject caused loneliness to wash over Zetta, but she knew that was the end of the discussion—for now. Wordlessly, she pulled the paper and a pencil from the top kitchen shelf. Without looking at her, Asa nodded his thanks and sat at the table. Zetta stared at him for a few moments but finally turned to the dishes waiting in the pan of now cold water.

* * * * *

Long after she had washed and dried the dishes, Zetta lingered in the kitchen, wrapping hand pies for the next day's sale to the boarding miners and cutting slivers from the bar of brown lye soap for tomorrow's wash. And always she looked out the back window, hoping to see her brothers returning from the meeting. Asa had stopped entering numbers on the paper but continued to stare at the columns. Finally, Zetta sat down and picked up the discarded pencil.

"If you are finished with this, I reckon I'll write a letter," she said.

Asa tore away the top sheet of paper with its column of numbers and pushed the tablet toward her.

"If my figures are right, we're going to be just a few dollars shy of paying off the land in the spring," he said. "It would have taken us years to be in this good of shape without my working coal."

As Asa studied the numbers, Zetta frowned. Instead of replying, she started the letter:

Dear Paw and Mama Becky,

I hope these few words find you and the boys well. We had a nice Christmas. I fixed a big ham dinner, and Sister and Brother got spoiled with all the new toys. It snowed here a little but most of it melted already. We're keeping the little Christmas tree decorated for a few more days for Brother and Sister. Come spring we're looking to plant it on the rise above the house.

Zetta tapped the pencil against the paper, determined not to confess her homesickness.

Asa looked up. "You all right?"

"Just wishing we was home—and trying not to let them know."

"Now, Zetta—"

"I know, Asa. But you asked." She turned back to the letter.

We had a sweets party Sunday night. The shift boss and his wife was here along with a neighbor couple and the granny woman who will help me when my time comes.

Loren and Luttrell are out this evening, but we expect them back soon. Sister and Brother are asleep now and Asa's sitting here at the table with me. Kiss Hobie and Frankie for me. Love, Zetta.

Asa looked up as Zetta folded the paper. "I'll mail that for you tomorrow morning, but that's kinda a short letter," he said.

"Not much I can rightly say. Leastways, they'll know we're still kicking."

* * * * *

As Zetta stood to get an envelope, Loren and Luttrell stepped through the back door. She studied their faces, looking for black eyes or bruises. Seeing none, she stammered, "How'd the meeting go?"

Loren pulled off his jacket and hung it by the door. "It was a bunch of nothing," he said. "Perton just yammered like he did here, saying we gotta be ready for whatever's coming."

Asa folded the paper with the wage totals and shoved it into his pocket. "Did he say what that might be?"

"Don't seem like much is coming just yet," Loren said. "Sure not more money."

Asa leaned back in his chair. "Who all was there?"

"Just about everybody," Loren said. "Even the colored miners. They stood in the back, respectful like. If you and your old buddy Jim Reed had been there, the two of you would have invited them to sit on the front row."

As her husband's jaw tightened, Zetta held her breath, waiting for another argument. Instead Asa swallowed hard, then asked, "Did Perton say anything about me not showing up?"

"Nope. Didn't call your name at all. But he did look hard at me and Luttrell when he said what hits one hits all."

Asa grunted. "Well, I just hope they hold off on a strike 'til after we're gone. I'm concerned Perton's making this out to be more than it needs to be."

Luttrell, who had been leaning against the back door, looked at his brother.

"Tell what Perton said about the thugs."

"Oh, yeah," Loren said. "At the end, when Clarie hadn't lit her warning lamp, I asked what happened to the thugs since nobody had seen them. Perton allowed how Old Man Golden's visit appears to be social but stressed we got to be ready."

"For what?"

"Didn't say exactly. He did say that just to be on the safe side not to fire any guns this coming Sunday night to see in the New Year—so's not to stir up trouble. And he said not to pay attention to any rumors. Strangest thing, he looked at the colored miners then."

Loren rubbed the back of his neck. "Well, that durn whistle will be getting us up pretty soon, so I'm hitting the sack."

Luttrell patted Zetta's shoulder before he followed their brother. "Sleep well, Sis."

But a good night's rest was something Zetta wasn't planning.

* * * * *

Just as she feared, Zetta did not sleep well. Each time she drifted off, coal-covered hands reached for her, causing her to jerk awake. At last she dressed and went into the kitchen. By the time the camp whistle blasted, she had kneaded the dough for the next batch of hand pies, made gingerbread cookies and started breakfast. Her main satisfaction, though, was in pulling another counting bean from the pint jar.

After a quick trip up the lane, Asa lit the fire under the wash kettle and dipped his hands in the porch wash pan before taking his place at the table.

Zetta served breakfast automatically as she pondered the tins. Lord, they are carrying death in their pockets and acting like it's nothing. Please protect them. And help me not fuss at Asa all the time.

Long after the three men had disappeared into the morning darkness, Zetta wrapped more prayers around them. Finally, she poured warm water over a washcloth and smiled at Rachel and Micah.

"Let me wash your hands. Then get one toy to play with whilst I do the wash."

With the children sitting on the floor near the open back door where she could see them, Zetta skimmed the coal dust from the top of the water that had settled there during the night. She started with the children's clothing and her dresses, pushing them under the heating sudsy water with the wash paddle. When those went into the rinse kettle, she pushed towels into the wash kettle then pulled the garments from the rinse kettle and wrung the water from them. As she stacked the clothing on the porch step, she glanced down the lane, hoping to finish the wash before Julia made her morning rounds.

As Zetta pushed the men's work clothes into the now boiling water of the first kettle, she saw Clarie coming down the path from her house. Her basket was covered with the blue cloth.

She smiled as the woman drew closer. "Morning, Clarie. I'm glad to see you got eggs for sale. How many can you spare me?"

Clarie set the basket on the step. "Some of my other girls said they'd be needing eggs, too," she said. "But I can let you have a dozen. My hens outdid themselves today."

She turned toward Rachel and Micah. "Good morning, you little sweeties."

Zetta put the work clothes into the rinse water. "Come inside so I can pay you," she said.

Clarie pushed her sleeves up. "First, let me help you wring the men's clothes out," she said. "I declare, you can break a wrist over that heavy material."

Pulling the separate items from the cold rinse water, each woman took an end of the material and twisted. Clarie added each item to the stack on the steps, then tipped the rinse kettle toward the fire under the wash kettle. As the dying fire hissed, she said, "I'll empty the wash kettle, too, when it has cooled off. All that water sure makes a mess in this mud. Come spring, most of the women put out little gardens in the back so the wash water ain't wasted. The gardens help keep down the mud, too. But I recollect what you said about not being here then."

Zetta picked up the shirts. "I'd leave here today if Asa would let us."

Clarie grabbed the egg basket in one hand and the remaining clothes in the other and started up the steps.

"I know, honey. But already I can tell I'm gonna miss you."

Zetta turned toward the woman. "Oh, I meant no disrespect, Clarie," she said. "You've already helped me tolerate being here."

Zetta nodded to the children. "Come on, Babies. Let me get you a sweet for being good."

* * * * *

While Clarie took off her coat and draped it over the back of a chair, Zetta handed each child a gingerbread cookie.

"You both were so good whilst I was doing the wash, you can eat your cookies in the front room," she said as she steered the children toward their toys. After she and Clarie hung the damp clothing around the kitchen, Zetta gestured toward the table.

"Here, sit down, if you've got time. The coffee is still hot from this morning and will go good with the cookies."

Clarie eased herself into a chair and pulled back the blue material covering the eggs.

"You know I always have time for your good sweets," she said. "Where do you want me to put these eggs?"

Zetta handed her a bowl then reached for the jar holding the coins from the food sales to the boarding miners.

"How much do I owe you?"

"Twelve cents will do, honey," Clarie said. "Same as what Roscoe pays down at the store. It's pitiful he pays one cent when he buys but three cents when he sells. It's no wonder most miners never get out of debt to the store. But it don't do no good for me to complain. I notice the bosses don't ask for my opinion on how to run things. I'm just glad my chickens laid good despite that commotion with the meeting last night."

Zetta counted out two nickels and two pennies and handed them to Clarie.

"Luttrell went to keep an eye on Loren," she said. "But Asa wouldn't go. Said he don't want any part of trouble."

Clarie put her faded coin purse back into her pocket then pulled the cookie plate closer.

"Oh, I knew there wouldn't be any trouble," she said. "I'd

dreamed of big ears of sweet corn even before Perton told me about the meeting. Corn's a good sign."

Zetta sat down. "I've been meaning to talk to you about dreams," she said. "I've been having some bad ones—cut timber and fresh dirt and hands covered in coal dust. And I dreamed about an evil crow the night you helped the woman who miscarried."

Clarie stopped chewing. "Well, now. That's bad all right."

Zetta clasped her hands together. "I even told Asa about the dreams, but he's determined we're not leaving before March thirty-first. I'm afraid to go to sleep anymore."

"Honey, sleep is when the good Lord talks to us," Clarie said. "We run hither and yon during the day, but at night we listen to him better."

"But why would he send us bad dreams?"

"He's telling us what to pray about," Clarie said. "Sometimes our prayers push away the bad. Sometimes our prayers get us ready to meet what's coming. But either way, we gotta keep talking to him and not let our fretting put our daytime fears into our nighttime dreams."

Zetta pulled her handkerchief from her sleeve and swiped at her eyes.

"I wanted to come here," she said. "I really did. But then I dreamed death signs that first night. I was ready to go home the next morning."

Clarie leaned forward and put her big hands over Zetta's smaller ones.

"You gotta ask the good Lord to help you each day."

"I do that," Zetta said. "But the fear keeps coming back."

Clarie sighed. "I know, honey. Some days we have to talk to him all day long about whatever is troubling us," she said. "I can't quote you chapter and verse, but remember in the Bible when Jesus said, 'Come unto me,' he didn't add come just once or come all cleaned up. He just said, 'Come.' That's the best invitation any of us will ever get."

"Asa's worried about a strike," Zetta said. "But I wish there was one—a big one that would force us to go back home."

Clarie reached for another cookie. "Oh, there's not gonna be a strike any time soon," she said. "The last couple years have been filled with some bad times, but all that is settled for now. Parts of the north are having a rough winter, and they're paying good money to get coal."

"But Mr. Golden was in town."

"He wasn't here about any strike, honey," Clarie said. "One of Ruthie's daughters is a maid up at the Gray's place and overheard Mr. Golden talking to Mr. Gray about maybe buying First Creek mining camp. After the noon dinner, she slipped off to Ruthie's to tell her. I was still there and when I said I was surprised they talked business in front of her, she laughed. Said white people never see her. Said as long as she's standing next to them holding a plate of food, she might as well be a picture on the wall."

Clarie sighed again. "I pondered that news about First Creek for the rest of the day. When Perton showed up yesterday morning to tell me about the union meeting scheduled for last night, I told him the real reason Mr. Golden was here. But Perton already had his mind made up. You know the old saying that 'a man convinced against his will is of the same opinion still.'"

"You told Perton? But I thought you don't like him."

"Honey, I don't like Perton when he's drinking," Clarie said. "Other than that, we tolerate each other. He worries about his men the same way I worry about my girls."

"But why the meeting last night?"

"The men needed to talk out their worries about Mr. Golden," Clarie said. "We all figure he's keeping closer track of his companies after that bad business with Sid Hatfield and his deputy last year."

Zetta glanced toward Rachel and Micah as they played quietly, then leaned toward Clarie. "That's twice I've heard his name in the past two days," she said. "And I didn't know a thing about it when it happened."

"Asa probably figured you had enough to think about with taking care of two youngins," Clarie said. "Besides, you know men. They're always trying to protect us."

"Well, that's wrong," Zetta said. "We need to know what's going on so we can better prepare ourselves and better protect our youngins."

"I'm not arguing, honey. I'm just saying how men can be."

Zetta rubbed her abdomen. "Do you know the men carry little tins of morphine?"

Clarie put her hand to her forehead but finally answered. "Yes, I do, honey. I was wondering how long it'd be before you found out. Most of the men don't tell their women. They figure they've got enough to worry about."

"Perton made Asa and the boys pull them out of their pockets when he was trying to get them to go to the union meeting. After he left, me and Asa had a big fuss. We was never like this at home."

"I know, honey. Coal camps do more than just tear up the ground."

Clarie pushed herself up from the chair and reached for her coat.

"Well, I better get the rest of the eggs delivered. You mind what I said about praying against those bad dreams. And I'm gonna be praying, too."

Zetta watched the older woman go down the back steps and then dump the wash kettle. As she watched the sooty water run into the black mud, Zetta put her arms across her abdomen and shivered.

CHAPTER 15

Zetta watched Clarie raise her hand in farewell after dumping the water from the wash kettle. She closed the kitchen door and started toward the bowl holding the rising bread dough, but sank into a chair instead.

"Lord, I can't do this," she whispered. "Clarie agrees my dreams are warnings. And I don't know what to do except beg you to keep them from coming true. Asa won't listen to me. But please keep him and my brothers safe. Please keep my youngins—born and unborn—safe."

Then fear, like some giant clawing animal, settled around Zetta, causing her to sob. Rachel was quickly at her side.

"You hurt, Mama?"

Zetta swiped at her eyes then wrapped her arms around the little girl.

"No, Sister. I was just thinking sad things. Tell you what. Whilst I fry the cabbage for the hand pies, why don't you shape little rolls for you and Brother? After I bake them, y'all can eat them with jelly. Would you like that?"

The little girl's face brightened. Zetta watched her run back into the front room to collect her rag doll and then clamor into a chair at the table.

Zetta sighed, swiped at her eyes again and pushed herself up.

* * * * *

122

As the cabbage cooked in Zetta's largest skillet, Rachel flattened small chunks of dough and watched as her mother placed them in a small pan.

"There! Now we'll let those raise again," Zetta said. "You can tell me when you think they're big enough to go into the oven."

At Rachel's nod, Zetta caressed the child's hair. "Before you know it, you'll be making the bread all by yourself," she said.

As Zetta turned toward the stove, she saw Dosha coming up the back steps. Before the young woman could knock, Zetta opened the door.

"Come in," she said. "Clarie was just here. I'm glad to see you, too."

Dosha flashed her bright smile at Zetta but swooped toward Rachel.

"Morning, Pretty Girl," she said. Then she saw Micah. "Oh, Sweet Boy, too."

She turned back to Zetta, who was stirring the cabbage. "I'm on my way to the store. Do you need anything?"

"Not today, thanks," Zetta said. "But let me get you some coffee before you go."

"I can't stay long," Dosha said as she plopped into the chair nearest the window. "Jack's got a hankering for rice pudding with raisins, so I need to get busy," she said. "I swear that man's got the biggest sweet tooth I've ever seen. He had a big time the other night at your party."

"We did have plenty with everybody bringing things," Zetta said as she set the coffee in front of Dosha. "But with Perton's shenanigans, I kindly forgot all the table was holding. Here. Have some cookies."

Dosha reached for the plate. "Could you believe the mean things he said about Polly? And to think he threatened to hit her."

Zetta sat down. "Perton scares me every time I see him. When he came here last night talking about the union, my stomach was all in knots. Did Jack go to the meeting?"

Dosha swallowed a bite of cookie, then nodded. "Sure did," she said. "He wanted to hear what Perton would say. The men don't talk to him much on account of his stuttering. It's like they figure he can't think right just because he can't talk right."

Zetta watched Dosha take another bite, wanting to ask if she knew Perton made the men carry tins of morphine. But, with a sigh, she decided against it. *No need to put my worry on her shoulders if she doesn't know,* she thought.

Dosha brushed her tiny hand across her mouth. "Well, that was right tasty."

Zetta leaned forward. "Do you ever wish you weren't here?"

Dosha looked bewildered. "The best place to be is wherever Jack is," she said. "And good-paying jobs don't come easy for men who don't talk good." She stood up. "Well, I reckon I better get to the store."

Long after she waved goodbye to Dosha, Zetta pondered her comment about the best place to be. *How can I be so miserable here when Dosha is so happy?*

* * * * *

After the evening whistle, Zetta opened the back door to put the pan of hot water and a towel on the porch. As she straightened, the men appeared.

Zetta called to the children, "Poppy's home!"

Immediately, Rachel and Micah ran to the open door. Asa splashed hot water onto his face, then scrubbed his hands with the lye soap and ran them over his face. As he rinsed the black lather and picked up the towel, he greeted his family.

"Seeing y'all here sure beats lining up at the boarding lady's house to wash," he said.

Loren nudged him. "And now you're making us line up behind you," he said. "You ain't the only hungry feller on this porch."

Zetta wanted to stall another argument. "Supper's waiting."

Asa tossed the towel to Loren, kissed Zetta and patted the children's heads before pulling nickels and dimes from his sooty pocket and dropping them into Zetta's hands.

"I told the boarders not to depend on your food much longer since your time is getting closer," he said.

"I'll make them as long as I can," Zetta replied. "But we'll see."

Loren stepped through the door. "You've got the boarders wanting to move in here, Sis."

Zetta ignored him as she watched Luttrell toss the black water into the yard beside the porch. As he handed her the empty pan and dirty towel, Luttrell nodded.

"I heard one of the boarders say he hopes he's smart enough to get a good woman like you when he's married."

Zetta smiled as she turned to dish up the food. "I'll still feed y'all even without your pretty words. Now, sit down."

Asa helped the children into their chairs as Loren punched Luttrell in the shoulder.

"Speaking of being smart, you better get a move on and speak to that pretty teacher," he said. "She was coming out of the store just now as we walked past. You didn't even see her."

Luttrell's face reddened. "Oh, I saw her all right. But I figured she wouldn't know who I was with all the coal dust on my face."

"Well, come Sunday, you'll be all slicked up," Loren said.

"Aw, I'll just be wearing the same thing we all wear—a clean white shirt and clean pants," Luttrell said.

"Well, compared to how we usually look, that's slicked up."

"I wouldn't know what to say to her, anyway."

Loren turned to Asa. "Hurry and pray for the food so I can give my pitiful brother a lesson in love."

At Asa's *Amen*, Loren broke off a chunk of cornbread and pointed it at Luttrell. "When you see her after work, you touch your hand to your cap—coal dust and all—and say, 'Howdy, Miz Pryor. You're looking pretty.' And you look her straight in the eyes and say it strong like. That way, she'll remember your eyes and your voice, so when you say howdy to her on Sunday, she'll know you."

Loren broke open the bread and spread it heavily with butter. "And on Sunday as you say howdy, you take off your church cap and hold out your hand to her. Then you ask for the honor of sitting with her."

"What if she says no?" Luttrell asked.

"She ain't gonna say no to a big handsome feller like you!" Loren said. "But you won't know that if you don't ask. Sometimes I can't believe we're of the same blood!"

Luttrell rubbed his chin. "Come on, now. Let me eat in peace."

Zetta handed Loren the cabbage. "Was Miz Pryor at church last week?"

Loren nodded. "Yep. Sat right in front of you. I had a big time watching Luttrell watch her as she watched the preacher. That's when I decided this here boy needed my help."

"Since I was new last week, I didn't notice her," Zetta said. "I'll watch for her next time."

She studied the discomfort on Luttrell's face and changed the subject. "Asa, was Mr. Gray in the mine again this morning?" she asked.

Asa reached for the bowl of fried sweet potatoes. "Just for a while," he said. "The little bit he was there, he seemed to be watching Perton."

With his mouth full of cornbread, Loren commented, "Perton was talking about a union getting us more money. I'd like to see me and Sarah living on all the money Old Man Golden makes—or even what Mr. Gray makes."

Asa shook his head. "Nah. It might be more fun to watch them try to live on the money we make," he said.

He started to take a bite of sweet potato but put down his fork.

"Speaking of that, when we get paid Saturday, don't forget you each owe Zetta $17.50 for boarding here for the past two weeks," he said. "The house rent comes out of my pay, but since she does your washing and cooks for you, she gets the money."

He picked up his fork again. "Besides, she's buying the groceries now."

Luttrell nodded. "I ain't forgot. That's only fair."

Loren snorted. "I ain't forgot, either. No need to be reminding us."

Zetta gasped. "Asa, that's thirty-five dollars. I can't take that much from my brothers."

Asa speared another potato with his fork. "Now, Zetta. A dollar twenty-five per day is the same price we paid the boarding lady when we stayed down there," he said. "And she didn't do our washing and she didn't feed us this good. Besides, you said yourself you'll have to start buying meat from Roscoe soon. So, that's the end of it. I'm just glad we get paid in real money here. A lot of the mines pay just in script. And that isn't worth the paper it's printed on. The only place it can be used is at the company store. That's just another form of slavery."

As Asa bent over his plate, Zetta saw Loren frown and lean forward. But Luttrell put his hand on his brother's arm and shook his head.

Zetta sighed. Lord, my every breath is a prayer from this day on.

* * * * *

For the next three days, a misty rain fell from the gray sky that seemed no higher than the tree tops. Each morning after the men left for the mine, Zetta cooked, washed dishes and tended the children. And she rubbed her tightening abdomen as she watched the puddles of soot grow in the yard. She was dismayed by the black water but grateful the rain kept Julia away.

By Saturday quitting time, the rain stopped just before Zetta put the hot water and towel on the back bench. But the water was cold before she saw the men step onto the porch.

"I was starting to worry about y'all," she said. "I made applesauce cake, and supper's been ready for a long while."

Asa washed then reached for the towel. "We got paid today since tomorrow is a Sunday," he said. "There's just Roscoe and one of his clerks for all of us, so it takes a while for them to read off our charges and then count out the remaining money due each man. There's still plenty of men standing in line down there."

Loren splashed water onto his face. "The feller ahead of me told Roscoe he could come up with a better system. Roscoe told him if he didn't like it, he could go to the end of the line. That shut him up pretty quick."

Asa tossed the towel onto the bench and touched Micah's and Rachel's heads.

"The feller in front of me got only three dollars for the whole month's work because he owed so much at the store. The company took out for house rent, the replacement shovel he broke in the mine moving coal, the carbine to refill his cap light, the Christmas gifts and all the food his woman charged in the store."

He kissed Zetta and said. "I sure am glad you brung so much from home."

"But we're going through it pretty fast," Zetta said.

Asa didn't comment.

After Luttrell tossed the water into the soot-covered yard, he dug into his pocket for a fistful of bills and coins before taking his seat at the table.

"Here's what I owe you, Sis. I appreciate how hard you work."

Loren handed her the same amount. "Here's mine, too. You're getting a good chunk of my pay, but you deserve it."

Asa looked up from counting the dollar bills from his own pocket. "She wouldn't be getting such a chunk if you'd stop throwing your money away. Every time I turn around, I see you buying some fool thing."

Loren clinched his jaw. "What's that to you? As long as I pay my bills, I can spend my money any way I want."

Zetta was in no mood for another argument. "Asa, with it being New Year's Day on Monday, will y'all be off?"

He shook his head. "Nah. We only get Christmas Day off. Good thing Easter comes on a Sunday or we wouldn't get that off neither."

Loren joined Luttrell at the table. "That still galls me nobody can shoot off rifles to welcome the New Year. That's a bad start to the year."

Asa put his arm around Zetta as she ladled soup beans into a large bowl.

"No. This will be a new year we always will remember," he said. "We'll have a new baby and the farm will be paid off. Soon, we'll have a whole new life, huh?"

Zetta nodded, but she thought the new life couldn't come soon enough.

* * * * *

The next morning, Zetta put pork chops and sauerkraut into the oven before pulling on Asa's coat for the walk to church. Holding onto Asa's arm, she pondered how the men still kept the tins of morphine out of sight during their baths last night.

As though keeping the tins from me keeps me from thinking about them, she thought.

In the church yard, Loren and Luttrell set the children down next to Zetta. Asa joined them as they walked toward the other miners.

When the men stepped away, Clarie whispered to Zetta. "I've been praying extra for you this week."

Zetta nodded her thanks and kept her voice low. "I told the Lord my every breath is a prayer now. I'm sleeping some better."

Then she looked around. "Where's Polly today?"

"She's staying close to home," Clarie said. "It'll take her a while to get over Perton shaming her the way he did at your sweets party."

"But she didn't do anything," Zetta said. "Perton was the one acting a fool."

"I know, honey."

What was I doing thinking I could help Polly that first day we met? Zetta thought. I can't help myself, let alone somebody else.

Dosha and Jack arrived, holding hands. Jack had his dulcimer in the same old quilt.

Jack nodded to the miners but didn't release Dosha's hand even when Loren gave one of his obnoxious cat calls. Dosha smiled and waved to the women but stood with Jack near the church door.

As Zetta turned to look at Asa, she saw Loren nudge Luttrell and nod toward the path. There, walking briskly and smiling, was Miss Pryor, the school teacher. As she approached the church yard, Luttrell—with another nudge from Loren—took off his cap and stepped toward her. But to Zetta's dismay, another miner cut in front, took off his own cap and put out his hand.

No. No. Zetta wanted to shout as Miss Pryor smiled at the miner. Luttrell, looking as though he wanted to be any place but there, stepped back. Loren shook his head.

In that same moment, Preacher Howard arrived. He raised his hand in greeting but didn't stop to shake hands as he walked somberly into the church.

As the worshippers followed him, everyone took their usual seats—with the exception of the miner who was now sitting next to Miss Pryor. Zetta looked at Luttrell, ready to give him a sympathetic look. But he was studying his shoes.

After Clarie eased down next to Zetta, she looked around, as though taking roll.

"Grays ain't here," she whispered. "Mr. Gray and Julia always come even if his wife don't. Something's up."

Preacher Howard stood with his Bible tight against his chest. When everyone was settled, he said, "I'm glad y'all are here."

He looked at Jack. "We won't sing today, if that's all right. And we won't have testimonies since I'm short on time. But I'll tell you about that in a minute."

Clarie leaned toward Zetta. "I told you something was wrong."

Preacher Howard pushed his glasses higher on his nose. "Today, I want to talk about Solomon's decision in I Kings 3:5-9."

He pulled his open Bible close to his face. "Verse five of I Kings 3 says that in Gibeon, the Lord appeared to Solomon in a dream by night and asked him what he should give him."

In a dream by night. Zetta sat straighter.

The preacher continued: "Then in verse seven, Solomon said he was but a child and didn't know how to go out or come in." Preacher Howard lifted his head. "The best prayer any of us can pray is 'I'm just a child. Help me.' Then in verse nine, Solomon asks for an understanding heart to judge God's people so he could discern between good and bad and be able to judge the great number of people before him.

"When Solomon asked to be able to discern between good and bad, he was asking for wisdom. And because he asked God for wisdom, just a few verses later he was able to make good decisions such as when those two mothers both claimed the living baby was hers. Nothing can wear a man out faster than a nagging woman."

As the preacher paused, Zetta saw—from the corner of her eye—Asa turn toward her. She ignored him.

The preacher continued. "But instead of sending the women away, Solomon's wisdom allowed him to know which woman was the rightful mother of the baby.

"We're still talking about Solomon's wisdom today. We wouldn't be doing that if he had asked God to kill all his enemies. No, sirree. We wouldn't be talking about his wisdom today if he'd asked for money. We talk about Solomon's wisdom because we hanker after it for ourselves."

Then Preacher Howard closed the Bible, but held it close to his chest. He was silent as he looked from face to face.

In the quiet moment Zetta thought, Lord, Solomon listened to you and then he did what you said. He was king. He didn't have anybody telling him he was wrong or all worked up. He didn't have Asa telling him not to worry.

Zetta gasped then looked at Asa as though asking him to forgive her wicked thought. But he was pulling a sleepy Micah onto his lap.

Preacher Howard clutched the Bible. "I'm needing God's wisdom right now. When Mr. Golden was in town last week, he told me I'm no longer needed here. So within the hour, I'm catching the train and gonna head back to Harlan County. My things are already at the station."

Zetta looked first to Asa, who shrugged his bewilderment. She turned to Clarie, but the woman frowned and shook her head.

Several calls tumbled over each other: "That's not right." "But we need you." "Who's gonna be our preacher?"

Preacher Howard held up his hand. When the room was quiet,

he said, "I don't know who will take my place," he said. "Maybe nobody. Mr. Golden said the colored men take turns preaching at their church. He thought y'all could do the same."

He pushed his glasses up again. "I wish I could give you a proper goodbye," he said. "But we don't have that choice—just like a lot of times in life. So I'm gonna pray and leave. I'd appreciate it if after I say *Amen* you stay in your seats as I go out the door. And please don't come to the station to see me off. Let me say my sad goodbyes now."

He again looked at each one. Then he took a deep breath and said, "Well, let's pray.

"Father God, we sure are glad You don't get surprised by things like this." Here his voice wavered, so he waited for a moment before continuing. "And we're glad you are with us during sad times. Help us hang onto you all the tighter then. And help us remember that whilst each day is hard here, we have a sweet rest waiting someday with you. In the name of your son, Jesus. Amen."

With his Bible still clutched to his chest, Preacher Howard strode out the door as calls of "God bless you" and "I'm praying for you" followed him.

After the preacher left, no one spoke. Then Clarie said loudly, "Well, that beats all."

Other comments followed hers: "We're no preachers!" "How we gonna teach our youngins about church when we don't have one?" "Wait 'til Perton hears what they've done now."

Zetta took a deep breath as she heard the dreaded name. Then she thought of what Julia had said. The first day that child showed up, she'd said her mother called this a godforsaken place. I reckon I was too quick to disagree with her.

Loren stepped across the aisle to pick up the sleeping Micah.

"Perton said nobody can shoot off rifles tonight," he grumbled. "Now old Rusty Hinge himself takes away our preacher. I'm starting to like this place less and less."

Amen to that, Zetta thought as she gripped Rachel's hand and reached for Asa's arm for the walk back up the sooty path.

CHAPTER 16

Before Zetta could take Asa's arm, Luttrell leaned over the home-made pew to swoop up Rachel.

"I'll see you back at the house," he said as he hurried toward the church door with the little girl in his arms—but not before Zetta saw him glance toward the pretty teacher listening to whatever the other miner was saying.

As Zetta sadly watched her brother leave, Clarie leaned forward.

"I saw what happened to Luttrell," she whispered. "Clarence, that boy who moved in ahead of him, fast talks women all the time. Make sure you tell Luttrell not to give up."

Zetta signed. "He's not one to pick a fight—even when he's right."

Clarie lowered her voice even more. "Well, I don't like seeing him being outdone. Especially by the likes of Clarence. And you can tell him I said so."

Asa put his arm around Zetta and gently pulled her toward the aisle.

"Clarie, come home with us," he said. "Zetta's got a good dinner waiting."

The older woman smiled. "I thank you," she said. "But I've got chicken baking."

She turned back to Zetta. "I'll be around tomorrow. Tell Luttrell what I said."

Zetta merely nodded.

* * * * *

When Asa and Zetta arrived home, they found Luttrell inspecting the decorated Christmas tree with the children solemnly watching him.

He motioned for Asa to look at the branches. "You've been keeping the soil moist just like Clarie said. But the needles are falling off."

As Asa leaned toward the tree, Zetta looked at Luttrell. "I'm sorry that other feller stepped in front of you at church this morning."

Luttrell shrugged. "Don't give it another thought," he said. "It just wasn't meant to be, I reckon."

"Well, Clarie saw it, too," Zetta said. "And she said he's a fast talker and for you not to give up."

Luttrell's face reddened. "Was the whole church watching me make a fool of myself?"

"No. No. I don't mean that," Zetta said. "It's just that Clarie sees everything. She likes you and don't like Clarence."

"Well, it's done now," Luttrell said. He put his hands behind his head and stretched. "Now that y'all are home, I'll run up to the outhouse. Loren'll be back from there directly."

Zetta sighed as she watched him open the back door. She turned to Asa, who was running his hands along the branches.

"Is the tree all right?"

Asa shook his head as he faced the children.

"Well, Babies, I reckon we better take the decorations off after we eat," he said. "Then we'll set the tree on the front porch where it can get more sunlight. It's got another long while before we can put it in the good soil at home."

And we've got another long while before we can get back there too, Zetta thought.

* * * * *

While the men washed up, Zetta slid the skillet of cornbread batter into the oven. Quickly, she sliced the last two tomatoes from home and placed thick chunks on the platter next to the pork chops. As she dished up the sauerkraut, Loren gestured toward the tomatoes.

"We must be the only ones in camp to have fresh tomatoes this time of year, Sis. Where'd you learn to wrap them green in news-paper?"

"From Sally Reed," Zetta said. "I don't know where she learned it."

"Jim's wife? I swear you and Asa are thick as thieves with that bunch." Loren spat the words.

Zetta gave him a scolding look, but he had already turned his attention to Luttrell as he pulled out his chair at the table.

"You ready for another love lesson?" Loren asked.

Luttrell shook his head. "I told you on the way home from church to leave it alone. It's over and done."

Loren leaned forward to spear a tomato slice and two pork chops.

"So you're gonna give up? Just like that? Nothing would ever get done if men gave up."

Zetta set the bowl of hot sauerkraut on the table. "And nothing would get done if women didn't keep putting one foot in front of the other," she said. "Now don't go eating before Asa prays."

Loren made a show of folding his hands. "I'm just letting the meat cool."

* * * * *

As soon as Asa said *Amen*, Loren grinned at Luttrell. Zetta didn't give him a chance to start more teasing.

"I liked Preacher Howard," she said quickly. "What'll we do without him?"

Asa reached for the sauerkraut. "Well, Mr. Golden told him the colored men preach at their church. But nobody comes to mind to do such at ours."

He turned toward Loren. "Unless you want the job. You can talk about anything in the world even when you don't know a thing about it."

Loren swallowed the bite of meat. "All right, Smart Mouth. Yep, I can talk up a storm, but I ain't called to do any preaching. You're all the time telling us what to do, so why don't you take a crack at ordering church folks around too?"

Asa shook his head. "If church folks argue as much as you do, I wouldn't last five minutes."

Zetta waved her hand. "I'm tired of having you two at each

other all the time. Maybe if the miners talked to Mr. Gray, he'd ask Mr. Golden to let Preacher Howard come back."

Loren scowled. "Mr. Gray won't go to the outhouse unless old Rusty Hinge tells him to."

"Watch your mouth," Zetta said. "We're eating."

Loren shrugged. "Well, in case you ain't noticed, Sis, we do what we're told. We'll go along with losing our preacher just like we'll go along with Perton telling us not to shoot off our guns tonight to welcome the New Year."

"Speaking of Perton, somebody said this morning he won't be happy when he hears Mr. Golden fired Pastor Howard," Zetta said.

"Nah. Perton's gonna be real happy," Loren said. "That's just more fuel for his fire. The coal fields had plenty of strikes last year to bring in the union. Perton wants a strike here. Wants to bring rich owners to their knees."

Asa handed a chunk of cornbread to Micah. "And whilst they're going to their knees, they're cutting jobs on their way down," he said.

"Well, something's going on," Loren said. "I don't trust old Rusty Hinge. He's fired the preacher for a reason."

Asa ignored him. "Come on, Babies. Hurry and eat. We'll take care of the tree whilst Mommy washes up the dishes."

* * * * *

The next morning, Zetta had biscuits baking before the whistle blew. Then she pulled another bean from the counting jar as fatback sizzled in hot grease.

"Lord, thank you for this first day of the new year," she whispered. "Please protect us. And please get us home soon."

As Zetta dropped the bean into the ever-present kettle of soaking beans, Asa appeared behind her and kissed her neck.

"Happy New Year, sweet wife. Now I can say the farm will be ours *this* year."

Zetta jumped. "Asa! You scared the living daylights out of me!"

He grinned as he turned her toward him. Then he leaned to kiss her abdomen. "And Happy New Year to you, Little One. Soon I can kiss you, too."

Loren stepped into the kitchen. "Quit your lollygagging, Asa.

We can't be late today. Whatever you do on the first day of the year, you'll do for the rest of the year."

Asa pulled out his chair. "You're liable to be late before I ever am."

Zetta grabbed the coffee pot from the stove. "Here, you two," she said. "Hush up and start on the coffee whilst I fry the eggs. Oh, here's Luttrell. Happy New Year!"

Luttrell nodded. "And you, too. That coffee's gonna taste mighty good."

Asa smiled as Zetta filled his cup first. "What you got planned for today?"

"I thought I'd check the clothes for the new baby," she said. "Make sure I've got everything ready. I probably won't get around to making extra hand pies today. Seems like the bigger I get the slower I move. You better tell the boarders not to count on me for a while."

"I did," Asa said. "And they're complaining already."

* * * * *

After the men left, Zetta crumbled biscuits into the gravy for the children.

"Now I'm gonna look at what I've got for your baby brother or sister," she said. "I'm just in the bedroom, so you go ahead and eat."

Within minutes, Zetta was back—holding a small white gown.

"I thought I got all the stains out, but I sure didn't do a good job on this one," she said to the children. "Maybe I can scrub it with the lye soap."

Just as she reached for the wash pan, she heard Julia's unwelcome voice.

"Hey, open the door!"

Micah stopped eating and looked toward the back porch.

Rachel clutched her doll to her face. "It's that bad girl again, Mama."

"Now don't you worry, Babies. I'm right here."

Zetta took a deep breath as she opened the door. Before she could greet Julia, the child stepped past her into the kitchen.

It's time somebody taught that child some manners, Zetta thought.

"Miz Julia, I told you before the polite thing to do is wait 'til you're invited in."

Julia shrugged. "And I told you before you're the one who opened the door."

Zetta forced herself to speak slowly. "I haven't seen you for a while. You been sick?"

The child flipped her blonde hair back from her shoulders.

"No. Daddy said I have to be more ladylike, so he's been making me stay home. But this morning Mama told him nobody can be a lady here with all the hillbillies. So she let me leave."

Julia ignored Zetta's glare and pointed to the baby gown still in the young mother's hand.

"What's that?"

Zetta wanted to say, "It's none of your business." Instead, she said, "It's a little gown. I'm getting everything ready for when Miz Clarie brings my baby."

Julia frowned. "She doesn't bring babies." She pointed at Zetta's abdomen. "You've got it right there."

Zetta saw Rachel's eyes widen as she followed the direction of Julia's finger.

Zetta jerked open the back door before she could ponder her action.

"Well, Miz Julia. I've got things to do and I'm sure you've got more people to spy on. So you run along now."

Zetta stood motionless with her hand on the door knob but her heart was pounding.

And I hope you tell your daddy what I said, and he kicks us out of here, she thought.

Julia flipped her hair back from her face again and sauntered out.

* * * * *

Zetta wanted to slam the door while Julia was still on the back steps, but she managed to close it quietly. Then she turned to find Rachel staring at her middle.

Zetta straightened and tried to pull in her stomach.

"Now you never mind what Miz Julia said. Let me get you and Brother a jellied biscuit."

As Zetta, with trembling hands, spread jelly on biscuit halves, she saw Clarie coming down the path, a jar of milk in one hand, her walking stick in the other. Zetta jerked open the door.

"Come in. Come in. I've done a terrible thing," she said. "Not two minutes ago I told Julia to go spy on other people."

Clarie put her hand to her chest as laugher rolled out.

"Oh, I'm sorry I missed that!"

"It's not funny," Zetta said. "Asa's gonna have a fit."

Clarie stepped onto the porch and handed the milk to Zetta. "What all happened?"

"I just wasn't in the mood to put up with her questions," Zetta said. "And she said right in front of you-know-who"—she inclined her head toward Rachel—"where the baby is right now. So I told her she had other folks to spy on and opened the door for her to leave."

"Ohhh! You were in a mood, all right." Clarie laughed again.

"I don't care if she tells her daddy, and he fires Asa," Zetta said. "Fact is, I hope she does tell. Having to pack would suit me just fine—no matter how mad Asa is."

Clarie shook her head as she took off her coat and eased into the chair.

"Oh, honey. Julia's not gonna think another minute about you sending her away," she said. "She'll just go pester somebody else. And even if she tells her daddy, he'll probably thank you for setting her straight. Ruthie's daughter, the one who's a maid up at the Grays, is all the time saying what a time that poor man has with that child—as though his troubles with his wife ain't enough. He's a big boss in the mine but he's a small man in his own house."

"But Asa said she got a family kicked out last year," Zetta said.

Clarie nodded. "That's the talk all right. But the man got the shakes ever time he went into the mine. He wanted to leave, but his wife liked the things she could buy at the store. So he picked a fight with Gray right in front of the men."

"How'd he do that?" Zetta asked as she poured glasses of milk for the children.

"He said Gray didn't know what it was like to work with a whole mountain pressing in," Clarie said. "And he said Gray couldn't control his own bratty girl."

"Oh, that tickles me!"

"Tickled the miners watching, too," Clarie said. "So Gray fired the man on the spot. I hear tell that miner just smirked, turned on his heels and went home to tell his woman to pack. Word got around that Julia got the family run out, but there wasn't a bit of truth in it."

"Then you mean we're not gonna have to leave?"

Clarie shook her head. "I'm afraid not, honey."

Zetta ran her hands over her abdomen and gave a little huff. "And for one pretty moment, I had some hope."

The young woman looked out the front window, toward the tipple. Finally she turned back to Clarie.

"Let me get you some coffee. I'm sorry I don't have anything sweet to go with it except leftover biscuits. I haven't done my baking yet since I was taking stock of the baby clothes and counting diapers."

"Good for you," Clarie said. "Plenty of times I've had to make diapers from an old sheet for new mothers."

She nodded toward Rachel and Micah. "How'd you know when these two was ready to show up?"

Zetta set two biscuits and a jar of jelly before Clarie. "My water broke both times. Scared me to death when it broke with Rachel, but with Micah I knew what was happening."

"Then your water will probably break with this one, too," Clarie said. "Sure makes it easier. When that happens this time, send Asa after me and start walking from room to room. Walking makes the birth go faster."

Clarie pulled the jelly jar closer then asked, "Did you tell Luttrell what I said about not giving in to Clarence?"

"Yes, but he just wants to leave the whole matter alone," Zetta said.

"I reckon that's another thing we need to pray on," Clarie said. "Hiding don't solve a thing."

* * * * *

Zetta moved slowly the rest of the day, thankful Rachel and Micah were content to play quietly. As she cooked, she glanced out the window, waiting for Asa to storm home after being fired. The lane remained empty.

That evening as Zetta set the pan of hot water on the bench, only Asa stepped onto the porch. Zetta searched his eyes to see if he was angry. But he smiled.

"Another long day made better by seeing you," he said.

Well, my plan to get Asa fired didn't work, Zetta thought. She sighed and looked down the path. "Where are the boys?"

"They'll be along," Asa said. "Loren talked Luttrell into stopping at the store. He's hoping they'll run into the school teacher. I swear Loren can wear a man out."

"That's just as well since I'm moving a little slow tonight," Zetta said. "I was busy making sure I've got everything ready for the baby. And Clarie stopped by for a while."

She watched Asa lather his hands. "Was Mr. Gray in the mine today?" she asked carefully.

"Nope. He prefers being on top of the ground. Can't say I blame him. But I hear tell that girl of his wears him out going in and out of his office all day."

Zetta sighed. Then she could've told on me if she had a mind to, she thought. Well, Clarie was right. Sending Julia away won't get us home any sooner.

She turned to dish up supper.

CHAPTER 17

Zetta's dead mother stood on the front porch, next to the undecorated Christmas tree with its browning needles. Blood ran down her white nightgown and dropped into the soot at her feet. Her mother watched the red and black colors run together and then looked into Zetta's face.

"Oh, my dear, dear child," she whispered.

Zetta awakened with a gasp. Heart pounding, she caressed her abdomen. *I thought I was finished with bad dreams. Then Mama shows up like this.*

She pulled herself to the edge of the bed and mouthed a quiet prayer. "Lord, Clarie said I've got to pray against the dreams, but I don't know how. All I can do is beg you to make them stop. Please help me."

Rachel stirred in her sleep, and Zetta leaned forward to pull the quilt around both children's shoulders. At last, she eased back onto her own pillow. Fitful sleep finally came.

* * * * *

Zetta awakened before the camp whistle. In the kitchen, she pondered her mother's sorrowful face as she reached for the counting jar and poured a single bean into her palm.

For the next week, one gray day rolled into the next as Zetta tried to push aside thoughts of the dream. Often she looked out the window at the soot hanging in the damp air and longed for the view from her own kitchen. Clarie's short visits provided some comfort. Most of all, she was grateful Julia didn't appear.

She moved slowly each day, but Sunday morning a new energy surged through her limbs. By the time the rest of the family was ready for breakfast, she had baked a double batch of biscuits, cooked extra apples and had chicken and dumplings simmering.

Asa looked at the stove as he seated Rachel and Micah at the table.

"What's all this?"

Zetta smiled. "I'm feeling good today, so I cooked extra to heat up later," she said. "The baby probably will come tonight. Tomorrow for sure."

"You acted this way the other times," he said. "The granny woman back home called it nesting. But it won't do for you to work like this, it being Sunday."

"I'm just trying to get a jump on the meals," Zetta said. "Now sit down and pray so we can get breakfast over with."

At Asa's *Amen*, Zetta handed him the plate of steaming biscuits.

"I'm glad I'm feeling good," she said. "But today seems all out of kilter with no church."

"I know," Asa said. "We talked about this in the mine when Mr. Gray wasn't around. It don't seem right to be at church with no preacher, so we decided to have church in our houses. The folks that like singing are up at Jack and Dosha's. Clarie's got the ones that like reading the Bible."

Zetta gasped. "I hope you didn't oblige us one way or another."

"No," Asa said. "I figured we're better off here. Just us."

* * * * *

When he had finished eating, Asa pushed back from the table.

"Zetta, whilst you clear the dishes, I'll get the Bible. Leave my coffee."

As Zetta stacked the plates in the dishpan, Loren pulled Micah onto his lap and Luttrell held out his hands for Rachel. She and her rag doll settled against him just as Asa came back into the kitchen. He sat down and thumbed the pages of the Bible until he found what he wanted.

"The first week me and the boys arrived, Preacher Howard said Psalm 40:1-2 are miners' verses," Asa said. "Listen now. 'I waited patiently for the Lord, and he inclined unto me, and heard my cry. He brought me up also out of an horrible pit, out of the miry clay and set my feet upon a rock, and established my goings.'"

Asa kept his finger on the verse as he looked up. "I like that. So when we go into the mine, I ask the Lord to bring us back up out of the miry clay."

Zetta's jaw dropped. "Asa, you never told me that."

"No need to."

He looked toward his brothers-in-law. "That's what I think on. You boys ponder a verse?"

Loren shrugged, but Luttrell cleared his throat.

"I like the ones about praying," he said. "I think about the one that says, 'I will call upon God and the Lord shall save me.'"

Zetta looked at each man. "No money can be worth what y'all face every day," she said.

Asa ignored her. "Speaking of prayer, I heard about this church that had a house of ill repute move in just down the street."

Zetta gasped. "Asa, don't be talking about places like that."

"Now Zetta, let me tell the boys this story," he said. "Anyway, the good folks didn't want that type of place near their church, so they held special prayer meetings to ask God to remove it. Lo and behold, the house burned down the very next week. Well, the gal owner got wind of all the praying the church folks had done, so she marched to the courthouse and demanded the church rebuild her house. Of course, the judge called the preacher in. But the preacher said they wudn't the ones that burnt it down.

"The old judge rubbed his chin. 'Well,' he finally said. 'This beats all. Here I've got me a preacher who don't believe in prayer and a sinner who does.'"

As her brothers laughed, Zetta shook her head. "Asa Berghoffer! Where do you find these wicked stories?"

Asa smiled. "If you think that's bad, you ought to hear the ones I don't tell you!"

"Asa!"

"Anyway, my point is that God always answers. Just not always how we expect or want."

Luttrell eased Rachel off his lap. "You said that real good."

Loren chuckled. "Yeah. But if Preacher Howard was still here, he wudn't worry about you taking his place."

Zetta frowned at her brother before turning to her husband.

"You did good, Asa, but we need a real preacher," she said. "One like we got at home."

At the word *home*, Zetta thought of her mother's sorrowful face in the dream.

"Asa, I want us to go back home right now."

"Zetta, why do you beat a dead horse?" he said. "We've got less than three months to go. For that little time, we can stand on our heads if we have to. Now what do you reckon Preacher Howard is doing in Harlan County this morning? I hope he's sitting at a rich widow's table."

Zetta gave a defeated sigh. "What's Harlan County like?"

"I hear tell the mountains are so close together there, the sun sets at two o'clock."

"Asa Berghoffer, the things you come up with." But this time Zetta smiled.

* * * * *

Zetta chose her largest iron skillet to cook extra sweet potatoes while the men kept the children busy in the front room. When the slices had browned to her satisfaction, she pushed the skillet to the coolest part of the stove and stepped into the front room. All three men were seated on the floor, watching Micah try to balance pennies on the pig's snout of the mechanical bank. Rachel sat nearby, folding and refolding the little quilt around her rag doll.

"I'm gonna rest for a while. When I get up, we'll eat," Zetta said.

Asa smiled but didn't look up from watching Micah. "We'll be here."

Suddenly Zetta felt weak. She leaned against the door frame for a moment, but as she entered the bedroom, a gush of water burst from between her legs.

"Asa! Come quick!"

She could hear him clamoring to his feet. As he rushed to her, Zetta gestured at the puddle.

"My water just broke!"

"Wait right here! I'll get Clarie."

"Hand me those towels hanging by the dresser to put between my legs," Zetta said. "Throw the blue one on the water on the floor."

Asa nervously snatched the towels from the nail. "Here. Lay down."

Zetta waved her hand. "No. Clarie told me to walk. Go get her."

Asa yelled toward the front room as he swiped at the liquid on the floor.

"One of you get Clarie. Now!"

Zetta heard both men bolt out the back door. "Asa! Go back to Sister and Brother," she said. "Don't let them come in here."

* * * * *

As they waited for Clarie, Asa tried to keep the children occupied while Zetta walked awkwardly from room to room with the towel between her legs.

Within minutes, Loren was back. "Clarie's church folks was still there," he said. "But she shooed them off and said she'll be right here. And she sent Luttrell to tell Dosha to come, too."

Loren turned toward the back window.

"They're coming," he said. "That carrot-top gal is running to beat all get out."

He opened the door as Dosha reached the porch. She rushed past him, her eyes sparkling as she gently hugged Zetta.

"Oh, I'm glad I get to help," Dosha said.

Luttrell and Clarie followed her in the door. Clarie carried her black satchel in one hand and clutched two old quilts against her chest with the other hand. She thrust the quilts at Luttrell.

"Here. Put these on the bed whilst I get settled," Clarie said. She put the satchel on the table and pulled a starched long white apron from it.

"Now you men stay out of my way," she said as she tied on the apron. "Loren, take the youngins to my house. Don't forget coats."

She bent toward Rachel and Micah. "Kiss your mommy and then go to my place," she said. "I keep a box of toys by my big chair. When you come back, the new baby will be here."

Loren held each child for Zetta to kiss and then hurried them out the door.

Clarie turned to Asa, whose arm was around Zetta.

"I'm staying here," he quickly said. "In case I'm needed."

"You've already done enough, I reckon," Clarie said.

Dosha spoke. "I'd want Jack holding my hand if I was having a baby."

"He won't be there if I'm the one catching your child," Clarie said. "Years ago, I let a husband in. Just as the baby's head showed, he fainted dead away and cut his lip. I ignored him 'til I got the baby out. Then I had to tend to him *and* the mother."

"Oh."

"No, sirree," Clarie continued. "Men ain't any use at a birthing. But I don't like sending them to work in the mine, either, since they're liable to be thinking of what's going on at home rather than paying attention to their job."

She turned back to her satchel. "Here, Luttrell. Take the hand scales and the twine to the bedroom. Then tote more water and heat it so I can bathe Zetta later."

Luttrell took the items from her, but stood awkwardly.

"I'd druther work a double shift under the mountain than do your job, Clarie," he said. "About all I've ever done like this is help the cows back home when they was calving."

Clarie chuckled. "When you have to do something, you can. Now get me that water."

* * * * *

As Zetta walked, gripping Asa's arm, she often stopped to catch her breath. Clarie continued pulling items from her satchel.

"One time, I had a feller tell his wife to dish up supper before she took to bed," she said. "I spooned up his meal and told him to sit on the porch 'til I called him in. And I said I'd take a broom stick to his backside if he didn't shape up. I figure Perton will be about the same way when it's Polly's time."

She dropped scissors into a pan of boiling water.

"Robert E. Lee's wife had her youngins in a closet scrubbed with borax. We can't scrub rooms in a coal camp, but I make sure everything is as good as it can be. None of my girls get childbirth fever from things not being clean."

She set a small jar of brown powder on the table.

"What's that?" Dosha asked.

"Scorched flour," Clarie said. "I brown it in a skillet to get rid of any little critters. That'll go on the raw end of the umbilical cord and be covered by these here belly bands."

She pulled several narrow strips of soft cotton material from the satchel then turned to Zetta. "Did you use scorched flour with your other youngins?"

Zetta rubbed her sleeve against the sweat on her forehead, then managed, "Granny at home used mutton tallow."

Clarie nodded. "That gets the job done, too. But with all the soot around here, I like the flour since it dries the cord out faster."

She turned back to Dosha. "When you're helping Zetta this week, change the band every day. Put scorched flour on the cord, then tie a clean band around the little belly. Do that 'til the cord falls off. That'll be a week or more."

Clarie moved to the stove and poured warm water into a smaller pan. Then she added the contents of a bottle of clear liquid.

As she dipped her hands into the water, she turned to Dosha.

"This here is bleach water," she said. "Wash your hands in it, too, and don't touch another thing other than those towels in my satchel."

She motioned to Asa. "Bring Zetta to the bedroom. Luttrell, you bring the pan of water with the scissors. I'm ready to catch a baby."

* * * * *

As Luttrell put the pan of water on the dresser, Asa eased Zetta onto the bed and kissed her forehead softly. Clarie waved both men away.

"You go on now," she said. "And close the door quiet like."

As they left, pain swept over Zetta, and she grabbed Clarie's arm.

"My bad dreams are back," she whispered. "My dead mother even showed up with blood dripping down her nightgown and into the soot on the porch."

Zetta's eyes remained on the old woman but she heard Dosha gasp.

Clarie pushed damp hair back from Zetta's forehead.

"That was fear talking, honey," she said. "Now, whilst I help you put on this short birthing gown, I'm gonna pray."

As she tugged off Zetta's dress and slip, she spoke aloud.

"Lord, thank you for being here with us. And thank you for the new life about to come into this pitiful world. Guide my hands and keep Zetta and the baby safe. And tell that old Enemy Devil to quit his tormenting through bad dreams. Thank you for hearing us and loving us. In your son's name. Amen!"

Her *Amen* was close to a shout as she pulled the yellow gown over Zetta's shoulders.

"Lay back and bend your knees now," she said. "That's it. Dosha, you hold her shoulders and help her push when I say."

Another contraction hit, causing Zetta to grimace. Clarie gently parted the young mother's knees.

"You've done this before, honey," she said. "You know to push when the pain comes. Rest when it stops. Some folks put an axe under the bed, saying it cuts the pain. But that just gives the men something to do. The Bible says women will go through suffering in childbirth, so there's nothing to do about the pain but bear it. There now. Rest a minute."

Zetta barely had taken a breath before another pain hit. She grabbed Dosha's arm.

"You're doing fine," Clarie said. "The baby's head is starting to show. I'm gonna be moving your skin around now to keep you from tearing."

Zetta gritted her teeth and pushed as another pain captured her.

Clarie gave a pleased whoop. "Here's the sweet little face," she said. "Another push now and we've got the first shoulder out. There! Now here's the other one. Take a deep breath then push again. The rest is easy now!"

With the next push, the baby was in Clarie's hands and howling. Clarie looked up at Zetta and smiled.

"It's a fine boy," she said. "I'll tie off the cord then you can have him."

Dosha released her grip on Zetta's shoulders. "Oh! He's got the sweetest cry," she said.

Asa shouted through the door. "Everything all right, Clarie?"

"You got yourself another boy," Clarie said. "Now leave me be. I'm not done."

She turned to Dosha. "You did a good job for your first time at a birthing," she said. "Now I need you down here. Get the twine and cut two pieces four or five inches each."

She waited as Dosha followed her instructions.

"That's it," Clarie said. "Now put one tight around the cord about three inches from the little feller's belly whilst I clean him up."

148

Dosha hesitated as she looked at the squirming, crying baby. "Oh, won't that hurt him?"

"No," Clarie said. "Tie the other string down from the first. I'll cut between 'em."

Dosha yelped, "Oh!" as the cord was cut, but Clarie ignored her.

"Just two more pushes, Zetta, and we'll have the afterbirth. Dosha, you might as well check it, too. It's supposed to be smooth. If there are chunks out, that means some is left in."

With Zetta's second push, the mass appeared. Dosha gasped as Clarie turned the grayish pink tissue over to examine the bloody underside.

"It's all here, Zetta," she said. "I'll burn it later. Let me push on your belly now."

Zetta moaned as wide hands encircled her abdomen.

"Good," Clarie said. "Your womb is tight. And nursing will firm it more."

Clarie gently placed the baby in the hand scales. "He's a little shy of eight pounds," she said. "But I'll claim an even eight. I always put the weight up to the next pound for boys since that makes their daddies proud. Now, where's this little feller's clothes?"

Zetta gestured toward the dresser. "Bottom drawer."

Clarie dipped a towel into the pan of water on top of the dresser.

"Dosha, wrap him in one of the soft blankets. We'll diaper him later. Right now he needs to meet his mommy as soon as I get her washed."

* * * * *

When the baby was handed to Zetta, she kissed his head. Then she pulled back the blanket to look at his tiny fingers and toes.

Clarie smiled. "Every good mother I've ever tended inspects all the parts."

She pulled a small pouch from her apron pocket and handed it to Dosha.

"This here's some strong tea," she said. "Make a cup for Zetta. That'll help her rest after her hard work. And tell Asa he can come in now and meet his boy."

As soon as Dosha opened the bedroom door, Asa burst in. Zetta's brothers followed with Rachel and Micah.

"I sent Luttrell up to get Loren and the youngins soon as I heard the baby squall," Asa said as he tenderly kissed Zetta's cheek and the top of the sleeping baby's head. Then he turned to his other children.

"Come see what Miz Clarie brung us."

As both children eased toward the bed, Zetta held out her hands.

"There's my big youngins," she said. "This here's your little brother, Isaac."

Both children stood on tiptoe to look at the baby, their eyes wide.

Luttrell nodded. "That's a fine name for a fine boy."

Loren leaned toward Isaac. "Well, you sure can tell that's Asa's boy," he said. "Looky at those ears. The other youngins got your ears, Sis. But this poor little guy got his daddy's. I sure hope he grows into them."

Zetta pulled the blanket around the baby's head. "You hush, Loren," she said. "This is a beautiful child."

Clarie gestured toward the bedroom door.

"Y'all have gawked enough," she said. "Zetta needs her rest. Dosha will mind the youngins and cook whilst y'all are at work, but Zetta's not to get out of bed for three days other than to use the chamber pot. Now you go dish up your meal and figure out how you're gonna get along 'til then. And make sure you take some time to thank the good Lord everything is all right."

As Clarie ushered the others from the room, Zetta thought about being able to take *four* beans at once from the counting jar when she returned to the kitchen. Then as Zetta whispered her own "Thank you, Lord" for the new life, Dosha entered the bedroom with the steaming cup of tea.

CHAPTER 18

Zetta awakened when the baby stirred against her. As she drowsily pulled him to her breast, she realized she was out of the short birthing gown and into her own warm one. And she saw her own quilts over her instead of the old ones Clarie had provided. She looked around the bedroom, which was lit only by the moonlight. Asa snored gently beside her, and Rachel and Micah were asleep in their own little bed an arm's length away.

"Lord, did I drink some of Clarie's tea?" Zetta whispered. "I don't remember. And I don't remember the others coming to bed. But I do remember you being with me. Thank you for this precious child. Please protect him. Please protect us all."

She caressed the baby's head as he nursed. Then she whispered again, "And please don't let anybody say anything about his sweet ears."

As she listened to the baby's tiny smacking sounds, Zetta heard the back door quietly open. Startled, she looked toward the sleeping Asa.

Why hadn't he locked up? Holding her breath, she strained to hear the intruder's whispers. Suddenly she recognized Dosha's voice.

"Jack, honey, put the lantern on the table," she said. "I'll stir up the fire. Between what Zetta made up ahead and what we brung, I'll conjure up a good breakfast."

Zetta huffed. Oh, it's just Dosha. I've turned into a regular 'fraidy cat, she thought.

As she switched the baby to her other side, Zetta realized he was diapered and in one of the gowns from the bottom drawer.

When did they get him dressed? But that thought was interrupted by Dosha's giggles from the kitchen.

"Jack, I declare," she said. "What if they was to catch us? Now you sit over there and keep your hands around this coffee cup whilst I fry the eggs. That old whistle is gonna sound any minute."

Zetta stifled a chuckle, waiting to hear more. But the mine whistle blasted then, causing Asa to moan and sit up. He turned to smile at Zetta.

"Morning, little mother," he whispered. "You sure slept hard last night."

Zetta nodded, her voice low. "I don't remember a thing after the baby."

"Well, Clarie came in a couple of times to check on you and get you in your own gown," he said. "She dressed the little feller, too, and even gave him a sugar tit she made up. Dosha will be here directly to cook and watch Sister and Brother."

"She's here now," Zetta said. "She's fixing breakfast. Jack and her come in the back door a few minutes ago. Like to scared me to death. You must've left the door unlocked for them."

As Asa nodded, Zetta heard her brothers enter the kitchen.

Luttrell's quiet greeting was swallowed by Loren's.

"Well, looky at this," Loren said. "When did y'all get here?"

Zetta heard Dosha giggle. "Just a minute ago. Here's coffee. Do you take sugar or milk?"

"Nope," Loren said. "I take it just the way it comes out of the pot. Hey, Jack. You ready for another long day under the ground?"

As Zetta imagined Jack smiling and nodding, Asa leaned over to kiss her.

"I better get in there before Loren eats all the biscuits."

* * * * *

With Rachel and Micah still asleep, Zetta finished feeding the baby and patted his back as she listened to the voices from the kitchen. Back home, her stepmother, Becky, had helped after the births of Rachel and Micah. Now it was strange to listen to another woman waiting for Asa to pray and then asking how to serve her men.

"Now you fellers will have to tell me how Zetta does this,"

Dosha said. "Every woman has her own way of doing things."

"Dosha, we appreciate you helping out," Asa said. "You just do what you normally do, and we'll be fine."

"Well, I hope you don't mind Jack taking his meals with us."

"He's welcome as long as we get buttermilk pie," Loren said.

Zetta knew Asa surely frowned at Loren then. "You are welcome, Jack, even without pie," he said. "No need for you to be alone with your woman helping here."

Zetta heard the chairs being pushed back from the table. Asa stepped into the bedroom, pulled the quilt over the shoulders of the sleeping Rachel and Micah, and leaned to kiss Zetta.

"Did Dosha pack your dinner buckets?" Zetta asked.

"Yep. Did that whilst we had breakfast."

Then Asa patted his shirt pocket. "I wrote your paw last night about the baby," he said.

"I'll mail it on my way to the mine," he added. "You're in good hands, but I'll sure be glad to get home."

As Zetta drew Asa's face closer to hers, Dosha whispered from outside the bedroom.

"Would it be all right if Jack was to see the baby?"

Zetta jerked the quilt up to her neck, feeling indecent, as Asa gestured for them to enter.

"Oh, Jack," Dosha whispered. "Isn't that sweet little thing pretty as a speckled pup? And to think I helped bring him into this world."

Jack nodded. "He…he plum…plumb pretty, Miz Ze…Zetta."

Asa patted the man's shoulder. "Well, we better head down the hill, Jack," he said. "The boys are gonna be waiting for you to drive us into the mountain."

* * * * *

As Dosha brought Zetta's breakfast in, Rachel and Micah awakened. The young woman helped Zetta sit up, plumped two pillows behind her back and spread a towel across her before putting the filled plate on her lap.

Rachel watched, wide eyed. "Do me and Brother get to eat in here?"

Dosha smiled. "Why, sure—if you're sick like your mommy and gonna stay in bed all day. But if you're feeling good and want to help me make cookies, then you need to come to the table."

Both children clamored out of bed and reached for their clothes.

Dosha giggled. "Holler if you need anything, Zetta." And she scurried into the kitchen behind the children.

With Isaac sleeping beside her, Zetta studied the filled plate. My lands. Dosha sure shot the pepper to the gravy, she thought.

As she dipped her biscuit into the black speckled mixture, she heard Clarie's voice.

"Howdy, Dosha. Here's milk for the youngins. How's Zetta this morning?"

Without waiting for an answer, Clarie strode into the bedroom. "Well, ain't you the Queen of Shebee," she said. "Looking all pretty and eating breakfast in bed."

The bed springs creaked as Clarie sat at the end of the thin corn shuck mattress.

"I saw Asa," Clarie said. "He mentioned you was feeding the little feller even before the whistle blew. You feeling all right?"

"Yes, but I don't remember much," Zetta said.

Clarie nodded "You were pretty tired, all right."

Then she motioned toward the plate as she stood up.

"Eat up," Clarie said. "You gotta make plenty of milk for this little feller. Do you recollect what I said about not getting out of bed for three days except to use the chamber pot?"

Her mouth full of biscuit and peppered gravy, Zetta nodded.

"Good. Come Thursday morning, you can get up after breakfast if the bleeding's normal," Clarie said. "You remember from the other times that you'll bleed five, maybe six weeks. It starts out red and then gets brownish before it quits."

Clarie stood up. "And don't have any dealings with your man 'til then."

Then Clarie shook her head. "Here I am talking like you was a first time mother," she said. "You already know everything I'm saying."

Zetta smiled. "I wish my granny woman back home had told me all this when I had Rachel," she said. "I kindly had to figure things out by myself."

"Well, go ahead and eat," Clarie said. "I'll check on you directly."

* * * * *

To Zetta's surprise, having nothing to do but sleep, eat and nurse the baby was pleasant. Between naps, she listened to Dosha's prattle as she entertained Rachel and Micah while she cooked. The smells of peppered meat, cinnamon squash, gingerbread cookies and buttermilk pie filled the little house and helped Zetta sleep all the deeper. Still, she eagerly awaited the men's return and smiled when she finally heard their voices at the back door.

She couldn't make out Asa's words but she heard Dosha's usual giggle.

"Oh, she's doing real good. And me and the youngins had us a big time today."

Loren's voice reached the bedroom. "Jack, when are you going to get busy and have your own youngins?"

Zetta imagined Jack shrugging and looking to Dosha to answer. Leave it to Loren not to mind his own business, she thought.

Dosha didn't giggle as she spoke that time.

"That's all in God's time, Loren Davis, not ours," she said. "And I'll thank you to hush if you want buttermilk pie tonight."

Zetta nodded. Good for you, Dosha.

She heard Asa laugh. "That's putting him in his place," he said. "After I see Zetta, I'm gonna enjoy that pie even more."

* * * * *

As Zetta listened to the supper conversation in the kitchen, Loren sounded contrite as he bragged on every dish Dosha set on the table. Rachel and Micah ate with the men while Dosha brought a plate to Zetta. As Dosha spread a towel across the quilt, Zetta grabbed her hand.

"I heard what Loren said when they was washing up," Zetta whispered. "He had no business saying that."

Dosha sighed. "Well, he just hit a sore spot," she whispered back. "Every month, I hope it's our turn to have a baby and then every month I get disappointed. Jack says we ain't been married long enough, but my mother used to say it took only once. God must love you special to give you three sweet babies."

Zetta started to tell Dosha that God loved her and Jack just as much, but Asa appeared.

"That was a mighty fine supper, Dosha," he said. "You go on and eat now. I'll keep Zetta and little Isaac company."

Zetta smiled as Asa sat carefully beside her, but Dosha's comment stayed in her mind.

* * * * *

The restful days passed quickly. As soon as the men left for the mine on Thursday morning, Zetta heard Clarie arrive.

"Howdy, Dosha," Clarie said. "You done a good job here, but I'm letting Zetta up today."

Dosha giggled. "Oh, I'm glad I could help out."

Clarie stepped into the bedroom as Zetta finished feeding Isaac.

"You're getting up now, but don't take on the world just yet," Clarie said. "If the weather is still clear come Saturday, I'll take you to the store to get you outside. We'll walk real slow. And we'll take Brother and Sister, too."

"I can't leave little Isaac," Zetta said.

"Hush," Clarie said. "It ain't like we're planning to walk to Hazard. Getting outside will give you something to look forward to."

"The only thing I'm looking forward to is going home," Zetta said.

"Grumbling's not going make that happen any sooner," Clarie said.

She turned to the few dresses hanging from nails near the children's bed. "I reckon we'll put you in the blue dress today."

Zetta pulled her nightgown over her head and held out her arms.

* * * * *

Dosha finished the breakfast dishes as Zetta entered the kitchen, leaning on Clarie's arm. Zetta glanced toward the shelf where she kept the bean jar as Dosha gestured toward the stove.

"I've got soup beans simmering and I made a gingerbread cake," she said. "I'll come back and help with supper if you want."

Zetta shook her head. "You've outdone yourself already," she said. "Asa and the boys will just have to put up with my sorry cooking now."

Dosha hooked a loose strand of bright red hair over her ear and then bent to hug Rachel and Micah.

"I had fun with y'all," she said. "Now you be good for your mommy."

As Dosha reached for her shawl, Clarie spoke. "I'll go, too. I need to check on Polly."

She turned to Zetta. "That is if you feel up to being alone."

Zetta was eager for them to be gone. "Y'all go on," she said. "I'm fine."

As the two women stepped off the back porch, Zetta pulled the counting jar from behind the dishes and poured four beans into her hand.

"Four more days closer to home, Lord. Four!"

She held the jar up to the light, trying to remember how many beans were left. There were still too many to count.

* * * * *

That night, Zetta watched as Jack and Dosha, carrying small graniteware pails, approached the blackberry patch behind the smokehouse. The clusters of ripe fruit caused the branches to dip almost to the ground as the young couple plucked handfuls of berries from the thorny branches. Dosha giggled and held an especially large berry at Jack's mouth.

As he leaned forward, the berry fell from Dosha's hand and hit his shoe, splashing black juice across his foot. Then Dosha began to cry, tears running down her face and mingling with the juice. Her sobs grew louder until they caused Zetta to claw her way out of another horrible dream.

Heart pounding and still hearing Dosha's sobs from the dream, Zetta quickly put her hand to Isaac's chest as he slept beside her. His tiny chest rose and fell with gentle breathing.

She looked toward Rachel and Micah, then Asa. All were sleeping soundly.

Lord, are you trying to tell me something I can't do anything about?

* * * * *

As she packed the men's dinner buckets that morning, the dream still was very much on her mind.

157

"Lord, what am I supposed to do with these dreams?" she whispered. "Asa's let me know he doesn't want to hear about them. Clarie's told me they're fear talking. But they keep tormenting me. Please help me. And please protect everybody I love."

Even after she saw the men off to work, she replayed the sound of Dosha's sobs in the dream. She was so deep in thought Clarie startled her as she came up the back steps. Zetta jerked open the door.

"I had another awful dream," Zetta said. "Dosha and Jack was picking blackberries and one fell on his shoe and Dosha's crying woke me up."

Clarie took off her coat as she stepped into the kitchen.

"Blackberries are a bad sign, all right," she said.

She pulled a chair out from the table and eased her bulk down.

"But the trouble with dreams is that you can read them different ways," Clarie said. "Some folks say 'dream out of season, worry without a reason.' You're all the time worrying about getting out of here, so maybe the Lord is telling you to stop your worrying and find something good in each day to think on."

"How am I gonna stop worrying when my men are working under a mountain and carrying tins of death in their pockets?" Zetta said. "And Asa is the one carrying dynamite!"

Clarie took a deep breath. "I was hoping you didn't know about all that."

"You mean you knew?"

"Oh, honey. I know more than I want to," Clarie said. "You got any of Dosha's gingerbread left?"

CHAPTER 19

After Saturday's breakfast, Zetta wrapped her usual prayers around the men as they disappeared into the sooty darkness leading to the mine, their filled dinner buckets swinging by their sides. As soon as she nursed Isaac and put him between two pillows on the bed, she fed Rachel and Micah breakfast.

She smiled as she spooned gravy over their biscuits.

"Make sure you eat real good now," she said. "Miz Clarie will be here directly, and we'll go to the store whilst Miz Dosha stays with little Isaac."

She pulled a slip of paper from her apron pocket. "Last night I made out my list of what we need," she said to Rachel. "Ham hocks, yeast, coffee, food paper and such. And I told your daddy I'll pay for the bag of flour this morning, but he'd have to tote it home tonight. I need to get started making hand pies for the boarders again."

Rachel smiled. "And cookies, Mama?"

"Yes. Cookies, too."

Before Zetta could say more, an unwelcome shout came from the back porch.

"Hey, open the door."

Julia.

Both children looked at their mother, but Zetta put her hands on their shoulders.

"Now don't you worry," she said. But she took a deep breath as she thought of how quickly that girl could ruin a decent day.

Zetta opened the door, but stepped in front of Julia as she started to enter.

"Well, Miz Julia. What brings you here so early?"

"I wanna see the baby."

I'm not giving in to this rude child, Zetta thought.

"Remember what I said before? It's polite to wait 'til you are invited in."

Julia put her hands on her hips and huffed, but she remained on the porch.

Zetta smiled with feigned courtesy. "Good morning, Miz Julia," she said. "Won't you come in?"

Julia gave another huff as she stepped into the kitchen. "So, where's the baby?"

"He's in the bedroom," Zetta said. "You sit here at the table whilst I get him. But you can't hold him and you can't say mean things. Are you willing to do that?"

Julia shrugged. "I guess."

"There's no guessing about it, young lady. If you want to see my baby, you have to follow my rules."

Julia shrugged again. "Okay."

Rachel and Micah slid from their chairs and followed their mother into the bedroom. Zetta hurriedly folded a small blanket around the sleeping baby, covering his ears, and carried him to the kitchen with the other children close behind.

As Zetta held Isaac toward Julia, he awakened momentarily, then yawned and squirmed, causing the blanket to fall from his head.

Zetta quickly tucked the material around his head and said, "Can you believe you were ever this little?"

Julia ignored the question. "His ears are ugly."

Zetta took a quick step to the door and opened it while she cradled Isaac in one arm.

"You didn't mind what I said, Miz Julia," she said. "You've visited long enough."

Julia huffed as she stepped onto the porch. "Well, his ears *are* ugly."

"Goodbye," Zetta said. "Next time you come, make sure you bring better manners."

* * * * *

Zetta was still smiling over her dismissal of Julia when Clarie and Dosha arrived.

"Well, now. That smile looks good on you," Clarie said. "Any reason?"

Zetta waved her hand. "Oh, I just sent Julia away instead of putting up with her shenanigans."

Clarie chuckled, and Dosha swooped toward Rachel and Micah.

"Oh, I've missed taking care of these sweet youngins," she said. "I'll stay with the little feller, Zetta, but don't you want to leave these two here, too?"

Clarie answered for her. "No, the wind's blowing the right way, so being outside will be good for them."

She turned to Zetta. "I'm ready if you are. I brung my basket to carry your food home."

* * * * *

The store was unusually quiet that morning, so Roscoe was sitting behind the counter with his straight-back chair tipped against the shelf. The chair thudded against the wooden floor as he stood to greet his customers.

"Morning, Clarie," he said. "You're making a regular habit of coming here."

"Well, you're easy on the eyes, Roscoe," Clarie said.

The man ran his hand over his bald head. "You beat all, Clarie," he said. "What can I do for you today?"

Clarie gestured toward Zetta. "She's got her list. I'll check our mail whilst you help her."

Roscoe nodded. "Now what's the name?"

"Berghoffer, sir," Zetta said. "But I'm paying cash today. And I'll buy a sack of flour, but my husband will pick it up after his shift."

Roscoe pulled a black ledger from the shelf.

"You can pay cash only for what you tote home," he said. "I'll add the flour to the books. That way, I don't get confused when a miner claims his wife already paid."

He flipped open the pages. "Let's see. Here it is. Berghoff."

He took the pencil from behind his ear and wrote "One sack of flour charged."

"Sir, our name is Berghoffer," Zetta said. "With an *er* on the end."

Roscoe shrugged and continued writing.

Clarie waved a letter as she came back to the counter.

"Nothing for you today, honey," she said. "But I got a letter from my Hindman cousin. I can't wait to read what she's got to say about the happenings over at the school. Reading her letters is as good as reading one of them fancy store-bought books."

After Roscoe added the last of the items from Zetta's list to Clarie's basket, he took a red and white peppermint stick from the glass counter case, snapped it in two and handed the pieces to Rachel and Micah.

"What do you say to Mr. Roscoe?" Zetta urged.

Roscoe smiled as Rachel chirped, "Thank you, Mr. Roscoe," and Micah smiled at him.

Clarie chuckled. "You've never given me anything for free, Roscoe."

He winked at her. "That's because you give me more trouble than these cute children do."

Clarie laughed. "Can't argue there."

* * * * *

Clarie was still smiling as the little group stepped onto the porch. At that moment, Perton hurried past, his jaw set and his face black with coal dust beneath his miner's cap. In his right hand, he carried a second miner's cap and a dinner bucket.

Clarie called to him. "Something wrong, Perton?"

He kept walking as he hollered over his shoulder. "Slate fell on Jack. I'm on my way to tell Dosha."

Clarie dropped the basket with a thud and slapped her hand to her chest.

"Wait! Is he. . . is he dead?"

Perton stopped and turned to her. "No. No. A big piece hit his right side but missed his head," he said. "His foot got the worst of it. He's over at the hospital. The doctor has him all ethered up."

Zetta, heart pounding, gripped the banister as she thought of Asa and her brothers.

She bit her lip then as she realized she hadn't thought of Jack first. As she turned toward Clarie, she suddenly remembered her dream of the blackberry hitting Jack's foot. The older woman, cheeks flushed, stood with one hand still on her chest, her other hand gripping her walking stick. Zetta wondered if she was remembering her own husband being killed by slate.

Perton turned to leave. Suddenly Clarie straightened her shoulders.

"Wait," she said. "Dosha ain't to her house. She's taking care of Zetta's baby."

She grabbed the basket and thrust it toward Perton. "Here, take this."

He took it and started up the path as Clarie turned to Zetta.

"Can you get home all right?" she asked. "I'll stay with the baby 'til you get there."

The young mother nodded, but Clarie already was hurrying after Perton.

Zetta gripped the children's hands and carefully walked down the store steps to the path.

"Lord, this is awful. Be with Jack—and Dosha. And please protect Asa and the boys from harm. And get us out of here," she whispered.

* * * * *

When Zetta and the children arrived home, Clarie was jiggling a howling Isaac.

Zetta cooed, "Oh, my hungry baby," and she reached for the child and opened her blouse even without shedding her coat. Clarie helped Rachel and Micah out of their coats, then eased into the chair across from Zetta.

"Dosha took the news awful hard," Clarie said. "She sank right down on the floor over there. But before I could say anything, she pulled herself up and said that wasn't gonna help Jack one bit. Then she grabbed her shawl and rushed out the door for the hospital. Perton had to hurry to catch up with her."

Zetta caressed Isaac's head as he nursed. "This is just like the end of my dream," she said. "Remember me telling you the one about the blackberry hitting Jack's foot?"

Clarie nodded solemnly, so Zetta continued. "What good does it do for us to know bad is coming if we can't do anything about it?"

163

"Oh, honey," Clarie said. "I give up trying to figure things like that out a long time ago. I just hang on to the Lord and ask him to help me each day."

"That don't help my worrying none," Zetta said.

"I know, honey. But that's all I've come up with over the years."

Zetta puffed out her cheeks, then asked, "Did Perton tell you what happened?"

Clarie nodded and put her hands to her forehead. "When I caught up with him, he said Jack had just returned from taking the men to the mine face," Clarie said. "He was gonna pick up Mr. Gray and take him in, but the slate fell first. That slate falling is awful stuff. Awful."

Zetta waited a moment, pondering how to form her question. Finally, she said, "Are you remembering your own long ago bad news?"

Clarie nodded. "Of course," she said. "But this is Dosha's time. Me telling her about my troubles won't help her none."

"Oh."

"Dosha did ask Perton why the whistle didn't blow when Jack was hurt," Clarie said. "He told her that happens when it's an accident deep in the mine. Like fire or men being trapped."

Zetta gasped. Trapped. Like those men Perton talked about gasping for one last breath.

Clarie interrupted her thoughts. "I'm going up to their place and start packing," she said. "If you feel up to it, you might want to come and help wrap dishes."

"Wrap dishes?"

"Why, yes, honey. We need to help Dosha pack since they have to be out of the house within two days."

"But Jack's hurt," Zetta said. "They can't expect them to leave 'til he's well."

"Honey, that's just another way the coal company reminds us this isn't a mission group," Clarie said. "They make money off men's blood and don't care how much of it is spilled."

Then Clarie took a deep breath. "Well, now. I better get on up to their place," she said. "The company will have the packing crates on their porch by now."

She nodded toward the growing stack of empty crates in the corner of Zetta's kitchen. "I see you still got yours."

"Yes. And I can't wait 'til March thirty-first," Zetta said. "I'll have them filled by the time Asa gets home that evening and be ready to catch the next train out. I don't care if we have to sleep at the station that night. I won't spend one more night here once our time is up."

"Oh, honey. I've heard that before," Clarie said. "I hope you're right. But life has a way of doing what it's gonna do."

As Zetta watched Clarie leave, she thought of how happy Dosha had been the morning she was on her way to the store to get raisins for Jack's rice pudding. How quickly that happiness had faded.

* * * * *

After nursing Isaac, Zetta wrapped her heaviest quilt around him and buttoned Rachel's and Micah's coats.

"Now both of you can take one toy to Miz Dosha's to play with whilst I help pack her dishes," she said. "And I don't want any shenanigans? You hear me?"

Both children nodded solemnly.

The gray sky hung even lower as Zetta and the children left the house. But as soon as Clarie opened Dosha's door, sunshine seemed to spill from the kitchen. Yellow cushions covered the seats of the chairs and the table was hidden by an orange flowered tablecloth that matched the curtains.

Dosha's house is bright and warm—just like her, Zetta thought. Look at those curtains. And me without even a feedsack on mine.

Clarie reached for the baby. "I'll put him on their bed."

She stopped and pointed to the end of the table where Jack's dulcimer lay.

"Ain't that sad?" she said. "It's just like he was playing it this morning and planned to come back to it at suppertime. Oh, well. There's the stack of towels to wrap around the dishes."

* * * * *

Dosha came through the back door before the first crate was filled. Both Clarie and Zetta grabbed her in a long hug and held her while she spoke.

"The doctor sent me home to pack whilst Jack sleeps off the

ether," she said. "They won't let me sit with him. What if he wakes up and I'm not there?"

She pulled a crumpled handkerchief from her sleeve and walked to the front window where she stared down at the coal tipple rumbling with that day's tonnage. When she turned back to Clarie, tears were running down her cheeks.

"We was so happy here," she said. "What'll we do now? Where'll we go?"

Clarie had picked up an ironstone bowl, but set it down. "You mean you don't have a soul to meet you at some train station?" she asked.

Dosha fought a sob. "No. Jack's people is all dead, and mine can't take us in," she said. "They mighta had room for us if Jack could work, but he'll be crippled. The doctor says every bone in his foot is crushed."

Clarie moved toward the young woman as she began to twist the flowered curtain.

"Why'd this happen to Jack?" Dosha asked. "He's never had anything good happen to him in life, except me, I reckon."

Suddenly Dosha lifted her young face to stare into Clarie's wrinkled one.

"Did this happen because we're bad?" Then she paused, gulping air. "Did God do this because we sinned together before we was married?"

Clarie wrapped her arms around the now sobbing young woman.

"Oh, Dosha, honey. God don't work like that," she said. "If he broke our legs every time we sinned, we'd *all* be crippled."

Clarie rubbed Dosha's back and stared at the dulcimer on the table.

"Honey, don't you worry," she said. "God's gonna work all this out for you."

Zetta saw Clarie's mouth move in silent prayer. It was as though she was receiving instructions as she went along.

"First off, you and Jack are gonna move in with me 'til he's fit to travel."

Dosha blew her nose. "But the camp rule says we have to leave within two days."

"No, the rule says you have to leave *the house* within two days," Clarie said. "All they care about is having it available for the next miner. Nobody's gonna come looking for you if you stay out of sight. Then whilst Jack's foot is mending, you and me is gonna finish piecing a quilt I've been working on. And I'm gonna show you how to make a vinegar poultice to help heal his foot."

Then with her hands still on Dosha's shoulders, Clarie pulled back to look at her.

"And I'm gonna brag on y'all in a letter to my cousin over at the Hindman School across the mountain," she said. "Then when Jack can stand a couple hours in a jolt wagon, you're gonna show up with your belongings and one of your buttermilk pies and get introduced to the two women who run the school. As soon as they taste your cooking, they'll take you on. When Jack gets well, they'll find something for him to do, too. They can't pay much, but you'll have a good roof over your heads."

Dosha rubbed her sleeve across her eyes. "You'd do that for us? But we're not even kin."

"You're one of my girls," Clarie said. "That's kin enough for me. Now get packing. This is gonna work out. I'm going down to tell that doctor to get Jack up to my place as soon as he's able to be moved."

"But what if he reports you to Mr. Gray?" Dosha asked.

"Honey, there's not a man in this camp who would dare do that," Clarie said.

Zetta and Dosha watched the older woman grab her coat and walking stick and hurry out the back door. Then they hugged each other and sobbed.

* * * * *

That night, a grim-faced Asa placed the bag of flour on the kitchen floor before stepping back outside to wash up. He didn't kiss Zetta.

She was fighting tears as she followed him onto the porch.

"Did y'all hear about Jack?" she asked.

"Not 'til we got to the mantrip after our shift and Clarence told us," he said.

"Clarence?"

167

Loren was waiting for his turn at the wash pan.

"Yep, Sis," he said. "Good old Clarence. He beat Luttrell's time with the school teacher and now we get to watch him jerk the controls on the air donkey. He liked to have jerked our heads off trying to get that thing stopped."

As Asa reached for the towel, Loren plunged his hands into the black water and turned to Luttrell.

"How about come Monday morning, we push Clarence in front of the engine?" Loren said. "Then you can court that pretty little teacher."

Luttrell scowled. "You sure know how to make a bad situation worse."

Zetta hurriedly changed the subject.

"I took the youngins up to Dosha's, and me and Clarie helped her pack," she said. "When I was leaving, folks stopped by to tell Dosha goodbye, so Clarie told them she wouldn't be holding Bible reading church for a while. Truth is, she needs y'all to tote the crates with Dosha and Jack's household belongings up to her barn tomorrow. She's keeping that sweet couple hid 'til Jack's fit to travel."

Loren stepped around her and took his seat at the table.

"Well, that'll eat up the morning," he said. "Sure knocks holding our own church in the head. You'd think Rusty Hinge would cut a feller a break and give him a few more days to get out of his house, it being Sunday tomorrow and all. But they wouldn't care if poor old Jack had been kilt."

Hearing him say *kilt* was too much. Zetta grabbed Asa's arm and began to sob.

"That could have been any one of you," she cried.

Asa pulled her close, but offered no comfort. "Zetta, this won't do," he said. "We're sorry Jack got hurt, but we're okay. Now we're gonna eat and then we're gonna take our baths. And you're gonna straighten up."

Zetta pulled back to look at him, wiping her nose with her sleeve.

"You want me to straighten up?" she said. "I dreamed Jack would get hurt—and he did. I told you I have bad dreams all the time here, and you won't pay them any mind. I want to go home before something worse happens."

Without another word, Asa abruptly turned and left the house.

Stunned, Zetta watched him disappear into the darkness. Vaguely aware of Rachel and Micah watching her, their eyes wide, she turned to Luttrell. Her words were choked by sobs.

"Why can't I make him listen?"

As Luttrell put his arms around his sister, Loren reached for the cornbread.

Chapter 20

Zetta cried against Luttrell's shoulder for several moments then realized she was breathing in the coal dust clinging to his shirt.

She pulled back from her brother and swiped at her eyes.

"When you was little, I was the one comforting you," she said. "Now you're all growed up and patting *my* back."

"Oh, Sis. I don't know what to tell you," Luttrell said. "Working coal is hard, but seeing what it's doing to you and Asa makes it all the worse."

Zetta pulled a handkerchief from her sleeve and blew her nose.

Rachel burst into tears. "Mama, I'm scared."

So am I, Zetta thought. But she leaned down to kiss both children.

"I'm all right, Babies."

She straightened, but her hands remained on the children as she watched Loren smear butter on a chunk of cornbread.

"I'm with you, Sis," Loren said. "Asa sure drove his ducks to a bad market this time."

Zetta wanted to defend her husband's decision to move to the camp, but couldn't. Instead, she turned to dish up the rest of the supper.

* * * * *

The five of them ate in silence—the children and the brothers watching Zetta as she pushed her food around the plate and

170

glanced repeatedly toward the back porch.

Asa still wasn't home by the time supper was over, and Luttrell and Loren had toted in the water for the baths.

Just as Zetta finished bathing Rachel and Micah and pulled their little nightshirts over their heads, Asa stepped through the back door.

"Poppy!" both children shouted in unison.

He spoke to the children and didn't greet Zetta.

"Well, now. Don't the two of you look fine," he said.

"Asa . . ." Zetta said.

He kept his eyes on Rachel and Micah.

"How about I put y'all to bed whilst your mommy takes her bath?" he said. "And I'll even tell you a story about a talking squirrel."

He swooped up both children and carried them into the bedroom. Tears rolled down Zetta's cheeks as she added a kettleful of hot water to the water in the galvanized tub. Then she blew out the lantern and took her bath.

* * * * *

With Baby Isaac asleep between them, Zetta couldn't snuggle against Asa's warm back after he finished his bath and slipped into bed without speaking.

It's just as well, she thought. Even asleep, Asa probably would pull away.

Zetta couldn't get comfortable. She'd doze, awaken with a jerk and then doze again. Finally, she gave up trying to sleep and went to the kitchen. As she pulled another bean from the counting jar, she held the container toward the kerosene lamp. The jar still was more than half full.

"Won't you ever get down to the final bean?" she whispered. With a tired sigh, she set the jar back in its hiding place.

She had just started to mix the biscuits when Asa came into the kitchen. She started to greet him, but the sight of his set jaw wouldn't let her form words. He pulled his jacket from the nail by the door, then stepped into the cold air and headed up the lane to the outhouse.

Zetta sighed. Well, if that's the way he wants to be, I'll have to wait 'til he's ready to talk, she thought.

At breakfast, Asa's prayer was unusually short.

"Thank you for this food," he said. "Bless the hands that prepared it. And help us all bear our present load."

At Asa's *Amen*, Loren pointed toward the biscuits.

"Start those this way," he said. "Here it is our one day of rest and we have to spend it toting Dosha's crates up to Clarie's barn."

He looked at Asa. "Even listening to your preaching would beat that."

Asa frowned. "You always got to be complaining, don't you?" he said. "Like I've said before, you'd complain if you was being hung with a *new* rope."

As Loren took a biscuit from the offered plate, he said, "Careful. Or you'll be toting those crates by your lonesome."

* * * * *

To keep from seeing the men carrying the crates filled with bright cushions and curtains, Zetta nursed Isaac facing away from the kitchen window while Rachel and Micah finished breakfast. Just as she buttoned her blouse and patted the baby's back, Julia's voice sounded from the back porch.

"Hey, open the door."

Zetta was tempted to ignore her visitor, but then Julia's voice sounded again

"Hey, I'm here!"

Zetta sighed as she positioned Isaac against her neck and then draped the small blanket around his head before opening the door.

"I'm not in the mood for company today, Miz Julia," she said. "One of our good friends was hurt pretty bad yesterday, and I've been trying to help his wife."

Julia shrugged as she peered around Zetta and made a face at Rachel.

"Daddy told us that at dinner last night," she said. "Mama says hillbillies are stupid. And she says anybody who works in the mines deserves whatever happens."

Zetta clutched Isaac closer as she realized she wanted to slap Julia.

"Well, your mother is wrong," she said. "And you can tell her I said so. Jack Conley is a decent man. He would never say the mean things about your mother that she says about miners."

172

Zetta closed her eyes and forced herself to take a long breath. When she opened her eyes again, Julia was staring at her.

Zetta pointed her finger at the girl. "I'm tired of your mother calling us hillbillies. And I'm tired of you repeating her meanness. Go home."

Julia's mouth formed a surprised "Oh" as she turned to go down the steps.

* * * * *

The sky was dark by noon, so Zetta lit the lamp on the kitchen table before adding extra water to the simmering beans. She kept looking out the window, waiting for the men to return.

Finally, she saw Loren hurrying ahead of Asa and Luttrell.

When he opened the back door, he tossed his jacket onto the nail hook and immediately sat down at the table.

"Hey, Sis. Let's eat," he said. "Toting all of Dosha's pretties wore me out."

Zetta set the bowl of steaming beans before him.

"Now leave 'em be 'til I get the rest of the food dished up," she said. "Is Jack out of the hospital yet?"

"Nope," Loren answered. "But Clarie said the doctor will bring him up to her place tonight. I reckon that feller is only too happy to have his hospital empty again. I'd like to know what he does down there. He sure don't do much doctoring."

As Asa and Luttrell came through the back door, Zetta spooned dumplings into a bowl without looking directly at her husband. But from the side of her eyes, she watched him hang up his jacket and pull a letter from the pocket. He stood awkwardly for a moment then cleared his throat twice. Finally, Zetta turned to look at him.

"You got a letter from your paw," Asa said. "I forgot to tell you yesterday, what with all the commotion over Jack."

Zetta bit back the words she wanted to say about their argument. Instead she said, "I'm trying to get food on the table. Read the letter to me whilst I pour the coffee."

Asa sat down and tore open the envelope as he leaned close to the lamp.

"'Dear Zetta and all. Was sure glad to hear about little Isaac's safe arrival. Will be glad to meet him come spring. We had a good Christmas but it would have been better to have you here with us.

Your little brothers are learning good in school.'"

Asa paused. "Why does he always call them 'your little brothers'? Doesn't he remember their names?"

Zetta shrugged. "Oh, you know Paw," she said. "He'll be calling them my little brothers when they're growed. Go on with the letter."

Asa continued.

"'I saw Jim Reed in town at Court House Days. He tipped his hat to me and stepped aside. I nodded and started on my way, but he said to tell you your chickens and the cow is getting along good. Well, your Mama Becky is setting supper on the table so I best close for now. Write soon. Love, your Paw—John Davis.'"

Zetta set a cup of coffee before Asa. "What do you reckon it will take for Paw to stop carrying a grudge against Jim?"

Asa shook his head. "It's a wonder he don't make me tip my hat to him, too, my family having been Union and all. Sometimes I think this country is never gonna be free of all that happened during the War Between Brothers."

Zetta quickly looked at Loren, her eyes daring him to start his usual argument about the different sides the two grandfathers and their families had chosen years before. Loren shrugged and took a sip of coffee as Asa folded the letter and handed it to Zetta. She knew the letter was a slow beginning but at least her husband was talking again.

* * * * *

The next morning, after the men left for the mine and before the children awakened, Zetta saw Clarie coming down the lane. The bright blue cloth covered her egg basket.

Zetta jerked open the door. "Oh, I'm glad to see you. Come in. Come in. I've been about to bust waiting for news about Jack."

Clarie smiled as she climbed the back steps.

"I figured you'd be about out of eggs, so I saved you two dozen," she said. "My hens laid extra good. I reckon it was because Dosha was out there talking to them after the doctor shooed her out of Jack's room yesterday. I talk to the chickens too, but whilst Dosha tells 'em them how pretty they are, I tell 'em if they don't lay, they'll make mighty fine eating."

As Clarie sat down at the table, Zetta reached for the change jar.

"Did the doctor get Jack to your place all right?" Zetta asked as she counted out 24 cents.

"Sure did," Clarie said. "Ruthie's son, Lloyd, and three of his buddies brung him in real gentle like soon as it got dark."

"Ruthie?" Zetta asked.

"You remember," Clarie said. "The colored granny woman."

"Oh, that's right."

"Well, they eased Jack down on the bed and then stepped back whilst the doctor checked his leg. Then everybody disappeared."

"How's he doing now?"

"The ether was out of his system this morning so he got a good look at his foot when I showed Dosha how to change the bandage," Clarie said. "Right away he started crying about black feet and death in that pitiful way of his. And Dosha was crying and trying to tell him it was all right, that he wasn't gonna die."

Clarie rubbed her forehead as she continued.

"I'll never forget her looking at me with big tears running down her face and saying Jack remembers how a few years back the feet of people—like his mother and sister—suffering with that awful influenza would turn black. When that happened, they were dead right quick."

Zetta sat down next to her. "Magoffin County was hit bad, but our family didn't get it," she said. "My stepmother, Becky, always claimed all the onions she made us eat kept us from getting sick. When Asa and I got married to take care of his mother, Becky gave us a bushel of onions as a wedding present!"

Clarie laughed. "Well, that beats getting something you gotta dust all the time."

Then her voice softened.

"I kept folks around here supplied with my teas," Clarie said. "And I told them to stay away from the aspirin the camp doctor we had back then was handing out. He finally moved to Lexington to help over there. But as many people as I heard they was losing each week, he must not have done much good. And the doctor we got now ain't any better."

Zetta leaned forward. "Did many folks die here back then?"

Clarie shook her head. "We did lose some, and that like to have broke my heart because they all were so young," she said. "But we weren't hit nearly as hard as the other camps. Most of 'em around here shut down for a full six weeks. The men were digging graves instead of coal. It was an awful time…. But I forgot about the feet turning black 'til Jack was hollering about it this morning."

She folded the blue cloth and put it back into the basket as she continued.

"It took me and Dosha a while to get him calmed down enough to understand the foot was black from the injury," Clarie said. "We had to show him his other foot, that it was still the right color, before he could settle down. Finally, I gave him some of my strong tea to make him sleep for a while. Then when he was awake and more clear headed, Dosha was all excited to tell him about moving to Hindman soon as he's fit to travel. Poor old soul was plumb pitiful trying to thank me."

Zetta smiled. "Oh, I remember your sleeping tea when Isaac was born," she said. "I didn't know what hit me."

Suddenly she gestured toward the leftover biscuits.

"Lands, Clarie. You've been here all this while and I haven't offered you a thing to eat. How about some jelly to go with these? And the coffee is still good and hot."

Clarie shook her head and stood up.

"Can't today," she said. "I'm on my way to mail the brag letter about Dosha and Jack to my cousin over at the Hindman Settlement School."

She opened the back door, then turned to Zetta.

"That reminds me," she said. "Dosha wants to see the baby again. So any time you and the youngins want to come up to my place, you come right on. This afternoon would be fine. Seeing little faces will be good for Jack, too."

Zetta smiled. "I'd like that. I was thinking I'd make my gingerbread cake this morning. How about I make two—and bring y'all one?"

Clarie shifted her walking stick to her other hand and reached for the banister.

"Now you know I'm not about to refuse your good gingerbread," she said. "We'll see you when you get there."

* * * * *

As soon as the little group reached Clarie's porch a few hours later, Dosha jerked open the door and ran toward them, arms flung wide.

"Oh, I've missed y'all," she said. "Come in where it's warm."

Clarie greeted them as they stepped into the old fashioned cabin, which had one large room. A stone fireplace held a roaring fire at the far end. The mantel was a split log and was crowded with jars of dried leaves. Crisp quilts hung on each wall, their colors matching the large braided rugs covering the wooden floor. Herbs and flowers hung upside down from wooden pegs near the fireplace, their muted colors and subtle fragrances almost dizzying in the warm room. Two large beds filled the corners closest to the fireplace. A few straight-back chairs were sprinkled throughout the room, but a large wooden rocking chair was pulled close to the fireplace. Jack sat there, one leg propped up on a stool and covered by several bright quilts.

Beside the rocking chair was the toy crate.

Rachel and Micah tolerated Dosha's hugs and coos but quickly scooted toward the toy crate and began to pull out wooden animals, tiny farm wagons and brightly painted blocks.

As Zetta gave Clarie the gingerbread cake, Dosha held her hands toward Isaac.

"Let me hold that precious child," she said. "I swear he's growing by the minute."

Dosha gently cradled the baby in the crook of her arm, then held him toward her husband.

"Look who's come to see you, honey," she said.

Jack smiled. "Gl. . . glad to se. . . see ya lit….little fell….feller."

Zetta had forgotten how painful it was to hear him speak.

Quickly she said, "I'm sorry you got hurt, Jack."

He nodded and turned to Dosha, waiting for her to answer.

She looked up from cooing at Isaac. "We're just glad it wasn't worse," Dosha said. "Clarie's been telling us how God brings his good out of bad things, so we're trusting that."

Clarie spoke. "Right now, we need to concentrate on getting Jack well. By my reckoning, a week here ought to mend him enough to get him over to Hindman. I hear they've got an infirmary set up a ways overlooking the school. It beats our camp hospital all to pieces."

Dosha interrupted her. "I don't want anybody taking care of Jack but me."

Clarie chuckled. "I feel sorry for anybody who tries to tell you what's best for your man."

CHAPTER 21

Zetta stood in front of her home and watched the muddy creek swirl. As the water reached the sycamore trees overhanging the creek banks, snakes abandoned their lairs beneath the roots and swam toward her. She chopped at them with her hoe as they reached the dry tangled grass at her feet, but several slithered past her and disappeared under the porch. As she whirled to chase the creatures, stones from the chimney rolled onto the roof's wooden shingles and thudded to the parched ground. The dust from the falling stones made her fight for breath.

Zetta gasped and clawed her way to wakefulness.

She gulped air, trying to calm her pounding heart. As Asa's gentle snores reminded her she was still in the coal camp, Zetta took another deep breath and put her hand softly upon the baby beside her. Isaac's breathing was even, and his little chest rose and fell as he slept. With her hand still on the baby, she leaned toward Rachel and Micah, holding her breath as she listened for theirs. Both slept soundly.

Isaac wiggled beneath her hand and whimpered. Zetta hurriedly changed his diaper, then opened her gown so he could nurse. Asa grunted and turned over, falling asleep again despite Isaac's little smacking sounds. As she caressed the baby's head, Zetta tried to push the frightening dream from her thoughts. Still it lingered.

Lord, I know you're trying to warn me about something but I can't do a thing about whatever it is, she prayed inwardly. Asa won't listen to me. So if you're wanting somebody to take action, you're talking to the wrong person. Try talking to him for a while.

When the baby was full, Zetta gently patted his back until he belched. Then she wrapped his blanket tightly around him and placed him between two pillows beside his sleeping daddy.

As she eased out of bed, she leaned over Rachel and Micah to listen to their breathing again before hurrying to the kitchen. There she struck a match to light the lamp on the table. She glanced into the dark corners, looking for snakes, before she pulled the counting jar from the back of the shelf. She dumped another dry bean into her hand and reached for the coffee pot.

* * * * *

Zetta, still pondering the awful dream, barely nodded as the men came to breakfast. As soon as Asa asked the blessing, she put their filled plates in front of them and poured the coffee.

Asa watched Zetta for a moment.

"You're acting poorly this morning," he said. "Didn't you sleep good?"

"No."

"You want me to have Clarie check on you?" Asa asked.

"No need."

"Well, you gonna be all right?"

"I guess."

Loren reached for the biscuits as Zetta filled his cup.

"The boarders are asking for your hand pies, Sis," he said. "You about ready to start making them again?"

Zetta huffed and turned to look into Asa's questioning eyes. "Might as well," she answered.

* * * * *

Zetta rubbed her arms for warmth as she stood on the porch and prayed as the men disappeared into the predawn darkness. Asa's dinner bucket held the last of the sliced sweet potatoes.

"Oh, Lord, please protect them today and every day. I wonder, Lord. Are you tired of my constant prayers for their protection? I hope not. But I'm tired of watching them being swallowed by the darkness as they go to the mine. I'm tired of begging to go home. I'm tired of the soot and all this mud."

At her mention of the mud, Zetta made a sweeping gesture across the backyard, which pulled her gaze toward Dosha and Jack's former house. There, a tall woman leaned against the front banister, looking across the lane and into the blackness surrounding the tipple. As she saw Zetta looking her way, she raised her hand in greeting. Zetta returned the gesture but quickly stepped back into her own kitchen.

My goodness, Clarie's right about the camp filling the houses up again right quick, she thought. It sure didn't take them long to get somebody else in there.

Zetta huffed as she pulled the ironstone bowl from the shelf, remembering how Dosha had greeted her that first morning in the camp.

Well, I'm not running up there to meet this woman, she thought. I've got babies to tend. And I'm sure not making her a pie. The camp ought not to have put people in that house so soon. Yes, I know I'm not being very neighborly, but I miss Dosha. Besides, we're leaving here next month. I don't need to be traipsing around making new friends.

As Zetta opened the flour bag, she leaned one hand against the kitchen wall. Then she stared at the rough boards beneath her fingers.

What family lived here before we moved in?

She looked at the stove. What woman cooked here before? Why did they leave? Was he hurt like Jack? Or was it that family folks say Julia got run out of the camp?

She ran her hand over the rough walls again.

Is their sadness held in these boards? Does it leak out every time I'm in this kitchen? Is their pain causing my bad dreams?

The thought caused Zetta to jerk her hand away and rub it against her apron. As she turned away, she saw Clarie heading up the back steps, a jar of milk cradled in her arm.

Clarie can tell me, she thought. But I'll not ask her. I don't want to know.

Zetta opened the door to welcome the older woman but held a finger to her lips.

"Come in," she whispered. "But the youngins are still sleeping. You're out awful early."

Clarie handed the milk to Zetta then pulled off her coat and eased into the kitchen chair.

"Dosha fixed a big breakfast and then was acting like she wanted time alone with Jack," Clarie whispered back. "So I went down to check on Polly as soon as Perton left for the mine to make sure she's getting along good."

"Polly still hiding?" Zetta asked softly as she set biscuits and jelly on the table.

"Pretty much," Clarie said. "I told her it was time to see your new baby. She tried to argue, but I flat out told her to stop letting Perton's drinking keep her from life. I swear, Perton's the one who acts like a fool with moonshine, but she worries about it more than he ever does."

Clarie reached for a biscuit and smeared it with jelly.

"But at least Jack is coming along good since he's able to sleep better at night," she said. "You and the children can visit again any time. He enjoyed seeing y'all before."

Zetta remembered his painful stuttering when he had greeted them during the earlier visit. She looked around the kitchen, searching for an excuse.

"I don't know," she said. "I've got to make the hand pies for the boarders again. Besides, I didn't sleep too good last night and I'm moving kinda slow."

"Your bad dreams back?"

Zetta nodded. "They never really left. Last night, I was watching fast moving muddy water and snakes and brown grass. And, to top it all off, our chimney at home was falling down."

"Muddy water is a sign of bad news all right," Clarie said. "Ruthie's daughter, a maid up at the Gray's, says a lot of letters have been going and coming between him and Mr. Golden. Something's up. I don't know if they're gonna buy First Creek Camp or if something else is brewing. I guess we have to be ready for whatever it is."

Zetta hugged her arms. "I'm glad we're leaving here next month," she said. "Next month. That sounds good. But next week would sound even better."

Clarie nodded. "I know, honey. But March thirty-first will finally get here. But about you dreaming of that broke chimney. We gotta pray against anything bad coming to your place at home. Who's looking after it?"

"A neighbor man, Jim Reed."

"He reliable?" Clarie asked as she bit into the biscuit.

"Oh, yes," Zetta answered. "Asa stuck up for Jim one time when some of the men threatened him for saying the poll taxes levied against colored people was an ugly plan to keep them from voting. He'll do anything for Asa and me now."

Clarie swallowed the last of the biscuit.

"That's good," she said. "But the snakes in your dream. Did you kill them?"

"Some. But not all."

"Well, you be on the watch," Clarie said. "Snakes are a sign of enemies. Around here, the first person I think of is that Miz Julia. When I see her heading up my way, I make sure I start for the store. Jack is doing real good at my place. I don't want anything to change that."

"How's his foot?"

"Pretty good for being hurt that bad," Clarie answered. "I check the skin every morning when Dosha changes the poultice. With so many bones broke, he's still gonna be laid up for a while. But by my reckoning, he can travel by this Sunday. You recollect I wrote my cousin over at Hindman about him and Dosha?"

Zetta nodded as Clarie reached for a second biscuit.

"I already told Perton I'm gonna need a wagon and two mules for the day, if he didn't have plans for 'em," Clarie said. "He looked like he was about to ask why, but I straightened my shoulders and looked him square in the eyes. That let him know he better not ask. So he just shrugged and said he'd tell the stable boy to have everything waiting for any man I send over there. I reminded him he'd better not get to drinking and forget."

"Who's gonna drive the wagon?"

"Ruthie's son, Lloyd. We got this all figured out," Clarie said. "And if Asa and the boys help Lloyd pack the crates in the wagon, he can leave that much sooner," Clarie said. "We'll make a pallet for Jack in the middle of the goods. And we'll put Dosha back there, too, so nobody sees her riding with a colored man. Perton's all the time sending Lloyd to Hazard. Folks won't think twice about seeing him with a wagon load."

Clarie reached for her coat as she stood up. "Make sure you and the youngins come up before they go."

Zetta nodded, but she dreaded saying goodbye to Dosha.

* * * * *

As soon as Clarie stepped onto the back porch to leave, Rachel and Micah awakened. After getting them dressed and fed, Zetta steered them toward their toys in the front room so she could mix the bread ingredients. Micah thumped the jumping man against the floor boards while Rachel accepted a pinch of dough to shape into pea-sized lumps for her play oven.

As Zetta placed the kneaded dough into the ironstone bowl to rise, she heard Julia's unwelcome voice.

"Hey, open the door."

Rachel and Micah looked up from their toys, but Zetta shook her head.

"It's okay. You go ahead and play."

If Clarie hadn't warned me about snakes being dream signs of enemies, I swear I'd send that youngin on her way again, Zetta thought. But she took a deep breath and opened the door.

"Well, Miz Julia," she said. "You're making your rounds extra early this morning. But if you're visiting me you better know how to behave. Think you can do that this time?"

"I guess," Julia said.

Zetta frowned. "There's no guessing about it, young lady. You're not gonna say mean things about my baby or the way we do things or about any of the miners. And you're not gonna call us bad names. You hear me?"

"Okay," Julia answered as she shrugged.

Zetta ignored the shrug and opened the door wider.

"All right. You can come in."

As Julia entered the kitchen, she looked at Micah and Rachel sitting with their toys in the front room. Zetta quickly turned her toward a chair at the table.

"Here, let me help you with your coat," Zetta said.

Then she turned to the ironstone bowl and pinched off a chunk of dough, which she offered to Julia.

"What's this for?" the child asked.

"To shape a yeast roll," Zetta answered. "Don't your mother make bread?"

Julia sneered. "No. That's the colored maid's job."

Zetta shook her head. "Don't your mother cook?"

"Why should she? We've got maids."

"Well now. What does she do all day?"

Julia shrugged. "Sits in her bedroom 'til Daddy comes home. Then she yells at him."

Zetta forced herself not to laugh at the unexpected news. Mrs. Gray hollers at her man. I plead with mine, she thought. And neither one of us can change their minds.

Zetta plopped the dough back into the bowl. "Well, how about a jellied biscuit instead?"

Julia shrugged. "I guess."

As Zetta opened the biscuit, she surprised herself by smiling at the child.

*****

Even though Julia's visit was calm, Zetta still was glad drizzly rain kept the child away for the rest of the week. After the men left for work Saturday morning, Rachel and Micah played with their toys while Zetta made apple cake. As she set it on the table to cool, a welcome voice called from the front of the house.

"Hello in the cabin."

She hurried to the door and found Clarie at the bottom of the steps with Polly at her side. The young woman stood with her head facing the sooty mud at her feet.

"Why, good morning," Zetta said. "Polly, It's good to see you again."

Polly glanced up then lowered her head again, causing her limp brown hair to fall across her eyes. "Good to see you, too, I reckon," Polly whispered.

"Come on in," Zetta said. "I just took apple cake out of the oven."

Clarie knocked the mud off her shoes with her walking stick.

"Well, we sure timed our visit right, huh, Polly?"

At the top of the steps, Clarie noticed the little Christmas tree with its browning needles in the porch corner.

"Well, now. It's still hanging on," she said. "But it'll do a heap better once Asa gets it planted in that sunny spot he's told me he's got picked out on your farm. You'll have to write me and let me know how it does."

Zetta nodded. "Believe me, that's one letter I can't wait to write."

As Clarie stepped into the front room, she smiled at Rachel and

Micah. "Morning, sweet youngins," she said. "I brung Miz Polly to see your little brother. Reckon that'll be all right?"

Both children nodded and turned back to their toys.

Clarie faced Zetta. "I told Polly she needed to see your new baby before he got all growed. I hope that's all right."

Zetta smiled. "Clarie, anything you do is all right. Y'all sit down. Let me dish up the cake and then I'll bring Isaac in."

Clarie waved her away as they took off their coats.

"Honey, I know how to maintain these hips," she said. "I'll take care of the sweets whilst you get the baby."

As Zetta picked Isaac up from the bed and returned to the kitchen, she folded the blanket around his head. When she held the sleeping baby toward Polly, the expectant mother murmured a soft "oh" and held out her arms.

Zetta glanced at Clarie, who nodded as she took a bite of the warm cake. Zetta placed Isaac into Polly's arms but stood by her side.

With the baby in her left arm, Polly hesitantly stroked his head with her right hand. As she did, the blanket fell away.

Zetta held her breath, waiting to hear a comment about the baby's ears. But Polly's face held only wonder.

"He's perfect," Polly whispered. "And to think a marvel like this is growing inside me right now."

She gently traced Isaac's tiny jaw with her finger.

As Polly concentrated on the baby, Clarie leaned toward Zetta.

"I saw your men this morning," she said. "I told them I'll need help tomorrow."

As Clarie inclined her head toward her house, Zetta understood she meant help loading the wagon with Dosha and Jack's goods.

"Loren complained, of course, saying he'd done enough toting last time," Clarie continued. "But I just told him the good Lord will repay him. He was still grumbling when I left them, but he'll be there."

Before Clarie could say more, Polly turned to her.

"Do you reckon my baby will be this pretty, too?" she asked quietly.

Clarie laughed. "Sure enough. Long as it takes after you instead of its daddy!"

* * * * *

185

The next morning, the sun struggled through the sooty haze as Asa, Luttrell and a grumpy Loren left for Clarie's after breakfast. Zetta poured hot water over the plates in the dishpan, then turned to Rachel and Micah.

"Now we ain't going inside Miz Clarie's this time, so don't be asking to play with her toys. We're just gonna say goodbye to Miz Dosha and Mr. Jack. And don't you be acting up when I tell you it's time to come home. You hear me?"

Both children nodded emphatically.

Zetta buttoned their coats, wrapped Isaac in a quilt and opened the door.

As they arrived at Clarie's, Asa and Zetta's brothers were handing the crates to Lloyd as he stood in the wagon bed. After he placed the last two crates beside the pile of quilts and pillows in the middle of the wagon, Lloyd jumped down and pulled off his hat as he stepped toward Dosha. Only then did Zetta realize how much taller he was than even her own brothers.

"Miz Dosha, we done got everything in," Lloyd said. "I'm gonna carry Mr. Jack out now, if y'all is ready."

Dosha's small hands fluttered near her face. "Lloyd, I still wish you'd let us pay you a little something for going to all this trouble," she said.

Lloyd shook his head. "Miz Dosha, you know I can't take nothing for helping you and Mr. Jack," he said. "Mr. Jack treated me and the other colored men real decent. Always raised his hand and looked us right in the face when we spoke to him, just like he done for the white miners. But Mr. Clarence now, he look right past us when we says, 'Morning, Mr. Clarence' or 'Thank ya, Mr. Clarence' and he act like we ain't even there. No, sirree. I won't take a nickel."

Dosha's eyes filled with tears. "Oh, what a good heart you have," she said. "I'll be praying the good Lord repays you."

Lloyd smiled broadly. "Now that I'll take, Miz Dosha. Sure will."

Clarie gestured toward the cabin. "Come on, Lloyd. Jack's waiting. "

Dosha watched Lloyd go up the steps, then turned to Zetta.

"I'm gonna miss you special," she said.

As she threw her arms around Zetta and Isaac, tears rolled down her cheeks.

Asa and Luttrell picked up Micah and Rachel as Lloyd carried Jack down the steps and gently placed him on the pile of quilts. Asa and Zetta's brothers stepped forward to shake hands with Jack. By this time, Dosha was sobbing as she hugged Clarie.

"What you done for us means the world," she said.

Clarie patted the young woman's back. "Now, honey, I'm glad I could help. Y'all are gonna be just fine. You'll see."

Then Lloyd helped Dosha into the wagon bed and pulled two crates across the back before climbing into the wagon seat and releasing the wheel brake.

As the mules started down the path, Dosha raised up from the pallet to look back at the group watching them go.

"I'll write y'all soon as I can," she called.

Clarie took a step forward. "For crying out loud, Dosha. Stay out of sight!"

Chapter 22

Zetta clutched the baby close to her face as the little group watched Lloyd guide the wagon down the lane and turn left onto the main street in front of the company store. Then he flicked the reins across the mules' backs, and the wagon and precious cargo were out of sight.

Clarie let out a long sigh.

"I'm gonna miss them two," she said. "Dosha sure enough spoiled me with all her cooking. I know they'll get along good, but this place won't be the same without 'em."

Clarie turned toward her home. "Well, y'all want to come in for a while?"

Zetta shook her head. "No, I reckon we'd better get on back."

Loren stepped forward and pulled Micah from Asa's arms.

"You go on, Sis," he said. "Since the sun is trying to shine, Luttrell and me will take the youngins over to the school swings. We'll be along directly."

Before Zetta could protest, Loren turned a giggling Micah upside down and turned toward the schoolhouse. Luttrell followed with Rachel in his arms. The little girl smiled and waved.

Zetta watched them before turning to Asa.

"Maybe you better go along and make sure Loren don't drop our boy on his head."

Asa put his arm around Zetta's shoulders. "Good idea. But let me see you and little Isaac back first."

As they started down the path, Zetta looked toward the street once more.

"I hope they get along good over at Hindman," she said.

Asa nodded. "They will. Between Dosha's cooking and Jack's playing, it'll be like they was meant to be there. Watch your step here."

* * * * *

After Asa left for the school, Zetta took Isaac to the bedroom, changed his diaper then sat on the bed to feed him.

She stroked his head as he gulped at her breast.

"If we was home, we'd be sitting near the fireplace in that big old rocking chair whilst you filled your little belly," she said. "And any rain would sweeten the ground instead of making coal dust mud holes."

Zetta switched the baby to her other side. "Once we're home, I won't have to worry about what you and Brother and Sister are breathing outside," she said. "So you keep growing and I'll keep pulling beans outta my counting jar 'til we can leave here."

When Isaac's eyes began to close, Zetta held him to her shoulder and thumped his back. When he released a sleepy belch, she placed him in the middle of the bed and pulled pillows around him.

"You are the best little feller for sleeping," Zetta said as she buttoned her blouse. "Now I'm gonna fix dinner and ponder what all I'm gonna have to buy at the store."

As Zetta reached for her kitchen apron, she could see her family coming back from the schoolhouse. Loren still was carrying Micah upside down.

The men stomped the soot from their shoes before stepping into the kitchen. Loren flipped Micah right-side up and set him next to Rachel before turning to Luttrell.

"Did you see that smart-aleck grin Clarence give you when he passed us just now?" he asked. "You know good and well he's on his way to call on the school teacher. I swear that man aggravates the living tar out of me and I'm not the one who lost a pretty woman to him."

Luttrell turned to hang up his jacket. "I've told you before to let that be."

Zetta turned to Asa and nodded toward her brothers as a signal for him to interrupt their conversation.

"Here, Loren. Put my jacket there, too, whilst you're at it," Asa said. "I'm more concerned about Clarence still not having the hang of stopping the air donkey. Jack could stop it smooth as butter when he drove the mantrip. Clarence is still jerking our heads off."

Loren hung Asa's jacket on the nail then turned to punch Luttrell's shoulder.

"Well, I bet old Clarence is smooth as butter when he's with your girl. I swear you don't have the sense God give a goose."

Asa quickly turned to Rachel.

"Sister, reckon I ought to tell about that talking squirrel?" he said.

Talking squirrel? Zetta wondered. Oh, the story he told Sister and Brother after our awful fuss when Jack got hurt.

Rachel giggled. "Oh, Poppy! Yes. And do his little paws like this."

She curled her hands near her face and wiggled her fingers.

Asa chuckled. "That beats all. You look just like a sweet little squirrel when you do that."

Rachel smiled. "Tell it, Poppy. Tell it."

Asa sat down at the table and pulled both children onto his lap.

"I heard tell about a little squirrel going into a store that sells coal," he said.

"He run right up to the man behind the counter, stood on his hind legs and put his little paws up next to his face just like this."

Zetta smiled as she watched the children's faces as their daddy wiggled his fingers and twitched his nose.

Then Asa said in his best squirrel chatter, "You got any hickory nuts for sale?"

Micah giggled and Rachel nodded excitedly for the rest of the story.

"Well, the store owner was mighty surprised to hear a squirrel talking," Asa said. "But he got over that real fast and said, 'No. I don't have hickory nuts. I sell coal. Don't let me see you in here again.' But, the next morning that little squirrel was right back in the store and asked the man if he had any hickory nuts for sale. Now the man was mad and he said, 'I told you no yesterday and I'm telling you no today. I sell coal, not hickory nuts. And if you come in here tomorrow, I'm gonna nail your bushy tail to the floor board.'

"The store owner thought that was the end of that, but sure enough the very next morning there was the little critter again. He stood up like he done before with his little paws up by his face like this and said, 'You got any *nails*?'

" 'No, I don't have any nails,' the store owner hollered. Then that little squirrel grinned his little squirrel grin and said, 'Well then. You got any *hickory nuts*?' ' "

As Rachel and Micah giggled at their Poppy's wiggling fingers, Zetta smiled and turned to her brothers. Both were smiling, too.

* * * * *

At the noon meal, there was no more mention of Clarence. Afterward, the men played with the children while Zetta washed the dishes and put the next day's beans in her largest pan to soak. When Asa tucked Micah in for a nap and didn't come out of the bedroom, Zetta knew he had stretched out on the bed, too, next to Isaac. Gradually, Loren and Luttrell drifted to their own bedroom. Only Rachel was left in the front room, content to repeatedly fold the little quilt around her ragdoll.

Just as the afternoon light started to fade behind the mountainside trees, Zetta saw Clarie coming up the back steps.

Zetta whispered as she opened the door. "Most everybody's sleeping good."

Clarie nodded. "I can't stay," she said. "I just stopped by to tell you Lloyd's back. He said he got Dosha and Jack to the Hindman School without any problems. And he said the school grounds are real pretty and the buildings overlook a creek. He said the folks there was expecting them because of my letters and had a room all ready. He carried Jack inside and then unloaded the crates and stacked them along the far corner. He said Dosha was pulling out pillows and quilts before he got everything unloaded, and she had their place all fancy looking even before he left. That girl is a sight."

Then without comment, Clarie opened her arms to Zetta as tears rolled down both their cheeks.

* * * * *

The next morning, after Zetta saw the men off to work and had fed the children, she mixed the crust for the fruit hand pies. As she reached for her rolling pin, she saw Julia standing on the back porch, her hands on her hips and frowning.

Zetta sighed. Might as well get her visit over with, she thought.

She opened the door. "Well, good morning, Miz Julia. You here for a visit?"

"Yeah."

"Well, have you been pondering how to show better manners when you're here?"

"Yeah."

"Then you can come in."

As Julia stepped inside, she looked toward Rachel and Micah playing in the front room. Then she turned to Zetta.

"You still got that dumb game you play with rocks," she asked.

"You mean the Fox and Geese game," Zetta said. "Yes."

"Can I play?"

The child's request surprised Zetta. But before she could answer, Isaac awakened and howled for his mid-morning meal.

Zetta looked toward the bedroom then back at Julia.

"I don't have time to show you how to play now, Miz Julia," she said. "I reckon school will be letting out soon for recess. Maybe you could play with those children."

Julia gave her usual shrug. "Nobody plays with me there."

Zetta refused to feel sorry for her. As Isaac's howls increased, she opened the back door.

"If you went where the swings are and asked to push some little girl real gentle like and didn't call anybody bad names, I bet they'd play with you."

Julia huffed as she turned to go. "I bet they won't."

Zetta opened the door wider. "You'll never know if you don't ask. Just be nice."

As the child walked across the porch, Zetta noticed her thin slumped shoulders.

* * * * *

After she fed Isaac, Zetta finished the peach hand pies. As she pulled the last one from the skillet of hot grease, she saw Clarie starting toward the back steps. A jar of milk was in one hand and the egg basket in the other. Her walking stick was tucked under her arm.

Zetta smiled as she opened the door. "Why you bothering with your stick this morning?"

Clarie chuckled. "You never know when it might come in handy to beat off some deranged wild cat or a drunk miner," she said.

She handed the milk to Zetta then pulled back the basket's blue cloth. "I've just got five eggs left. I know that's not enough to do you, but I'd druther you get them than the store."

Zetta reached for her coin jar and fished out a nickel.

"I'll take all the eggs you can spare," she said. "I've been trying to stretch our food goods, but right soon I'm gonna have to give in and start buying from Roscoe. Don't know how I'm gonna do that with three little youngins to take to the store, though. I sure do miss Dosha's help. I was thinking about asking Polly if she could watch the Babies."

Clarie shook her head. "No. Polly's too much of a worrywart. I'm all the time down at the store, so I can tote back a little each day even if it's ham hocks or potatoes. I'll stop by each morning, you tell me what you need and I'll tell you about what it should cost since you'll be paying cash money."

Zetta smiled. "I declare, Clarie. I don't know what I'd do without you. But don't you get tired all the time helping people out?"

Clarie took off her coat and eased into the chair nearest the window.

"Life's hard in these hills, so we have to help each other," she said. "If I needed help, you'd find a way to be right there."

Zetta put a hand pie on a saucer and set it in front of Clarie.

"You're giving me more credit than I deserve," she said. "New people moved into Dosha and Jack's place and I haven't had the decency to greet 'em. I returned the woman's wave one time, but that was it."

Clarie nodded her thanks for the pie.

"You needn't have worried," she said. "I figured on taking you up to meet her but she didn't no more than get settled in when she got a telegram down at the camp office saying her sister was bad sick. She took their little youngin and went to tend her."

Clarie bit into the pie. "This is right good," she said. "But back to that woman. Her man's up there fending for hisself and complaining every minute. Says the only decent meals he gets are the hand pies Asa sells."

"Oh, that's too bad about her sister," Zetta said, trying not to sound relieved.

"That's probably just as well, though," Clarie said. "This way you don't have to see another woman in Dosha's kitchen. Oh, that reminds me, Dosha sent us letters. I swear I'd forget my head if it wasn't attached to my neck. Anyway, I took the liberty of checking your mailbox when I checked mine. Sure enough, she sent one to you, too."

Clarie pulled two letters from her apron pocket and handed one to Zetta.

"I'll read mine to you first," Clarie said.

She leaned toward the light of the window and began: " 'Dear Clarie, I hope this letter finds you doing good. Jack and me sure do thank you for all you done for us. You said God brings his good out of problems when we give them to him and you was right. Whilst Jack mends, he does a lot of sitting in the sun and says it sure beats working in the dark. We've got a real nice room near the students that has to stay here since they live too far away. And you ought to see the school kitchen with them pretty stoves! I'm having me a big time cooking. Tell Polly I'm praying for her and the baby. I'm sorry I won't be there to help you bring the little feller into the world. Thanks again for all you done for us. Love, Dosha and Jack Conley.' "

Clarie folded her letter. "Read yours now."

Zetta unsealed the envelope and opened the folded paper.

" 'Dear Zetta, I hope this finds you and yours fine. I miss you and your sweet babies. I'm hoping Clarie lets you know what's in her letter so you'll know we're getting along good. I wish you could visit. I'd like you to meet the two women heading up this here school. The folks around here talk about their ways being so different. But they have good hearts. They could have been leading lives of leisure back home, but their spirits was too big for that fancy world. Here they know they are helping. Well, it's time for me to get to the kitchen. Kiss your babies for me. Tell Asa and the boys hello from Jack. Love, Dosha Conley.' "

Zetta stared at the paper for a moment and then clutched the letter to her heart.

Clarie nodded. "I know that feeling, honey. One of these Sundays, you and me will have to get a wagon from Perton and go visit that sweet girl."

* * * * *

Dreary day folded into dreary day as Zetta tended her family. And each morning she counted out dollars for Clarie to buy their groceries. But while it worried her to see the dwindling amount in the money jar, she happily watched the beans in her counting jar diminish.

But the sameness of the days stopped when Perton showed up the night before payday.

Asa heard the heavy footsteps on the front porch and left the supper table even before a knock sounded. As Asa opened the door, Perton stepped inside without waiting to be invited.

"Well, I hope you're happy," Perton said.

Asa frowned. "About what?"

"I'll make the general announcement tomorrow before everybody gets paid," Perton said. "But I'm telling you now because this is what happens when we don't stand together. You didn't want a union. Well, starting in two days on the first of March, the mine runs *seven* days a week."

Asa didn't turn at Zetta's gasp.

"But we was told we'd always have Sundays off," he said.

Perton snorted. "And you believed everything they said. Now you know the real truth."

Loren stood up from the table. "Old Rusty Hinge thinks just because he owns the mine, he owns the men, too," he said. "Well, he don't own me."

Perton nodded at Loren then glared at Asa. "Now that attitude is what I like hearing," he said. "I'm talking to some people. We'll work this first Sunday all right, but things are gonna change after that. When Old Man Gray told me the news, he said we ought to be thankful we got jobs. Here they are working us worse than the mules and he wants me to kiss his feet."

Then as quickly as he came, Perton was gone. Asa went back to the table with his head lowered. As Loren started to speak, Asa raised his hand and said, "Not now. Give me time to think on this."

Suddenly Zetta remembered her dream of the snakes crawling out of the muddy water and endangering her home. Another dream was coming true.

* * * * *

When Clarie arrived the next morning, Zetta was eager to talk about the extended work week. The older woman shook her head.

"Mr. Golden musta been planning that all along when he fired Preacher Howard. Perton's gonna get the men worked up about this, so I figure there'll be a strike before long."

Zetta brightened. "A strike? Then we can go home sooner."

Clarie nodded. "Yep, if it comes to that," she said. "But I sure pity the ones who ain't got any place but here. If there's a strike, the store won't let 'em get food. And the company will turn 'em out of their houses. We've always had plenty to pray about. Now we got even more."

* * * * *

When the men arrived home that evening, they were somber as they washed at the back porch bench. Zetta studied their faces and decided Asa's and Luttrell's held only concern. Loren's held anger.

As her brothers wordlessly handed wrinkled dollar bills to Zetta for their February board and room, she merely nodded. But as Asa tossed the dimes and nickels from that day's sale of the hand pies onto the table, Zetta took a deep breath.

"How'd it go when Perton said the mine's gonna run seven days?" she asked quietly.

Asa pulled a long breath into his lungs then huffed it out.

"The men was pretty mad," he said. "Some of them was yelling for a strike right now."

Loren turned from hanging up his jacket.

"Yeah, and you didn't help matters much by saying a strike won't fix anything," he said. "How else we gonna get old Rusty Hinge to listen? Talk don't amount to a hill of beans!"

"Is there gonna be a strike?" Zetta asked, trying to keep hope out of her voice.

Asa shook his head. "Not just yet," he said. "Perton wants time to meet with the shift bosses over at Benham and Lynch. I'm counting on that taking a while."

He gestured toward the food waiting on the stove.

"But right now, I'm thinking about my belly."

Zetta sighed as she turned to dish up the meal.

* * * * *

Sleep didn't come easily for Zetta that night, but at least she was spared more bad dreams. She changed and fed Isaac the next morning before the others were awake then hurried into the kitchen. She dumped another bean into her hand and smiled as she held the counting jar toward the lamp on the table.

Well, look at that. The jar's just one-third full now, she thought.

As Zetta marveled at the few beans, Asa suddenly was beside her. Zetta thrust the jar behind her back.

He grabbed her around the waist and swung her in a circle.

"Today's the first day of March," he said. "Just one more payday and then we're going home! I've been marking off the days on a dynamite crate just like you been doing with your bean jar."

Zetta gasped. "Turn me loose," she said. "How'd you know about that?"

Asa chucked. "I saw the jar when it was my turn to put the carbide in our hat lanterns," he said. "You didn't pick a good enough hiding spot."

Then he leaned close to her. "It's about time you wore that pretty sweater I got you for Christmas. By my figuring we got two things to celebrate. Us getting closer to home and the woman birthing time almost up for you. I'm been missing you something awful."

Zetta's face flushed. "Hush before the boys hear you," she whispered. "Just a couple more days I reckon on the woman thing. And I'll wear the sweater for you then."

Asa whirled her around the kitchen once more and kissed her soundly.

CHAPTER 23

Asa climbed onto the mule and waved a cheery goodbye as Zetta stood near the pear trees, the bare branches moaning as they rubbed against each other. She turned toward the house, knowing the children were waiting for her. But before she could climb the steps, the mule came back through the gate—without its rider. Zetta touched the saddle, which was still warm. She ran her hand across the leather then realized her hands were stained with blood.

A strangling sob tore from Zetta's throat as she lurched upright in bed. Her cries of "No! No!" awakened Asa. Only when she felt his hand on her shoulder did she open her eyes. Mindful of the baby between them, she gripped his arm in the darkness.

"The mule came back alone," she sobbed. "And there was blood on the saddle."

"There's no mule here, honey," Asa said as he leaned to stroke her cheek. "It was just one of them old bad dreams of yours. Now, let me hold little Isaac and you scoot up close to me. Everything is okay. Everybody's safe. You just go on back to sleep."

Zetta gave a jagged sigh as she gently placed the baby on her husband's chest. Asa curled his left arm over the child and then spread his right one to give her room to snuggle against him. Within moments, he was asleep again.

Zetta stared into the night, listening to Asa's steady breathing and remembering the bloody saddle.

"Lord Jesus, please help me," she whispered. "Oh, Lord. Please help. Nobody else will."

* * * * *

For the next two days Zetta continued to be troubled by the dream as she watched Asa and her brothers move toward Sunday. She wondered if they were dreading being deep in the mine and wouldn't see the sun that day either. Or if they were pondering a strike. But all three men became quieter. Asa wasn't telling jokes, and Loren wore a constant frown. But at least he wasn't making smart aleck remarks to Luttrell about losing the pretty school teacher.

Even Saturday morning, after a hurried breakfast, the three men toted water from the community pump without comment. They dumped pail after pail into the wash kettles in the backyard before Asa lit a fire under one. But this time there was no banter between them.

Zetta studied their set jaws, feeling the heaviness.

Is every house in the camp like this? she wondered. I wish they'd say something. But Asa won't talk even about my bad dreams, so why do I think he's gonna tell me what's happening in the mine?

After the men left for work that morning, Zetta pushed the clothes into the boiling water with the wash paddle and watched the sky, wondering how soon the threatening clouds would release cold rain.

I hope the storm holds off for a while. I'm tired of all this mud, she thought.

She glanced toward the lane leading to Clarie's house. But there was no sign of her friend. She wanted to talk to her and have her mind filled with comforting thoughts. And she wanted to tell Clarie her female birthing time was almost finished. But Clarie wasn't around and the only sound Zetta heard was the rumble from the mine tipple. She sighed.

I guess everybody is staying inside today because of this damp-ish weather.

Suddenly she realized she'd welcome even a visit from Julia.

* * * * *

After Zetta rinsed and wrung out the clothes, she carried them into the kitchen to hang them around the stove. Inside, she smiled at the noise from the front room where Micah stacked his blocks and then knocked them over.

"I'm back now," she called.

Rachel came into the kitchen and sat at the table, still clutching her ragdoll. Zetta smiled, happy for the company.

"Know what we can look forward to when we get home, Sister?" she said. "The dogwood trees blooming soon after. Do you remember them from last year?"

The little girl stared blankly at her mother.

"Oh, honey, you're gonna love seeing those white blossoms against the brown mountainside before the rest of the trees show their leaves."

Rachel smoothed the doll's dress as her mother shook out another shirt.

"When I was little, my mama told me that the dogwood tree used to be great big—as big as the chestnut trees alongside our lane at home," Zetta said. "And because the tree was so big and strong, the old time soldiers took it to make the cross Jesus died on. Well, the dogwood tree felt real bad the Savior of the world was having to die on its wood, and Jesus felt its sadness. Then he said never again would dogwood trees grow strong enough to be used in such a way. Instead their trunks would be slender and twisted, and on their small branches would be wide blossoms shaped like a cross. And the middle of the flower would look like the crown of thorns the soldiers thrust on his head. So to this day, when we see the dogwoods, we're to remember Jesus dying for us."

Rachel hugged her rag doll. "I like that story, Mama."

"And I liked telling it, honey," Zetta said as she hung the last of the clothes beside the stove. "Now what do you say we make a cobbler for your daddy before Baby Isaac wakes up? I've got one jar of blackberries left. That'll be a special treat before our baths tonight."

* * * * *

At supper, the men ate the beans and cornbread and fried cabbage in silence. But when Zetta set the cobbler on the table, Asa smiled.

"Now that's a fine end to a good supper," he said as he reached for the serving spoon.

Loren watched Asa scoop a large portion onto his plate.

"Don't be so hoggish with that," he said.

Asa pushed the pan toward him. "There's plenty left," he said. "I'm just fixing to build up my strength for toting more water up the hill for tonight's baths."

Loren's frown deepened as he plunged the spoon through the crust.

"I don't know why we're even bothering with baths tonight," he said. "No reason to get all slicked up since we're just going to work and get all dirty again tomorrow."

Luttrell patted his brother on the shoulder as he reached for the cobbler.

"Think of it this way," he said. "We're getting rid of last week's grime before having to start adding more layers."

* * * * *

Despite the warm bath, Zetta couldn't get comfortable once they went to bed. She lay in the moonlight, listening to her family's breathing as she prayed silently.

"Lord, I'm all out of kilter thinking about that awful dream and the mine running Sundays now. And I worry about the men worrying about a strike. About the only good thing that happened yesterday was them talking at supper again. Help these next four weeks go fast."

Finally, she fell into a fitful sleep.

The next morning, Zetta was awake before the whistle blew. After using the chamber pot, she smiled at the whiteness of the cloth as she tilted it toward the pale morning light seeping through the sooty window.

Well, my female birthing time is totally up, she thought.

She looked toward her still sleeping husband.

I hope he wakes up before the boys do, so I can tell him.

In the kitchen, Zetta lit the table lantern then pulled the counting jar from the dish shelf. Before opening the lid, she shook the beans against the glass.

"By my reckoning there's only twenty-eight of you left in there," she whispered. "And I can't wait 'til every one of you is gone."

She opened the jar and smiled as another bean rolled onto her palm. "Now there's just twenty-seven of you left. Just twenty-seven more breakfasts to fix 'til we're home."

As she put the jar back on the shelf, she heard her brothers' corn shuck mattress rustle.

Loren was the first one into the kitchen, but he merely nodded to Zetta as he opened the door to go up the lane to the outhouse. Luttrell and Asa soon followed. When they returned, they ate in silence as Zetta filled their dinner buckets. But as they started to leave for the mine, Zetta grabbed her shawl.

"Asa, let me walk with you whilst the youngins are still asleep," she said.

Asa held his hand out. Together they walked down the back porch steps and around a mud puddle. Zetta glanced toward her brothers who were farther ahead then leaned closer to her husband.

"I just wanted to tell you my woman's birthing time is up as of this morning," she whispered.

Asa grinned and grabbed her by the shoulders. Then he kissed her soundly.

Zetta pulled away, horrified.

"Asa, not here in public," she said. "People will wonder what ails you."

He pulled her even closer and kissed her again.

"Anybody watching will know here's a man who loves his woman," he said. Then he whispered, "And a man who can't get this day over fast enough."

Zetta blushed as Asa kissed her once more and then ran to catch up with her brothers.

She returned to the kitchen and found Rachel and Micah awake and sitting in their chairs. As she spooned gravy over their biscuits, she smiled softly as she thought about being with Asa that night.

* * * * *

When Isaac awakened, Zetta changed his diaper. As she picked him up to feed him, a flash of red caused her to turn toward the window. A cardinal landed on the porch banister, but the noise from the tipple drowned out his song.

"Sister, come look!" Zetta called "Bring Brother here and see this little red bird telling us spring's finally coming."

As both children clamored to the window and pressed against the glass, Zetta unbuttoned her dress and sat on the bed to feed Isaac.

"He's got his red feathers all shiny so's he can court him a mommy bird," she told the children. "Maybe he's thinking about building a nest in that little tree your poppy set on the front porch. You can't hear him plain right now but if we was home you could hear him calling *ta-peter, ta-peter* real sweet like. Now that the red birds are back, the other birds will show up, too. When we get home, I'm even gonna be happy to hear the blue jays jabbering and them old crows cawing and scolding each other."

Rachel turned away from the window and pointed outside.

"Mama, Uncle's running."

"What?"

Rachel gestured toward the tipple again. "Uncle's running."

Still holding the baby as he gulped milk, Zetta stood up to look. On the path well below the house, Loren was running toward a man carrying a miner's hat and a dinner bucket. As Loren caught up with him, he grabbed his arm so quickly the man's own hat fell off.

"Oh, no!" Zetta gasped as she recognized Perton and remembered the morning he had delivered bad news to Dosha.

Then she saw Loren grab the dinner bucket and hat with one hand and gesture beyond the house with the other.

"Oh, please, Lord," she said as she pulled Isaac away from her and put him in the center of the bed. The baby howled at the interruption of his meal as Zetta buttoned her dress with trembling hands.

"Sister, you mind the baby," she called over her shoulder as she rushed into the front room. Just then Loren burst through the door. He dropped the hat and dinner bucket.

"Asa's hurt bad," he said.

Zetta slapped both hands to her chest and took a jagged breath.

Loren's words rushed out. "We got him at the train station. Taking him to Lexington. Doc here can't do nothing. Hurry. You ain't got much time to see him before we go. Perton went after Clarie for the youngins."

Zetta followed Loren as he rushed out of the room. On the porch she looked back at the children. Through the bedroom window she could see Rachel bouncing her hands against the bed as she tried to quiet a still howling Isaac. Micah stood with his face against the glass, his eyes wide with fright. Then Zetta lunged for Loren's arm as they hurried toward her injured husband.

* * * * *

Both Loren and Zetta were out of breath when they arrived at the train station. Luttrell stood with his hand on Asa's shoulder as he lay on a baggage wagon, one arm across his eyes and his leg tightly wrapped by blood-soaked material.

Zetta gasped and gripped Loren's arm all the harder. Then she took a deep breath and leaned over Asa, her back to his leg.

"Oh, honey," she whispered as she touched his ashen face.

He took his arm away from his eyes and blinked several times as he looked her way. When he spoke, his words came slowly.

"I'm not kilt," he said. "But I reckon I'll be a one-legged man."

Zetta brushed the damp hair away from his sweaty forehead.

"The doctors in Lexington are real good, so don't worry about that," she said. "You just get well."

He closed his eyes. "I should've listened to you about going home," he murmured.

Zetta wanted to scream "Yes!" Instead she merely stroked his clammy cheek, wishing she had grabbed her shawl to wrap around him.

In that moment, the station master appeared with a folded blanket and shook it out. Zetta reached for one end and helped him spread it over Asa. Before she could express her thanks, a train whistle sounded from down the track.

"Right on time," the station master said. He turned to Loren. "Since y'all are the only ones outbound, we'll get it out of here right quick."

Zetta bent over Asa again. "The train's coming," she said and gently kissed his pale lips.

Asa closed his eyes. Then he opened them again as though startled.

"Take...take care of...our babies," he stammered.

Zetta nodded, not trusting herself to speak. As the train noisily pulled in, the station master opened the baggage car and spread another blanket on the floor. Then he helped Loren and Luttrell gently lift Asa into the car. As they climbed in, he ran toward the engineer shouting, "Leave now. Everybody's loaded."

Zetta stretched her hand toward Asa, but his eyes were closed.

As steam began to build within the engine, the station master ran back to the baggage car and tugged on the heavy door. Before he could close it, Loren stood up and yelled to Zetta.

"I'll be back tomorrow to help you pack up the house," he shouted.

Help me pack up the house? Zetta thought as she watched the train chuff away from the station. Then she remembered the camp rule of having to vacate within two days.

Oh, Father God. I didn't want to leave like this!

She wanted to scream toward heaven as she turned away from the tracks. Then Perton stepped toward her.

"Miz Zetta, Clarie is with your youngins. I'll walk you back. I'm right sorry."

Zetta swallowed. "How'd it happen?"

"Got pitched off when the mantrip stopped. It run over his leg," he said.

Zetta gasped. Clarence. Clarence did this.

* * * * *

Perton left as soon as Zetta stepped numbly through the front door. Clarie stood near the kitchen table, holding a whimpering Isaac in the crook of one arm while she handed biscuits to Rachel and Micah. But as soon as they saw their mother, they scurried from their chairs and clutched her legs. Tears ran down Zetta's face as she hugged them.

Clarie moved to her side and put her free arm around the young woman's shoulders.

"Perton told me how bad it is," she said. "I've been praying ever since."

She steered Zetta to a chair, gently handed Isaac to her and then pulled a handkerchief from her sleeve.

"Here. Go ahead and have a good cry," she said. "This is bad all around. But this little feller needs to eat. I tried fixing him a sugar tit, but he wouldn't take it."

She turned to Rachel and Micah who were leaning against Zetta. "Your mommy's here now, so you gotta eat."

She gestured toward a burlap bag near the door. "And after you eat real good, I'll let you see the toys I brung from my house."

Both children craned to look toward the bag then hurried back to the table.

Clarie turned to the stove and brought a filled cup back to Zetta.

"Drink this," she said. "It'll make your milk come down good. Soon as that little feller gets his belly full, you and me will start packing."

Zetta swiped at her nose and nodded. "You're right. Sooner I get home, the sooner I can tend Asa when he gets out of the hospital."

As she unbuttoned her dress, Zetta looked at Clarie.

"My birthing time was up this morning," she whispered. "We was gonna be together tonight."

As tears flowed down Zetta's cheeks, Clarie patted her shoulder then began to unstack the corner crates.

* * * * *

As the women wrapped the dishes, heavy rain began to fall. Zetta turned toward the kitchen window to check the widening puddles in the yard. But instead, she saw Loren on the porch, cold rain dripping from his hair as he stood with downcast eyes.

She jerked open the door.

"What you doing back so soon?" she asked, fear rising in her throat.

As Loren lifted his head, Zetta fought a scream.

"No! I will not let you tell me anything bad."

Loren stepped into the kitchen and held out his hands.

"Oh, Sis. He's gone," he said.

The room seemed to tip for Zetta. But she threw herself at her brother and hit his chest with her fist.

"No! Don't you tell me that!"

Loren hugged her, pinning her arms to her sides as Clarie patted Zetta's back.

"Oh, honey," Clarie murmured.

Loren's words came slowly. "We didn't get even to Jackson before he started shivering real bad," he said. "When we put our jackets over him, he tried to say something but his words were all slurred. Then he was gone."

Loren tightened his arms around Zetta and continued.

"When we got to the Jackson station, we put him on the next train coming this way after that ticket agent called in a doctor. The doc said Asa lost too much blood…." Loren's voice trailed off.

Then he gently raised Zetta's face to his.

"We tried, Sis. Me and Luttrell tried our best."

Zetta pulled away from Loren and reached for the wall.

"My dreams told me something bad was coming, but Asa wouldn't listen," she wailed. "He wouldn't listen."

Clarie eased her into a chair. There Zetta rocked back and forth, moaning.

Suddenly she turned to her brother.

"I gotta know," she said. "Did he swallow what was in that death tin y'all carry? Tell me the truth."

Loren shook his head. "No, Sis. He didn't swallow a thing."

Zetta hugged her arms then, fighting sobs. But sounds like a wounded animal rolled out, causing Rachel and Micah to run to her.

As she hugged the children, her voice was filled with terror.

"Why didn't God help us? Asa can't be dead. We need him!"

Clarie leaned down and hugged the three of them until Zetta's sobs settled into breathless gasps.

Then Clarie stood up. "Where is he?" she asked Loren.

Loren cleared his throat. "At the hospital death house for the time being," he said. "Luttrell's at the camp office sending a telegram to Paw to meet the last train into Salyersville tonight. Asa will be on it. Luttrell, too. I'll stay here and take Sis and the youngins home in the morning after we pack up."

Zetta turned to her brother.

"No. I'll not stay in this house another minute without Asa," she said. "We're going home with him tonight."

Loren ran his hand through his still wet hair. "But, Sis, the rules say we have to get everything packed up."

Clarie shook her head. "No. Zetta's right," she said. "Y'all need to leave tonight. Me and some others will finish packing and send everything on tomorrow's train."

Loren looked at his sister. "Well, you'd probably have the Big Eye anyway and not sleep," he said. "Sure, we'll all go tonight."

At that moment, the back door opened and a slump-shouldered

Luttrell stepped into the kitchen followed by Perton.

Luttrell knelt before Zetta and wordlessly wrapped his arms around her and the children.

Perton cleared his throat. "Clarie, it's time for your camphor and whiskey."

Zetta pulled away from Luttrell and turned to Clarie.

The older woman nodded as she looked into Zetta's questioning eyes.

"Honey, my concoction will keep his skin from turning dark. I'll get Ruthie to help me. We've done this together before."

Then she faced Loren. "You bring down his Sunday shirt and pants in a little while."

As Clarie closed the door behind her, Loren sorrowfully turned to his sister.

"Well, I reckon it was a good thing we took our baths last night after all."

CHAPTER 24

With Rachel and Micah huddled at her side, Zetta pulled baby Isaac even closer as Clarie left. Then determined not to sob with Perton in the room, she took deep breaths and imagined the old woman stepping into the rain, her walking stick making little splashes in the dirty puddles.

An awkward silence filled the kitchen with Clarie's absence. Finally Perton cleared his throat again and turned to Zetta.

"I'll see to getting your man's coffin on the train tonight and then be back in the morning to see you and the youngins off."

His name is Asa. Say his name, Zetta thought. But she turned to Loren.

He answered Perton for her.

"No, we're all going tonight," he said.

Loren then turned to his brother, who still squatted beside Zetta.

"I didn't have a chance to tell you yet," he said. "But Sis says we're all going home with Asa. Clarie will tend to the packing and send everything tomorrow."

Luttrell's gentle expression let Zetta know he agreed with her decision. Then Perton cleared his throat once more.

"Well, all right," he said. "Remember that normally y'all wouldn't get paid for leaving before the month is up. But under the circumstances, I reckon Mr. Gray will okay me sending the little that's due you come payday."

As he paused, it struck Zetta he was waiting for praise for his supposed generosity. She leaned over the baby, remembering Asa's pale lips as she kissed him goodbye.

When no one commented, Perton opened the door, then turned back.

"I'm sorry, Miz Zetta," he said. "I hope you and the youngins get along good. But it's things like this that make it necessary to get a union in here. If the mine owners cared about safety the way they care about lining their pockets…."

Luttrell stood up. "Perton, union talk can wait for another day—and another family."

Then he thrust his hand deep into his pocket and pulled out two small tins.

"Before you go, take these with you," he said.

Loren glanced at the tins and pulled his own from his pocket.

"Yeah," Loren said. "We ain't never gonna need these again."

Perton merely closed his hand over the tins and went out the door.

Luttrell had two death tins, Zetta thought. Why'd he have two? Oh, the second one was Asa's. Oh, Asa.

Luttrell put his hand on Zetta's shoulder.

"If we're gonna make that last train tonight, we need to get a move on. Tell me where your satchel is so I can pack the clothes for you and the youngins."

Clothes for me and the youngins? Oh, that's right. Asa's clothes will be packed later. Lord, I can't do this. Zetta put her hand to her forehead as she wondered why her mind was working so slowly when everything else was moving so quickly.

* * * * *

Still clutching a sleeping Isaac and with Rachel and Micah at her side, Zetta sat on her bed and numbly watched Luttrell shove clothes into the satchel.

"You're packing for me," she said. "And earlier Clarie fixed a basket with this morning's biscuits and fried fatback for the train. I'm just sitting here, not doing a thing for nobody."

Luttrell looked up. "You always been doing for us. It's only right we do for you now."

Just then, Loren entered the room.

"Sis, Clarie said for me to bring Asa's Sunday shirt and pants," he said.

Zetta swiped at her eyes.

"They're hanging on the nail behind the door," she said.

Loren grabbed the items and hastily rolled both before shoving them under his jacket.

"I'll be back right quick," he said and hurried out of the room.

Luttrell pulled the final pieces of clothing from the drawer. On top of the stack was the red sweater Asa had given Zetta for Christmas.

I never did wear that for him, Zetta thought as tears started down her cheeks again.

Then Luttrell held out an envelope stuffed with money.

"This was in the drawer corner," he said.

Zetta groaned. "That's Asa's pay these months," she said. "He was working for the four hundred dollars we owe on the farm. Whatever amount is there cost his life."

As Luttrell shoved the envelope deep into the satchel, Rachel turned to her mother.

"What's he doing with our clothes, Mama?"

Zetta pushed down a strangling sob. "We're going home, Baby."

Rachel looked at Luttrell and then back at Zetta.

"Is Poppy going too?"

Zetta opened her mouth to answer but nothing came out.

Luttrell knelt before the little girl and took her soft hands into his rough ones.

"Your Poppy can't be with us like he was before," he said. "But he still loves you and your little brothers."

Zetta heard the back door open. For one lopsided moment, she thought Asa was home.

Then Loren stepped into the bedroom. "I give the things to Clarie," he said. "She'll meet us at the train station in a little while to say goodbye."

Zetta rubbed her forehead again.

"Did you see Asa?" she managed.

Loren shook his head. "Nah. Clarie met me at the door and took the clothes," he said.

He shifted his weight awkwardly.

"Perton showed up then, too, and had me pick out a tombstone from the back room," he managed. "That's the least thing I wanted to do. But I saw one saying something about a sweet face, and it reminded me of the first night here when you said that to Asa."

Zetta closed her eyes. *Now I'll miss his sweet face for the rest of my life.*

* * * * *

Loren and Luttrell quickly gathered their own clothes and shoved them into another satchel while Zetta wordlessly bundled Rachel and Micah into their coats in the kitchen. Isaac, still asleep, lay within the folds of a quilt on the table. As Zetta picked him up, she looked at the stove and thought of all the meals she had cooked since she had arrived.

Suddenly she took a deep breath and gently placed Isaac back on the table. Then she stepped to the dish shelf and pulled the counting jar from behind the stack of plates.

Every morning I pulled another bean out and was happy we was one more day closer to home, she thought.

She unscrewed the lid and poured the contents onto her palm, ignoring the few beans that fell onto the floor. Then she shoved the remaining ones back into the jar and jerked open the back door. With the rain falling on her dark hair, she leaned over the porch rail and tipped the jar toward a mud puddle. She watched the beans plop into the sooty water before stepping back inside the kitchen where her brothers waited. Luttrell held Rachel in one arm and clutched a satchel and the basket of food in the other. Loren had the second satchel and held Micah—right side up this time.

"I'm ready," was all Zetta said as she put the empty jar on the table and picked up Isaac.

* * * * *

At the station, Perton and Clarie stood under the roof overhang. As Clarie greeted her, Zetta realized the woman had been standing in front of a long plain box. A coffin. *Asa's* coffin. Zetta knees weakened, and she gripped Luttrell's arm.

As he whispered, "I'm right here, Sis," Clarie reached for the baby and gestured for them to move closer to the station and out of the rain.

But Zetta continued to stare at the wooden box.

"Where'd you get a coffin?" she whispered.

"The back room at our little hospital has a stack of 'em," Clarie said sadly.

Then as though she wanted to change the subject, she said, "Polly wanted to come to see you off, but she's feeling poorly. I took her some tea and told her to stay in bed. But she sure was sorry to hear about Asa. She cried and took on so, I was sorry Perton told her."

Then Clarie said, "Speaking of Perton, him and Lloyd brung Asa down to the station after me and Ruthie got him dressed."

Zetta turned to see Ruthie's tall son standing near the coffin. He looked at her sorrowfully and shook his head. As Zetta moved to touch the top of the wooden box, Perton fumbled for something in his pocket and held out slips of paper to her.

"Mr. Gray asked me to buy your tickets home on behalf of the Golden Gate Coal Camp and said to express his condolences."

Then Perton's face hardened. "There. I said it just like he said to. But all his fancy words ain't worth a hill of beans to us working coal. And one of these days, he's gonna find that out."

When Zetta merely looked at the tickets in Perton's outstretched hand, Loren took them and shoved them into his jacket.

Clarie moved toward Luttrell, reached into her apron pocket and pulled out a small bottle. Even though Clarie's voice was low, Zetta could hear her words.

"This here is camphor and whiskey me and Ruthie put on the white rags over Asa's hands and face," Clarie said. "Take those off when you get him home. The good color will last through the day, but put more of this on the rags and cover the skin each night 'til the funeral."

Zetta saw Luttrell nod as he put the bottle into his jacket pocket.

As Clarie turned to speak to Zetta, Julia ran around the corner and onto the station platform. The little girl stopped in front of the coffin and studied it for a moment. Then she ran to Zetta and threw herself against the young mother so hard that Zetta put her hand out to steady herself. But just as quickly as Julia had arrived, she turned and ran back the way she had come.

Clarie faced Zetta. "If I hadn't seen that with my own eyes, I never would have believed it," she said. "I've never seen that child hug anybody in all my life. Not even her own mother or daddy. That girl took a shine to you."

Zetta put her hand on the coffin. I don't care, she thought.

* * * * *

When the train arrived, Lloyd, Perton and her brothers gently loaded Asa's coffin into the baggage car. Zetta turned away, trying not to remember saying goodbye to him just that morning. Clarie, still holding Isaac, took the young mother by the elbow.

"Come on, honey," she said. "I'll help y'all get settled."

Inside the train, Clarie directed them toward seats facing each other as she unwrapped the sleeping baby and kissed his forehead before handing him to Zetta. She touched Rachel's and Micah's cheeks then turned to their mother.

"I'm gonna keep praying, honey," she said. "The good Lord will get you through this."

Zetta shook her head as tears began to flood her cheeks. "Prayers weren't much help before. Asa's gone."

Clarie hugged her tightly. "Oh, honey. I remember those dreams. I truly do. But keep talking to the Lord."

Zetta didn't let go until Loren arrived and stowed the satchels and food under the seats.

"Luttrell's staying with Asa, so I'm sitting with you and the youngins," Loren said.

He held out his hand to Clarie. "We appreciate all your help."

She merely glanced at his hand as she threw her arms around him.

"Loren Davis, you take care of my girl here. And take care of yourself, too."

Then Clarie was gone. Zetta didn't watch her go as she directed Rachel and Micah to seats near the window before wearily easing herself down and rearranging the quilt around Isaac.

Loren dropped into the seat across from her. As the train began to pull away from the station, Zetta looked at Rachel and Micah.

"You poor little things must be starved," she said. "Here, Loren. Hold Isaac whilst I get these youngins something to eat."

214

Loren held the baby awkwardly as Zetta gave the children biscuits from the basket. She watched them eat for a moment, then reached for Isaac.

"Loren, this morning Perton told me only that Asa got pitched off the mantrip," she said slowly. "What all happened?"

Loren leaned back for moment. When he faced her, his eyes were angry.

"That fool Clarence jerked the handles on the air donkey extra hard when he tried to stop at the coal face," he said. "It threw Asa off and run over his leg."

Then Loren leaned forward. "You don't need to hear this, Sis," he said. "It ain't gonna help Asa or you one bit now."

Zetta shook her head. "I have to know no matter what you got to say."

Loren huffed. "Okay, but it was bad."

He glanced at Rachel and Micah biting into the biscuits then lowered his voice. "Us that seen what happened, jumped off and was hollering for Clarence to stop whilst we was trying to pull Asa free. When Clarence saw what he done, he got rattled. Then right stupid like, he reversed the controls and run over Asa's leg again."

Loren grimaced and paused, but Zetta said quietly, "Go on."

Loren took his sister's hand into his. "Asa was groaning something awful," he said. "When Clarence realized what he done, he took off running. Some of the men went after him."

Loren's voice was harsh. "I hope they beat the living daylights out of him."

Zetta shook her head and motioned toward the children.

Loren nodded. "Anyway, what with Clarence gone, there wasn't nobody to drive the mantrip out of the mine. Lloyd, that big colored man, ripped off his own shirt and tied it around Asa's bleeding leg. Then he run to a nearby handcar and pulled it over to the track. Then him and Perton helped me and Luttrell put Asa on the handcar real gentle like. With two of us on each side, we started pumping those handles for all we was worth to get him out of the mine."

Loren paused then said, "I ain't never gonna forget Lloyd saying, 'You stay awake Mr. Asa. You stay awake. We's getting you to the doctor soon's we can.'"

Loren ran his hand through his hair. "That's it, Sis. You know the sorry rest of it."

Zetta pulled her hand away from Loren's and clutched Isaac tighter.

"This is the worse thing that ever was," she whispered.

Loren rubbed the scar on his chin. "You know Asa and me didn't always see eye to eye," he said. "But he was a good man."

Then Loren pulled Micah onto his lap and moved to sit next to Zetta. As she leaned against her brother's shoulder, she felt his stifled sobs.

* * * * *

The rain followed them to the Salyersville station. Through the train window, Zetta could see Paw Davis standing in front of the mules at the wagon.

Loren led the way out of their seats. As Zetta stepped onto the platform, Paw was there to greet them. He patted Rachel and Micah on their heads, then turned to his daughter.

"I was afraid of something like this," he said. "But Asa was bound and determined to work coal. It's a wonder I'm not collecting more than one body."

Zetta forced herself only to say, "Want to see your new grandson?"

Paw shook his head. "Keep him covered up what with this rain. I'll see him at the house. Becky and me figured it's best to have the funeral at our place since yours has been closed up these months."

Loren glanced around the station. "Didn't nobody come with you?"

Paw shook his head. "Didn't want 'em," he said. "Jim Reed was close to begging to come, but I told him no. I just wish we didn't have to pass his place to get to ours. Knowing him, he'll be standing there waiting for us."

Then Paw asked, "Where's Luttrell?"

Loren gestured toward the baggage car. "Down there with Asa," he said.

"Well, standing here ain't gonna get this done," Paw said. And he started toward the back of the train.

* * * * *

When the three men had loaded the coffin into the wagon, Paw gestured for his sons to get in before handing the children and satchels up to them.

"I got quilts in that far corner to put over the youngins heads," he said as he helped Zetta climb into the wagon seat. Then he walked in front of the two mules and patted their noses before getting into his own spot.

As Paw picked up the reins and released the wagon brake, Zetta turned to check on Rachel and Micah. The little boy sat on the wagon floor, huddled under the quilt near his uncles who sat on top of the coffin, their eyes downcast. But Rachel leaned against the box, her head uncovered as she patted the wood.

That child knows her Poppy is in there, Zetta thought. She pushed down threatening sobs.

"Luttrell, honey, get that child covered up," she said.

When Rachel was under the quilt again, Isaac awakened.

As he started to cry, Zetta jiggled him in her arms.

"You gotta wait a while," she whispered. "I can't feed you in this rain."

By the time they turned onto the lane leading to the Davis house, Isaac was howling.

Then through the darkness, Zetta saw Jim Reed's house ahead. Lantern light shone from every window. And just as her father had predicted, Jim waited by the road. As the wagon drew closer, Jim pulled off his hat and stood bareheaded in the rain.

Zetta saw her father nod as though to continue past, but suddenly Jim stepped in front of the wagon and raised his hand. As Paw reined in the mules, Jim's wife, Sally, ran to the wagon.

"Oh, Zetta. We're so sorry this happened," she said.

Jim joined her and choked out, "Asa was the finest man I've ever met."

He turned to Zetta's father. "Mr. Davis, sir, I'd be much obliged if you wouldn't mind me attending the funeral."

Her father muttered something in reply, but Zetta didn't hear it over Isaac's howls. Sally reached up and pulled the quilt bundle from Zetta.

"Let me have that baby," she said. "You and the youngins come into the house right now. I've got supper and warm beds waiting for you."

She turned to Paw. "Mr. Davis, you and the boys take Asa on to your house," she said. "You can come for Zetta and the youngins in the morning."

Zetta started to refuse, wanting to stay with Asa. But then she thought about having to face all the people who undoubtedly were waiting with her stepmother. She looked at the well-lit house again and nodded at its beckoning.

Chapter 25

Before her father could stop her, Zetta stepped down from the wagon seat and reached for Rachel and Micah as Luttrell handed them down along with her satchel. The three of them hurried after Sally as she carried the still howling baby into the welcoming cabin.

"Take off your coat," Sally said as she unwrapped Isaac from the quilt and handed him to Zetta. She gestured toward a chair at the table.

"You set right there and feed this baby whilst I feed your other sweet youngins."

Zetta glanced toward the door.

"Don't be looking for Jim and the boys," Sally said. "They're staying in the barn tonight. And our girls are already upstairs asleep in the loft. You go ahead and feed that child."

Zetta opened her dress and drew Isaac to her. His howling ceased.

As Sally pulled the coats from the children, she saw that Rachel's rag doll was soaked.

She gently reached for the toy. "Let's put your dolly here by the fire to get warm."

After she placed the wet coats, quilt and doll in front of the fireplace, Sally washed Rachel's and Micah's hands and spooned chicken and dumplings into bowls for them.

She turned to Zetta. "Since your paw don't talk to Jim, we didn't hear what you had," she said. "I don't know if you'd got a boy or a girl."

Zetta looked up from stroking the baby's head as he nursed.

"This here is Isaac," she said. "He's a fine little boy."

Sally sighed. "It's a shame he won't remember his good daddy."

She reached for another bowl. "Our oldest boy was working at the train station when Luttrell's telegram came in. Fact is, he's the one that delivered the awful message to your paw. That's how we heard about Asa as quick as we did."

Zetta sighed. "I'm sorry Paw's still holding a grudge."

Sally nodded as she placed chicken and dumplings in front of her guest.

"Men folk can get set in their ways, all right."

* * * * *

The baby fell into exhausted sleep as soon as his stomach was full. Sally placed him in the waiting cradle before changing Rachel and Micah into their night clothes and lifting them into the big bed by the fireplace.

"Don't you worry," she said. "Your mommy will be right next to you soon as she eats."

Zetta had no appetite. But to keep from insulting Sally, she choked down a few bites before she joined the children. As she reached into the satchel for her nightgown, tears ran down her cheeks. Sally put her hand on Zetta's back.

"I don't know how to best help you," she said. "I keep thinking what if it was my Jim that was dead. I don't know why a good man like Asa was taken when there's plenty others I'd druther we was burying."

Zetta pulled the nightgown to her face to keep from replying.

Sally patted her back again. "I'll leave off washing the dishes 'til morning and join the girls upstairs," she said. "You get some sleep. Holler if you need me."

Zetta swiped at her tears as Sally turned down the lanterns and climbed the loft ladder. In the glow from the fireplace, Zetta looked at Rachel and Micah. They already were asleep. As she took off her damp clothes and pulled the nightgown over her head, she thought of Asa's hearty kiss that morning on his way to the mine.

"Oh, Asa. I didn't know that was the last time," she whispered. "I thought we was gonna be together tonight and then talk about coming home to our farm in just a while."

She swiped at more tears as she eased next to the children. She longed to lose herself in sleep, but knew sleep wouldn't come. As she stared at the hand-hewn ceiling beams, she whispered toward the shadows.

"Lord, this ain't the way tonight was supposed to be," she said. "How can Asa be gone? My whole world is turned upside down."

She crossed her arms hard over her chest as she thought of Asa's final words.

"Oh, Lord, help me. Please help me," she whispered. "Asa told me to take care of our babies before they put him on that train. Did he know *then* he was gonna die?"

Micah stirred beside her, and Zetta touched his hair.

"How am I gonna raise these youngins without their Poppy?" she whispered.

Hot tears dripped onto her pillow. More fell throughout the long sleepless night.

* * * * *

The rain had stopped when Paw arrived after breakfast the next morning. He barely nodded as Sally greeted him. Without speaking, he helped Zetta and the children into the wagon seat before slapping the reins across the mules' backs. As the animals strained forward, Rachel hugged her doll and looked back into the wagon bed before turning to her mother.

She's thinking about the coffin being there yesterday, Zetta thought.

Paw's voice was gruff. "Your Mama Becky had a good supper waiting for you," he said. "I don't know why you had to go and stay with the Reeds."

Zetta decided not to answer.

"Just as well, though, since you put off meeting the new preacher's wife," Paw said. "She's right big and bossy. In fact, your little brothers hid out from her."

Their names are Hobie and Frankie, Zetta thought. Ain't you ever gonna call them by their given names? And little Hobie was just a few days old when our own true Mama died.

Paw continued. "Loren was so disgusted with her, he took off to see Sarah even though it was late."

Zetta sighed. "Is he back now?" she asked.

Her father nodded. "Yep. But him and Luttrell set out for the cemetery first thing this morning when the rain quit," he said. "Jim Reed and his oldest boy showed up, too. Asked if I minded if they helped. I told them to suit themselves. I figured with four of them working, it won't take long to get the grave dug."

The grave? Oh, Asa. We have to put you in that cold ground. Tears rolled down Zetta's cheeks again.

* * * * *

Zetta clutched Isaac tighter as the mules turned onto the lane leading to Paw and Becky's cabin set against the brown hillside. As the wagon drew closer, she could see the wide front porch where Asa had dropped to one knee the night they finished school.

Oh, Asa. You told me you would always watch out for me and you'd work hard to give me a good life. Now this.

As the mules stopped at the steps, two little boys ran out the front door and waited as Paw helped Zetta and the children out of the wagon. On the porch, Zetta called each boy by name as she gave him a one-armed hug before Becky appeared. The woman patted Rachel's and Micah's heads before reaching for bundled up Isaac.

"Let me see that youngin," Becky said. But as she cradled the baby in one arm and opened the quilt with the other, she chuckled.

"Loren was right," she said. "He told us last night this child got more than his share of ears. Well, maybe he'll grow into them. Not that his daddy ever did."

Becky handed Isaac back to Zetta, ignoring her frown, and gestured toward the cabin.

"I don't know why you didn't come right on here from the station," Becky said. "Folks was here. And we had everything ready. We cleared out that front room for the coffin and put the extra beds in this next room all ready for you and the youngins to sleep."

When Zetta didn't answer, Becky patted her shoulder.

"I know you think this is terrible, but you'll get over this," she said. "You ain't the only widow woman left with youngins. When my first man died, there I was with three little boys."

Zetta stared at her without comment, but her mind was racing.

Yes, and gave 'em up without a second thought when you married Paw and had Frankie.

Becky opened the cabin door. "Come on in," she said. "It being the tail end of winter, there ain't no flowers to set around. I would've liked a wreath of dogwoods like my sister made when my first man died, but I had to settle for pussy willows and evergreens now."

Under her breath, Zetta muttered, "I don't care one way or another," and she stepped into the front bedroom now crowded with extra beds. Before she could unbutton the children's coats, a large woman came from the kitchen, wiping her hands on her apron.

"I'm Mable Collins, the preacher's wife," she said. "You must be Zetta."

Paw wasn't kidding about her being big, Zetta thought. She'd make three of me!

The woman swooped toward Rachel and Micah.

"And these are your poor little fatherless youngins," she said.

Both children pulled away and clutched Zetta's legs.

Mable turned back to Zetta. "I hear Asa was a good Christian man," she said.

Zetta tried not to stare at the rolls of fat that formed the woman's neck.

"Yes, he was," she stammered.

"Well, that makes my husband's job easier when he preaches the funeral tomorrow," Mable said. "Ain't nothing worse than having to preach knowing a person is in torment and not with Jesus. My husband's job is to preach, and my job is to comfort and help those grieving when there's a laying out."

Mable leaned toward Zetta, her breath smelling of sausage grease. "First thing I always do is make sure the family's clock is stopped and the mirrors covered," she said. "It's bad to let a clock stop by itself in a grieving house. That's a sure sign somebody in the family will die within the next year."

The woman waved fat fingers toward the black cloth draped over a nearby mirror.

"Same with the mirror," she said. "If you don't cover it when there's a dead body in the house, the next person who looks in it will die."

Zetta bent over the baby in her arms and wished the woman would go away.

* * * * *

223

When her father stepped through the door after putting the mules in the barn, Zetta was grateful to be rescued from Mable Collins. Paw set the satchel at the foot of the closest bed without looking at his daughter.

"You seen Asa yet?" he said.

Zetta shook her head as dread surrounded her. "No. Not yet," she said.

"Might as well get it over with," Paw said as he gestured toward the next room. "We'll keep the youngins here for a while."

Aware the others were watching, Zetta slowly placed Isaac on the closest bed then tugged off Rachel's and Micah's coats and placed them on each side of the baby. She bit her lip as she pulled off her own coat. Finally, with a deep breath, she took the four steps to the hallway.

From the doorway, she could see Asa's coffin positioned on two straight-back chairs facing each other. The coffin lid leaned against the wall behind a cluster of gallon jugs filled with pussy willow stalks and pine branches. A few straight-back chairs were against the other wall.

Zetta moved slowly toward the open coffin lined with black cloth. She took a jagged breath as she saw Asa's face.

His head rested on a small black pillow, and his lips were relaxed and slightly parted, as though he was about to take a gentle breath.

"Oh, Asa. What am I gonna do without you?" she whispered.

His sandy-colored hair was across his forehead, the way it was each morning. Zetta pushed it up then snatched her hand away as she felt his icy flesh.

Rubbing her arms, Zetta studied the small bowl of salt on Asa's chest just above his folded calloused hands. Another bowl was near his head. Zetta bit her lip, knowing the salt's purpose was to slow decay. She forced herself to study the Sunday shirt beneath his hands.

"You should've been wearing that yesterday, and we should've been in church instead of you having to go off to the mine," she whispered.

She studied the blue trousers below the white shirt, remembering the bloody material that had bound his leg at the train station. She put her hands to her face, trying to push away the memory.

Then she looked at his shoeless feet covered in unfamiliar new black socks.

Clarie must have supplied those, she thought. Oh, Clarie. How I wish you was here with me right now.

* * * * *

After Zetta had been alone in the room for several moments, Becky and Mable entered—holding Rachel's and Micah's hands. Paw Davis remained in the doorway.

"Poppy!" Both children pulled away from the women and ran to the coffin, their fingers outstretched. Zetta grabbed their little hands to keep the children from touching their daddy's cold skin.

"He sleeping," Micah said.

"Why is he still in a box, Mama?" Rachel asked.

Before Zetta could answer, Mable swooped the little girl up and held her over Asa.

"Put your hands on his," she said.

Zetta released Micah's hand and snatched Rachel from the woman's arms.

"I'll not have her remembering his skin," she said.

Mable's eyes narrowed. "They both need to touch their daddy to keep from having bad dreams about him."

Becky nodded. "And they both need to kiss him goodbye, too," she said. She leaned toward Rachel whose arms were around her mother's neck.

"Child, your daddy is with Jesus now," Becky said. "But you ain't never gonna see him again in this life."

Clutching Rachel with one arm, Zetta grabbed Micah's hand again and backed toward a chair across from the coffin.

"Leave my youngins be," she said.

Becky and Mable huffed and stomped out of the room. Paw Davis looked solemnly at his daughter and nodded as he turned away.

* * * * *

For several minutes, Zetta held Rachel and Micah close as she tried to slow her pounding heart. Only then did she notice how tightly Rachel clutched her doll.

"You don't need to worry none," she whispered. "I'm right here."

But the words were barely out of her mouth before Becky, still frowning, appeared.

"The boys are getting cleaned up from digging the grave," she said. "And your little feller is starting to work up a cry. You need to feed him before folks start arriving."

Zetta, still clutching the children's hands, turned to the door just as Luttrell entered. He had on clean clothes and his dark hair was freshly combed. He studied Asa for a moment.

"Even with all the rain, Sis, his resting place is good and dry," he said.

Zetta stared at him, her eyes brimming with tears.

Luttrell patted her on the shoulder then held out his hands to Rachel and Micah.

"Hobie and Frankie said the mommy cat out in the barn is act-ing like she had kittens," he said. "Let's go see if we can find 'em."

Both children grabbed his hands and pulled him toward the door.

"Get coats on," Zetta called. But she thought, thank you, sweet Luttrell.

Loren entered the room then, freshly washed and in clean clothes. He didn't look at Asa, but flopped into the closest chair.

"Well, that was a bad job," he said.

He leaned forward, his hands resting on his knees. Dirt was still under his fingernails. Dirt from Asa's grave.

He glanced toward the doorway and lowered his voice.

"I reckon you met old Large and In Charge Mable, huh? She's getting potatoes out of the root cellar now, but whilst we was set-ting up Asa's coffin last night, she was hovering around telling us how to position the coffin. Like we don't know how to do any-thing. And when Becky brung out the dishes of salt to put with Asa, she said they ought to be bigger."

Loren ran his hands through his hair.

"Luttrell told her we'll change the salt right often," he said. "You know how he is with folks. But that woman wears me out."

Loren stood up and quickly faced away from the coffin.

"I'm glad me and Luttrell are meeting tonight's train and taking everything up to your place. Sure beats dealing with that woman."

Isaac's hungry cries spared Zetta from having to hear more.

* * * * *

Zetta had changed into her black Sunday dress by the time people began arriving at mid-morning. From their mule-drawn wagons, solemn faced men unloaded straight-back chairs while their wives shushed children and tried to find space on the kitchen table for more fried chicken, dumplings, shuck beans, sweet potatoes, cornbread, stack cakes and cobblers. Zetta could hear Becky thanking the women for their offerings as she shoved platters closer together. She imagined Mable Collins standing nearby, inviting newcomers to eat heartily as she replenished her own plate.

Once the food and the chairs were positioned, visitors murmured condolences to Zetta.

She accepted hugs and handshakes as she listened numbly to meaningless words: "God needed Asa with him, honey. Heaven is a sweeter place now." "We was born to have nothing but trouble in this life, child." "Your grief will wear out after a while. You'll get over this."

One of her father's cousins frowned as he greeted her. "I coulda told you something like this would happen," he said. "God didn't mean for men to dig in the earth like ground hogs."

When Loren's sweetheart, Sarah, arrived with her parents, she tried to look sorrowful, but a giggle bubbled just beneath her quiet words.

"I'm sorry this happened," she said as she hugged Zetta. Then she whispered, "We're gonna be sisters sooner than I thought. Loren asked me to set a wedding date last night."

Zetta tried to smile, pondering how the news once would have made her ask for details. But she had no energy now and barely noticed when Sarah and Loren slipped away for the rest of the day. The only ones who brought comfort were Jim and Sally Reed. Sally hugged Zetta tightly then stepped back as Jim took her extended hands into both of his.

"Miz Zetta, I'm dreadful sorry this happened," he said. "I've lost a good friend, but so has this pitiful world."

Zetta nodded, not trusting herself to speak.

* * * * *

Throughout the morning, Zetta was grateful to tend to Isaac as an excuse to get away from all the people.

Oh, Clarie. I wish you was here, Zetta thought as she changed Isaac. You know what it is to hurt. And you wouldn't be saying wearying things. Just as Zetta wrapped soft flannel around Isaac, Rachel burst into the bedroom. Luttrell followed, carrying Micah.

"Mommy! We didn't know where to find you!" Tears were running down Rachel's face.

Zetta wrapped her arms around the child.

"I'm right here, honey," she said. "I was just tending the baby."

Rachel took a deep breath. "I thought you was in a box like Poppy."

Zetta pulled her tighter, fighting her own tears. Luttrell shook his head.

"I'm sorry, Sis," he said. "I kept them playing with the kittens long as I could, but they got to missing you."

Before Zetta could answer, Mable Collins appeared.

"There you are! Folks is asking for you," she said. "You need to come out and greet 'em. Bring your poor little fatherless youngins, too."

Zetta waited until Mable was beyond hearing, then turned to Luttrell.

"Why does she call them that every time?" she said. "I'm already tired of her, and we ain't even had the funeral yet. I wish Clarie was here."

Luttrell gently set Micah down. "I know, Sis. Me, too. Know what's strange, though? I keep wondering what Asa would think about all this."

Zetta's shoulders sagged.

"And I keep wondering how I'm gonna raise these youngins," she said. "People keep telling me I'll get over this. But nobody tells me how."

Luttrell rubbed his knuckles against Zetta's cheek.

"Sis, you don't ever have to get over this," he said. "All you have to do is keep putting one foot in front of the other."

CHAPTER 26

With Isaac comfortable again, Zetta turned to Rachel and Micah as they watched her—their eyes wide. She gripped both children's hands and started back to Asa. Becky stopped her.

"I keep forgetting to tell you that Asa's sisters from over at Royal can't come," she said. "One is having a baby any minute now and the other is keeping the youngins."

Zetta blinked. *I never even thought about his sisters.* "How'd they hear?" she said.

Becky shrugged as she turned away. "Luttrell got word to 'em."

Zetta put her hands to her forehead. *That's so like my tender-hearted brother.*

As Mable approached from the kitchen, Zetta grabbed the children's hands again.

"I been watching you," Mabel said. "You feed your poor little fatherless youngins but you yourself don't eat enough to keep a bird alive."

Zetta wanted to say, "You've been eating enough to make up for me." Instead she murmured, "I'm all right."

Mable wasn't finished. "You gotta eat more for the baby's sake."

Luttrell appeared at her side.

"Pardon me, Miz Mable," he said, "But I need to tell Zetta where me and Loren will be for the next while."

Mable frowned and turned back to the kitchen.

Luttrell gestured outside where Loren waited with the wagon.

"We're gonna meet the train," he said. "If Clarie got your goods on it, we'll take 'em to your house and be gone a long while. If they ain't on that train, we'll be back sooner."

Zetta put her hand to her forehead again.

"What would I do without you?"

Luttrell patted her arm. Then with six quick steps he was out the door.

* * * * *

When her brothers didn't return within the next hour, Zetta knew her household items had arrived. For the rest of the afternoon, she sat with Rachel and Micah leaning against her in front of Asa's coffin. She nodded at the comments from numerous visitors, but didn't care whether they stayed seated next to her or moved to the front porch or to the kitchen. The preacher meandered from room to room as he greeted the men. The comment from Sarah's father swirled down the hallway.

"Howdy, Preacher. You must've been praying the rain would hold off today," he said. "I do hate putting a person in a wet grave."

Tears filled Zetta's eyes.

Oh, Asa. How could all this happen just since yesterday morning? she thought. Right about now, I should be finishing supper and waiting for you and the boys to get back from the mine. But instead here you are dead, and I'm sitting in this room waiting for them to unload our things in our empty house. We was supposed to be going back there together. You wanted to give our youngins a better life than you had. Now this.

The slamming of the front door startled Zetta as another visitor carried a filled plate onto the porch, forgetting to catch the door behind him. As Zetta jumped at the sound, Becky appeared and didn't try to hide her chuckle.

"You liked to have jumped out of your skin," she said. "But I reckon I was jumpy like that when my first man died."

I'm tired of hearing about your first man, Zetta thought.

Becky held two folded papers toward her.

"I forgot to give you these locks of Asa's hair," she said. "I cut them from the back of his head last night. One's to put in your Bible and the other is for your hair album."

Zetta stared at the papers. "Hair album?" she said. "I don't have such a thing."

"You mean to tell me you don't have a lock of your mother's hair?" Becky said. "Didn't you love her?"

Zetta took a long breath before she answered.

"I loved my mother more than I can say. And I still miss her."

Zetta didn't watch Becky leave the room, still holding the papers. She merely smoothed the skirt of her Sunday black dress and pulled her children closer.

* * * * *

At last, Zetta saw the wagon pass the window on the way to the barn. Luttrell held the reins while Loren slouched next to him. Eager to talk to her brothers, she grabbed Rachel's and Micah's hands.

"Let's go check on Isaac and get you something to eat," she whispered.

She hurriedly put two fried chicken legs and two biscuits on a plate and steered the children into the bedroom where Isaac slept between pillows on the middle bed.

Her brothers entered together.

"I reckon the crates come in," Zetta said.

Loren nodded as he rubbed the scar on his chin. "Yep. And we stacked 'em in your kitchen," he said. "We thought about unpacking them but we didn't know where you'd want everything. You women like things in certain spots."

Luttrell pulled a letter from his shirt pocket and held it toward Zetta.

"This here is from Clarie," he said. "She tied it to one of the crates."

Zetta sat down on the nearest bed. "I'm tired. You read it to me."

Luttrell opened the envelope and unfolded the paper as Loren leaned against the wall.

"'My sweet Zetta. I sure am sorry this awful time has come upon you. It hurt me to pack up your things like this. But with everything I packed, I prayed for you all the more. That child Julia stood on your back porch the whole time I was in your house and just looked pitiful. Clarence ain't been seen since the accident. Probably a good thing for him since the men are pretty mad. And after Perton helped me get everything to the station, he went off on a drunk.'"

Loren snorted. "Like his getting drunk does anybody any good."

Luttrell continued reading. " 'The crate holding Asa's clothes has your money jar from the kitchen. I put it way down in the bottom. I didn't send Asa's shoes since they was in bad shape from the accident. And I didn't send your little Christmas tree since it is looking so pitiful. I'll put it back in the ground here and send it in the spring if you want it. But don't think about that now. Just remember I sure am sorry this happened. I'm praying for you and the youngins with every breath. Keep hanging onto the Lord, honey. He's with you even in this. I wrote Dosha over at Hindman. I know her and Jack will be ever so sorry. I'm closing this letter with more prayers and a sad hug across the miles. Love, Clarie.'"

Zetta pulled a handkerchief from her sleeve and wiped her eyes. "Clarie's the only thing I miss about that camp," she said.

She looked at Luttrell. "Was the tombstone on the train, too?"

Loren answered for him. "Nope. Perton told me when I picked it out that the camp will send it once the stone cutter from Hazard carves the name and dates in."

He ran his hand across the scar on his chin. "Knowing old Rusty Hinge, they won't be in any hurry," he said. "They push a miner's family out right now but then forget about 'em. It's untelling when you'll get that stone."

Zetta closed her eyes.

* * * * *

As evening approached, Becky lit several lanterns as neighbors began to leave, apologizing for needing to go home for milking time but promising to be back in the morning. Zetta murmured her thanks to each one. She especially was relieved to say goodnight to Mable and the preacher. Sarah's father was next.

"My Sarah is a good hand to drive a team, so she's taking the rest of the family home," he said. "I'm staying to sit up alongside your paw and brothers."

Zetta merely nodded.

As Sally and Jim Reed started to say leave, Jim abruptly turned to Zetta's father.

"Mr. Davis, sir, I'd be much obliged if you'd let me sit up with y'all."

"Suit yourself," Paw said.

Zetta, surprised at her father's answer, turned toward him. As her paw returned her gaze, he puffed his cheeks as if wrestling with a thought. He looked at Jim.

"And I reckon Asa would want you to help carry him to his resting place tomorrow."

Jim's eyes widened. "Thank you, sir. I'd be honored." Jim quickly turned to his son. "You get your mother and others home," he said. "I'll see y'all back here in the morning."

* * * * *

After putting the children to bed, Zetta went back to Asa just as Luttrell poured the pungent contents of Clarie's bottle into a wash pan. After wringing out the white cloths, he placed them over Asa's face and hands as Becky positioned a fresh dish of salt on his chest.

Zetta looked away from Asa and watched her father and Loren pull five chairs forward and gesture for Jim Reed and Sarah's father to sit down. She stood awkwardly for a moment, feeling useless, before meandering back into the bedroom. There she hurriedly changed into her nightgown and eased into bed next to the children just as Becky entered.

"That bed is gonna feel good tonight," Becky said as she tugged off her dress. "I been working so hard, I'm dead on my feet."

No, Zetta thought as she turned away. Dead is being cold and still and in that front room.

After Becky got into the next bed, Zetta could hear the men sitting with Asa settling into their chairs. Sarah's father cleared his throat.

"I wish we was here for a wedding instead of a funeral, huh, Loren?"

He didn't wait for Loren's answer. "I remember the first time I ever set up with a body," he said. "My daddy's sister was took by fever just a month before she was to be married. Her women friends set up with us and sung church songs. But long about midnight, they was wore out from crying. And Dad and me was wore out from digging the grave. So when things got quiet, we all dozed off."

Zetta heard a chair creak as someone shifted his weight.

Sarah's father went on with his story. "I don't know how long I slept with my head bobbing, but at one point I woke up and found all the lanterns out. But the strangest light was right by the coffin and standing there was a woman I'd never seen. She had her right hand up like this over her heart, and I could see two of her fingers was missing. Then next thing I knowed, she up and disappeared."

Loren's holler of "Well, now!" was so loud Zetta turned toward the children, expecting them to awaken. But they didn't move. Even Becky merely grunted in her sleep.

Sarah's father continued. "Yessir, scared the daylights outta me so bad I nudged my daddy to ask if he's seen her. He was all groggy 'til I told him about her hand. He jumped up to light the lanterns again and said their grandmother had been missing fingers like hers."

"That'd make a feller's hair stand up," Loren said.

Sarah's father chuckled. "Yessir. You better believe the next time I set up with a body, I made sure we had plenty of lanterns. That time it was for a cousin."

Zetta doubled the pillow and pushed it under her head, wishing he'd stop talking.

Instead, Sarah's father cleared his throat again. "Now that cousin had been like a brother whilst we growed up. But I gotta admit he was a hot head. Got hisself shot. It was so bad that we couldn't show him. The weather was real hot, so we had the windows open. And all night long we was knocking strange puffed up cats off the coffin lid. That worries me to this day about his soul."

Jim's gentle voice reached Zetta. "We don't have to worry about Asa's soul."

Oh, Lord. I couldn't bear this if I didn't know he's with you, Zetta thought.

The men were quiet for several moments. Then Loren spoke. "Speaking of souls, that preacher shook a lot of hands today, but I don't think he said two words when his wife was around. I told Zetta that's a woman who's large and in charge. I swear she wears me out."

"Well, at least we got us a preacher," Sarah's father said. "Used to folks would do the burying and then have to wait 'til the circuit preacher come around."

"I recollect that," Paw said. "Sometimes we'd have a funeralizing long after the person was buried. Maybe even nine or ten months later."

"Yessir. And the widow woman might be living with her second man," Sarah's father said. "Might even be in the family way with his child. And there she was, crying and carrying on about her husband. So the preacher would preach a funeral and then marry the new couple. Yessir, I like it better that we got our own preacher and don't have to do any funeralizing."

My goodness, Zetta thought. I never knew he talked so much.

Luttrell quietly asked, "How old you reckon Asa is now. Is he this age? Or the age of a child—since heaven is for the pure?"

Asa will always be this same age to me, Zetta thought.

She imagined her gentle brother leaning forward with his head down and clutching his rough hands.

"You asked a good question," Sarah's father said. "My granddaddy was 24 when he died. And his little boy, my daddy, was five. My daddy growed up, got married, had me and a bunch more, saw his grandchildren born and then died when he was seventy-five. So in heaven there was my seventy-five-year-old daddy meeting his twenty-four-year-old daddy. That hurts my head trying to figure that out."

"I think they both was in their prime," Loren said. "So they was in their twenties when they met again."

"But what about children that dies?" Jim asked quietly.

Oh, I remember, Zetta thought. Him and Sally had a little girl die a few years back.

Jim continued. "Do they stay that age or are they the age they would have been if they'd growed up?"

Luttrell's voice was low. "I reckon we'll get the answers when we get there."

Isaac stirred then. As she pulled the baby to her, Zetta's tears dropped onto his head.

* * * * *

Zetta didn't sleep even after the men's conversation ceased. As she waited for dawn, she stared into the shadows. The neighbors began arriving shortly after breakfast. They filed into the front room, nodding at Zetta as she held a quilt-wrapped Isaac on the skirt of her black dress. Rachel and Micah huddled against Zetta while the rest of the family sat nearby.

Mable and her preacher husband were the last to arrive. She remained by the door while he stepped to the foot of the coffin. As he looked at the group, Zetta studied his craggy face.

I wish Pastor Howard was here, she thought. I heard him just those two times but at least he had a kind face.

Preacher Collins checked his pocket watch. "It's time to start," he said.

As he put away his watch, he began to sing the opening words to "Blessed Assurance." The others joined in.

Zetta didn't sing the mournful familiar words, but stared at Asa.

This is the last time I'll see you on this earth, she thought. And I won't ever again kiss you or hear your jokes or cook for you.

She pulled the handkerchief from her sleeve and held it to her eyes.

At the final line of the song, Preacher Collins raised his right arm.

"Yes, even during sad times just like the song says, we can still praise the Savior," he said. "Jesus told us about the many mansions in his Father's house. And he said he was going to prepare a place for us. That's what he's done for Asa."

Mable Collins began to sob. Between deep breaths, she cried out, "Oh, Sweet Jesus. Yes, that's the good truth." Becky began to wail, and the sound annoyed Zetta.

Go away, she thought. All of you leave me and my youngins alone.

The preacher raised his voice above their cries: "Psalm 23 says, 'He prepareth a table in the presence of mine enemies.' Yessir, Jesus hisself is preparing a table for Asa right now. But not in the presence of enemies, but in the presence of God Almighty. This man's suffering is over. But we're still here, having to face dark days. But all our pain here on earth just makes our going to heaven all the sweeter."

Mable's cry of "Yes, Jesus" encouraged Preacher Collins to raise his voice even more.

"Parents, live right before your children. You want to be in heaven someday and you want your children there with you. They won't get there without your good example. Heaven promises a sweet reunion, but in that place of torment where there's wailing and gnashing of teeth, there'll be no such thing."

He looked directly at Paw. "Parents, change your ways and get right with God before it's too late. Let your family see you in church with them each Sunday."

Paw frowned. "Get on with it," he said. "Sky's starting to cloud up again."

The preacher shook his head, but muttered, "All right. We'll pray at the grave. Y'all say your last goodbyes."

As neighbors filed by Asa, many touched his cold hands in the mountain belief the act would prevent bad dreams of him.

Then it was Zetta's turn. She held Isaac close as she took Micah's hand.

She turned to Rachel. "Take Brother's other hand and don't let anybody pick y'all up."

Tears rolled down her cheeks as she looked at Asa one last time. This didn't have to happen, she thought.

As the mourners waited in the yard, Zetta and the children stepped outside onto the porch. Jim Reed's oldest son approached.

"Miz Zetta, I'm to take y'all on ahead to the graveyard," he said.

As Zetta nodded, she could hear nails being pounded into the coffin lid. She knew that sound would stay with her forever.

* * * * *

Under the darkening sky, Jim's son guided the wagon carrying Zetta and the children up the hill to the graveyard. Gray tombstones leaned beneath pines, white oaks and poplars. Near a bare dogwood tree, four shovels were thrust into the dirt piled beside an open grave.

Zetta took a raspy breath. Asa's grave.

As they drew closer, a hawk left its perch in a poplar tree and swooped down on a chipmunk. Zetta looked away as the little creature dangled from the hawk's talons.

Death comes so sudden, she thought.

Jim's son pulled the wagon behind the dogwood tree and helped Zetta and the children down. As they waited, other wagons came up the hill. The last one carried Asa. Paw drove while Loren, Luttrell, Jim Reed and Sarah's father sat on the coffin. As Zetta clutched Isaac, Rachel and Micah pushed themselves tightly against her legs.

After pulling the wagon close to the grave and setting the brake, Paw jumped down, holding two coils of sturdy rope. As Luttrell and Loren pulled Asa's coffin slowly from the wagon, Paw looped the rope under it as Jim Reed and Sarah's father steadied it against the wagon bed. Then lifting the coffin to their shoulders, the five men slowly approached the grave.

Mable Collins rushed to the men.

"Make sure you've got him facing east," she said. "He's got to face the rising sun for when Jesus comes."

Loren's answer was close to a growl. "You ain't the only one knowing to do that," he said. "You're standing in our way."

As Mable moved aside, the men set the coffin down and picked up the ropes to lower Asa into the grave. When it was just a few inches from the bottom, one man on each side pulled the ropes up, causing the coffin to thud onto the dark soil. At the sound, Micah hid his face in Zetta's skirt. She pushed down sobs, determined not to frighten her children—or give onlookers more to talk about.

Preacher Collins stepped forward as the others moved closer to the grave.

Lifting his hand, he prayed, "Lord, you saw fit to take this young life," he said. "So we ask you to give his family strength for the days ahead. And now we trust his spirit to you."

He picked up a clod of dirt and held it over Asa's coffin.

"You said we was made from the dust and we will return to dust. We accept your will."

As he dropped the dirt onto Asa's coffin, Luttrell, Loren and Jim pulled the shovels from the dirt pile and began to toss soil onto the coffin. Zetta's father slowly picked up the last shovel.

Rachel covered her ears and sobbed, "Don't let 'em put dirt on Poppy!"

Tears rolled down Zetta's face as she put her free arm around her little girl.

Chapter 27

As the men pivoted from the dirt pile to fling soil into the grave, shovelful after shovelful of wet dirt thudded against the wooden coffin.

Sally Reed stood behind Zetta and the children, one hand on the young mother's back. Becky stood nearby, her sobs growing in volume. Finally, Luttrell and Loren tossed the last of the dirt, and Paw and Jim Reed slapped their shovels against the mound to pack it down.

No one moved until an old woman said, "Well, another short life under a pile of mud."

Suddenly a strong wind swept up the hill, bending limbs over the wagons positioned beneath bare trees. As the men hurried to quiet the mules, Mable Collins appeared at Zetta's side.

"Well, that's over," she said.

This won't ever be over, Zetta thought as she stared at the mound of dirt.

Mable continued her prattle. "Yes. Yes. Now you and your poor little fatherless youngins will have to go on living. And you'll have to be strong for them."

Zetta turned away so quickly she bumped into Becky, who was reaching for Isaac.

"Mable's right," Becky said. "You ain't the only one who's ever suffered."

Zetta clutched the baby and stared at Becky. A minute ago, your sobbing was heard to the next mountain, she thought. Now your

239

voice is clear. Who was you putting on that show for?

Luttrell stepped in front of Mable and Becky to take Zetta's elbow.

"Sis, let's get back to the house before the sky opens up," he said.

* * * * *

Zetta remembered little about the ride. She vaguely was aware of both children looking back toward the grave as the wagon pulled out of the cemetery.

Then Isaac awakened and began to whimper. His whimpering had turned to hungry howls by the time they reached Paw's house.

As Zetta and the children climbed the steps, she was glad Isaac was crying since his hunger would allow her to escape to the bedroom. The neighbors filled the room where Asa's coffin had been and balanced plates of food on their laps as they ate. Zetta nodded as she passed them and hurried to the bedroom. Rachel and Micah were close by her side.

In the bedroom, she closed the door and leaned against it for a moment. When she realized Rachel and Micah were watching her, she gestured toward the bed.

"Sit up here whilst I change Isaac," Zetta said. "Soon as I feed him, I'll get you something from the kitchen."

The bedroom door opened, and Zetta's younger brother Hobie stepped in.

"Ma said for y'all to come eat before folks start taking their food home," he said.

Oh, I wish he'd known our own mother, Zetta thought.

She turned to Rachel and Micah. "You go on with Hobie," she said.

Both children took Hobie's outstretched hand, and he closed the door behind them. Zetta quickly changed the howling Isaac and unbuttoned her dress. But as she started to pull the baby to her, she looked at the thick winter quilt on the bed. Her arms felt heavy as she pulled off her dress and tossed it onto the foot of the bed, but soon she and the baby were under the warm quilt.

She stroked Isaac's head as he nursed.

"Oh, sweet little boy," she said. "What's gonna happen to you without a daddy? He loved you even before you was born. And he was so proud of all you youngins. Dosha said God loves me special to give me three sweet babies. But how am I gonna raise y'all alone?"

The bedroom door opened, and Becky stepped in. "There ya are," she said. "The youngins are eating good, and the Reeds just left. Sally was wanting to stay, but I told her you'd be fine. I told her you needed to rest, but I sure didn't think you'd be in bed this time of day."

"I didn't sleep much the last two nights," Zetta said without looking up. But she thought, I wish you had let Sally stay. And I wish Clarie was here instead of you.

When Zetta didn't answer, Becky muttered, "Well, all right," and left the room. Zetta fell into exhausted sleep with Isaac still nursing.

Within moments, she was in the green meadow above their barn. The rich blue sky held a sprinkling of bright translucent clouds. As she lifted her face toward the sun, Asa appeared at her side and pointed to the little Christmas tree they'd had at the camp and which he had just planted. As she admired its plump green needles, Asa beckoned for her to look at the small primrose flowers at his feet. She smiled, and he stooped to pluck a yellow blossom for her. She touched the delicate petals and leaned against her husband's shoulder as he put his arm around her waist.

As Asa gestured at the beauty around them, the bedroom door opened. Becky's voice pulled Zetta from the peaceful scene.

"Folks are starting to leave," she said. "Don't you want to see 'em off?"

Zetta could hear neighbors loading dishes, chairs and children into their wagons and saying goodbye to others. Someone laughed in parting.

She squeezed her eyes shut, trying to return to the dream.

"Tell them I'm feeding the baby," she murmured. "Say I appreciate them being here."

* * * * *

Asa turned from the pear trees, which were heavy with white blooms, and grinned as Zetta and the children stepped from the house and onto the porch to greet him. Rachel called, "Poppy!" and held her hands out. Asa bounded up the steps, but before he could pick up the child, the bedroom door opened again.

"Zetta, honey? I brung you something to eat."

Sarah.

Zetta wanted to yell, "All of you leave me be." Instead, she kept her eyes closed.

She could sense Sarah leaning over the bed.

"I brung you a boiled potato," Sarah said. "Whenever my mother is sick, nothing satisfies her like a potato sliced all thin with a little butter."

"Come on, Sis. You gotta eat something." Loren.

Zetta opened her eyes and looked at her brother. "I'm just tired," she said. "I'll eat in a while. Where are the youngins?"

"Hobie and Frankie are with 'em whilst they finish eating," Loren said. "Everybody left just before the rain started up. Mable sent us in here to get you to eat something."

Zetta sighed. "Mable's still here?"

Loren nodded. "Oh, yeah. Says it's her duty to help during this time of grief. She sent her husband on home, though."

He leaned closer. "Just between you and me, I think he was glad to get away from her."

Sarah started to giggle but stopped as Mable stepped into the room.

Mable picked up Zetta's dress from the foot of the bed and hung it on a nearby hook. Loren stepped around her and quickly left.

"You know, you should be thankful Asa died in one piece," Mable said. "Before me and my husband got into preaching, he worked the mine over at Eccles, West Virginia. About nine years ago, a big explosion killed more than 180 men. It didn't happen on his shift, but he helped pick up the bodies—or what was left of 'em."

Zetta heard Sarah gasp. Mable ignored her and continued her story.

"He said the explosion picked those strong men up just like rag dolls and throwed them against the walls and broke them apart. And all those women and poor little fatherless youngins didn't have the comfort of saying goodbye like you did. So you can thank the good Lord for that blessing."

Zetta closed her eyes. No part of this will ever be counted as a blessing, she thought. She was grateful when she heard Mable and

Sarah leave the room.

But before she could fall asleep, the door opened again. Paw cleared his throat.

"You doing all right?"

Zetta gave a quiet huff. "I reckon."

"Well, you stay right where you are. Me and the boys are fixing to take these other two beds back to the other room. Now that everything is over, Becky wants the house back in order."

"All right," Zetta murmured. She could hear someone outside the bedroom sweeping the floor. The sound annoyed her.

Everybody's all fired up to get things right again, she thought. Just like nothing ever happened. Oh, Lord. Please help me.

* * * * *

Heavy rain fell on the little cabin all afternoon. Zetta drifted in and out of dreamless sleep as she thought of the rain hitting the fresh dirt of Asa's grave.

After the men moved the extra beds back into the room where Asa's coffin had been, Zetta heard them leave to do chores in the barn. Becky took Rachel and Micah into that room.

"You two sit up here now whilst I finish up," Becky said.

Micah's little voice reached Zetta. "Poppy?"

That poor child. He's remembering his daddy's coffin being in there.

"Now I already told y'all he's with Jesus," Becky said. "So y'all need to be good for your mommy 'cause your daddy and Jesus are watching."

Tears dripped onto Zetta's pillow, but she swiped at her eyes as the bedroom door quietly opened. Rachel and Micah entered and stood by her bed.

"Climb up here, both of you," Zetta said. "I know you're wore out, too."

With one arm around Isaac, she lifted the quilt.

"Here. Stretch out next to me."

As both children kicked off their shoes and clambered into the bed, Becky looked in and shook her head. Zetta ignored her and cuddled the children until she left. Micah fell asleep immediately, but Rachel reached across him to pat her mother's hair. Soon she was asleep too, her breathing in sync with Micah's. As Zetta closed her own eyes, she heard voices coming from the kitchen.

"Loren's tore up and says Zetta didn't deserve this," Sarah said.

"Well, a lot of folks—like me—don't deserve what they get," Becky said. "She's in there acting like the world has come to an end. Acting like she knows something we don't know."

"Don't you worry," Mable said. "The truth will out. God has his ways of doing things."

"What do you mean?" Sarah asked.

"Why, child, the Bible plainly says in Psalms that the Lord knows the way of the righteous: but the way of the ungodly shall perish," Mable said, "God protects his people, so she must be holding some secret sin."

Zetta wished she had the energy to stomp into the kitchen and argue with the woman. Instead she thought, what about those people over in Eccles you talked about? Surely, those 180 men and their wives wasn't all bad.

"That stands to reason," Becky said. "After all, if the spring don't bring rain, the dogwood blooms will be small. And if a person holds sin inside, bad things happen."

Lord, are they questioning Asa's goodness now, too?

"You just never know what's in a person's heart," Mable said, sounding as through she had a mouthful of food.

"How long is Zetta gonna stay in bed?" Sarah asked.

"Can't never tell," Becky answered. "When I was growing up, we had a neighbor who pined away and died after her man was throwed from a horse. And their two little youngins wound up having to be raised by their grandmother. When my man died, I thought about her and was bound and determined not to take to my bed."

Zetta frowned. Maybe not, but you gave up your little boys to be raised by their uncle, she thought.

Mable cleared her throat as though she had just swallowed.

"When we was over in West Virginia, I saw a lot of women take to their beds after the explosion," she said. "But the worse was one that lost her son that day. Her husband was still alive, and they had a house full of other youngins, but she thought the sun rose and set in that one boy. I gotta admit he was a sweet young feller, but she wasn't the only mother that lost a son. But she took to her bed and never got up again."

Sarah gasped. "She died, too?"

"No. No. Just never got up again except to use the chamber pot," Mable said. "Her oldest girls had to bring food to her and bathe her and change her nightgown right there in bed."

"Surely Zetta won't be like that," Sarah said.

"Well, I just hope she's out of bed before Easter gets here the first of April," Mable said. "We're planning a fancy egg roll at church, and I'll be needed there."

You sure ain't needed here, Zetta thought as she closed her eyes.

* * * * *

Asa plunged the tin dipper into the bucket of cold spring water and started to take a drink as Zetta approached. When he saw her, he smiled and held the dipper out. As Zetta's lips touched the water, someone dropped a pan in the kitchen.

Zetta fought opening her eyes, wanting to stay with Asa. But the women were preparing supper and not keeping their voices down as they pondered Zetta's plight.

Don't y'all have anything better to do than talk about us? Zetta thought. A good man is dead. And this terrible thing will follow me and my children for the rest of our lives. And they'll talk about their daddy dying just the way Asa talked about his daddy dying on Christmas Eve.

And there you are, talking against us. Asa and me didn't do anything wrong. You're making up a bunch of stuff, thinking nothing bad is ever gonna happen to you. Well, y'all ain't as smart as you think you are. Clarie said there are some things in life that all we can do with 'em is bear 'em. Well, I have to bear this. I wish Clarie was here. Y'all are miserable comforters.

Yes, God has allowed this terrible thing, but he will help me through it. Y'all are wearing me out even more than God has, Zetta thought. And she drifted off to sleep again.

* * * * *

Isaac's hungry whimpers awakened Zetta the next morning. As she pulled him to her, she wondered where Rachel and Micah were. Just then Becky opened the door. Zetta jerked the quilt higher to cover the baby and herself.

"I got biscuits and gravy here for you," she said. "Even if you don't feel like eating for yourself, you need to eat for that baby," Becky said. "You don't want your milk drying up."

"I'll eat directly," Zetta said.

Luttrell knocked softly on the open door.

"How you doing this morning, Sis?"

"I'm getting there," Zetta said, relieved to have him interrupt Becky's lecture. "Come on in. Where are Sister and Brother?"

Luttrell gestured toward the barn.

"Frankie and Hobie been keeping them busy with the kittens," he said. "I reckon when y'all go back home, you're gonna have to take a couple of the critters with you."

Zetta watched Becky leave then turned back to her brother.

"I'm dreading going home the worst in the world," she whispered. "How am I gonna go back there without Asa?"

Luttrell nodded. "Me and Loren's been talking about that," he said. "So we're gonna take turns staying there 'til you get used to it. We can make up a pallet in front of the fireplace each night. And next month, we'll do the planting for you."

"Asa woulda been plowing his own ground this time," Zetta said. "Now he won't ever be out there again."

"Don't think on that right now," Luttrell said. "Here. Dosha sent you a letter."

He pulled an envelope from his shirt pocket and held it toward Zetta.

She closed her eyes. "You read it for me."

Luttrell pulled a chair closer to the bed and opened the envelope.

" 'Oh, sweet Zetta,' " he began. " 'I'm writing this with tears running down my face. Clarie wrote us the bad news as soon as she got your goods packed and gave us your address. Me and Jack cried hard when we read what happened. Jack said Asa always had a smile for him and wouldn't let the men tease him about stuttering. And Jack loved his jokes. He'd tell them to me over supper. I know I could have wound up being in your shoes when Jack got hurt, so I'm praying for you in special ways with every sad thought. But I'm glad you are there with your family all around you. I know they are a comfort. We are happy here, but we still miss the camp. I miss you and Clarie most of all. Well, I'll close for now but I'll keep praying for you. Kiss your sweet babies for me. Love, Dosha Conley.'"

Zetta was fighting sobs by the end of the letter.

As Luttrell patted his sister's hand, Becky and Mable came into the room. He stood up and offered his chair, then quietly left.

"The sun is trying to come out," Becky said, "So Sarah got Loren to build a fire under the wash kettle so she can wash the baby's diapers."

"She don't need to be doing that," Zetta said. "He's got enough."

Mable frowned. "Some folks know life goes on," she said.

"Things need doing."

Zetta pulled herself into a sitting position, careful to keep the quilt over her and Isaac.

"No, *your* life is going on," she said. "I'm trying to get used to my new one. I been hearing y'all talking about God's punishment and wondering about any secret sin. Hear me tell you this—you are accusing an innocent person.

"I'm a good woman who lost a good man. At the camp, the supervisor's wife always was acting like she's better than she is. Well, I'm not gonna pretend I'm worse than I am."

Zetta pointed her finger at the women. "It was good when Asa was here. We did good things, and people appreciated us. But now that I need your help, y'all are talking behind my back, badmouthing me and saying we deserved this."

Zetta looked directly at Becky. "If I was a bad person, I would deserve this," she said. "But you know I was faithful to Asa even in my heart. If I hadn't been, yeah, maybe I would deserve to have him taken away. But I was true to him and I tried to help others. Whilst he was working in the dark, I befriended a pitiful woman named Polly and tolerated a spoiled rich child named Julia. I helped poor and rich alike—and now I've got you two telling me I had this coming."

As Zetta paused, Mable stormed out of the room. Becky quickly followed.

Lord, I probably should've kept my mouth shut, but now maybe they won't be so quick to talk about me, Zetta thought.

Then she smiled. And eased back under the quilt.

CHAPTER 28

Asa was working on a piece of plow harness as Zetta stepped from the children's bedroom. She watched his strong hands stitch the broken straps together and thread them through the buckle. When he realized she was watching him, he stood up and pulled a chair closer to the fireplace for her. As she sat down, he stood behind her and rested his hands on her shoulders.

"Oh, Zetta. I'm sorry how things turned out," he said. "I married you because I loved you. But I also knew you were strong. Now you know you are strong, too."

He kissed the top of her head. "I appreciate how you handled those two women. I wouldn't have done as good. Too often, I avoided arguments by telling a joke. But there was truth that needed telling, and today you told it."

Zetta leaned against Asa's rough hands as he caressed her cheeks.

"I'll always be with you," he said. "And as long as you remember me, I'll never really be dead."

In the fireplace glow, Zetta turned to face Asa. But before she could kiss her husband, Paw burst into the room.

"Daughter, if you die, who's gonna take care of your youngins?"

Zetta pushed her face deeper into the pillow, trying to stay with Asa. But he was fading even as she held her hands toward him.

Paw pulled up a chair. "Mable says you're talking outta your head."

Zetta groaned. "I wasn't talking out of my head," she said. "I was telling the truth."

She forced her eyes open and turned to her father.

"And I ain't gonna die," she said. "I'm just wore out. Wore out from thinking about Asa dying the way he did. Wore out from wondering what I coulda said to get him to come home. Wore out from crying. Wore out from knowing the mine wasn't supposed to be working on a Sunday. Wore out from wishing Jack coulda been driving the mantrip. Wore out from worrying about raising these youngins alone. And wore out from listening to women who think they know what's in my heart."

Her father leaned back. "Well, now," he said. "So what can I do for you?"

"Tell them to let me sleep," Zetta said. "Me and the youngins go home tomorrow."

* * * * *

Exhaustion claimed Zetta for the rest of the day. At dawn the next morning, the rooster's crowing awakened her. As she sat up to nurse Isaac, Rachel and Micah awakened, too.

"Good morning my sweet babies," Zetta said. "I need you to hurry and use the chamber pot and then get dressed. After breakfast, we're going home."

"And see Miz Clarie?" Rachel asked as she helped Micah from the bed.

Tears sprang into Zetta's eyes. "No, honey. We're going back to our own farm."

Sarah quietly opened the bedroom door.

"Oh. Y'all are already up," she said. "I was just wondering what sounds good for me to bring you to eat."

"I appreciate that," Zetta said. "But when I finish feeding Isaac, I'm coming to the table. That is if Mable's not tempted to poison my food."

Sarah giggled. "Oh, she ain't here. Yesterday evening her husband come to get her the regular time, and I heard her tell Luttrell she wouldn't be back. Said her job was done."

Zetta nodded. "It sure is. At least I won't have to face her for a while."

She switched the baby to her other side. "I'd appreciate if you wouldn't mind helping Sister and Brother get dressed whilst I finish up with this little feller."

Within a few minutes, Isaac's tummy was full, and Sarah had taken Rachel and Micah to the kitchen. As Zetta pulled a dark green dress from the sachet and shook it out, the red sweater came with it. She gasped and shoved the sweater back into the case, wishing she could shove away her regrets about not having worn Asa's gift for him. She dressed quickly, brushed her hair without looking in the mirror and stepped from the room.

In the kitchen, Becky glanced at her, nodded and turned back to the stove. Zetta sat down as Sarah handed her a plate.

"Luttrell and y'all's paw are doing the barn chores," Sarah said. "So me and Loren are gonna take you back to your house. That is, if you're still going today."

Zetta glanced at Becky. "Today's as good a day as any. I've done wore out my welcome here."

Becky put a plate of biscuits in front of Zetta without looking at her. "I fried up a chicken for y'all to take for your noon dinner," she said.

Zetta murmured, "Thank you."

She managed to force down a few bites of cooked apples and drink a glass of milk. But before she could offer to help wash the dishes, Loren bounded up the steps and into the kitchen.

"I got the wagon waiting," he said. "I'm ready when you are."

Zetta took a deep breath. "I'm as ready as I'll ever be. I'll get Isaac."

* * * * *

On the porch, Becky hugged Rachel and Micah goodbye before Loren swung them into the wagon, but she didn't say anything to Zetta.

That's just as well, Zetta thought. It's gonna take us both a while to get over all those words from yesterday.

As Zetta started down the steps with Isaac, Hobie and Frankie ran from the barn with Luttrell close behind. Hobie held a tabby kitten, which he thrust into Rachel's arms. Frankie handed a black kitten with white paws to Micah. Both children smiled as they cradled the kittens.

Zetta looked at Luttrell. "*Two* cats?"

Luttrell shrugged. "When Hobie told me which ones the youngins liked, I checked to make sure they're both female. Their mother's a good mouser. Maybe they will be, too."

Loren positioned Zetta's satchel in the back of the wagon then helped her and Isaac into the wagon seat. Sarah climbed next to the children.

Zetta didn't look back as the mules pulled the wagon away from her father's cabin.

* * * * *

Zetta clutched the baby as the wagon turned onto the lane lined with chestnut trees. She could see her little white house ahead. How could I leave with such high hopes not even three months ago and come back like this? she wondered.

As they continued under the limbs of the trees, Loren interrupted her thoughts.

"With all the rain, these trees should have been showing spring buds by now," he said.

Before Zetta could study the branches, Loren hurried the mules to the pear trees in front of the house. As he called "Whoa" and pulled tightly on the reins, Zetta sighed.

Lord, I'm dreading this the worst in the world, she thought.

Loren helped Zetta and the baby down first. Then he lifted Sarah and the children down from the back of the wagon. As Rachel's feet touched the ground, she ran up the porch steps clutching her rag doll and the kitten. Zetta followed slowly.

At the front door, Loren pulled a key from his pocket. "Paw put a padlock on the door to keep any riffraff from meandering through whilst you was at the camp with us," he said.

As soon as the door was open, Rachel rushed into the front room.

Suddenly, the child began to sob. Zetta hurried in and found her standing in front of the picture of Jesus near the door and looking at the holy face.

"Mama Becky said Poppy is with Jesus," Rachel sobbed. "But he's not there! I wanted to see him, but he's not there! Jesus is all by hisself."

Tears rolled down Zetta's cheeks as Rachel sobbed against her leg.

How do I explain all this to a child when I don't understand it myself?

* * * * *

As Loren brought Micah into the room, he looked sorrowfully at Rachel who leaned against her mother's leg. Sarah followed with the small basket of fried chicken Becky had provided. The three adults stood awkwardly for a moment, as Zetta looked around the front room with its deep green painted floor and braided rug.

"Well, here we are," she said.

"I'll build a fire," Loren said. "Take the chill out. Me and Luttrell checked the chimney the other day. No bird's nest is in there, so we're good to go."

"All right," she said. "I'll put Isaac to bed first."

With Rachel close by her side, Zetta took the sleeping baby into the bedroom. The thin mattress was still rolled up on the bed frame. As she placed Isaac in the cradle, Zetta stared at the bed. I'm gonna be in there all by myself from now on, she thought.

Sarah was right behind her.

"You tell me where the quilts are, and I'll get the beds made up," she said.

Zetta gestured toward the kitchen as she stepped back into the front room. "Everything's in those crates," she said.

Just then a man's voice called, "Hello in the cabin."

Micah cried, "Poppy!" and ran to the front room as Rachel hurried behind him.

Zetta put her hand against the wall. Lord, this is too much for any of us.

Loren swooped up Micah and opened the door. Jim and Sally Reed stood on the porch.

Jim took off his hat. "Morning, Loren. We saw y'all passing our place and figured Zetta was coming home. So we brung back her milk cow and chickens."

He gestured to the wagon beyond the porch where the cow was tethered. Four crates of clucking chicken were in the wagon bed.

Jim held out a small pail as Zetta approached. "Here's milk from this morning," he said.

Sally peeked around Loren. "Zetta, I've come to help you with the house."

Zetta nodded her thanks to the couple and turned to her brother.

"Whilst you men tend to the animals, we'll unpack."

Still holding Micah, Loren took Rachel's hand. "Let's take your cats up to the barn and find a good bed for 'em," he said. "Animals don't have any place in the house."

The three women watched the little group walk down the porch steps and toward the barn. Then Sally turned to Zetta.

"Where do you want me to start?" she asked.

* * * * *

The women worked quickly—and silently. By the time Loren and Jim returned from the barn with the children, the beds were made, dishes were on the shelves, clothes put away and the Christmas toys lined up in front of the fireplace. Only the crate holding Asa's clothes remained.

Sally hugged Zetta goodbye before joining her waiting husband in the wagon.

"I know you've got your brothers," she said. "But if you need anything at all, you know we're just up the road."

And then they were gone.

Zetta turned to Loren.

"I appreciate you letting Jim work with you in the barn."

He shrugged and turned to Sarah.

"If you're ready, I'll take you on home," he said.

When Sarah nodded, Loren looked at Zetta. "I'll be back after supper to stay the night."

As the young couple started down the steps, Zetta turned to face a watchful Rachel and Micah. She closed her eyes as panic welled up. *Lord, I can't do this.*

Finally, she took a deep breath. "Here, Babies. Play with your play pretties."

She looked at the crate holding Asa's clothes, knowing she should pull out the jar with the money from her sale of hand pies and add that amount to the envelope holding Asa's saved wages. But the farm payment wasn't due until next month. She'd figure that out later. And she turned to check on Isaac.

* * * * *

For the next week, one day bled into the next. Each evening, Loren or Luttrell showed up, milked the cow, ate supper, slept on the pallet of quilts in front of the fireplace, milked the cow the next morning and stayed with the children while Zetta gathered the eggs and fixed breakfast. And each day, Zetta's goal was to keep putting one foot in front of the other.

One evening, Luttrell held out a letter from Clarie as Zetta mixed cornbread batter.

"No. I like how you read," she said.

He cleared his throat. "All right," he said. He sat at the table and tore open the envelope.

" 'Dear Zetta. I'm writing to remind you that you and your youngins are in my every prayer. By now most everybody else around you is going on with their lives and probably telling you to do the same. But I want you to be good to yourself for the next while. Just keep the children clean and fed, and everything else can wait. How I wish we didn't have all these miles between us.' "

"Oh, I wish so, too," Zetta said. "I miss her more than I ever thought."

"I know, Sis," Luttrell said. He turned back to the letter.

" 'As far as the camp goes, there's not much news from here. Polly is still poorly and still in bed. Perton is still trying to stir things up about getting a union. And Julia is still moping around. Clarence hasn't been seen since the accident. And that school teacher he was seeing is as bewildered as the rest of us as to his whereabouts. Well, I'll close for now. But I want you to remember I'm holding you close in my heart. Hugs and prayers across the miles, Clarie.' "

Zetta pulled her handkerchief from her sleeve and wiped her eyes.

"Oh, Luttrell. Everything was supposed to be so different."

"I know," was all he said.

With sagging shoulders, Zetta poured the cornbread batter into the hot skillet.

* * * * *

The next night was Loren's turn to stay. As Zetta washed the supper dishes, he paced in front of the fireplace.

"What's wrong?" Zetta asked. "You and Sarah getting along good?"

"Oh, yeah," he answered. "I'd get married tomorrow if it was up to me, but she wants to wait 'til the dogwoods are in bloom."

"So what's wrong?"

Loren set down at the table.

"Sis, Asa's tombstone arrived at the train station today."

"Well, it's about time," Zetta said. "I'm been wondering about that."

She looked closely at him. "Ain't you glad? You thought it might take longer."

Loren rubbed the scar on his chin.

"Sis, the camp didn't add the *E-R* on the end of his name. It's got Asa *Berghoff* instead of *Berghoffer*. Me and Luttrell remember how that bothered you when we was at the camp."

Zetta looked out the kitchen window toward the spot where Asa had planned to plant the Christmas tree from the coal camp. Finally, she turned back to her brother.

"Are the dates right?"

"Yep, those are okay."

Zetta took the kettle from the stove and poured more hot water over the dishes in the pan.

"Set the stone," was all she said.

* * * * *

Four days after her brothers set Asa's tombstone, Zetta stood on the porch and breathed deeply of the warm spring air.

She smiled at Rachel who was watching her from the doorway.

"We got another long day stretching before us," she said. "So we're gonna take us a walk as soon as I bundle up little Isaac."

But before Zetta moved, a tall man stepped from the side of the house.

"Good morning, Zetta."

Jesse Allen.

Zetta gasped, wishing one of her brothers was still there. Especially Loren.

Jesse pulled off his hat and remained standing below her.

"I didn't mean to scare you."

Zetta put her hands behind her back so he wouldn't see them trembling.

"I wasn't scared," she said. "I just wasn't expecting to see anybody. Least of all one of the Allen boys."

Jesse nodded. "I reckon I know that," he said. "Me and my brother was pretty hard on Asa when we all was growing up. That's why I didn't come to your paw's house for the funeral, figuring I wouldn't be welcome. But I come by now to tell you something I want you to think about in the days ahead."

He studied his hat brim for a moment then lifted his eyes again to Zetta.

"I was always partial to you even when we was little," he said. "But you never paid me no mind. Asa was the only feller who got your attention. Made me plumb mad. Wasn't nothing to do but give him a licking now and again."

Zetta took a step backward. "Why you telling me this?"

Jesse smiled. "Because I'm still partial to you," he said. "And after a respectable time, I plan to come calling."

Zetta gasped then drew a deep breath slowly through her nostrils to regain her composure. "You still ain't welcome here, Jesse Allen."

The man nodded. "Maybe not yet, Zetta," he said gently. "But Asa's dead, and I'm not. And neither are you."

As Jesse turned quietly away, tears rolled down Zetta's face.

* * * * *

Zetta stayed on the porch for several minutes so Rachel and Micah wouldn't see her crying. At last, she stepped inside.

Rachel followed her into the bedroom. Zetta wrapped Isaac in his quilt, then looked at the dresser for several moments. Finally, she opened the bottom drawer and pulled out the red sweater. She held it toward the window then thrust one arm and then the other into the sleeves.

What ailed me that I didn't wear this for Asa? It don't matter what folks think.

Rachel smiled. "You look pretty, Mama."

Zetta choked back a sob. "Thank you, honey. Got your rag baby?"

As they went out the door and down the porch steps, Zetta folded the quilt lightly across Isaac's face then walked slowly with Rachel and Micah holding hands next to her. She glanced at the side of the house where Jesse Allen had been, but no one was there. Relieved, she talked to keep the children company, but knew she was talking more to herself than to them.

"All of us was gonna come home March thirty-first," she said. "I had it all planned out. I was gonna have everything all packed and the water toted up for the men's baths even if I had to tote water all day. And I was gonna have everything packed in the crates and their clean clothes all laid out. I was gonna put their dirty work clothes in a pillow case, and we'd take everything to the station and get on the last train outta that place. I bet your daddy would have said we'd leave first thing the next morning. You know how he didn't like to be rushed. But I would've made sure we got out of there as soon as we could."

As the little group was nearing the Reed's place, Zetta whispered, "Oh, please, Lord. Don't let Jim and Sally see me. I gotta do this just with the youngins."

When no one appeared by the time they passed the house, Zetta whispered, "Thank you, Lord," and continued her story.

"And with Dosha not at the camp, the only person I would've said goodbye to would've been Clarie. Well, maybe Polly, too. But here I am back home without your daddy and trying to figure out how I'm gonna raise you sweet youngins all by myself."

As they turned onto the lane below the cemetery, Zetta stopped at the bottom of the hill.

"That's where Poppy is," Rachel said.

Zetta nodded and walked slowly up the gentle slope with the children. At the top, the sun shone on the new gray rectangular tombstone standing upright near the dogwood tree.

She put the quilt-bundled Isaac on the dry ground.

"Sister, you and Brother sit here with the baby."

She stepped to the side of the grave and leaned toward the stone:

Asa Berghoff.

"Our name is Berghoffer—not Berghoff. Couldn't the camp that killed him have the decency to bury him with his rightful name?" she whispered.

She read the dates quietly. "Born May 12, 1900. Died March 4, 1923."

Then she mouthed the inscription cut into the stone beneath the dates: "We knew no sorrow, we knew no grief 'til thy sweet face was missed."

"Oh, Asa. I do miss your sweet face," she whispered. "I miss having you here with us. But all my missing you ain't gonna bring you back. But I'll take care of our youngins. And I'll tell them stories about you. And they're gonna know their daddy loved them."

A gentle breeze stirred the dogwood branches above her. Zetta studied the swollen buds on the tree then looked again at the mound of dirt.

"I want to talk to you so bad, Asa," she whispered. "You'd never believe who showed up this morning. Jesse Allen, of all people. You told me I'm strong, but I'm afraid of so many things. How am I gonna face the future without you?"

She pushed down sobs. "Well, I'm wearing the red sweater you got me for Christmas," she whispered again. "And I'm wearing it right out in the open. Nobody's seen me in it yet, but I don't care if they do. I'll just tell 'em you bought it for me. I might even wear it to church when I go. Well, maybe not. I already give Mable Collins enough to talk about."

She read the inscription again quietly. "*We knew no sorrow, we knew no grief 'til thy sweet face was missed.*"

She looked beyond the top of the dogwood tree. "That's the truth, Asa Berghoffer," she whispered. "And when I'm an old woman, I'm still gonna miss your sweet face."

As a cloud crossed in front of the sun, Zetta tugged at the bottom of the red sweater before turning to pick up Isaac. She took Micah's hand.

"Sister, take Brother's other hand," she said. "We're going home."

Together she and the children slowly walked down the hill and away from the grave.

* * * * *

AUTHOR'S NOTES

One cold November afternoon as my husband, Don, and I were coming to the end of our battle with his brain cancer, my paternal grandmother, Katy Dunn Picklesimer Lovely, and I took a walk through Oak Grove, our town's cemetery. As we walked past the ancient tombstones marking the graves of the area's founding families, I wondered how soon I would be back there to bury my beloved husband. How could I get through something as awful as the death of my funny Scotsman? Grandma Katy had been widowed young, too, but by a Kentucky coal-mining accident. Quietly I asked, "What was it like when Grandpa Ted was killed?"

I wanted—needed—encouragement. Something I could hang onto to give me hope that I would get through the dark valley ahead. I wanted her assurance I would be able to face the challenge of raising our two young children alone. But instead of offering strengthening words, Grandma Katy whispered only a somber "It was the worst thing that ever was."

The chilly air suddenly moved into my very being, and we walked in silence for the rest of our time together. Since that long-ago day, I've written much about my widowhood journey. Now it's time to write about Grandma Katy's.

I know very little about my paternal grandfather, Ted Picklesimer, who was killed at a coal camp near Hazard, Kentucky in 1923—nine weeks before his 23rd birthday—and buried under a misspelled tombstone. So, this story is just that—a story. The jokes the character Asa told are ones I heard from relatives during my childhood. Few of these characters existed, and for the ones who did, I've made up the conversations. The names I chose are common among Kentucky mountain families and are in no way indicative of actual people. This is nothing more than the story I wish Grandma Katy had been able to tell me on that cold, long-ago Michigan afternoon.

Like the character Zetta, Grandma Katy had been left with three children under the age of four: Reva, Mitchell—who became my father—and Ishmael. All three lived into their senior years and now are in heaven, reunited with their mother and young Poppy. I am grateful for their love and their stories.

I'm also grateful for the several folks who encouraged me during this writing process. My son and daughter-in-law, Jay and Marianne (nee: Reddin) Aldrich asked for details each time we shared a meal. Jay especially was helpful with discussions of specific dreams and Zetta's rebuttal of the women in the days after Asa's funeral. My daughter and son-in-law, Holly and Eric Hulen cheered me on as well. And I still smile as I ponder my Birthday Friends—Libby Paddle, Mim Pain, Elizabeth Robinove and Mary Wells—who threatened to withhold the walnut prawns at our dinners until I had read the latest chapter of *Zetta's Dream* to them.

My mother, Wilma Picklesimer, and sister Thea Picklesimer helped with details of mountain funerals. Kay Hulen, R.N. and Linda Williams, M.D. provided the medical details for Isaac's birth and Asa's death.

Deb Landers, Bobbie Valentine, Kelly Crowther, Candy Lindley, Ruth Lund, and Joyce Riter asked about the book in every phone conversation.

Nancy Emens provided a 1970s photo of the actual coal tipple at the camp where Grandpa Ted had worked. The creative designer, Nicole Miller, used that photo for the cover.

All these dear folks helped make this family story a reality.

GLOSSARY OF APPALACHIAN TERMS

All fired up: Eager.

Bank the fire: Rake the coals together. In the morning, the coals are raked apart to expose the innermost red ones to be used as the base for the new fire.

Beholding: Obligated.

Big eye: Insomnia.

Cash money: Actual money—as opposed to payment in goods or work.

Crops laid by: The weeds have been conquered for the rest of the growing season, but the harvest isn't ready

Don't amount to a hill of beans: Of no value

Drove his ducks to a bad market: Made a bad choice

Druther: Rather—as in "I'd druther go fishing today."

Food paper: Wax paper. Name of the inventor is greatly in dispute. Some sources cite Thomas Edison; others his assistant Thomas Conners. Still other sources name Gustave LeGray for inventing it in 1851 for use first in photography.

Fried corn: Fresh corn kernels cut from the cob, seasoned with lard and cooked in an iron skillet. Not at all like the modern-day corn on the cob that is battered and deep fried in hot oil.

Gall: Highly irritating, exasperation.

Gom: To make a mess.

Granny woman: An older woman of the community who was skilled in knowledge of herbs, country medicine and childbirth.

Gray graniteware: Metal cookware covered in heavy gray paint. Contained lead.

Green lumber: Fresh-cut lumber that has not been allowed to dry properly. The resulting warping left cracks between the boards.

Gritted bread: Field corn or other overripe corn would be scraped against a board into which several small nails had been driven. This would make a coarse cornmeal, which would make a heavier cornbread batter.

Hanker after: To long for.

Hardtack: A hard, unsalted cracker. This was carried by the soldiers during the War Between Brothers (aka: the Civil War) and was often infested by weevils

Heard tell: Heard.

Hillbilly: First found in 17th century documents to describe supporters of English Protestant King William III who were called "Billy Boys." Most of the early American colonists were from Great Britain, and some scholars believe the British soldiers of the 1770s applied the term to those immigrants living in the Appalachian Mountains/hills. The term became derogatory after a 1900 *New York Journal* article gave an unflattering definition that became the basis for modern stereotypes.

Hoe cakes: Griddle cakes usually made with cornmeal. So named because they could be baked on the blade of a garden hoe.

Hog wild: Unrestrained.

Hunker: To crouch or squat.

Laying out: The viewing of the body before the funeral.

Lazy man's load: Carrying several heavy objects all at once rather than dividing the load and making two or more trips.

Lye soap: Water is added to clean wood ashes and boiled in a kettle. To test the strength of the resulting lye, a chicken feather is dipper into the liquid. When the soft part of the feather is eaten away, clean kitchen grease collected from cooked meats can be added.

Mantrip: The railed vehicle taking the miners to their work stations. The engine or "air donkey" pulled several open cars and would be stopped by throwing it into reverse.

Marble stone: A large, hard stone in which several small round holes had been drilled. A creek pebble would be placed in each hole, and the stone would be placed under the gentle part of a waterfall. The constant bouncing of the pebbles against the stone eventually would produce round pebbles used as marbles.

Malarkey: Foolish talk.

Mine face: The area of unmined coal where the miners will work on any given day.

Obliged: Obligated.

Pallet: A pile of quilts placed on the floor or in the back of a wagon and used as a bed.

Peter out: To diminish in size, strength or amount.

Purple fever: Childbirth fever. Medical term "puerperal fever," which developed from a piece of the afterbirth remaining in the uterus, causing an often fatal infection.

Reckon: Guess.

Recollect: Remember.

Riffraff: Undesirable people.

Sallet: Various greens mixed together for salad. Especially important as a spring tonic after a long winter.

Shenanigans: Rude or questionable conduct.

Sore eyes: Medically known as trachoma, this highly contagious infection of the inner eyelid and front of the eyeball caused blindness if untreated.

Sugar tit: A small piece of cotton material, shaped like a cone and filled with sugar. Given to babies shortly after birth to help with their sucking reflex.

Thick as thieves: Questionable association.

Unthoughted: Thoughtless.

War Between Brothers: The Civil War or, more rightly, the War Between the States. Since the loyalties of Kentucky inhabitants were split between the Union and the Confederacy, members of the same family often were on different sides. In fact, the Kentucky Commonwealth motto is "United we stand, divided we fall."

Widow woman: widow

Won't think twice: Won't give the situation a second thought.

Wore out my welcome: No longer welcome to stay.

Youngins: Young ones or children.

Dosha Conley's Buttermilk Pie

3 eggs beaten
1-1/4 cups sugar
1 stick butter, melted
1-1/2 teaspoons flour
½ cup buttermilk
1 teaspoon vanilla
Pinch of salt
Unbaked pie shell

Blend first 7 ingredients together.

Bake in unbaked pie shell at 325 degrees for about 45 minutes or until firm. Enjoy!

Note: More authentic coal camp recipes are in *Zetta's Coal Camp Recipes,* available through Amazon.com.

POPULAR BOOKS BY SANDRA P. ALDRICH

Bless Your Socks Off: Unleashing the Power of Encouragement

Heart Hugs for Single Moms: 52 Devotions to Encourage You

HeartPrints: Celebrating the Power of a Simple Touch
(with Bobbie Valentine)

Honey, Hang in There! Encouragement for Busy Moms

Men Read Newspapers, Not Minds—and other things I wish I'd known when I first married

One-Year Women's Friendship Devotional
(with Cheri Fuller)

Will I Ever Be Whole Again? Surviving the Death of Someone You Love

101 Upward Glances: Watching for God's Touch in the Ordinary Days

21 Bible Encounters: Stories of Transformed Lives
(with Thomas Youngblood)

SANDRA'S BLOG

Hugs Across the Miles: Encouragement from an Appalachian Woman: http://sandraaldrich.wordpress.com/

About The Author

SANDRA P. ALDRICH, a Harlan County, Kentucky native, is an international speaker and author or co-author of 24 books. Known for her Kentucky story-telling style of speaking and writing, Sandra loves the Lord, family and all things Appalachian. Eastern Michigan University granted her a Master of Arts degree, but she says life granted her a Ph.D. from the School of Hard Knocks. Currently she resides in Colorado Springs, Colorado because of its lack of copperhead snakes. Well, that and the fact that her two grandsons, Luke and Noah, are also there. Learn more at www.sandraaldrich.com and www.facebook.com/sandra.aldrich.

Made in the
USA
Monee, IL